To Italy, *with* Love

Nicky Pellegrino

ORION

An Orion paperback

First published in Great Britain in 2021 by Orion Fiction,
This paperback edition published in 2022 by Orion Fiction,
an imprint of The Orion Publishing Group Ltd,
Carmelite House, 50 Victoria Embankment,
London EC4Y 0DZ

An Hachette UK company

1 3 5 7 9 10 8 6 4 2

A CIP catalogue record for this book
is available from the British Library.

ISBN (Mass Market Paperback) 978 1 3987 0102 1
ISBN (eBook) 978 1 3987 0103 8

Typeset by Deltatype Ltd, Birkenhead, Merseyside

Printed in Great Britain by Clays Ltd, Elcograf S.p.A.

MIX
Paper from
responsible sources
FSC® C104740

www.orionbooks.co.uk

Nicky Pellegrino was born in Liverpool but spent childhood holidays staying with her family in Italy. It is her memories of those summers that flavour her stories: the passions, the feuds, but most of all the food. Nicky now lives in Auckland, New Zealand with her husband, two dogs and two horses.

Find out more at www.nickypellegrino.com

'If you don't know where you've come from,
you'll be lost your whole life.'

Anon

Assunta

A girl in a white dress was standing beside the fountain in the main piazza of Montenello. There was nothing unusual about that. Almost every day, from spring to late summer, a different bride was there, smiling into the face of her groom. Today a breeze gusted through the hilltop town, catching at this bride's veil and ruffling the blossoms in her bouquet, making the photographer's job more difficult.

This was an ideal place to pose for a wedding portrait. With the fountain so pretty, especially when the sun was sparkling through the jets of water that cascaded over its scalloped stone tiers. With it being only a few steps from the Town Hall, where the ceremony had taken place, and a short stroll to the hotel where the reception would be held.

At first the weddings were a novelty. People used to pause and watch the scenes unfold, smile to share the joy and feel the love in the air. But there had been so many weddings now that it hardly seemed worth glancing up from whatever you happened to be doing to pass judgement on the bridal gown, to see how young or old the newlyweds might be, and watch them exchanging kisses for the camera.

From the kitchen of her low-ceilinged *trattoria*, Assunta had a view of the whole sweep of the piazza. Rarely was she in too much of a hurry to stop work and gaze through the window for a while. But what interest did Assunta have in weddings? None at all.

When she was much younger, Assunta had assumed marriage would be somewhere in her future. It was what everyone did, pair up and make a life together, and she hadn't expected to be any different. But people had gone from Montenello since then – almost everyone who had been in her class at school, her friends and their families. Shops had closed and more houses been boarded up as they moved to the cities in search of work, or emigrated to distant countries.

Assunta wasn't tempted to follow. As others left, she only put down deeper roots into the rocky earth of this small town that rose like a fortress from the peak of a southern Italian mountain.

It was a busy life running her small *trattoria* with its rough plastered walls covered in bright ceramics. At mealtimes hungry people crowded in, shouting conversations from one table to the next as she ladled out food and ferried plates. During the lulls she would go next door to the bar run by her half-brother Renzo, enjoy a drink, smoke a cigarette and talk about nothing important. At the end of the day there was always her house, with its garden to tend and a comfortable bed to rest in.

She was in her mid-fifties now, with a comfortably round body and salt-and-pepper hair, and it was a long time since Assunta had imagined being married. She let those thoughts go years ago without too much regret, telling herself a husband wouldn't make her happier than she already was.

Assunta had never changed; it was the town around her that did. For many years Montenello could be relied on to be isolated and quiet. This was a place where not much happened and there weren't many young people left. Empty buildings crumbled, weeds forced their way through cracks in the honey-hued stone, and slowly it was turning to dust. The same was happening in hilltop towns all over Italy. No one seemed interested in doing much about it.

Then along came a new mayor, full of energy and ideas. He promised that Montenello wasn't going to become yet another ghost town; he would find a way to save it. Everyone had assumed this was the usual bluster and he would talk loudly but do nothing. To their surprise the new mayor was a man of his word, and now, bit by bit, their town was being transformed.

Most of the changes didn't touch Assunta. She carried on with life as usual, even if it was against a soundtrack of drilling and hammering as houses were saved from ruin and the hotel was restored. When the foreigners began to come, Assunta noticed them milling round the piazza. Some even found their way into her cramped little *trattoria* but when they saw that she didn't have a proper menu and there was no choice at all in what they were given to eat, they soon backed out again.

There was a new restaurant in the hotel serving modern Italian food and Assunta was certain they would be better served there. Her cooking was for the people who had always eaten it. Traditional dishes made slowly and with love, served with a basket of hard-crusted bread and a carafe of fruity white wine.

The rhythm of Assunta's life stayed the same, changing only season by season like the food she cooked. Each morning the mirror showed her a woman who was small, round and entirely unremarkable; not someone love was ever going to find. She might not have dwelled on it if it hadn't been for the brides, standing there beside the fountain so full of hope and love; if she didn't keep seeing them day after day throughout the wedding season, all those girls in white dresses reminding Assunta of what she would never have.

This morning's bride was pretty with pale skin and high cheekbones. The wind was whipping at her too-long veil, the groom trying to control it. They were laughing together as a stronger gust breezed through and the gauzy veil flew up, rippling in the air behind them, while the photographer hurried to capture the moment.

Looking away from the window, Assunta turned her attention to the beef she was braising. If she had found love at that girl's age, surely it would have burned out its brightness by now. Still, as she pushed her wooden spoon through the rich ragu of wine and tomatoes, she couldn't help imagining what it might be like to have someone beside her as she moved through the rest of her life; a person to talk to and laugh with, to lean on whenever it seemed she couldn't stand alone.

Sarah-Jane

It was all going so well, right up until the moment when everything went wrong, and the very first thing I thought was how many people were going to tell me, 'I told you so.' For a moment I was nothing but infuriated, then I started to panic. My little car, which had carried me for so many kilometres without a hint of trouble, died all of a sudden in the main piazza of a small Italian hilltop village.

I only visited Montenello because I read a newspaper article about the place, how the mayor had been selling off properties for one euro and his scheme was now regenerating what had been a dying town. It sounded intriguing so I planned to have a quick look around and then keep heading south. It was the kind of impromptu thing my trip was about, after all. Freedom to do whatever I liked was the whole point in coming.

The town was nice enough and I walked its narrow streets for a while, paused in the piazza to watch a bride and groom as they posed for their wedding photographs, and visited a *pasticceria* where I bought a little cake made of the lightest sponge filled with custard cream and spun sugar. After a couple of hours, having apparently exhausted Montenello's possibilities, I decided to be on my way.

Baxter and I got in the car and I turned the key in the ignition. As the engine stuttered to life there was a loud bang as if I had crashed into something, which obviously I hadn't because we were stationary. A few people turned to stare but then looked away when it became clear there was nothing interesting to see; just me in a car that wasn't moving. I tried the ignition again, and nothing.

'Shit,' I said. 'Shit, shit, shit.'

Baxter shot me a worried look from beneath his bushy eyebrows as if he had been fairly certain all along that something like this would happen.

I stared back at him. 'It'll be OK, I'll find a mechanic, it's probably nothing major.'

I didn't feel as confident as I sounded. The inner workings of cars are a mystery to me; before I started on this trip I just about knew how to drive one. It was the main reason my friends were so certain this trip was a terrible idea. Tackling the chaos of Italian roads when, despite getting my licence years ago, I had spent hardly any time behind the wheel. Depending on who you listened to, it was at best reckless and at worst they imagined I was going to kill myself and probably several others.

The only one not to discourage me was my mother. She knows how determined I can be once my mind is set on something. Also Mum had been right there, watching and listening, as everything collapsed around me. We went through the whole thing together and she understood better than anyone how I must be feeling.

I'm close to my mum, far closer than most of my friends reckon is normal. I had a little self-contained flat in the basement of her house in Notting Hill and we were in and out of each other's places all the time. Perhaps it's because my father died when I was a child and she brought me up solo, but we're best friends. My mother is a lot of fun and she never tries to tell me how to lead my life.

Still, Mum hadn't needed to say a word for me to know she had a few reservations about Tom. It's never the greatest idea to fall for your boss, is it? In retrospect, I can see that.

But who could resist Tom Whiffen? Anyone who has seen him judging TV cooking contests, or followed him on

Instagram, or bought his books, or had him make a brief personal appearance at their table in his Soho restaurant, would be charmed. There is that strong jaw and the broad shoulders, and the deep masculine voice. And Tom has a way with him; he is outrageously appealing. Like I said, who could resist him? Not me, ordinary never famous me, drawn to him like some sort of glittering jewel I was mesmerised by. Just being near Tom made me feel happier.

We were together for a year, although most people didn't know about us. Not because Tom was married – he most definitely wasn't; it was to do with his public profile and wanting to keep his personal life out of the tabloids. Also, there is one thing most of Tom Whiffen's fans don't realise: he's not that great a cook. Oh, he's fine at making things look pretty and isn't short on business acumen, but if you've cooked a recipe of Tom's in the past five years – whether it came from his website, one of the books or a magazine – it was me who created it, one hundred per cent me, every time. While Tom has been out in the world putting on a big show, I've been in the background devising and perfecting the dishes he attached his name to.

Plenty of celebrity cooks have help – it isn't uncommon. But Tom has this thing about the public believing he does everything himself. 'Made With Love by Tom Whiffen' is his motto; it was the name of the first book and his magazine – he even used it for the restaurant.

I never minded not being asked to accompany him to launches and parties. Couldn't have cared less about not getting a credit in his books or my photo on his website. I didn't want to be the star, I preferred not to be the centre of attention. My thing was doing the work I loved, steeped in deliciousness every day, at home in my little kitchen, creating lovely foods. And when it all changed with Tom, when our work partnership turned into something deeper, I was amazed he had chosen me, out of all the women he could have had.

We didn't do any of the things other couples do; never went out for lunch or to a movie, and we couldn't take a walk in the park for fear of the paparazzi stalking us. Keeping our relationship quiet was a challenge but it was important to Tom and that was fine by me. We were close, talking every day and spending weekends together at my place, mostly in bed or curled up on the sofa, eating whatever I had cooked and binge-watching Netflix.

'Are you happy, Sarah-Jane?' my mother asked every now and then, her brow slightly creased.

'Absolutely,' I always replied. 'Couldn't be happier.'

I expected things to change eventually. There would come a moment when we outed ourselves as a couple, but in the meantime, I quite liked it being just the two of us. It felt as if the outside world didn't matter, and what we had was too special to be touched by it. I wasn't in any hurry to push for more, sure that in our quiet way Tom and I were building a relationship that would last. All those days and nights together, just him and me, listening to his plans, sharing his dreams. I was important to him.

Then Tom started expanding his business even more ambitiously and working longer hours. He took on an assistant called Jo to look after the social media and merchandising – there was a range of Made With Love by Tom Whiffen cookware and crockery by then. I dealt with Jo almost entirely by email and she seemed efficient. Next, Tom opened his first Made With Love restaurant. The plan was for it to be the flagship of a chain and naturally he wasn't going to be manning the kitchen himself.

He hired an executive chef, a French woman called Dominique Clairmonte, who was so lean and elegant it was difficult to believe she took even the tiniest taste of any dish she cooked. Tom always liked my curves, he had praised my food too, but once she appeared on the scene, nothing about me seemed good enough.

'Dominique has been reviewing the last six months of the magazine and thinks we're not paying enough attention to the latest food trends,' Tom told me in the first of a series of excruciating sit-down meetings. 'We need to be thinking about the way people are eating right now and the new ingredients that are exciting them.'

I ran my eyes down the list she had provided. Filipino food was having a moment apparently and she suggested I start with the desserts. We had missed out on the plant-based trend (irritatingly I had said that to Tom myself ages ago) and there were several Asian ingredients that Dominique thought I could be making more of.

'Gochujang, really?' I said, wrinkling my nose. Not that I have anything against Korean fermented red chilli paste but it didn't seem to me that it belonged in a Tom\Whiffen recipe. It wasn't mainstream enough, not yet.

'Our readers don't want to invest in lots of jars that will only be used once and end up cluttering the fridge,' I reminded him. 'They're looking for simple, fresh and fast, that's what they tell us.'

'Dominique thinks we ought to be challenging them. She's using gochujang in the restaurant a lot. She did this thing with sweetcorn that was fantastic. Honestly, I've never tasted anything like it.'

'Most of her restaurant food isn't going to work in a home kitchen. There are too many elements, too much fuss,' I argued.

'Dominique says there's no reason that the recipes can't be streamlined. And this is the direction my food is going in now. I need you to be on board with it, OK?'

For the next week or so gochujang dominated my cooking. Fermented red chilli was dolloped into stews and soups. I used it in tacos and devilled eggs, marinades and dipping sauces. It packed such a punch of flavour, was thick and sticky, earthy and hot, an explosion of umami. Even using a small amount, and thinning it down with water or broth, it seemed to shout loudly from every dish I tried it in.

I really care about the recipes I develop. They may not have my name on them, but I get a buzz thinking about people in their kitchens recreating a dish I came up with. On the Made With Love social media pages, fans will often post photographs of their attempts at Tom's world-famous carrot cake (the secret is a hint of curry powder) or his decadent raspberry chocolate brownie stack. I love seeing the personal twists they put on dishes and don't want them led astray with recipes that will never work or be disappointed with flavours that won't appeal to their palates.

The gochujang was the start of a nagging sense that things were changing, and not in a good way. Over the next few weeks I saw less of Tom. He was often too busy to come over at weekends and my phone didn't ring as much. A day or two might pass without us talking and now, whenever we had our usual brainstorming meetings in the office, Dominique joined us, so instead of relaxed chats over coffee and interesting thoughts jotted down in a Moleskine notebook, there were spreadsheets and proper planning. Some of her ideas were good but it hurt to have so many of my own dismissed as dull. At the end of every session I was the one left with a long to-do list, while they went off together.

'Tom's got a lot going on at the moment,' I told my mother. 'The restaurant was a big financial risk and things have been so difficult.'

I waited, hoping life would get back to normal but Dominique's influence only grew stronger and soon it felt as if she was my boss, not him. It was crushing all the joy out of my job and for the first time, work felt like work.

'You don't think there's something going on between them?' my mother wondered.

'Definitely not,' I told her. 'Dominique is a lesbian and in a fully committed relationship. He's crazy about her cooking, not her.'

For me the most obvious sign there was a problem came when the latest issue of the *Made With Love* magazine arrived in the post. I happened to notice that one of my recipes had been altered. For some reason saffron had been added to a fish soup. Saffron is one of the more expensive spices and normally I don't use it. Looking closely at the recipes on other pages, I found more tweaks, usually to the ingredients. Not only unexpected spices but teaspoons of agave nectar where they didn't belong, and butter where I had used olive oil, as though someone had decided my original recipes lacked flavour. That sort of thing wasn't supposed to happen. Tom might edit an introduction, so it sounded more like his voice, but the recipes themselves were my territory and I was always meticulous.

I rang the magazine's editor who sounded embarrassed as she told me that Dominique had been given final approval.

'For the website recipes too,' she admitted. 'There's nothing I can do ... sorry, Tom authorised it.'

I felt sick. Was Tom not happy with my work anymore? But then why hadn't he told me so himself? I tried his mobile and it went straight to answerphone. When I called the office, Jo said he was in a meeting.

Even though she was Tom's assistant, Jo and I hardly ever saw each other because our jobs were very different. I looked after the recipes while she managed everything else and any exchanges between us tended to be short but friendly. Jo might email for my advice about which saucepans to include in the Made With Love kitchen essentials range. I would call and check in with her if I needed to know about Tom's schedule. When we chatted, it was about the usual things that colleagues talk about – the weather, holiday plans, how busy we were.

Now I was speaking to her a lot more frequently as I tried

to get hold of Tom. Day after day there was always a reasonable enough explanation for why he hadn't had time to call. Jo said he was away on a shoot, then recording a podcast, busy in several more meetings, caught up with promotion for his latest book. She kept telling me how busy things were and how packed his schedule was. We chatted so much that eventually I confided in her, admitting my concerns about the changes being made to my work, and she was so reassuring that it made me think I might be overreacting.

'I know what Dominique can be like,' Jo sympathised. 'I'll make sure Tom calls you in the next day or so, when things quieten down, I promise.'

What Jo didn't mention during any of those long chats was that she had been accompanying Tom to events. So it was a surprise to see the item on the *Daily Post* website a couple of mornings later, a paparazzi shot of them together heading into a cocktail party at The Groucho Club. Tom's arm was around Jo, his hand resting on her rounded belly. The headline read: *MADE WITH LOVE: TOM WHIFFEN'S BABY JOY*.

I assumed the newspaper must have got it wrong. Jo did look quite pregnant (oddly she hadn't mentioned that either), but it couldn't be Tom's child; I didn't believe it. The more I looked at the picture though, the more I stared at that hand of his. It was a hand that had stroked the length of my body, touched every part of me, a square and strong-looking hand with neatly trimmed fingernails and it was resting very casually on Jo's baby bump. She was smiling, and Tom was ducking his head, looking slightly sheepish. He was wearing a shirt that I had given him – blue with a fine pink stripe, which I knew was one of his favourites.

I grabbed my phone to call him then changed my mind in case I ended up sounding needy and insecure. Sooner or later Tom would hear about the paparazzi picture. He would get in touch to explain everything and we would laugh about it.

Mum was away on a yoga retreat in Cornwall at the time, so I had a strange few days, waiting for my phone to ring, with only Baxter to talk to.

Baxter is my dog; he's one of those Border Terriers with an expression that always seems faintly worried and when I talk to him he stares at me, tilting his head to one side, so it seems like he's really listening. Baxter wasn't particularly fond of Tom, partly because he wasn't allowed to sleep on the bed when he was staying over, but also weirdly for someone who was charming to other humans, Tom was bad with animals. He always played with Baxter a bit too roughly, patted him a little too hard, and yelled at him to shut up on the rare occasions he barked. When Tom was around, Baxter looked even more pensive than usual.

After the third day of trying to get on with work and stay off the *Daily Post* website, I caved in and made a call. Tom didn't pick up but a few minutes later sent a text to say he was flat-out busy and would be in touch soon. I carried my phone in the pocket of my apron all afternoon as I tested recipes and rehearsed what I would say to him. The plan was to keep things light and breezy but drop into the conversation that I had heard about Jo's pregnancy and wondered what the plan was for her maternity cover. Hopefully that would lead to an explanation; he would tell me the newspaper had got it wrong, and everything would be cleared up.

Except he didn't call; instead later that evening I received an emailed meeting request. Tom wanted to see me the next day and I was to go into the office.

The Made With Love office is above the Soho restaurant and is actually just three high-ceilinged rooms with sash windows. Between travelling for so many TV shoots and live events, Tom doesn't usually spend much time there and the place always has an over-tidy, staged feel about it with everything painted white and too many pot plants.

I arrived to find the office empty aside from a youngish

guy I had never met before who was wearing a suit and sitting at the desk that Jo usually occupied.

'Hi,' I said. 'Tom around?'

His eyes moved from the computer screen he had been frowning at and he looked at me, expression unchanging. 'Tom's running late, but shouldn't be far away. Are you Sarah-Jane Santi?'

'That's right.' I sank down on the expensive but uncomfortable sofa.

'Did you bring a support person?' he asked.

'I'm sorry, did I what?' I sat up straighter. 'Who are you, anyway?'

'I'm Robert Matthews, I look after Human Resources for Made With Love.'

'You do?' It was news to me that we had hired another staff member but the company was growing so fast it was difficult to keep up and I hadn't been in the office for a while.

'I started here a couple of weeks ago,' he told me.

'Oh right ... and where's Jo?'

'Not in until later this morning – doctor's appointment.'

While I was waiting, I flicked through the pages of a rival food magazine without taking it in. Something here felt very wrong. I kept asking myself why on earth I might need a support person, and whether Tom was running late because he was with Jo at the doctor's appointment.

He was wearing a paisley shirt when he arrived, not one that I had given him. 'Sarah-Jane,' Tom said, not quite meeting my eyes. 'Thanks for coming in. Shall we sit at the meeting room table?'

He didn't say much after that, his new Human Resources manager did most of the talking, and I listened with a growing sense of disbelief. The company was changing, as I had probably noticed, and the restaurant was now its food hub. I had done so much to help Made With Love succeed and my contribution was valued but unfortunately it was time for my role to be disestablished.

'You're making me redundant?' I turned to Tom, confused and hurt. 'You can't.'

'Sorry, Sarah-Jane, but this is a business decision,' he said awkwardly. 'I have to make the best choices for the company. You'll find the redundancy package that Robert has put together is very generous. And you're so talented, you'll pick up more work, you'll be busier than ever.'

I tried to speak again but tears were dripping from my eyes and I couldn't seem to breathe properly. Robert passed a box of tissues and, by the time I pulled myself together, Tom had disappeared somewhere and the meeting room table was covered in paperwork.

'So you see, financially you're going to do really well out of this,' Robert was saying in an encouraging tone. 'Apart from the lump sum, which is far more than we're legally required to give, we'll pay out all holiday leave owed and that's a decent amount as you don't seem to have taken much time off.'

'Where's Tom?'

'Sorry, he's not available now.'

'What do you mean, not available?'

'He had another meeting.' Robert had the grace to sound embarrassed.

'I need to talk to Tom – properly.'

'You may want to seek legal advice,' he said stiffly, 'but I can assure you the company is treating you more than fairly. Change is inevitable with any business ... This hasn't been an easy decision but I think it will turn out to be the right one for all of us ... You should see this as an opportunity, a chance for personal growth ...'

Robert droned on and the urge to scream was almost overwhelming. Signing the paperwork, having barely scanned my eyes over it, I tried to shut out the sound of his voice. I had to get away from there. He was still talking as I slammed the door in my haste to escape the office. Down on the street, the first thing I did was try calling my mother's number although I knew there was a strict no-phones rule at the Cornish yoga retreat. The phone rang unanswered and I left a message:

'Mum, I need to talk to you, something completely crazy just happened.'

I was sitting on a bench in Golden Square, trying to steady my breathing and order my thoughts, when she called back.

'Sorry darling,' she said, her voice so hushed I had to strain to hear. 'My phone was on silent. We're supposed to be having a day of quiet contemplation.'

Mum forgot to whisper when I told her what had happened. 'Redundant? He can't do that, can he?' she asked.

'Apparently he can. Also Mum, I think he's been sleeping with his assistant. I don't know for sure but … she's pregnant.'

'The bastard.' My mother never swore, literally never, now she said the word again, this time more loudly. 'The total bastard.'

'The thing is, I don't know what to do.' I started to cry again.

'Just get home, Sarah-Jane. I'll be with you as soon as I can and listen …' Hang on, there's someone here …' She held the phone away from her face but I could hear her telling whoever had interrupted that she would speak on her phone if she damn well felt like it.

'Listen darling, we'll sort this out.' Mum was talking to me again. 'Just go home and make yourself a cup of tea – or even better, a gin – and I'll be there before too long.'

'Sorry to drag you away.' I knew she had been looking forward to the retreat.

'Silent meditation is doing my head in,' she said, 'so don't worry about that.'

I went straight home, made some tea and lay on the sofa with Baxter and my phone, trying Tom's number repeatedly. When it became clear he was never going to pick up, I left him a shaky-voiced message.

'You owe me an explanation. Please come over, or at least call back. We need to have a conversation about this. I deserve that at least.'

After that I took a long shower, letting the water mingle with the tears still running down my cheeks. I had that same sense of disbelief as when my father had died; this couldn't be happening, it was a disaster out of nowhere. At least, that was how I felt standing there, steaming up the bathroom and trying to wash it all away, the whole hideous day.

Later slumped on the sofa, pink-skinned and wet-haired, listening to 'Someone You Loved' by Lewis Capaldi on high repeat, I realised there had been signs that I hadn't wanted to recognise. All those unreturned phone calls, the weekends when he was too busy to see me, the continual excuses. That must have been his way of backing off. Because charming, affable, everyone-loves-me Tom wouldn't have been able to come right out and say he didn't want me anymore. That wasn't his style at all. And it made me ache to think how little I must have mattered to him, when he was everything to me.

Sitting there, wrapped in a towel, I hoped the phone would ring but when it did, it was Mum to say she was on the train, heading home.

'I don't know what to do with myself,' I told her. 'I keep thinking, is this my fault? Why wasn't I good enough?'

'Take some Rescue Remedy and have a lie-down,' she advised.

My mother was going through a phase of being devoted to all things natural so her cupboards were filled with special teas and homeopathic cures. I needed something stronger and searched my bathroom cabinet, where I found a pack of paracetamol and a few Xanax the vet had prescribed for Baxter's anxiety on Guy Fawkes Night. They seemed to work well enough for him so I took two and went to bed. I really needed to be unconscious, just for a little while.

Mum got home a few hours later and held me while I sobbed, then defrosted some cauliflower soup that I had stored away the previous winter, and watched me struggle to swallow a spoonful. 'Oh, Sarah-Jane,' she said.

'Is Tom ever going to get in touch and explain things?'

'Maybe he will,' said my mother. 'But I think you already know what's happened, don't you.'

'He's replaced me ... he doesn't need me anymore.'

She nodded, her expression as devastated as mine.

'I love him though.'

She hugged me again. 'He isn't worth your love.'

I looked at my mother, still so beautiful with her thick pale hair worn heavy-fringed and long, and her slightly hippyish clothes. Love hadn't been kind to her either. She was young when she lost my father in a helicopter crash and grief wrapped itself round her very tightly. Now it was finer and flimsier, but still always shrouding her slightly.

If love was always going to end in pain then it wasn't worth it. That was what I decided, curled up on the sofa, feeling betrayed and miserable. Love was hard, hurtful and much too risky, so from now on I wasn't going to have anything to do with it. I would fill my life with other things instead.

That is how I ended up sitting in a car that wouldn't start, parked in the piazza of a small Italian hill town on a bright summer's day. This was supposed to be my new beginning.

I tried not to cry, really I did. There had been enough tears in the past six months and I was totally over feeling sorry for myself. I looked at Baxter as he stared back, his tail thumping hopefully against the leather of the passenger seat, and I wasn't sure his faith in me was justified, not now everything seemed to have gone wrong again. Feeling helpless and alone, my head sank into my hands. The tears were beyond my control.

Assunta

The *trattoria* was empty but Assunta knew that customers would appear suddenly and all at once; it was the same every time she opened. Five lunchtimes and two evenings a week she served up a meal to the people of Montenello and it was a habit she was reluctant to break, even though, in the last year or so, the longer days always left her with tired legs and an ache between her shoulder blades.

While the work took a greater toll, the food she cooked seemed to taste better than ever; even those recipes she had made without change for over two decades. To Assunta it felt as if all those sauces and stews simmering away in her cast-iron pots were passing down their flavours, one to another, deepening the savoury, sweetening the sweet, clarifying the acidic notes.

She cooked instinctively, her body knew what to do, freeing her mind to think of other things, although hours might pass and afterwards she wouldn't remember what those thoughts had been.

This morning had been filled with distractions. First, the bride had stolen her attention, the wind billowing into her veil as if it were a sailcloth. Now, as she kneaded the dough for gnocchi, her eyes kept being drawn to a young woman sitting in a car parked right outside the *trattoria*, a woman with a long tangle of dark hair and a worried expression.

There had been a loud bang; that was why Assunta had glanced out first of all and noticed her. At that point she didn't realise that the car had broken down, only seeing how panicked the stranger looked and wondering why. Now the girl had her hands over her face and her whole body was shaking.

Watching her sobbing, alone aside from a small dog that was sitting on the passenger seat, Assunta considered going over to ask if there was anything she could do. But she had never been one to interfere in other people's business and, besides, it was nearly lunchtime and soon there would be a crowd hungry for the beef that had been braising gently in a sauce of red wine and tomatoes for the past six hours.

Assunta turned away and busied herself shaping the gnocchi dough. Several minutes later, when she looked out again, the girl was no longer crying. Instead she was holding her phone, stabbing at the screen with a finger, which was all the young people seemed to do in any situation nowadays.

As she was cutting loaves of bread into thick slices so she could set a basketful down on each table, Assunta glanced out of the window once more and saw the young woman now standing in front of the car, with its bonnet raised. It dawned on her what had happened, and she knew there was no way to help. Assunta didn't have a clue about cars, had never even owned one. All the supplies for the *trattoria* were delivered and any place she wanted to go to, she walked.

She was still staring out of the window when the truck pulled in and parked at the centre of the piazza. Francesco Rossi clambered out of the driver's side, and her father Augusto lowered himself carefully from the other. This wasn't unexpected. Each weekday the pair of them appeared at about this time to eat lunch at the *trattoria*, then retired to the bar to drink a *digestivo* and play a game of cards. At some point, when they had gathered enough strength, they would slide open one side of the truck and spend the remainder of the afternoon selling fresh fruit and vegetables to the people of Montenello.

Both men were so old now that Assunta was always relieved to see them arrive and took it as a signal to start piling plates with food. Today though she waited and watched, knowing how much Augusto loved to help others, how nothing made him happier; and that the sight of a pretty young woman with tear-reddened eyes and a broken-down car would be irresistible.

Not that her father knew anything about engines either. Still, predictably enough, he and Francesco had stopped beside the car and were peering beneath the bonnet. The young woman said something to them and Augusto listened with a hand cupped round his ear, because he was growing deafer but hated wearing his hearing aid.

A group was starting to form, with several other men who had been heading towards the *trattoria* pausing to take their turn to stare at the broken engine and offer an opinion. Augusto called for Renzo to come out of the bar, and beckoned over several friends. A lively discussion turned into a noisy argument, her father at its centre, waving his hands in the air, trying to shout down the others, although his lungs weren't strong enough to lend his voice much power.

The crowd had swelled and the girl was looking even more anxious. Assunta watched the scene for a few moments, exasperated. She was well aware the men could carry on like this for half an afternoon and it would irritate her beyond reason to watch them. There was only one thing to do. Tightening the apron around her thick waist, she sailed out of the *trattoria*, pushing her way through the mass of people. Reaching the young woman, she said in Italian. 'Come with me.'

The girl didn't understand her. 'I'm sorry?'

'Come inside.'

'You mean me?' She was still confused.

'Leave them to argue.' Assunta spoke in English this time. 'They are enjoying themselves. Come in and bring your little dog.'

The girl gazed at the cluster of noisy men, then at the even more useless engine of her car, and seemed to make up her mind. Clipping a lead on the dog, she scooped him up from the passenger seat and hugged him to her chest.

'I can't understand a word they're saying,' she told Assunta, following her into the *trattoria*. 'Even though I do speak a bit of Italian.'

'Don't worry, they make very little sense, even to each other.'

'Can you help me? I need a mechanic. Is there someone local I could call?'

'Later yes, but first eat.'

'Eat?' The girl sounded doubtful but took a seat anyway, pulling out her phone and tapping at its screen, creasing her smooth forehead with a frown.

Assunta busied herself warming a plate and covered it with food: a helping of gnocchi, a slick of meaty sauce and a shower of shaved pecorino cheese. She poured a glass of lightly chilled white wine and set it in front of the girl.

'Eat and things will seem better.'

Sarah-Jane

There was a really bad moment when I was surrounded by all those Italian men, trying to shout each other down, voices booming, arms waving, with no one paying me any attention, when I wanted to be safe on my sofa, with my mother bringing me a bowl of soup, Baxter curled up beside me and nothing more challenging to deal with than a crossword puzzle, a moment when all I could think of was home. Then a woman appeared, a solid and reassuring one, who took charge of the situation and ordered me to follow her. And I was so grateful, I didn't think twice about complying.

A comforting smell of cooking found me as I stepped inside her little *trattoria*. I would have sworn I wasn't hungry, until she put the plate of food in front of me and I breathed its steam. The first mouthful made me feel a little better. The gnocchi were pillowy clouds, the beef meltingly tender, the pecorino tasted sharp and savoury. It was a classic Italian dish and it was really good, even quite soothing.

Outside there was still a crowd gathered round my car. A couple of men were poking about under the bonnet, but I wasn't confident either of them had a clue what they were doing. As I had discovered, via Google, the nearest qualified mechanic was miles away and in another town. Hopefully there was a tow truck they could send because otherwise my car wasn't going anywhere.

The cook was back in her kitchen by now and busy serving food to those customers who, growing bored with the drama, were starting to trickle in. I realised she might have noticed me earlier, looking out through her window to see me huddled in my car, crying pathetically. It must have seemed an overreaction to a broken-down vehicle. She wasn't to know I was crying about everything, all the things that had gone wrong, and this was one more setback.

Being dumped by Tom was the start of a very rough time for me. I found it so difficult to accept that the life I loved had come to an end, and I was grieving for it. For a long time I couldn't work out how to move on, and to be fair I had been badly treated.

My severance pay was followed by a formal letter, signed by Tom's HR manager on his behalf. It thanked me for my contribution to the company, expressed regret that our relationship had been brought to an end and wished me the very best from the entire Made With Love family. That was it – a single piece of paper. All my work, all the love I had poured into Tom and his business, and he had ended the whole thing like that.

I stopped expecting my phone to ring, stopped caring really. With all the things that had given my days structure suddenly gone, I struggled even to get out of bed in the morning. A heaviness settled over me and, if Baxter hadn't needed walks, I might never have left the house. As it was, I slept a lot. Being awake meant endless repetitive thoughts about what I had lost and how messed up it all was.

'You're depressed and that's completely understandable,' said Mum, plying me with soothing essential oils and St John's Wort.

What worried her most was that I felt too sick to eat properly. Three times a day she persisted in putting food in front of me and, once all the meals stocked in my freezer were used up, she took over in the kitchen.

My mother isn't a terrible cook; I would describe her as over creative. She can't resist adding unlikely ingredients to every dish. Sometimes it works – a spoonful of jam in a pasta sauce – but disasters happen. Right now I didn't care either way. Everything tasted the same and I had to force down a few forkfuls.

'How's the bean burrito?' she would ask.

'Fine.'

'Is there too much chocolate? I read somewhere that South Americans use it in their food but maybe not Dairy Milk.'

'Maybe,' I agreed.

For weeks I ignored messages from friends, couldn't concentrate on reading a book or watching a TV show and instead cried endlessly. This wasn't me anymore. I was a stranger to myself and that was a terrible feeling. I waited for it to pass but it didn't.

Mum decided the most important thing was to keep busy so she subscribed to the *New York Times* crossword and insisted we tackle it every day. We listened to podcasts, did yoga together, played old board games she dug out of a cupboard and took Baxter for long walks.

Slowly, shade-by-shade, I began to feel a little lighter. Reading articles about Tom, I cried only a little. I managed to cook, starting with things that were easy to eat and make: buttery scrambled eggs, smooth vegetable soups. And I started talking to friends and telling them some of what had happened. All were sympathetic but most didn't understand. Their well-meaning advice was that I should boost my social media presence, shoot some cooking segment videos, start a blog. But I'm one of those people who are happier in the background. Yes, like everybody else I've got an Instagram account but I hardly ever post anything because I prefer not to put my life out there; I'd rather get on with it quietly. Chasing a higher profile would never have appealed to me even if my self-confidence had been at an all-time high, which it most certainly wasn't. Nor did I want to be an assistant for some other celebrity chef, or help in a café, or start my own catering business.

My life seemed like a thread that had frayed and broken,

and now I needed a stronger one to follow. Wherever that took me, it had to be strides away from before, somewhere completely different.

One afternoon my mother arrived back from her session volunteering in a charity shop and found me staring at the blank screen of my laptop.

'What are you up to?'

'Making a list of ways to reinvent myself. So far I have a complete lack of good ideas.'

Part of the problem was that I just wanted my old job back, the one I had loved.

'You've worked so hard since you left college. Now you've got your redundancy and some money saved, why not take a sabbatical?' Mum suggested.

'I thought you were worried about me spending too much time sitting around?'

'Yes, but I'm not talking about sitting around,' she said. 'You could do some volunteering or get into a new project.'

'I'll think about it.'

'Why not have another go at your father's family tree?'

We had always known Dad's heritage was Italian. The surname Santi was the main clue, but I liked to think it showed up in my appearance, in my olive skin and dark hair, and how fast I could eat a bowl of spaghetti with only a fork, no spoon.

After his death, as a distraction from her grief, Mum had tried to trace Dad's family history. I think it was a way to connect with him and, for a while, she really got into it, but the flow of Italian blood went back a long way through the generations and she never worked out where his ancestors came from.

Still, that link with another country made me feel special. I grew up loving everything Italian and most of all, the food. My gap year was spent working at an *agriturismo* in Tuscany, picking grapes and olives, and trying to learn the language. Since then I had been back once or twice for short breaks, and Tom always used to talk about us visiting Venice together although we never managed it.

'If you can discover which town the Santi family originated from, we could visit, wherever it is,' suggested my mother. 'So it's not a pointless project.'

'OK,' I agreed, mainly to keep her happy, because trawling through old files and records wasn't appealing and anyway I had started thinking about Tom again, the restaurants in Venice he wanted to take me to, and the dishes he couldn't wait for me to try. Piquillo peppers stuffed with a whipped cream of sea bass and lemon zest, cuttlefish ink risotto, salt cod baked in milk with yellow polenta, and the two of us together at some perfect little restaurant at the canal's edge with a gondola gliding past.

I forgot about tracing my genealogy and Mum didn't mention it again. But Italy was on my mind now and I started flicking through recipe books and craving its familiar flavours. In my mother's freezer, I found the carcasses of some roast chickens I had saved, and I simmered up a silky rich-brown broth then cooked a risotto of mushrooms and sage. There was semolina flour in the cupboard so I made pasta – little ears of *cavatelli*, sheets of lasagne – listening to Italian opera as I kneaded and rolled.

Next I turned my attention to the potted basil plants my mother was growing on a sunny windowsill. I caught the scent of them whenever I walked past and on grey days, catching a leaf between my fingers, it took me back to my gap year, the feeling of freedom, sunshine on my skin and days filled with possibilities.

Harvesting the plants to make a pesto, Italy felt closer than ever. When I crushed the leaves to a paste with pine nuts and garlic, I realised that I couldn't have the person I loved, but I could have the place. Italy was still there, waiting for me.

'I think I'm going to have that adventure,' I told my mother. 'You're right, it's exactly what I need.'

Over the next few days I formed the loosest of plans. I would revisit the places and people I knew, the *agriturismo* and the language school in Tuscany, drop in on Italian foodie friends I had connected with since then, and explore further afield. Mum could meet me for short holidays along the way, wherever most appealed to her.

'Good idea,' she agreed. 'I can always get a house-sitter.'

'To water the plants?'

'No, for Baxter, of course,' she said. 'Surely I'll be looking after him while you're away? I'd rather get a house-sitter than put him in kennels.'

We both turned and looked down at the dog. He stared back at us, wagging his tail and my heart sank. Baxter was my friend. He had seen me through the darkness of the past weeks.

'I can't leave him, I just can't,' I said.

'Well then,' my mother shrugged, 'I suppose he'll have to go with you.'

I dismissed the whole idea at first, as it seemed too difficult. But Italy stayed in my mind, filling its darkest corners with colour and brightness. I wanted to be there again.

My mother helped me navigate many of the things I needed to organise. For Baxter there was a pet passport, a microchip and a rabies shot. For me a second-hand car – a shiny red Saab convertible that I completely adored – and a few sessions driving round London to regain my lost skills. We started on the smaller roads then worked up to the busier routes. Once I could make it round Hyde Park Corner without either of us squeaking in fear, we decided I was ready.

The night before I was due to leave, I might have changed my mind, except it felt like I had to do this, not only to escape London but because I was sick of myself, of the heartbroken girl I seemed to be. If the old Sarah-Jane was lost, then it was time to become a new person, a better, bolder one.

'We're doing this, Baxter,' I told him, and the dog rolled over onto his back and splayed his legs like he does when he'd rather not move. 'We're definitely doing this, we have to.'

My mother waved me off one day in early spring without any admonishments to drive carefully, or stay in touch, or check I had my passport. She gave me only one instruction. 'Have fun, Sarah-Jane, enjoy this.'

Once my jittery excitement had settled, I did have fun. With all the time in the world, I took the slower back routes whenever I could. In my little car I drove onto a Channel ferry, soared up and down the undulating roads of France and braved Swiss alpine passes.

I like my own company, so I hardly ever got lonely, and when I did, there was Baxter to chat to. Of course there were wrong turns and near misses with other cars, days when I wished there was someone to share the driving and times I was tempted to turn back. And by no means was the journey trouble-free. Reversing proved especially tricky, and my car was already scarred from a minor collision with a lamp post. But nothing too serious happened and on sunny days, with the roof down and my dog attached to his safety harness on the passenger seat, there were times that felt fabulous. When I crossed the border to Italy, I cheered so loud that Baxter started barking.

I was convinced it made me look more like a local to have a dog beside me. And Baxter is one of those dogs that knows how to fit in. At cafés he sits politely under the table and never begs for food (although usually I slip him a little). If children want to pat him then he couldn't be more delighted. It is rare for him to tug on the leash, unless he happens to glimpse a squirrel, and he is happy to go wherever I take him. He is the perfect travelling companion.

For the first few weeks I revisited people and places I remembered, stayed with old friends or at any cheap *pensione* where Baxter was welcome. Mum came and stayed in Venice with me for a long weekend and then we met up again for a week in Amalfi.

After that I decided to venture south and cover new territory. The plan was to drive to Sicily, and round its entire coastline, before heading north again. This would be a relaxed journey. If I saw a place that looked intriguing, I would stop and spend some time there. When I wasn't impressed, I'd move on.

Maybe it was the steepness of the roads I had to tackle, or the wrong sort of petrol or something about my driving, but more than likely, the car was always going to let me down. Now it had happened, dramatically with a big bang, and I hoped this wasn't going to be the end of my adventure.

At least the food in the little *trattoria* was unexpectedly good. Once I had finished the pasta, wiping a crust of bread around the bowl to catch the last of the sauce, and eaten a side dish of wilted chicory with thin slivers of garlic and a bittersweet bite of lemon, and drunk a glass of wine, the day started to seem like less of a disaster. Cars broke down all the time and people fixed them. It would be fine.

The cook passed by my table, arms loaded with empty plates. She seemed to operate the place entirely by herself. There was no waitress or kitchen hand that I had noticed and yet she didn't seem rushed as she went about her work.

'Thanks, that was delicious, exactly what I needed,' I said when she stopped to collect my dishes.

She gave me an unsurprised nod.

'I think there's a mechanic in Borgo del Colle,' I added. 'They're not answering the number on the website right now. But hopefully they'll be able to tow my car there and fix it before too long.'

The woman frowned, deepening the web of fine wrinkles

on her face. Putting down the stack of plates she had been carrying, she turned and went outside. The two older guys were still there arguing loudly across the bonnet of my car, while a younger man was trying to mediate, and a few others were standing about looking on, apparently lacking anything more interesting to do.

The cook started shouting in Italian, pointed a finger and waved her hands around a bit. They all stopped talking and stared at her. Her hands were on her hips now. '*Andate subito!*' she ordered, and my grasp of Italian was adequate enough for me to understand that she was telling them to go somewhere straight away.

What I didn't expect was for one of the elderly men to slam shut the car's bonnet, while the other climbed into the driver's seat and released the handbrake, or for the crowd to come together and push, amid a clamour of voices. Slowly, they started to move my little Saab.

I hurried out of the restaurant, Baxter at my heels. 'What's happening? Where are they taking it?'

The cook looked at me, eyebrows raised in surprise. 'To the mechanic, like you wanted.'

Assunta

Assunta knew everyone who lived in Montenello, and most of their business too. What she didn't overhear while weaving between the tightly packed tables of the restaurant, her brother Renzo gleaned working behind the bar next door.

Not that they gossiped exactly, not with other people, but they exchanged information between themselves, usually in the afternoons when everything was quiet. Whether it was bad tidings or better news, it always reached Assunta before long.

And so Assunta knew that Carlo Mastrobuoni was lonely. For many years he had eaten a weekly lunch at the *trattoria* and ever since his wife had died, he came more often. Making time to chat, she heard about the Mastrobuoni family. How his youngest girl was struggling with too many small children and a husband who wasn't working; how he despaired of his older daughter who only cared about clothes and holidays; how his son was in Napoli, not properly settled yet, but working hard and doing well, because Riccardo was a good boy. Of all his offspring, Riccardo was the one most likely to come home and be with a father who needed some company. Sure enough, Assunta had seen the pair together only the day before. Now, as she looked out through the open doorway of the *trattoria* at the car that had stopped and the men standing around it, there was one more thing she remembered that she knew – Riccardo was a mechanic.

The Mastrobuoni house wasn't far away, down a slight incline and then a steeper hill, so the car could be pushed there, perhaps not easily, but it was possible. That was what she told her father and Francesco, who both knew her well enough not to try and argue.

Soon she was watching them trying to manoeuvre the vehicle, with Francesco calling instructions to Augusto at the steering wheel, and the others pushing together. Reaching a downward slope, the car began to move more smoothly and a cheer went up from the men.

'My bags are in there,' said the dark-haired young woman, sounding panicked. 'Where are they going exactly?'

'Not far.'

'I'd better run after them. I'll come back later and settle my bill, is that OK?'

Young people puzzled Assunta. She couldn't understand how they could waste half their lives looking at their phones and then, for the other half, be in such a hurry.

'No need to run,' she said.

'But ...'

'See how slowly they are moving? The mechanic's place is not far but still it will take them some time to reach it. And now it is afternoon; people are resting, no one is working. Later Riccardo Mastrobuoni may have other things to do before he looks at your car. Perhaps he will have to send for whatever your engine needs. This will take the time it takes.'

'Oh God, I'm going to need a hotel, aren't I?' The girl's phone was already in her hand. 'If there's one nearby, that is.'

'Tell me, what is your name?' asked Assunta.

'Sarah-Jane.' The girl was tapping at her phone screen again.

'Sarah-Jane, my suggestion for you is to relax. My brother Renzo will bring you a coffee and perhaps a *digestivo*. With so much stress on a full stomach ... you will become bloated and that won't help your situation.'

The girl looked up from her phone, almost smiling but not quite. 'It won't?'

34

'Later I will take you to meet the mechanic then show you the hotel which is also not too far to walk.' Resting a hand on the girl's shoulder, Assunta guided her back inside the *trattoria*. 'Everything will be OK.'

'Thank you so much. I'm sorry, I didn't ask your name.'

'Assunta.'

'You speak really good English, Assunta.'

'My father insisted I study; he has always been progressive. He was among the men who tried to help with your car, Augusto, the noisiest. You will meet him again, when he remembers that he hasn't eaten any lunch.'

Returning her to her seat, she supplied Sarah-Jane with coffee and a glass of Amaro Lucano. A few customers were still finishing their food. Maddalena Marino was wrapping slices of bread in paper serviettes, reaching into the baskets on the empty tables around her for more. The town's mayor, Salvio Valentini, was conducting a meeting that would most likely finish in the bar next door. Leonardo Gallo and his wife Giusi were bickering as they sipped the last of their wine.

There had been times over the years when Assunta had taken on staff to help wait tables or prep food. The younger ones never stayed long; no sooner were they trained than they moved away or found a better position. And the older ones grew tired or sick or died. So now she managed alone. While the days could be long, she had done this work her whole life, and never considered anything different.

Busy putting aside food for her father and Francesco, who would be hungry once the excitement was over, Assunta saw that the girl, Sarah-Jane, was on her feet. She was clearing away the mayor's plates, taking the stack of bread baskets from Maddalena and shaking out the crumbs, relieving Leonardo Gallo of his empty carafe. Next she helped load the large commercial dishwasher that took up too much space in Assunta's kitchen and cleaned the carafes by hand, carefully polishing them dry with a cloth before returning them to the shelves, finding the right place for everything.

'You have worked in restaurants,' Assunta observed.

'I waitressed when I was younger.'

'And now?'

Sarah-Jane hesitated. 'I'm on a sabbatical.'

'I don't know that word.'

'I'm taking time off, probably about a year, driving around Italy with Baxter my dog.'

'This seems a very nice thing to do.'

'So far it has been,' Sarah-Jane agreed. 'But now the car has broken down and so ...'

'You will stay in Montenello for a while, relax, walk your dog. It might also be a nice thing.'

'I guess it might,' said the girl, sounding unconvinced. She polished the last wine carafe, placed it carefully on the shelf, then turned and cast her eyes over the empty dining room. 'Are we nearly done here? I'd really like to go and check on my car now.'

Assunta unlaced the strings of her apron and hung it on a hook ready for the next time she needed it. The girl's help meant everything had been finished in half the usual time. Her kitchen was clean, the tables wiped, all was in order. But there was no hurry.

'One moment,' she told her.

Sarah-Jane

Everything took so long. As kind as these people were, I wished they would move faster. I needed to talk to the mechanic, find out how long fixing my car was likely to take, check into a hotel, call my insurance company and see if I was covered for any of this. There was a lot to do.

Helping with the clean-up at the *trattoria* didn't win me any time. Once everyone had left and the place was tidy, Assunta insisted on stopping at the next-door bar, introduced me to her brother, smoked a cigarette and drank a glass of the same herbal liqueur she had given me earlier. Since I didn't have a single clue where my car had been taken, I couldn't go anywhere without her.

I have worked in restaurants but never a place like the one she ran. The paying system seemed to involve her scribbling in a notebook that she carried in her apron pocket or taking cash from people, without bothering to check they had given the right amount. She was short and solid, with a mostly stern expression but when she smiled, it changed her face. Right now she was chuckling at something her brother was saying in Italian, as she lit a second cigarette. I despaired of us ever getting out of there.

'A few moments more, signora,' she promised, but I was pretty certain it was going to take longer.

She sipped at the liqueur, a dark black brew with a bitter-sweet flavour, then stubbed out the cigarette in an ashtray that her brother had produced from under the counter (although I am certain smoking in bars was banned in Italy years ago). When it seemed as if we were about to leave, her elderly father appeared, with his even more ancient friend, and that meant going next door to fetch the food she had put aside for them, and more chatter and laughter.

'Where exactly is my car?' I asked, raising my voice to be heard. 'I really need to go and sort things out.'

It was the old man, Augusto, who responded. 'Of course, of course.'

Slowly he tackled his meal, his friend drank a glass of wine, Assunta smoked yet another cigarette. The afternoon was passing by the time we set off, an entire troupe of us, wandering down the hill together.

'You will like Riccardo Mastrobuoni, he is very nice,' Augusto promised me.

'Is he the mechanic?' I asked.

'Of course.'

I didn't care about his level of niceness, only that he knew what he was doing. Still, I smiled at the old man because he seemed very sweet and I didn't want to seem ungrateful.

We headed off at a slow stroll and, halfway down the hill, stopped outside a house, although there was no sign of my car there. Assunta knocked on the door and a silvery-haired man poked his head out of an upstairs window. They proceeded to conduct a conversation at top volume, the man calling down to the street, the others yelling back. Not understanding a word, I glanced at Baxter who wagged his tail hopefully.

'Carlo says that Riccardo has taken your car a little further down the hill to his workshop,' Assunta told me eventually.

'Does he think it can be fixed?'

She shouted something else at the man, and another long back and forth ensued, this time involving laughter. Finally she turned to me with a shrug. 'He doesn't know.'

Together, we continued down the hill in search of the workshop. Eventually the row of houses ended and there was only a curving road and a wall of rock. That was when Assunta stopped again. 'We are here,' she declared.

It wasn't even a proper garage, more a hole in the side of the mountain, the ceiling barely above head-height, with its loosely hinged double doors thrown open. My slightly dented Saab was there, parked next to a white Fiat Cinquecento. Hanging over the open bonnet was a man wearing rolled-down overalls and an oil-stained T-shirt, staring at the engine, not doing anything much.

'Are you sure he's a mechanic?' I asked Assunta.

At the sound of my voice, the man turned. The first thing I noticed was that he had a striking combination of dark hair, olive skin and turquoise eyes. He had what my mother would describe as a strong nose, and the rise of his eyebrows hinted that he understood English.

'You are Signora Saab,' he said, bending to greet Baxter who had trotted over.

'That's right. Can my car be saved?'

Wiping his hand on a rag, the mechanic came to stand beside me. He wasn't especially tall but I still got an impression of physical power.

'Almost certainly, but there is one problem,' he said. 'Saab, they are finished making these cars, I think, and the parts aren't always easy to find.'

'Really?' I had bought my car seduced by the glamour of cruising along with the roof down, the breeze in my hair, the sun on my face. And on the back roads of Tuscany and the hilly winding routes of Umbria and Abruzzo, it had felt as good as I imagined. 'I suppose that's why it was such a bargain. What if you can't get the parts at all?'

'Signora, nothing is impossible. I have kept this Fiat going for my father for years. I will do the same for you, but I need some time.'

'How much time?'

He rubbed his chin, already smeared with oil, and shook

his head. 'I have no answer to that, not yet. As soon as I have fixed my father's car, I will take a look and see what is needed.'

Baxter was sitting at his feet, gazing up at him. At times my little dog seems almost like a person, and I had the distinct sense right then that he knew how important this mechanic was to us.

'Your bags are in the car,' Riccardo observed. 'The hotel will come and collect them later.'

'I don't even know if I can get a room there. It may be fully booked. I noticed earlier there's a wedding on in town.'

'There is always a wedding,' he said, matter-of-factly.

I was really reluctant to leave without my things. There was a suitcase and two smaller bags with my laptop and toiletries stowed in them. They were too heavy to carry far so I considered asking for a ride because this guy must have a functioning car somewhere if he had managed to tow the Saab. But what if he took me and all my bags to the hotel and they had no space there, or wouldn't accommodate Baxter? I let out a sigh. It must have been a loud and heavy one because everyone stared.

'They will have a room for you,' Riccardo reassured me. 'Leave everything else, I will take care of it.'

His bright turquoise eyes gazed into mine and I felt fractionally reassured.

'And the bags?'

'Don't worry, I will look after them until the hotel sends someone.'

It seemed my only option so, with a last glance at my unreliable car, I headed away with my new friends, not back the way we had come but up a series of steps that cut along the side of the mountain.

'I'm lost,' I told Assunta, who was walking beside me in silence. 'Is the hotel much further?'

'Not far,' she said.

We rounded a corner and there it was. Two storeys, with shuttered windows and an archway for an entrance, it looked boutique and worryingly small. As we entered, I could hear music playing and a hum of conversation.

We were in a reception area with a beautiful carved wooden desk. Beyond it was a large room where a party was taking place and a stairway with a sign pointing the way to a restaurant on the second floor.

'Hi there.' The man behind the reception desk sounded Australian. 'You must be the woman whose car broke down?'

'Am I famous?' I asked, startled.

'It doesn't take much to be famous in this town,' he said with a smile.

Coming out from behind the reception desk, he kissed me on both cheeks Italian-style. Tall and well-muscled, with a shaved head and a classy-looking suit, he even smelled expensive.

'I'm Edward,' he said, 'the owner/manager of this place.'

'Great, I need a room, but the trouble is I'm not sure for how long. Also I have my dog, so ...'

'We're pet-friendly,' he told me. 'Oh and don't worry you won't be disturbed by the noise from the wedding reception.'

'I'll just be relieved if there's a bed for me.' I could hear English voices among the party guests. 'You seem very busy.'

'We are but there are more rooms than you might think.' He gave me a leaflet with the words *Albergo Diffuso* emblazoned on it. 'This place is a little different. You can read about the concept here, but I'll give you the quick explanation. We don't accommodate our guests in this building. Here is where you'll find the traditional hotel facilities: a breakfast room, function centre and restaurant. You will stay in one of the restored houses of Montenello and experience being a part of the community.'

It sounded expensive and I was trying not to overspend

on accommodation. Also I didn't particularly want to experience being a part of a community I had been trying to leave. But by then I was past caring. My feet hurt and it was getting late and I needed to know where I would be sleeping.

'Most of our rooms are nearby,' he continued, 'but those are full because of the wedding. We do have a house a little further away that we are able to offer in busy times. It's charming and there are no other bookings, so you can stay as long as you like.'

'What would the cost be?'

'If you pay in advance for the week, and we don't service your rooms, then I can give you a good discount.'

The price he named wasn't too steep, and the house he went on to describe sounded perfect. Private, simple, beautiful views – my spirits lifted a little.

'I'll take it.' Knowing the deal was too good to turn down, I handed Edward my passport and a credit card.

'Welcome to Montenello,' he said. 'I hope your stay with us is going to be an enjoyable one.'

Assunta

Assunta had not been inside the hotel since everything was changed. She had walked past and stared through its lit windows, glancing at the chandelier in the function room and at the well-dressed people holding flutes of champagne, but had never been curious to see more.

Montenello kept on changing. Strangers came, places opened, but to Assunta it felt as if the new life of her town had been laid over the old one like tracing paper. Mostly she looked beyond it and focused on what was familiar.

She had visited this hotel when she was younger and it was always on the shabby side. Now stepping through its doors again, Assunta saw how it had altered and all the ways it was still the same. She was intrigued.

Everyone else had a place to be: Edward was taking the stranded English girl to her accommodation, while her father and Francesco were heading to their fruit and vegetable truck. Assunta only had to go home and she wasn't in any hurry.

First she explored upstairs, finding the restaurant. She had imagined it as one large space, but instead it was arranged through several rooms. The furniture was rustic and there was a clutter of small vases filled with flowers that might have been picked at the roadside. In the bathroom was an antique mirror spotted with age, as well as scented soaps and fancy cloths to dry your hands on.

There were other rooms upstairs, but they seemed to be for staff or storage, so Assunta went back down and walked through the wedding party. She took a glass of champagne from a tray and found a seat at the end of a chaise longue, beside an older woman.

From there she had a view of the bride, who had changed into an evening gown, and looked flushed from the wine and the warmth of the room. Catching Assunta's eye, she gave a half-smile, probably thinking this was yet another distant aunt she had been obliged to invite.

As a waiter passed, Assunta reached for a canapé and the woman beside her took one too. 'These are good,' she said in English. 'The ones with wagyu beef and truffled aioli are better though.'

Nodding and smiling, Assunta sipped champagne and enjoyed pretending to belong. This was a beautiful room, filled with pillars and archways, with the glittering chandelier at its centre and a grand marble fireplace against one wall. It was perfect for a party and the younger women, with their polished fingernails and sculpted hair, matched it for sleekness. Assunta had never been so attractive or self-assured, even at their age. In silky dresses and spiked heels, they seemed a different species.

A waiter offered to top up her glass, but Assunta shook her head. The hotel often hosted wedding receptions like this one. She could put on smart clothes and drink champagne with strangers almost any evening at this time of year, occasionally even in winter. She was amused by the idea, but knew she wouldn't bother again. Once was enough.

Putting down her empty glass, she moved unseen through the gathering, past the reception desk and out of the hotel. Heading first to the piazza, she checked on her father. Augusto had given up trying to sell fresh vegetables and was sitting outside the bar, chatting with some of the men who had helped to push the car earlier.

Seeing him well and happy, Assunta turned for home. It wasn't far and she took her time, stopping to exchange a few words with anyone she knew: an elderly woman sitting outside her front door shelling fava beans, the man who swept the streets, a neighbour who was watering window boxes filled with herbs, the mayor's wife out with her toddler in a buggy.

Inside her own house everything was still and the only sounds the ticking of a clock and the birdsong in her garden. Assunta breathed the smell of polished wood and lavender. When she had an evening free, her routine was the same. First she showered, to wash away the working day; then rubbed lotion into her skin to keep it soft, and dressed in something comfortable.

This evening Assunta was tired, but also quite hungry. Looking into her fridge and cupboards, she thought about what to cook. Her customers would assume she never bothered making meals for herself but lived on leftovers of whatever she had served in the *trattoria* that day. Occasionally this was what she did if she was exhausted, standing over the sink to eat something before falling into bed uncaring.

But there was a pleasure to be found in setting a table with her grandmother's china, her good crystal and bone-handled cutlery. In having a cloth napkin and pouring a glass of ruby red Aglianico wine.

In Assunta's cupboards were ingredients she never used when she was cooking for other people. Lately she had been attracted to Middle Eastern flavours, creating dishes that were smoky with tahini, soured with pomegranate molasses or spiced with cumin.

Tonight carrots were roasted with honey and harissa, aubergine was cooked until it was silky then topped with fresh herbs, garlic, lemon and warm spices. A dish of hummus, fried haloumi, warmed crusty bread, and Assunta sat down to her meal.

As she ate, she thought about the wedding. All those guests would be feasting on a banquet by now. She didn't envy them. It was the years the bride had ahead of her, eating at her own table, extending its leaves to accommodate the family she would have – the sons and daughters, the grand-children. All the people she would belong with. Assunta felt a pang when she allowed herself to think of that.

Sarah-Jane

Baxter and I had done a lot of walking, and there was further to go. Since I had no bags with me, the hotel manager thought it better to escort me to my accommodation on foot, so he could point out the quickest way, through the back streets and hidden stairways.

'Tomorrow morning you might want to come back for breakfast,' said Edward in his lilting Australian accent. 'Although there is an excellent *pasticceria* in town and the bar will be open for coffee. That's where you'll find a lot of the locals first thing.'

'How did you end up living here?' I wondered.

'You've heard about the scheme to sell off abandoned houses in Montenello for one euro?'

When I nodded, he continued.

'We entered the very first lottery and managed to win one. My husband Gino has a connection with this town; his parents left here years ago to emigrate to Sydney.'

'And you've ended up running a hotel.'

'That was Gino. He heard about the *albergo diffuso* concept and got the mayor onside with the idea, then things kind of snowballed. We don't own all the houses, some are sub-let from other people, but wherever possible, Gino oversees the restoration to be sure tradition is respected.'

'And it's been successful?' I couldn't imagine many people coming to such a remote spot for a holiday.

'We've had our ups and downs, but we're still here. The mayor's wife runs a destination weddings business and that's what keeps us going.'

47

I was breathing more heavily now as we scaled a row of steep steps, Edward pounding upwards ahead of me.

'We don't have many of the things tourists are looking for,' he conceded. 'Beaches, nightlife. What we have is peace and beauty.'

'The locals don't mind an invasion of outsiders?'

'Now and then feathers are ruffled when someone's favourite seat in the bar is taken, but this town was fading away so most of them are happy that its fortunes have been changed. The one-euro house scheme was the mayor's idea – him and Augusto came up with it.'

'The little old man, Assunta's father?' I was surprised.

Edward nodded. 'Augusto is a cool guy. If you're spending a whole week here, you should get to know him. He's got a lot of stories.'

A whole week in a town where I knew no one … the reality hit me. How was I going to fill so much time? Hopefully there were more things to see in Montenello than I had found so far.

At least the house was lovely. A cottage with a doorway swathed in flowering jasmine, inside was neat and bright, with far-reaching views across the valley. I loved its simplicity.

'Sweet, isn't it,' said Edward. 'One of my favourites.'

'Is the one-euro house that you won similar to this?'

He laughed at that. 'Absolutely not.'

Half an hour later my bags were delivered in a three-wheeled Piaggio Ape truck. I was pleased to be reunited with them and spent some time unpacking and putting things away, wedging the empty suitcase under the bed afterwards. Baxter was already curled up on its covers, worn out from our day's adventures, snoring a little.

Just as I was wondering where I would find some dinner, there was another knock and I found Edward on the doorstep, a jute bag in his hand.

'*Buonasera*,' he said, cheerfully. 'You're settling in? I've brought a few things.'

The bag was unpacked to reveal juicy tomatoes and apples with wrinkling skins, a wedge of waxy cheese in greaseproof paper, a loaf of crusty bread, a bottle of red wine and a carefully wrapped cake that must have come from the *pasticceria*. He hadn't forgotten Baxter; for him there were offcuts of meat.

Edward stayed for long enough to uncork the wine and pour me a very full glass.

'Won't you have one too?' I wondered, keen on some company, at least for a short while.

'Not this evening, sorry, we're a bit short-staffed and I need to get back. Another time though?'

'Sure – it seems like I'm going to have a few evenings to fill, so that would be great.'

Once Edward had left, I lay down next to my dog, pulled a rug over both of us and closed my eyes for a moment. This hadn't been the day I was planning, at all.

My mother is a big believer in the power of focusing on all the things that have gone right for you, rather than any disappointments. Her point is that it's better for the spirits and while I'm sure she is right, after the whole business with Tom I had struggled to find the good in anything for a while.

Now, curled up with Baxter's warm little body beside me, I decided to be grateful for the fact my Saab had broken down, not in the middle of nowhere, but right outside a little *trattoria*. People had been helpful and I had a lovely place to stay. And I was going to get a break from driving now. Thinking about the maze of steep streets I had navigated, with so many tight corners and badly parked cars to avoid scraping; that also seemed a thing to be grateful for.

By the time my mother called, I was in a better frame of mind. We chatted and I told her about Montenello, describing the way it seemed to rise up out of the mountain, its church spires soaring into a sky swirling with swifts.

'That sounds wonderful,' she said, wistfully. 'I wish I was there.'

'I really wish you were here too.' It wasn't that I minded being on my own – usually I quite like it – but a week seemed too long to spend in an unexciting little town where I didn't know anyone at all. 'It's going to be a bit boring, isn't it?'

'Remember when you were eighteen and you went off to university, my advice to you then?' said my mother.

Of course I remembered. I was staying in the halls of residence of a college that was miles from home, and she told me to knock on the neighbouring doors and introduce myself to the people living behind them. All these years later, I still knew some of the women I had found.

'You should do the same thing there,' Mum suggested. 'Make new friends.'

I wasn't about to start knocking on doors. Instead, once we had finished chatting, I stayed inside and ate a dinner of bread, cheese and tomatoes, looking out over my view of rooftops, sky and valley.

My day hadn't gone as planned, but it hadn't worked out too badly. And sitting there, as the light faded, what struck me was that I hadn't thought of Tom for hours.

Until then he had been with me all the way on this journey. Driving through France then Switzerland, I had imagined him in the passenger seat, held conversations with him in my head, viewed every detail of the trip through his eyes – the landscapes I passed, the places I slept in, the meals I ate – imagining what he would think, what he might say (he'd have hated the Saab, which was rattly and draughty if I'm honest), and how I would reply.

For some reason Tom didn't have a presence yet in this house, and I had nothing to say to him, not this evening.

*

I woke early with Baxter curled in the crook of my legs and it was tempting not to move. Morning sun was filtering through the curtains and warming the room. From outside I could hear birds chirping and someone was playing a piano, starting with scales then tentatively easing into a tune I recognised, Satie's first Gymnopedie. Closing my eyes, I let the music flow over me.

When the stranger had finished playing, I got up and let Baxter outside to sniff about and have a morning pee. Around us the town was coming to life, windows and doors had been opened and the air smelled of coffee. There wasn't any in the bag of supplies Edward had so helpfully provided the previous evening, and now I was craving my first cup of the day, so that meant getting dressed and finding my way back to the bar in the piazza.

Baxter breakfasted on leftover bread and cheese, while I took a shower, put on a bright yellow sundress and looked though the cupboards in search of a basket to use for shopping.

I couldn't remember the way back to the hotel and the map on my phone only led me astray in the twisty maze of lanes. Finally I came across a woman pulling a shopping trolley behind her, and decided to follow. She led me past a pharmacy, and a shop selling dried goods, cheeses and salami. A short way beyond was the piazza, and it was already bustling. There was a queue lining up beside a truck selling fresh fish and more women trundling shopping trolleys.

My first stop was the bar. Several people stared as I walked in, and the same barman who had been there the day before acknowledged me with a nod. On the counter was a tray of plump pastries and, choosing one stuffed with custard and dusted with slivers of almonds, I chased it down with two cups of coffee.

Fortified, I decided to walk down the hill and find the mechanic, Riccardo Mastrobuoni, in the hope there had been a chance for him to look at my car and see what was needed.

I followed the same route as the day before, on a wide road that curved around the mountain with views over the gorge below and a silvery stream that snaked through it. The doors of his workshop were thrown open and I heard a radio playing Italian pop music. Bits and pieces of engine were littering the road outside and, when I looked inwards, it was to see the bonnets of both the Saab and Fiat propped open.

'*Buongiorno*,' I called to Riccardo, who was dressed in rolled-down overalls and a tight white T-shirt, standing between the two broken-down vehicles, apparently deep in thought.

'*Buongiorno*,' I repeated, raising my voice.

Turning to me, he smiled.

'Ah, Signora Saab,' he called out over the racket of music.

I pointed to the engine parts on the ground. 'Which car does all of this belong to?'

'A little from both,' he admitted.

'So how do you know which part goes where?'

Riccardo laughed, as if I was joking but must have realised from my expression that I was genuinely worried. 'No problem,' he promised.

'Do you know what's wrong with my car yet?'

'The transmission,' he said. 'That is the main issue but there are other things that will need attention if you are going to make a long trip without it breaking down again. I am writing a list.'

'A long one?'

Leaning against the uneven rock wall of the workshop, Riccardo kicked at a tyre. 'What made you choose a car like this?'

'I fell in love with it,' I told him. 'It seemed like fun.'

'Did you have someone go with you when you bought it?'

'My mother, she loved it too.' We had taken it for a test drive through London with the roof down even though rain was threatening, and it felt stylish and adventurous. Both of us were convinced I had to buy it.

'Does your mother know about cars?'

'Not really,' I admitted. 'Not at all.'

He nodded slowly. 'OK.'

'It has low mileage for a car of its age,' I pointed out.

'That sort of thing can be falsified.'

'The salesman was great; he threw in four new tyres and replaced the window wipers. He gave me a really good deal.'

Riccardo nodded again, his expression serious and unchanging.

'You think it was a rip-off? That I shouldn't have bought it?'

He rested a hand on one of my Saab's red panels. 'I love old cars but they need lots of love. You can't expect them to keep going without regular attention.'

'Can you fix it?' I asked worriedly.

'Yes, but—'

'It's going to cost a lot, isn't it?'

'Not necessarily,' he told me. 'People have cars like this that they break up for parts so I can look to buy what is needed second-hand. It is time, more than money, which is needed. Do you have enough of that?'

'I suppose so.'

'Then there is no problem,' Riccardo said brightly. 'At least not one that is too big for us to manage.'

Looking down at the chunks of metal strewn over the ground, I hoped this oil-stained guy with the disconcertingly bright gaze actually knew what he was doing.

'Your bags arrived safely, yes?' he asked. 'Do you need anything else?'

'Only to get groceries – is there a supermarket?'

'Not here in Montenello, we have only a few small shops

and the trucks that come to sell fresh food. Meat one morning, seafood the next and Augusto with his vegetables every afternoon.'

'So I should be able to find everything?'

'I hope so, but if you want to drive to Borgo del Colle I have a car you can borrow, not as charming as yours, but more reliable.'

'Oh right, a loan vehicle? What would that cost?'

'Cost?' He looked at me blankly. 'It is my car and you are welcome to use it. Later this afternoon I must go with my father to an appointment, but most days it is available.'

'That's really kind.'

He shrugged off my thanks. 'No problem ... *tutto va bene* ... everything is fine.'

By the time I made it back to the piazza, the truck selling seafood had disappeared. I found the *salumeria* open so bought cheese, dried pasta, and a selection of cured meats, then wandered further, looking for a place that sold dog food, but only found a hardware store.

Tracing my route back to the house was easier; I only went wrong once or twice, even managing to find a shortcut Edward had shown me the previous day. But unpacking my shopping, I was irritated to realise I hadn't bought any coffee.

I tend to drink cup after cup of it in the mornings like a proper addict and at home there was a fancy machine. Here was only equipped with a stovetop Moka pot but that would have been perfectly fine with some coffee to put in it. Searching the cupboards again, I came across salt, pepper, half a bottle of olive oil and some vinegar, but no coffee. I checked the small freezer, finding it empty.

'Sorry Baxter, we'll have to go out again,' I said, and his ears pricked at the sound of my voice. 'Maybe we'll find some dog biscuits this time, too.'

At the *salumeria*, the man behind the counter shook his head when I asked if he sold coffee. With no more likely places in sight, I found myself back at the bar. A group of old men were playing cards outside and, walking in, I had the sense of arriving late at a party. There was a crowd standing at the counter and all the tables were taken, but a woman moved her expensive-looking handbag off a chair, gesturing for me to sit down. She was stylish, with a short pixie hair-cut and clothes that definitely hadn't been bought around here. I wondered if she was another of the one-euro house owners.

Pulling out my phone, I googled Montenello, coming across an article in the *Guardian* that detailed how it had been destined to become a ghost town until an energetic young mayor, Salvio Valentini, formed a rescue plan. There was a photograph of him, young and good-looking, stand-ing outside the Town Hall and smiling broadly.

If someone offered me a dilapidated house here at a bar-gain price, I was pretty sure I wouldn't be tempted. For a city lover, there didn't seem to be enough happening, in fact milling about the piazza looked like the extent of the excite-ment. Oh, and the weddings of course; there was another one happening now, a bride and groom posing for photographs in the piazza. I watched them gazing into one another's eyes, moving closer to kiss and walking hand-in-hand past the fountain.

'It's wedding season,' said the stylish woman, her accent London-posh. 'There'll probably be another couple there tomorrow, and the next day. You stop finding it so romantic after a while.'

I had never been one for dreaming about getting married. Some of my friends couldn't wait to climb into a poufy dress and there was a spate of summers that were hectic with hen parties and weddings. I never longed to be the one walking up the aisle or cutting the cake; there wasn't a moment of envy. Perhaps it was to do with losing my dad, but I didn't join the crush to catch the bouquet.

'Where do they all come from?' I asked the well-dressed, well-spoken woman.

'Lots are from England, but all over I think. They're always having to sieve confetti out of the fountain.'

Sure enough, this bride and groom were being showered in rose petals that were drifting over the fountain's scalloped edges and into the jets of water.

'It's very important for the town,' added the woman. 'There's money in the weddings for several businesses here. And fortunately there's no shortage of people falling madly in love.'

Until I met Tom, I never dreamed of getting married, but if he had proposed I'd have said yes, and stood with him in a cloud of rose petals. I loved Tom in a way that I could feel like a weight on my chest and would have married him in a heartbeat. Instead, here I was looking on as strangers celebrated, watching a bridal party parade across the piazza, bridesmaids and groomsmen, proud parents, cherubic flower girls, all heading to the next location.

As they disappeared from view, the fruit and vegetable truck arrived, rolling into the piazza and parking at its centre. I recognised Augusto and his friend climbing out and watched them ambling towards the *trattoria* for lunch. In the bar, the crowd was thinning. The pixie-haircut woman with the nice handbag was gone, the group of old men had abandoned their table, a whole wave of locals had ebbed and flowed into the place next door. Since I was hungry too, I decided to follow them.

Assunta's *trattoria* was busy, packed with people eating and talking. At the nearest table I saw my mechanic, Riccardo, who had changed out of his overalls and put on jeans and a clean white T-shirt, although he still wore the ghost of an oil smear down one forearm. He was sitting with the older man that I guessed was his father.

Standing in the doorway, I hesitated but Baxter was bolder, trotting inside and straight over to them. Riccardo leaned down to pat the dog's head and then smiled towards me.

'Signora, we have a space, if you would like to join Papa and I.'

'Are you sure? I'm not intruding?'

'No problem,' he said.

'This is a popular spot,' I said, taking a seat and encouraging Baxter to lie down beneath it. 'Is it always so busy?'

Riccardo nodded. 'It is best to come early because when Assunta runs out of food, she stops serving.'

He poured out some wine and introduced me to his father, a more weathered version of him, with eyes faded to a paler blue, hair silvering, jaw softening. There was a slightly awkward attempt at conversation, until Assunta rescued us, appearing with steaming plates: a tangle of spaghetti with tender squid and nutty chickpeas.

Riccardo's father ate with pleasure, scooping the tender bites of squid onto his fork with a crust of bread, and declaring it very good.

'It is always very good here,' he told me.

'Yes,' agreed Riccardo. 'In Napoli there are plenty of great restaurants but I always missed this one.'

'I loved Napoli,' I told them. 'I spent a few days there, staying in a little apartment on an island, right next to the walls of a castle.'

'Castel dell'Ovo,' Riccardo guessed. 'The garage where I used to work wasn't far from there. I loved it too, but it's good to come home.'

He looked to be in his early thirties, with fine lines round his eyes that crinkled when he smiled and his palms were roughened from years of manual work. Did he live with his father, I wondered, or had he brought a family back home with him?

'Montenello must be very quiet after living in the city,' I remarked.

'It is OK.' Riccardo shrugged. 'One thing that is difficult is finding a job, even now with all the improvements. I am fortunate because everywhere there are cars that need to be fixed and the mechanic over in Borgo del Colle is very expensive.'

'Lucky that Assunta stopped me taking my Saab there then.'

'I think so,' he agreed, eyes sparkling. 'Very lucky.'

We had a second course of crisply fried fish sprinkled with a smoky sweet crush of dried peppers, and a dish of lemony *broccoli rabe* flecked with garlic. Riccardo and his father left as soon as they had eaten, not wanting to be late for their appointment. Finishing the last mouthfuls of wine, I stacked up our plates, and carried them to the kitchen, adding them to the pile already mounting. There were other customers heading off and leaving a mess behind. Since Assunta seemed to have enough to do, I cleared their tables, as I had the day before, and then thought I may as well start loading the dishwasher.

'How did you make that pasta dish taste so good?' I asked Assunta, who glanced at me in surprise as I scraped and stacked plates. 'What did you put in it exactly?'

'Only what was needed,' she said, gruffly.

'What exactly though?' I pressed her. 'Would you give me the recipe?'

'Recipe?'

Assunta said the word with an expression on her face that suggested she was in pain. Over the years I had met a few cooks who guarded the secrets of their signature dishes. Some gave you instructions but forgot to mention a crucial ingredient. Others seemed set on taking the mystery to their graves. But I had never come across anyone who was affronted at the very mention of the word, spitting it out like an insult.

'There are no recipes here,' Assunta said, as if concerned I was going to start rifling through the kitchen for some hidden book or folder.

I think of recipes as stories about food. Reading through a complex one, imagining it step-by-step, conjuring up flavours and textures, is like an escape for me. I can never have enough cookbooks, whether they are glossy-paged volumes or old notebooks filled with spidery handwriting. I love recipes, if they are good ones then you can rely on them.

And every cook you meet has something to teach you, whether it's a special trick with pastry or a clever way with cauliflower. Some will share the knowledge passed down through families or picked up on travels, and I'm greedy for that; I want to collect and keep it, like a hoarder.

So I wasn't going to give up on Assunta, not now I had tasted her cooking. I wanted to know what made her gnocchi so light, why her ragu melted in my mouth and how a simple dish of pasta and chickpeas could be so comforting. There had to be recipes, there always were.

Assunta

There was no book of recipes in Assunta's kitchen – there never had been. She wasn't ruled by instructions, by a teaspoon of this and a cup of that. But how to tell this girl, who seemed so hopeful and helpful, that good food couldn't be reduced to ink on a page?

Being a cook was about understanding how to coax the flavour from ingredients, as Assunta had discovered as a young girl helping out in this *trattoria*, which had belonged to her grandmother back then. Growing up in the kitchen, standing on a stool to wash dishes in the sink, dicing onions and stripping the skin from cloves of garlic, Assunta had learned mostly by watching. There was no need to write down the things she knew: how to adjust the intensity of a broth or the silkiness of a sauce. It seemed there was no one left in the world with the time and patience to learn the way she had.

If it was recipes she had come for then Assunta assumed that Sarah-Jane would leave soon enough, empty-handed and disappointed, but instead she carried on tidying tables, found a cloth to wipe them down, finished loading the dishwasher, polished the wine carafes dry and started putting them away.

'Not on the shelf this time,' Assunta told her. 'I will need them again this evening.'

'You open at night?' She sounded surprised.

'Only twice a week. It used to be more but ...' Assunta didn't feel the need to talk about the way her knees ached after a long day, or that soon she would only manage lunchtimes, and fewer of those until eventually the place would close altogether.

'You don't have any staff? It seems a lot of work for one person.'

'I am used to it,' said Assunta. 'But thank you for your help.'

'Thanks for yesterday,' responded the girl, arranging the carafes on the counter where Assunta wanted them. 'It seemed like the last straw when my car broke down.'

'The last what?'

'Just one more bad thing, coming after a whole lot of others,' she explained. 'I've not been having the best time lately.'

Assunta wasn't even slightly curious to hear more. Strangers came and went in Montenello; there was no need for her to know anything about their lives.

'There are no recipes here,' she repeated.

'Would you show me then, let me hang out and watch while you prepare a few dishes?'

Assunta couldn't find any reason to refuse. 'I suppose so.'

'Really?' The girl brightened. 'That would be great.'

'This evening I make one course: spaghetti with sardines and *pangrattato*. I use a little nduja, do you know it, the soft and spicy sausage from Calabria? It disappears and you only get the flavour.'

'It's the secret ingredient.'

'If you like.'

Assunta took off her apron. Thanks to the girl, there was more time to spend next door resting her feet, smoking a couple of cigarettes, listening to whatever her brother Renzo might have to say.

The sound of the *trattoria* door opening was unwelcome. She looked up but didn't recognise either of the people who came through it.

'We are closed until later,' she said, in Italian.

'Oh no, really?' Sounding resigned, the man turned to his companion, an older woman balanced on a walking stick. 'Guess we'll have to see if we can find some lunch elsewhere, Mom.'

Standing her ground, the elderly woman stared at Assunta. 'Giuseppina? Is it you? Surely not?'

'Me? No,' Assunta said, taken aback by the question. 'But that was my grandmother's name.'

The woman threw her son a desolate look 'Of course, it was. Giuseppina is gone now, so many years and they have all gone. We should never have come.'

'You are tired and hungry, Mom,' he said. 'We'll go to the hotel and see if we can order something there.'

'There is a wedding at the hotel,' the woman complained. 'Too much noise, too many people.'

Assunta didn't mind the strangers in her town, but she wasn't so tolerant of those who came back, the ones who had left years ago, and expected Montenello to be the same, for nothing to have changed while they were busy leading new lives in other places.

'I will open again at six,' she said. 'One course, tonight it is sardines.'

'You couldn't do something for us now, just a plate of pasta maybe? We've had a long journey.' There was a pleading note in the man's voice and he spoke Italian haltingly, like it had been learned from lessons. 'This is my mother's first time in Italy since she left as a very young woman. She came from this town and wanted to see it again and maybe find some of the folks she knew back then.'

'Yes, yes,' said Assunta, impatiently, because when they came back, the ghosts of the people they used to be, it was always with the hope of being recognised. 'In the bar next door you can eat a *panino*, maybe a slice of pizza. There is coffee, *gelato* and it is open all afternoon.'

'We'll go there then,' said the man, turning for the door. 'Thanks.'

His mother stayed a moment longer, balancing on her stick, swaying slightly. 'You look a little like her,' she said softly. 'Like Giuseppina.'

Assunta's grandmother was a whirlwind. She had created this *trattoria*, and cooked in it with strength and passion while her husband played cards next door in the bar, or sat on a bench in the piazza holding long conversations about nothing. She never wasted time nagging him but shouldered the work herself as Assunta did now. Giuseppina wasn't a beautiful woman; her energy was her most striking feature and she always seemed to be moving.

When she was a child, Assunta's mother used to leave her at the *trattoria* before going off to one of her jobs cleaning houses or picking fruit. And so she had grown up in a kitchen around sharp knives and scalding pots of water. Very early on, her grandmother put her to work. Even when she was old enough for school, this kitchen was where she learned the most important lessons.

Assunta had never wanted more from life than to stay here, cooking at Giuseppina's side. But her grandmother died, too young and very quickly. Once that energy and passion was gone, the *trattoria* was all that was left of her.

Now each day Assunta grasped the worn handles of kitchen knives she had held, simmered sauces in her cast-iron pots, boiled pasta in her steel saucepans. It was Giuseppina who had hung the brightly painted plates on the walls, and there they stayed. It was she who had started putting out bread and wine on the tables, and Assunta continued with the custom. There was a memory in almost everything she did.

They were all gone now; her grandfather whose easy days finished suddenly one sunny morning in spring, her mother whose harder times petered out slowly. Assunta was thankful she still had Renzo – strictly speaking, her half-brother – and her father Augusto. But the *trattoria* was her life, just as it had been Giuseppina's.

She never thought she resembled her grandmother. Her features were not so sharp, her build much stockier. She was surprised that this woman, returned from who knows where, had stared into her face, and seen something of Giuseppina in it.

Opening the fridge, she pulled out the ragu left over from the day before. She would boil some pappardelle, shave a little pecorino, cut a few slices of bread; it wasn't much trouble, not really, not for a woman who remembered her grandmother.

Assunta reached for her apron. 'Sarah-Jane, could you do me a favour?'

'Yes, of course.'

'Go next door and tell those people I will bring a plate of pasta for them.'

Sarah-Jane

Assunta was brusque but it didn't disguise her kindness. When those Americans appeared, the elderly woman and her son, even though it was way past lunchtime and she needed a break, she fed them bowls of pasta blanketed in rich *ragu*, and a dish of cubed aubergine crisped in the oven and drizzled with an oily crush of herbs she had plucked from a jar on the window ledge. I helped her carry the meal over to the next-door bar then sat there, drinking coffee, while she smoked a cigarette and the Americans frowned at the wisps of smoke reaching them as they were trying to eat.

'Did he say his mother is from Montenello?' I asked, as although the man's Italian had been spoken slowly, I wasn't certain if I had understood correctly.

'That is what he said,' Assunta confirmed. 'There are lots of them who come here, looking for their memories.'

'Do they ever find any?' I was thinking of my father, and the town his family originated from, and whether there might still be memories of them there.

'Sometimes,' said Assunta. 'Papa tries to help, but his mind is not as sharp as it used to be, eh Renzo?'

Up until then I hadn't realised the barman understood any English. But now he looked towards the far table, at the Americans who were finishing lunch, and at Augusto who was engaged in an animated conversation with them, and Renzo nodded then smiled.

'Papa likes to talk about the old days,' the barman observed.

'I hope that they do find someone she knew back then,' I

65

said, because it seemed too sad, coming all this way and not seeing a trace of the life you'd once had. 'Or the house she grew up in, at least.'

'They found lunch,' said Assunta abruptly.

She seemed in no hurry to clear the empty plates and head back to the *trattoria*. Everyone in the bar appeared to be settling in for the afternoon. Augusto was calling for coffee and *biscotti* as the Americans were urging him to pull up a chair, Baxter was curled up in a pool of sunshine, Assunta's eyes were half closed and she was breathing more deeply.

Fiddling with my phone, checking news websites and social media, I tried to stifle my impatience. For these people it might be normal to fritter away hours of their lives, but I was used to being busy. I could only hope that Riccardo Mastrobuoni moved at a faster pace than this, or I was going to be stuck in this town forever.

Assunta was sitting upright in her chair but must have been dozing because when the American guy came over to settle his bill, her eyes didn't open.

'I'm sure it would be OK if you stopped by later to pay,' I said, as he pulled out his wallet.

'Later we may have to crash out. We're jet-lagged.'

'Tomorrow then,' I suggested.

'Sure, we won't forget.' He started to leave, then stopped. 'Also could you tell her that my mother thinks the food is as good as Giuseppina's was. She wanted me to be sure to mention it.'

Assunta dozed on for fifteen minutes more while people came and went, the coffee machine roared and the low hum of conversation was pierced by an occasional noisy greeting or bark of laughter, without any of it disturbing her.

When her eyes did open, she glanced at the old-fashioned clock on the wall and sighed, then easing herself up from her chair, she gathered up the crockery, called goodbye to Renzo, nudged the door open with a hip, and sailed through it, with me following close behind, as I hoped she was expecting me to.

Back in the *trattoria*, I did my best not to get in the way as she put on her apron, picked up a paring knife and cleaned the sardines. Kitchens make sense to me. I find them comforting because they are where food is made and I enjoyed seeing Assunta cook in hers, watching stale bread baked and crushed to crumbs, seeing onions diced and smelling them sizzle in oil, looking on as she layered flavours – herbs, garlic, a smear of soft chilli-spiked sausage.

Once the customers arrived she let me help, taking full plates to tables and bringing them back empty. The dining room was busy but people didn't linger over their meals, as diners might in a city restaurant; they came to satisfy an appetite then left early.

When everybody had disappeared, Assunta made up three final plates: a nest of spaghetti cooked al dente, sardines in a light lemony broth with a spike of chilli and a crunch of breadcrumbs, one for herself, one for me, and a portion of leftovers for Baxter.

'A simple dish, you see,' she said, as the three of us were eating. 'You will go away and write it down now?'

'Yes,' I admitted.

'It is the place and the people that make a dish like this, not the recipe,' she warned.

And I understood what she meant. If I tried to cook this at home, it wouldn't be the same, even if I could find fresh sardines and soft Calabrian sausage. This dish was only to be experienced right now, and I could write down every exact measurement but probably never recapture it.

'I'll read the recipe then, and it will remind me of today,' I told her.

She grunted and shrugged, as if she found the idea completely absurd but was too polite to mention it.

'Tomorrow I make *coniglio in agrodolce*, rabbit in a sauce

that is sweet but also sour,' she told me. 'It is very good. Come back and I will show you.'

'I will,' I said, already excited by the thought of a new dish and different flavours. 'Thanks.'

I helped with the last of the clean-up and the dishwasher was grumbling away, the tables wiped, and the kitchen all orderly, before we left the *trattoria* together. Assunta turned out the lights and pulled the door closed without bothering to lock it.

Outside the piazza was dark and empty, a chilly breeze stirred, and we said goodnight quickly before turning to walk in opposite directions.

I had a better night's sleep in my little jasmine-covered cottage than I ever seemed to manage at home in London. There was no background noise of traffic or screaming police sirens and I woke earlier than usual and with a clearer head.

I breakfasted on bread and cheese, and Baxter seemed happy to share it.

'We have to do better than this,' I said, feeding morsels to him and smiling as he did that funny thing of curling his lip and baring his teeth as he took each one from my fingers.

Neither of us could go much longer without a supermarket trip, so I decided to take up Riccardo's offer of his car. I would shoot over to Borgo del Colle, stock up on essentials and hopefully be back in time for another cooking session with Assunta.

Not wanting to waste any time, I dressed in frayed denim shorts and a flowery frilly sleeved smock top, and marched quickly to the piazza, still almost deserted at such an early hour. Skipping my morning coffee, even though the bar was already open, I found my way to Riccardo's workshop just as he was opening its doors.

'*Buongiorno*.' He was smiling, apparently pleased to see

me. 'This is unexpected. You are here to visit with your car again so soon?'

There were even more engine parts littered over the ground, and I tried not to look too closely as the sight of it was disconcerting.

'Actually, I need to get to a supermarket and wondered if I might borrow the car you mentioned?' I asked.

'Sure, help yourself.' Reaching into a pocket of his overalls, he tossed me a key. 'I will show you where it is parked.'

'Great, I really appreciate it.'

It turned out that it wasn't a car at all, but a tow truck, a great beast of a thing that somehow Riccardo had managed to wedge into the tightest of parking spaces.

'She is, what do you call it, a stick shift,' he told me, gazing at the thing proudly. 'Are you OK with that?'

'Not really,' I admitted. 'I did learn to drive in a manual car, but that was a while ago.'

'You would like me to give you a quick lesson? You will pick it up again.'

'I'm not sure that I can even get it out from where it's parked. And how do you manage down all those narrow streets?'

'You won't have any problem in Borgo del Colle,' he assured me. 'The streets are wider there.'

Sizing up the truck, I decided that Baxter might have to manage on leftovers for a few days longer and I would drink my coffee at the bar.

'Thanks but I'd rather not risk it.'

'Really?'

'I can't help noticing it's a little bit bigger than my Saab.'

Riccardo laughed. 'OK, maybe you have a point. My father refuses to drive it too. If you like, I could take you. It is no trouble.'

Now I was torn. Distracting him from his work seemed a bad idea, but I love Italian supermarkets. They have counters full of beautiful cheeses and cured meats, and shelves filled with amazing olive oils that cost the same as the ordinary ones do back home. Also I did really need some supplies.

'How long will it take, do you think?'

'We drive there, drink a coffee, we shop and come back. Not too long.'

'OK then, if you really don't mind.'

Riccardo swung the tow truck out of the tight parking space without the least trouble, and I climbed in the passenger door, Baxter jumping up behind me and sitting obediently in the footwell. There was an unexpected lack of mess, no oily rags, crumpled up invoices or old food wrappers.

'She is a beauty, yes?' Riccardo gave the dashboard a gentle pat. 'I bought her when I came home to Montenello and she is going to help me find lots of business, at least I hope so.'

'What brought you back?' I wondered.

'Mamma died,' he said, simply.

'Oh, I'm sorry.'

'It has been sad for all of us, but especially my father. He was with my mother for a long time. They were childhood sweethearts.'

'He must be struggling without her.'

'Yes, although he kept insisting he was fine by himself because he didn't want to bother us. Finally I realised he needed some company, and so here I am.'

'Are you back for good then?'

'That is the plan,' Riccardo said. 'If I can build a good business, there will be no reason not to stay.'

With a roar of the diesel engine, we pulled out onto the causeway that separated Montenello from the main road and I swivelled in my seat for a view of the town as we drove away. Lost deep in its tangle of streets it was easy to lose any sense of how imposing the place was, clinging to the mountain-top it seemed sculpted from, and visible for miles around.

Riccardo accelerated away along a forested road that twisted towards the nearest large town. Like most Italian men, he drove too quickly but there was a confidence in the way he handled the vehicle. Unlike me, he didn't see the threat of a collision in every oncoming car or the potential of disaster round every bend. He pressed hard on the accelerator and the car surged forward. Within twenty minutes we were in Borgo del Colle.

'We made good time,' he said, sounding satisfied.

This town didn't have the striking beauty of Montenello, but I could see it was going to be more useful. A wide tree-lined boulevard was busy with all sorts of shops and several restaurants, and groups of people strolled around the paved area at its centre.

'You would like to drink a coffee first?' Riccardo asked.

'Yes, please I haven't had a cup yet, and I'm desperate.'

'No coffee?'

'Not even a sip.'

'That is terrible. I wouldn't be speaking, I wouldn't even be standing,' he said, dramatically.

'I'm barely breathing at this point,' I pointed at a café we were passing. 'What about there?'

'There is a better place, just round the corner.'

He took me to a bar only slightly wider than a corridor, with a cramped space for people to stand, an impressive espresso machine and a youngish guy, tattooed and pierced, who greeted Riccardo with a lot of hugging and back-slapping.

'A good friend?' I asked.

'A new one,' said Riccardo. 'Most of the guys I used to know have moved away and, you know, I live with my father so ...'

'You need to hang out with people your own age,' I guessed.

'Exactly. I love Papa but he drives me a little crazy some-times.'

'Really?' Friends often said that sort of thing about their parents and I found it hard to understand. 'What does he do?'

'*Madonna mia*, so many rules.' Riccardo held his fingers to his head and pulled an imaginary trigger. 'There is a certain time to eat meals, a time when the lights must be switched on, when the television can be watched, when a snack can be enjoyed. Some doors in the house must be constantly closed and others left open. And so it goes on.'

'I guess when you're older, you get used to your routines.'

'Papa is in his mid-fifties. That is not so ancient, is it?'

'Not really,' I agreed. My mum was about the same age and I thought of her as young.

'Even the way he hangs out the laundry is the same as how my mother used to. She has gone but nothing else has changed for him.' Riccardo sounded sad. 'It has been two years now and he lives like he is expecting her to come home again and check that everything is in order.'

'It's good that you're here then,' I said. 'But also good that you've got new friends.'

'I think so.'

I was expecting Riccardo to wait in his truck while I did a quick dash round the supermarket to pick up my few essentials, but he came in and travelled the aisles with the trolley, apparently enthusiastic. In the vegetable section he pointed me towards pearly oyster mushrooms and blousy zucchini blossoms. At the deli counter there was a long discussion about the most delicious cheeses, with several other shoppers getting involved, and the man behind the counter handing out samples to one and all. Next we had to consider the cured meats, salami flavoured with sweet and spicy pepper, chilli-red soppressata and smoky prosciutto. We learned how good the local salami was when eaten with a shaving of pecorino, we tried marinated artichoke hearts and plump green olives, had so many little tastes it almost added up to a meal and, before we moved on, spent several moments saying goodbye to all our new deli-counter friends.

Riccardo led the way up an aisle lined with olive oils and vinegars, delicious dressers-up of food in unfamiliar bottles and jars. I couldn't resist putting several into my trolley next to the pile of paper-wrapped deli packages. By the time we reached the checkout, my small shopping trip had turned into an extravaganza.

'I'll never eat all this,' I said, as we were packing it into bags. 'I'm only here for a week.'

'Perhaps you will stay a little longer,' said Riccardo.

'Only if my car isn't ready, but I have total confidence in my mechanic.'

'He knows what he is doing,' Riccardo agreed. 'But if you find you like it here, then you might prefer not to hurry away, even when your Saab is fixed.'

'I don't think so – there's still so much of Italy to see,' I told him.

On the drive back I told him about all the places I wanted to visit and in turn Riccardo spoke about growing up in Montenello. He described the meals his mother had prepared and how much he and his father missed them.

'You don't cook?' I asked, surprised, as he had been so passionate about food while we were in the supermarket.

'I cook, but it doesn't taste the same, at least that is what Papa says. He prefers to eat in the trattoria; never goes anywhere else, tells me he doesn't see the point.'

'Surely there are other decent places?'

'Assunta's food is traditional, and my father prefers that,' said Riccardo. 'Still, you should be sure to eat at the new hotel one evening. The chef is a local so his menu also has the flavours of Basilicata.'

'Is there anywhere in Borgo del Colle you think I should try?'

'Not really, unless you want to eat a pizza,' he said dismissively. 'You need to go further for good food. There is a place I visited once, a restaurant in an olive grove in Puglia. It belongs to the mother of Montenello's mayor and it is fantastic.'

'Could I reach it without a car?'

'No, but I could take you,' he offered. 'Why don't we have lunch there together ... Sunday?'

I hesitated. As easy as it had been to spend a morning in Riccardo's company, as likeable as I found him, as kind as the invitation was, it didn't seem the greatest idea to be going out for lunch with my mechanic.

'If I eat well, I work better,' he said, his tone teasing. 'Whenever I am hungry I get confused, which piece of engine belongs in which car; I am not so sure I know any more.'

'Don't say that, not even as a joke.'

'It would be best to book a table,' he continued. 'The nicest ones are outdoors, among the olive trees – it is very pretty.'

'Perhaps your father would like to join us?' I suggested, because with him along it definitely wouldn't feel like a date.

'I can ask but, as I said, he only ever eats at Assunta's trattoria. It was where he went with my mother.'

'I lost my father when I was young.' I surprised myself with the words because usually I don't do that – trade my sadness for another person's, like grief is some sort of club or a competition. I'm private and tend to stay quiet.

'Then you understand how it is to want your life as it used to be?'

'But nothing can be the same, can it,' I said.

Those years after my dad had gone felt like the end of the world. None of our old routines seemed to make any sense. Lost in a grief that made her reckless with the rules, Mum let me skip school for days so we could spend them together. One winter she pitched a tent in the living room and we camped in it and had all our meals as picnics. She allowed me to stay awake till midnight, eat cake for breakfast and wear whatever I wanted. I suppose to other people we must have seemed eccentric.

'Life has to be different,' I said to Riccardo. 'It just does.'

'I suppose Papa will realise that eventually.'

He turned on the radio after that and we travelled the rest of the way listening to Italian pop music and watching the scenery flash past the windows. Soon we were driving over the causeway and into Montenello's steep-sided streets. While Riccardo did a masterful job of squeezing his car through the narrowest lanes, there was no way of parking close to the house, so he helped me carry my bags of shopping to the front door.

'I will see you on Sunday for lunch then,' he told me, as we said goodbye. 'You will be coming to visit your car again before that?'

'I don't want to keep interrupting you.'

'No problem, any time.'

As soon as he had gone, I started worrying that I might have given him the wrong idea. Riccardo seemed a nice guy – kind, good-looking, funny – but I wasn't looking for any of those things. I had no interest in men now, no matter how lovely they were. Baxter and me, we were a team, travelling Italy together and it was an exclusive relationship. My heart, like my Saab, didn't need any more dents in it.

Assunta

Assunta was never sick, she could rely on that, until in middle age the migraines started. When the first one struck, it seemed like she was going blind. Her vision began flaring and blurring; there was an entire part of the room she couldn't see properly as if it was fading into non-existence, and then the throb of a headache followed.

Those migraines were terrible, sapping her energy and leaving her useless. The first time she had struggled on, but now Assunta knew that it was better to stay at home with the curtains drawn and her eyes closed. Resting today hopefully meant feeling better tomorrow.

She was sure that her grandmother would have been stronger. Nothing kept her from the *trattoria*, even towards the end, and Assunta still carried a picture in her mind of Giuseppina, white-faced and frail, sitting on a stool while the meal was prepared and urgently sharing the last of her secrets. Assunta almost heard her voice. 'No sugar in the sauce if the tomatoes are sweet enough, always grow your own herbs in case they are expensive to buy, never serve too much bread or you will dull their appetites.'

Giuseppina wouldn't approve of closing the *trattoria* for an entire day. She would have frowned as she totted up the lost profits. But those were harder times and her grandmother had a family to support. For Assunta, living alone, there were no fears of unpaid bills and so when the migraines attacked, she surrendered.

Throughout the morning she dozed, off and on. By mid-afternoon the headache was a duller ache and she was impatient to move from her bed. Taking a shower, getting dressed and making a cup of camomile tea were all signs that she was feeling a degree or two better.

Even so, she didn't feel inclined to respond to the knocking on her door. Whoever it was could come back another time. When they were insistent, knocking again more loudly, Assunta gave a hiss of impatience.

'*Vengo, vengo*,' she called, putting down her tea and rising from her chair.

For a few moments she couldn't place the man she found standing on her doorstep. Then Assunta realised it was the American from the day before, the pushy one who had insisted on lunch for himself and his mother. She didn't bother concealing her irritation.

'What is it?'

'So sorry to bother you,' he began, 'but your restaurant is closed and I need to pay for the meal we had yesterday. My mother is talking about leaving in the morning. Being here hasn't been what she hoped for.'

People over-shared, thought Assunta. They were most interested in themselves and assumed others would be too.

'Mom had so many memories,' he said wistfully. 'This place was always home to her. So I thought, while she was well enough to travel, that we ought to come back.'

Assunta wondered if he was expecting to be invited inside. She angled her body more squarely in the open doorway, just in case.

'I've always been curious too,' he explained. 'I wanted to see where we came from and Montenello is beautiful, but it looks like we're leaving so I ought to pay you. How much do I owe?'

His wallet was in his hand, and he pulled out a sheaf of banknotes, pressing them on Assunta. Many visitors would have left without making such an effort. His generosity softened her.

'If they stay long enough, they can start to find their memories,' Assunta told him. 'The old ones, their minds move more slowly.'

'Mom recognised you,' the man said. 'At first she was confused but later on she realised that she remembered you as a child, always in the kitchen of your *trattoria*.'

'That was me,' agreed Assunta.

'I don't suppose you have any recollections of her? She is called Caterina Campanella.'

'None, but I must have been small then.'

'I think she was close to your grandmother.'

Giuseppina hadn't bothered with friends. Family and work had claimed her time, so it seemed unlikely that this woman had been important.

'Would you talk to her?' he asked. 'It might spark some more memories.'

Assunta couldn't help wondering if this stranger had known Giuseppina as a different person from the one she remembered. Everyone had a part of themselves they kept hidden, even from those they were closest to. Who else had her grandmother been?

'Not today.' She pressed the palm of her hand against her forehead. 'I have a migraine.'

'And I've disturbed you, I'm sorry.'

There weren't many photographs of Giuseppina, only a few black and white prints that Assunta had framed but hardly ever looked at. In life, her grandmother had been constantly changing – her moods, her expression, even her appearance. She wore brightly coloured aprons, a different one each day of the week. Her long grey hair was piled on her head in different styles: wound in plaits, or pinned up into a mass of curls, or pulled in a neat chignon. There were times she sang as she worked and others when she preferred silence. There were happy days and sad ones. The stiff woman who stared out of the old photographs, wearing her best clothes, wasn't the person that Giuseppina had been.

Closing the door, finding her way back to her seat, sitting down, shutting her eyes, Assunta allowed a hope to rise. Her grandmother was long gone, but if this stranger really had been close to her, maybe she could bring a part of her to life again.

Drifting towards sleep, Assunta's memories played in her mind. Those memories she held dear, that she took out and touched all the time; if they had been made of stone, they would be worn smooth.

Sarah-Jane

I kept changing my mind. While I was unpacking the shopping, I decided not to go out with Riccardo; he was my mechanic, and it was a bad idea to complicate things. By the time the fridge and cupboards were fully stocked, I was thinking one lunch couldn't hurt. As I set off towards the piazza, I flip-flopped again and was definitely going to cancel. But walking on further, my thoughts rearranged themselves. Riccardo was looking for company, that was all, and I was alone here, so perhaps it made sense for us to hang out together.

Reaching the *trattoria*, I stopped short. There was no sign of Assunta, and inside looked empty and dark. Remembering how the door had been left unlocked the previous evening, I pushed it open tentatively. No cooking smells, no customers, everything clean and silent.

'Hello?' I called out, not expecting a reply. She had promised to be here but for all I knew it was normal for Assunta to close the place on a whim if she needed a rest.

Why was I so interested in her recipes anyway? Cooking wasn't my job anymore and I had no real use for anything she showed me. I had finished working with food when Tom finished with me; written it out of my life, so if I learned a few new dishes I was only doing it to fill in time, and have something to show for the otherwise wasted days I was stuck in Montenello.

Settling on a bench in the piazza, I people-watched for a while. Already I was starting to recognise faces. The street-sweeper cleaning up the morning's shower of confetti looked familiar, two women pausing for a chat outside the *pasticceria* were the same pair who had been there the day before, a good-looking man dressed in a suit was surely the mayor. Having grown up in London, I'm used to feeling anonymous, and it was unsettling to think of living in a place where no one was a stranger.

What I love about cities is how they always seem so full of possibilities. I could get lost in London, there were some parts I had never seen, and others that changed from one visit to the next. But this town wasn't likely to hold many surprises. If you were born here, like Riccardo, you might prefer it that way, but to me it seemed unexciting.

Distracting myself on my phone, I browsed through the better lives my friends were leading, captured on Instagram and Facebook. The perfect sourdough loaves they had baked, the meals they had ordered, the views they were gazing at, the piles of books they were reading. It didn't make me feel any better.

Sitting there, an hour slowly passed, and I kept watching people. I saw several of them approach the *trattoria*, register it was closed, and turn away disappointed. Perhaps they would go and have lunch at the hotel restaurant instead, but places like that tended to be frequented by tourists. And I couldn't imagine many of the locals would bother travelling all the way to neighbouring Puglia, to a restaurant in an olive grove.

What was I going to do about Riccardo? I still wasn't sure and it wasn't like me to be so indecisive. All that time with Tom I had said yes to everything; it made me squirm to remember how keen I was to please. He had hired me when I was low on experience, declaring that he knew a natural talent when he saw it, and I tried to be what he expected. There was never a night that I wouldn't work late or a deadline I said was impossible. If Tom needed something, I made it happen and until the restaurant opened, I was a part of the

Made With Love business every step of the way. In tough times I was glad to take a pay cut, in good ones I was happy to share in the triumph.

Every time I remembered that meeting with his Human Resources manager, the redundancy agreement all drawn up and ready, every time I recalled Tom's face the last time I saw it, serious and distant, not mine anymore, I grew more determined that I wasn't going to let that happen again, not anything like it. I was better off on my own.

Eventually I got bored of sitting there and took Baxter for a long walk, circling up towards the tower at the town's higher point. The further I climbed, the more derelict things seemed. Some houses were abandoned, their doors and windows boarded up. Others might have been occupied but the shutters were tightly closed or the windows misted by dust so it was hard to tell. I suspected I was seeing the real Montenello now, silent and secluded.

The views were impressive, whenever I managed to glimpse a slice of one between the tightly packed buildings. The tower offered the best lookout point and, since there was nobody about, I tried its heavy wooden door, twisting the rusted metal handle, giving it a good push. Slowly and with a creak, it opened. Inside was a spiral of stone steps that seemed solid if uneven. I grasped the handrail and headed up carefully, reaching an opening that took me out onto the ramparts. There I found a low parapet and, careful to hold tightly to Baxter's leash, I peered over it taking in the view of a valley criss-crossed by roads and the blue hills beyond. Hopefully I would be on one of those roads before too long, in my Saab with its roof down and the sun on my face.

There must have been other people up on that tower recently as I found a scorched patch of stone where someone had lit a fire and a few empty beer bottles were littered about. Conscious that I was trespassing, I didn't linger for long, edging back down the spiral staircase and pulling the door closed with another loud creak. As I emerged it felt as if there were eyes on me, watching from behind the blank windows of the surrounding houses, while the street was silent and empty.

I took a route that looped downwards, returning me to a part of town where the shutters of the houses were freshly painted and flung open, and there were the sounds of people inside, music playing, the whirr of a drill, someone whistling cheerfully.

By the time I reached the hotel, Montenello seemed a prosperous place again and, stepping inside, I found another lavish wedding reception in full swing. A small boy in a tuxedo was chasing a flower girl past groups of people sipping champagne, and a harpist was playing but nobody was listening. I paused, leaning against a pillar, staring at the bride and groom. There was so much love in the air that for a moment it almost felt hard to breathe.

'Sarah-Jane?' The owner Edward was behind the reception desk and looking at me concernedly. 'Are you OK?'

'Yes, fine,' I managed.

'I was planning to check in with you today. Are you happy with the house?'

'It's great, yes,' I said, recovering myself a little.

'Can we organise a relaxing spa treatment for you, a massage or facial? There's a very good woman who comes over from Borgo del Colle.'

'Thanks, but I'm not really a treatment person.'

'Me neither if I'm honest, all that poking and prodding.' He pulled a face. 'Anything else we can help you with?'

'Actually I'm at a bit of a loose end. Is there a language school or a walking tour? Maybe a cookery school even?' I was looking for a rack stuffed with tourist leaflets but this hotel didn't appear to have one.

'There are a few experiences we can organise for our

guests but I'm afraid everything tends to be tailored to larger groups.'

'You mean bridal parties,' I said, as the pageboy pursued the breathless flower girl into the lobby, and the chitchat of the guests grew louder while the harpist played on anyway. 'I'm guessing you don't have too many solo travellers with dogs?'

'None until you came along,' he said cheerfully.

'Is there always a wedding happening?'

'Very often at this time of year ... you know what they say about Montenello.' At my blank look, Edward added, 'The most romantic town in Italy.'

I hadn't known that, definitely not.

'And the perfect setting for your love story,' he finished.

'Seriously? That's what they say?'

'It's the marketing slogan.'

'The most romantic town in Italy?'

He nodded. 'That's right.'

'I only stopped here because I heard about people buying houses for one euro. I thought that was what the town was famous for.'

'That too, of course.'

'I was meant to be staying for a couple of hours. I should be driving down through Calabria by now and catching a ferry to Messina.'

'Ah, you were heading to Sicily.'

'Instead, a mechanic is dismantling my car engine, who knows how long it will take him to put it back together and I'm the only person in town who's not here for a wedding.'

'Can I suggest—' Edward began, then there was the ringing sound of someone tapping glass with metal and the entire place fell silent. The groom started speaking, proposing a toast to lasting love, to his beautiful bride and the wonderful future they were bound to have together. 'Without your love everything else would be pointless,' he declared. 'You aren't only my life partner, you are my life.'

'Oh please,' I said, not quite under my breath.

'You're having a bad day,' Edward observed, as champagne glasses clinked. 'What say we get you out of here?'

'Yes, I should go,' I agreed. 'Definitely.'

'Do you have plans for the rest of the day?'

'A quiet afternoon with Baxter, then a quiet evening.'

'That sounds dull.'

'We'll be fine.' I looked down at my little dog, who stared up through bushy eyebrows, worriedly. 'Won't we?'

'If you're interested in the one-euro houses,' said Edward, 'how about I take you for a tour of mine?'

'Have you got time?' I was keen for the company as much as the chance to have a nose around.

'The thing about Montenello is there's almost always time. I'll have a quick chat to my colleague and then I'm entirely dedicated to making your day a better one.'

'That's extraordinary service.'

'I pride myself on it.'

Again I followed Edward into a labyrinth of stairways and back streets, keeping up with his longer stride and, before we had gone too far, I was disoriented. The houses in this part of town were grander, set behind high walls and ornate gates, and Edward pulled out a key as we neared a particularly lovely palazzo. Its walls were painted softest gold and it had plaster columns round an arched entranceway and a row of shuttered windows opening onto wrought-iron balconies.

'You own this?' I asked, impressed.

'The bank does, mostly,' said Edward.

He opened the door, standing back to let me step inside, and instantly I was in a different world. Crystal chandeliers glittered from high ceilings, a curving stairway swept upwards, the walls were frescoed or mirrored and the furnishings were elegant.

'Oh,' I said, gaping. 'Oh wow.'

85

'It wasn't like this when we bought it,' Edward told me. 'The ceiling was about to cave in and the stairs were a death trap.'

'So you did all this?'

'With my husband Gino – it was his vision and he was the one that made it happen. Gino is a furniture designer. He created some of the more fabulous pieces here. Do you want the full tour?'

'Yes, please.'

'Good – I would have insisted on it anyway.'

Edward led me through the reception rooms, pointing out details I might have missed: cupids decorating the ceiling in the dining area, fake-fur rugs to snuggle into while you were reading in the library, bespoke tiles designed by a local artist, art in gold frames and shelves cluttered with *objets*. He showed me several bedrooms with modern four-posters swathed in silk. The bathrooms were marble and I counted five. The whole thing must have cost a fortune and, while it was beautiful, I preferred the simplicity of the jasmine-covered cottage, with its few small rooms filled only with things that were useful.

'Gino believes in doing things properly,' explained Edward, as I admired a hand-carved dining table.

'It's all very impressive.'

'Yes, and so is our mortgage after such a huge renovation. The place gets used a bit by wedding parties. These days the trend is to have a series of celebrations. A wedding eve dinner, a lunch the next day and usually some sort of cocktail party, as well as the big reception.'

'Of course,' I said. 'It would be great for that sort of thing. The perfect setting in the most romantic town in Italy.'

'Sarah-Jane?' He glanced at me. 'It's not really my place to ask but I think I'm going to anyway. Your expression when you walked into that wedding today ... you looked like you'd been slapped – has there been a little bit of heartbreak?'

'You could say that.'

'Just a slightly cracked heart or smashed to smithereens?' he asked lightly.

'Smithereens.'

'Ah … and now here you are surrounded by newlyweds. Not ideal.'

'Not something I'd have done on purpose,' I agreed.

'Fortunately this house is equipped with a champagne fridge. Do we go Veuve or a rather good Prosecco? I'm paying.'

'In that case the good Prosecco please.'

Edward showed me through to a drawing room that was about the size of my London flat in its entirety and considerably more glamorous with etched velvet wallpaper in shades of old gold, tasselled lamps, deep sofas smothered in cushions and a vintage Persian rug that Baxter immediately curled up on.

He brought out a chilled bottle of Prosecco in a shiny champagne bucket and a tray of small dishes filled with snacks: plump green olives, salty nuts, crisp baked circlets of dough dotted with oregano, marinated chilli peppers stuffed with capers and silvery skinned anchovies.

'This feels decadent,' I said.

'I hope so,' he replied. 'Otherwise there's no point, is there?'

Sitting in the exquisite room, as the Prosecco foamed into my glass and Edward placed dishes of food on the copper-topped table at my elbow, I felt my mood start to soften.

He took a seat on the chaise longue opposite, sipped his drink and examined me. Not in a way that felt judgemental; it wasn't as if he was rating my look, marking me down for buying chain-store fashion and wearing my hair in a messy topknot, more that he was taking a moment to work out who I was exactly.

'Shall we talk about you or me?' he asked.

'You,' I was quick to say.

'What would you like to know?'

'Lots of things, let me see.' I looked for safe ground to steer the conversation onto. 'OK, first of all have you always worked in the hotel business?'

'No, back in Sydney I did journalism mostly.'

'What made you move to Italy?' I was expecting a story of redundancy or some sort of midlife crisis that had driven him to start again on the other side of the world.

'I was restless,' said Edward. 'Our life was fine, it was really good, but I wanted more than one sort of life. When I saw they were giving away houses here, I jumped at the chance to try something new. There were loads of applications and we were among the lucky ones; it's been a bit of a roller-coaster ride since then.'

'You're happy though?'

'Every day is a challenge, but I love it. Gino still has one foot in Sydney, that's where he is at the moment actually.'

'Montenello must seem very quiet in comparison.'

'If you think it's quiet now, you should have seen it before,' Edward said with a wry smile.

Reaching for the bottle, he topped up my glass then pushed the dish of salted nuts within my reach. I felt pampered in the nicest way, as I settled back into a pile of soft cushions.

'Let's talk about you now,' said Edward, 'not the heartbreak if you'd rather not, the other stuff. What do you do?'

'I'm a recipe creator.'

'Should I have heard of you?'

'No, I'm more like a ghost-writer, no one knows about me, they've only heard of the people I work for.'

'Such as?'

'Tom Whiffen.' Even saying his name, I felt a pang.

'I know him – the Made With Love guy. I've watched his TV show a few times. Is he as charming as he seems?'

'Yep,' I said, a bit tersely.

Edward gave me a searching look. 'And?'

'And I'm having a break from work right now, doing some travel while I've got the chance. So what is there for me to see in Montenello?'

Almost everything he suggested, I had already tried: enjoyed the view from the tower, tasted a pastry from the famously good *pasticceria*, eaten at the *trattoria*. There was a church with some frescoes he said were worth seeing, and a walking track through the forest on the far side of the causeway, but otherwise it seemed that I had done it all.

'I can suggest a couple of places to eat,' Edward continued. 'A restaurant in a converted monastery up in the mountains and another across in Puglia, set in an olive grove and more rustic but still very special ...'

'Is that the one that belongs to the mother of Montenello's mayor?' I asked.

'Don't tell me you've been there already too?'

'No, but I have an invitation for Sunday lunch,' I confided. 'My mechanic Riccardo asked me.'

'Riccardo Mastrobuoni?' Edward's eyebrows arched.

'Anyway, I don't think I'm going.'

'Because?'

'It seems a bad idea.'

'I'm sorry? The hottest guy in town asks you to lunch at one of the best restaurants within driving distance, and that seems like a bad idea?'

'Yes.'

'Because of this heartbreak that we aren't going to talk about?'

I nodded. 'Partly, I suppose.'

'Oh dear,' said Edward. 'This might need a second bottle.'

Usually I don't drink in the afternoons. But in this room that felt like a film set, all perfectly curated and arranged, with the windows open to a breeze that billowed into the gauzy curtains and candles scenting the air with cedar, it was easy to keep sipping and talking. Edward was sharp and funny. He had a fund of stories and a seemingly limitless supply of delicious snack foods. It would have been easy to share everything, the whole sorry Tom Whiffen saga, but I held back. Talking about it only made things feel worse.

If he was tempted to ask prying questions, Edward held back too. Instead he plied me with good wine and amusing conversation until the chiming of a gilded clock reminded us that the afternoon had passed and it was time to make a move.

'Thank you,' I said, as he blew out candles and closed up windows. 'This was exactly what I needed.'

'Hey, you're welcome. It's what life is all about in Montenello, spending time with each other, connecting ... well, that and the weddings.'

This time of day was when the town came to life. Church bells rang, and people took to the streets to stroll or stand about. An old woman was sitting on a chair beside the open doorway of her home, eyes closed against the last rays of evening sunlight. I said a tentative *'buonasera'* as I passed and she opened her eyes and smiled back at me. Baxter stopped to sniff lamp posts and touch noses with a fluffy white Maltese while I exchanged a few words with its owner. Our walk was a social one and for the first time I got it, the whole point of Edward's hotel, because it was a good feeling to be a part of things, even if only temporarily. When I got back, I pulled out a wooden chair and sat beside the doorway of my little house while I phoned my mum, messaged friends and caught up on my old life.

Once the sky darkened, I went back inside and left the chair where it was just in case I wanted to sit out there again, with my door open and my face to the world.

Assunta

Assunta woke with the faintest ghost of a headache. The trick with the days she lost to a migraine was pretending they hadn't happened and easing into her regular routine: drinking a glass of freshly squeezed orange juice, taking a shower, dressing in her work clothes, all the time thinking of what she would cook for her customers that day.

She liked to appear early at the bar, as her brother Renzo was opening – taking down chairs from the tables where he had put them the night before so he could sweep the floor, starting up the coffee machine, receiving his delivery of pastries from the *pasticceria*. That was her brother's routine and it was Assunta's habit to sit on a stool beside the counter, chatting as he went about it.

This morning she wasn't the first to arrive. Carlo Mastrobuoni was standing at the bar, sipping a *cappuccino* and eating a *cornetto con crema*. Assunta had known him her entire life. They were in the same class all the way through school and, after they had left and he got married, she served lunch to him and his wife Maria every Tuesday and Thursday, for decades, until Maria grew too sick to enjoy eating. Carlo was almost as familiar to her as the collection of worn wooden spoons she used to stir sauces in her kitchen.

'What are you doing here?' she asked gruffly.

In reply, he held up his coffee cup and waved the pastry in the air. 'Breakfast,' he said, in case it wasn't obvious.

'Yes, but why?' Assunta knew he didn't usually show his face in the bar at this early hour.

'I decided to take my breakfast here today, that's all. The *cornetto* is very good.'

'It is,' Assunta agreed, accepting a coffee from Renzo. For her first cup of the day she demanded two shots of espresso and a jug of steamed milk so she could add precisely the amount she wanted. The *cornetto* she preferred to be plain, fluffy and buttery.

Companionably, side by side, she and Carlo ate their breakfasts.

'How is Riccardo?' Assunta asked and, pulling out her cigarettes, offered him the packet.

He refused, with a shake of his head. 'Those aren't good for you.'

'So everyone says.' She lit up anyway. 'What about Riccardo – has he finished repairing the English girl's car?'

'Not yet, he is still working on it.'

'She will be impatient, wanting to be on her way.'

'It takes time. Riccardo will do a good job; that is more important.'

'True,' agreed Assunta. 'That is the most important thing.'

'It was kind of you to bring the work to him.'

'Business has been quiet?' she guessed. 'People are still taking their cars to the mechanic in Borgo del Colle?'

Carlo sighed. 'I told my son that he should stay in Napoli. He had a good future there. He didn't need to come home.'

'Perhaps he wanted to.'

'He had a regular salary and his own apartment.'

'You must be glad of his company though.'

Carlo frowned. 'I was fine on my own, I can manage, that is what I told him, but he wouldn't listen.'

'Riccardo is a good son.'

'He borrowed money to buy the tow truck and pay the rent on his workshop. He took a risk.'

'People will realise there is a mechanic in this town and

they don't need to go all the way to Borgo del Colle,' Assunta reassured him. 'Like you said, it takes time.'

Carlo signalled for another coffee, and Assunta nodded her request too. The second cup she liked to take strong and black, with a slick of golden *crema* on top and a little sugar stirred through.

'At Riccardo's age you always think you know best,' Carlo said. 'I suppose we must have been the same.'

Assunta moved her mind back through the years. She remembered Carlo when his hair was jet-black, and left to curl rather than kept close-cropped. He was always on the quiet side, never one of the stirrers of trouble, and even then Maria was usually somewhere nearby. It seemed inevitable they would marry.

'At Riccardo's age, I was wise enough to realise it was my grandmother who knew best,' said Assunta. 'The young people are different now. Their lives are nothing like ours were.'

'He says I am too set in my ways,' complained Carlo, finishing his coffee.

'If your ways suit you, then what is wrong with being set in them?' Assunta argued.

'Exactly, that is what I keep telling him. But he insists that I need to start making some changes.'

For years now Carlo had worked in the Town Hall. Assunta wasn't clear on exactly what he did, but in towns like Montenello, if you found a good job then you stuck with it, so she imagined he would remain there until it was time to retire.

'What are you giving us for lunch today?' he asked her. Since losing his wife he walked across the piazza for his midday meal more frequently, sometimes with one of his colleagues, but often alone.

'*Coniglio in agrodolce.*' She had plump green olives from Sicily to simmer with the joints of rabbit in a sauce singing with vinegar and sugar.

'Yesterday you were closed – were you ill?'

'Just the usual, a migraine.'

'Are you getting them more often?' Carlo sounded concerned. 'Should you see a doctor?'

Assunta shrugged off the worry. 'It is my time of life, that is all. I am healthy and strong, no need for doctors.'

His wife Maria hadn't been strong, even as a younger woman. She was delicate, a tiny woman with thin shoulders who Carlo towered over. All three of her pregnancies had been a trial and giving birth to Riccardo almost finished her. Assunta hadn't been surprised to learn she was dying; it seemed a miracle that she had survived so long.

'Yes, you are strong but still I think you should take the number of my *telefonino*,' said Carlo. 'Then if ever you need anything ...'

Assunta produced her own mobile phone, an old and very basic model, and managed to save the number he gave her. She couldn't imagine using it. There were plenty of neighbours to call on and Renzo was always right here.

'I will look forward to my lunch,' Carlo said, as he was leaving. 'Sweet-sour rabbit, very good.'

'I had better go and make a start on cooking it,' Assunta replied.

She stayed in the bar a little longer though, chatting with Renzo. Most days they conducted a similar conversation, usually with a snippet or two of something new. This morning she learned that the mayor was set to make another announcement and that the English girl had been sitting in the piazza for quite a long while the previous morning.

'Ah yes, she was expecting me. I have agreed to show her some of Nonna Giuseppina's dishes. Maybe she will come back again this morning.' Assunta found herself hoping the girl did appear. It felt almost like old times, with the two of them in the kitchen, sharing tasks and making the work easier.

*

Assunta left the bar when Renzo grew busy with the first drift of customers. Next door in her *trattoria*, everything was in its place. On the doorstep was the paper sack filled with loaves of fresh bread. As she reached for her apron the butcher's truck rolled up, delivering an order of lamb. Later the cheese man would come by, and then her customers, much the same group that had been eating there for years. This was her day and Assunta settled into it.

Sarah-Jane

I kept thinking about weddings, mainly because I kept seeing them. Day after day, people tying their lives together; the tulle dresses and bouquets of flowers that it took; the bottles of Prosecco. The more I thought about it, the less sense such a fuss made.

It was early and I was sitting in bed, propped up against cushions with my laptop on my knee, stalking Tom Whiffen online. His baby would have been born by now, but there had been no news reports; I was careful to check every morning. His website hadn't been changed much either. Since my last look, a couple of my old recipes had been pulled out of the archives and tweaked a bit, and the Made With Love range of spatulas put on half-price sale. There was nothing interesting showing up on any of the social media pages; whoever had updated them last was recycling old shots.

It was his assistant Jo who looked after all the digital stuff; at least she had when I was working there. Every time logging on, I expected to be devastated by shots of them together. Tom and Jo with their newborn. Tom and Jo in a smart suit and a white dress celebrating their marriage. I wasn't sure which would be worse, and yet I couldn't stop looking.

I heard a soft thump as Baxter jumped off the bed, then the sound of him shaking his head and flapping his ears. It was his way of signalling that it was time for us to get up and do something more interesting. Pulling a sweatshirt over my pyjamas, I padded barefoot to the door, and let him out for a pee. The chair was outside where I had left it the evening before and, once he had finished with all his sniffing at walls and corners, Baxter settled down beside it. For a while he sat sentinel, keeping an eye out for passers-by, but soon grew drowsy, curling up on the sun-warmed patch of ground, and starting to snore softly. I sat down too and ruffled his wiry-haired head, feeling such a rush of love for my little dog. He was my best friend.

Out there, away from the laptop and phone, Tom kept chasing around the edges of my mind. I had so many memories of our time together – meals we shared, lazy mornings in bed, quiet evenings on the sofa – and I felt cheated by those memories now because it seemed as if Tom couldn't ever have cared about me.

Closing my eyes against the morning light, I reminded myself of the three words my mother kept saying: 'You deserve better.' She had said them over and over until I agreed she was right, but the problem was it didn't make any difference. The future I imagined was Tom, living and working with him; I had even imagined our wedding day. Nothing fancy, just a quietly beautiful celebration with those closest to us, with a tulle dress and a bouquet of flowers, and bottles of champagne. Without him I didn't know what life was meant to look like.

So there I was, keeping company with my usual thoughts, drifting away with them, when a tall shadow fell over me.

'Good morning.' The voice lilted with an Australian accent.

'Edward,' I said, my eyes flying open.

'You looked deep in thought there.' He sounded amused.

In pink flower-sprigged pyjama bottoms and an oversized sweatshirt, with my face not so much as splashed with water and my hair unbrushed, what I looked was a state.

'I wasn't expecting visitors.' I tried to smooth down my hair, snagging my fingers in its knots.

'Sorry, I should have called first.' He held up a foiled silver bag. 'I forgot to put coffee in your welcome pack so thought I'd drop by with some.'

'Thanks, that's really kind of you but I managed to get to the supermarket yesterday and stocked up.'

'This stuff is special,' Edward insisted. 'It's locally roasted and very good. Gino and I won't drink anything else now.'

'I'd better try a cup then.'

'I'll make it,' he offered, 'while you ...'

'Sort myself out?'

He smiled and nodded. 'Nice jim-jams though – stylish.'

'Yeah thanks,' I said dryly.

I had the quickest of showers and climbed into a pair of hot-pink shorts and a turquoise smock top. By the time I emerged, Edward was pouring a dark stream of espresso into two tiny cups. 'Shall we drink it outside?' he asked.

'Sure,' I agreed.

He carried a second chair outside, and we sat in the jasmine-scented archway, enjoying the sunshine.

'I didn't drop by just because of the coffee,' Edward admitted. 'There's something I'm hoping you might do for me. A favour. It struck me that there might be an opportunity, when you mentioned having worked for the Made With Love guy.'

'Tom Whiffen,' I said flatly.

'We're at the stage with the hotel where we need to look at promotional activities, and connecting with someone like him, getting TV exposure or a feature in his magazine, it could make a real difference.'

'Sorry, but I don't think I can help.' This wasn't the first time people had tried to reach Tom through me. In the past I had been mostly happy to open doors, but now those doors were tightly shut, particularly to me.

'I wouldn't ask but to be honest, things haven't been easy,' Edward continued. 'Last year was tough for everyone and we almost went under. Things are picking up a bit now thankfully but we're too dependent on the weddings. I thought if we could showcase another aspect of what we offer ...'

'Tom wouldn't be interested in hearing from me.'

'It's worth a try though surely?' he persisted.

'We're not in touch.'

'I see,' said Edward, although of course he didn't. Picking up the empty espresso cups, he went inside, and I heard the tap running as he rinsed them clean.

'That coffee really is delicious,' I told him when he emerged, ducking his head to avoid the trailing branches of jasmine. 'Thanks for bringing it over.'

'No problem, enjoy the rest of your stay. You know where to find me if you need anything.'

'Edward, wait,' I said, as he started to head away. 'I'd love to help you out but ...'

'Don't worry, if it's not something you feel comfortable doing, that's fine.'

I liked Edward; I wanted him to like me. But the only person who knew the whole story about Tom and me was my mother, and I wasn't about to launch into it now.

'Made With Love made me redundant,' I said instead. 'It all ended badly.'

'Ah, right, sorry.'

I shrugged. 'These things happen.'

'Between that and what we didn't discuss yesterday,' Edward mouthed the word 'heartbreak' at me, 'you've had a rough time.'

'Sounds like you have too.'

'You're a guest; it's unprofessional of me to bother you with my problems.'

'I'm not your usual kind of guest though, am I?'

'True.'

'Do you want to sit down again? I can put on more coffee.'

'I'll make it,' he said. 'You stay where you are.'

The tale that Edward told me over the second Moka pot of coffee was all about big dreams and big debts, a lot of worry, a few close calls, and his determination to survive them.

'It was me who pushed us into taking such a risk with our lives. Gino was happy in Sydney and we were pretty secure there. Italy was my dream, and I have to make it work.' The way Edward's voice dropped to a low monotone told me how desperate he must have felt.

'Wasn't the hotel his idea?' His words came back to me. 'You said Gino heard about the *albergo diffuso* concept and then it snowballed.'

'It certainly did,' said Edward. 'He never does anything in a small way; I knew that when I brought him here. And I signed those loan agreements and agreed to it all.'

'Will you be able to keep things going?' I was worried for him and this husband I had never met.

'We're working as hard as we can. That's partly why Gino is back in Sydney now. He got a couple of big commissions for furniture and we couldn't say no to the cash.'

'You must miss him.'

'I really do, but it's only for a few months. He'll be back before the end of summer, hopefully. And in the meantime I've got plenty to keep me busy.'

'Weddings?' I guessed.

'Yes, lots and lots of weddings.' Edward raised his espresso cup. 'So here's to love saving us all.'

I didn't want to make a toast to love – it wasn't going to save me. The thought of walking over more fallen confetti, seeing women in tulle and men in morning suits, overhearing their speeches, wasn't appealing either.

'Here's to the success of your hotel,' I said instead, clinking cups with Edward. 'Although I may be avoiding it from now on when you're hosting a reception.'

'You won't be able to escape the weddings completely,' he told me, 'not in this town – they're everywhere.'

Hearing Edward's story was a reminder that other people had problems too, and I shouldn't get lost in my own. Things weren't so bad really. I had my mother and my dog, no immediate concerns about money and I was travelling around Italy, admittedly stalled for the time being, but with plans to head off again as soon as possible.

There was a chance that Riccardo wouldn't be able to fix my broken-down Saab and, if necessary, I would have to get a rental car, even though it wasn't in my budget. I wasn't sure how rental companies felt about pets but surely with a diligent vacuum and some air freshener I should be able to eradicate any signs of Baxter once I had finished with the car?

Glancing at him, I saw that he was trying to get my attention, circling my chair, stopping and staring, then pacing again. It was his way of saying he wanted something, generally a meal or walk, and usually he would nag until he got it, resorting to whimpering if I ignored the subtler hints.

'You're right, we haven't had breakfast,' I said, and Baxter pricked up his ears. 'Some biscuits and then a walk, OK?'

He approved of the plan, claws skittering over the tiled floor as I filled his bowl, and then he followed me attentively from room to room as I gathered my things and put on my white Converse shoes.

In London I preferred to keep Baxter on a leash, except at the park. Mostly he was obedient, but I didn't want to risk him being distracted by a cat and racing across a road busy with buses. In Montenello there wasn't much traffic, particularly in this part of town with the streets at their narrowest, and there were certainly no buses. I let Baxter trot on a little way ahead and felt relaxed about it.

'*Buongiorno*,' I said to a man strolling by, and he responded by remarking that the day was a hot one, speaking slowly to be sure I understood. I smiled at a woman leaning out of her window to water pots of red geraniums and she smiled back at me. A man puttering past on a Vespa raised a hand in a reflexive greeting. Ahead of me an elderly couple were walking together, his arm linked through hers, pulling twin shopping trolleys behind them. Perhaps this would be Riccardo some distant day, with stooped shoulders and silvered hair, taking his wife's weight as they made their way over the cobbles.

Ah yes, Riccardo – what was I going to do about him? By now I ought to have sent a message to cancel our lunch. I kept pulling out my phone ready to do it then hesitating.

With things like that, I never know what to say. I'm bad at it, really bad. The unspoken rules about when you're supposed to call and how keen you're allowed to be, the asking-out and the first date; to me it all seems fraught and awkward.

My mother, keen on me meeting people, was always persuading me to go along to the parties I had been invited to, even though I preferred staying at home to bake a cake or read a book. I went out with a few guys I knew, friends of friends, sat through movies shoulder-to-shoulder with them in silence. There were drinks in pubs and cheap-and-cheerful dinners, Sunday afternoon walks on Hampstead Heath, kite flying on Parliament Hill, guys I saw for a while but wasn't sorry to break up with.

When I met Tom, we seemed to come together naturally. He made it easy for me, perhaps because he was a bit older, and it felt right, it felt like what I'd been waiting for. There were many good things about being with him; the idea of never having to go dating again was only one of them.

Now here I was, despite myself, mired in it once more, needing to tell Riccardo I wasn't interested, without offending him so much that he left pieces of my Saab all over the floor of his workshop. It wasn't like a recipe. There was no exact quantity of anything, no blueprint to follow, no tried and true method. And so I kept putting it off.

I walked towards the piazza, with Baxter still leading the way. That wide sweep of cobbles hemmed by buildings was the hub of the town. Almost everyone must have crossed it at some point in their day. This morning there was the usual group of elderly men sitting outside the bar, a group of women were forming a queue beside a truck selling fresh fish and, looking through the windows of the *trattoria*, I saw Assunta moving around inside.

Smelling the smoky sweetness of onions slowly caramelising, I was drawn closer. The door was ajar and Baxter went through it. Before I could stop him, he trotted round the counter and into the kitchen uninvited. From the doorway, I tried to call him back, but he wasn't listening.

Assunta looked up. 'I have started already.'

'Sorry, I came by yesterday ... you weren't here.'

'Migraine.' She touched her fingers to her head.

My mother tended to get them, so I knew how bad they could be; often she was wiped out for days, napping under a blanket on the sofa. They made her feel slow and clumsy, as though she was living in a fog. I wondered if Assunta should really be working with sharp knives and hot flames today.

'Can I help?' I asked.

'Of course,' she said.

Assunta's *trattoria* was a calming place to be. Her hands had performed each task so many hundreds of times, her knives and spoons were worn to her grip, and she never seemed hurried, even if a few customers arrived before the food was ready to serve.

'They will wait,' she said with a shrug. 'And if they don't, then too bad.'

Just before noon the wedding party of the day flocked into the piazza. Assunta only glanced up briefly from her work then looked away, but my attention was caught for longer. They were a showy pair, this bride and groom. Her gown was figure-hugging, beaded with crystals that caught the light, and dazzling white. He was tall with a mane of fair hair and his suit was a bright maroon. The photographer appeared intent on capturing an image of them running across the piazza in a hailstorm of confetti, with bridesmaids and flower girls fanning out behind them. There was a lot of laughter, as they tried a second time, a third and then a fourth.

'I think I may be allergic to weddings,' I said aloud without thinking and, beside me, Assunta chuckled.

'You are staying in the wrong town then,' she observed.

'I know that now. But why are there so many?' Even after talking to Edward, I didn't completely understand how one place could attract such a surfeit.

'I am not really sure,' admitted Assunta. 'Perhaps because it costs much less to marry here than somewhere like Venice or Rome.'

She had been filling carafes with wine, but stopped to stare, just as the groom was scooping the bride up into his arms and executing a graceful twirl, white confetti fluttering down all around them, as cameras clicked, and phones were held aloft.

'They must still spend thousands, even here.' I counted off on my fingers. 'The clothes, the flowers, the catering, the photography, the hotel rooms, the big cake.'

'There is money in love,' Assunta agreed.

It was time for the obligatory shot of the happy couple kissing beside the fountain. Her head tipped back, his lips touched hers and they froze in passion for long enough to ensure it had been properly memorialised.

Assunta turned away from the scene, wielding her demijohn of wine and returned to topping up carafes with it. I ferried them over to the tables, along with clean glassware, as she sliced up bread for the baskets. We completed our tasks capably and in silence. By the time we were finished, and the room was ready, the wedding party had disappeared and customers were piling in.

Looking out through the window again, I noticed Riccardo and his father strolling across the piazza. They seemed to be heading towards the *trattoria* but then paused halfway, still deep in conversation. Riccardo laughed at something his father said, touched his shoulder and turned to walk off in the opposite direction, while Carlo Mastrobuoni continued on to the *trattoria* without him. As he came through the door, I watched Riccardo disappearing round a corner, and oddly what I felt seemed very like disappointment.

Assunta

Some days Assunta barely noticed the customers who came and went, the predictable mix of faces that she saw without really seeing. Whole weeks were so much the same that there was nothing worth remembering, whole months even. She assumed it must be the same for everyone. There were times you had no energy and dragged through a day, then moments when the sun shone and your spirits lifted. Things went smoothly or not so well. Time passed.

Today as she chopped stems of broccoli rabe, propped a wooden spoon beneath the cast-iron lid of the saucepan where rabbit cooked in its sweet-sour sauce, and as she spooned food onto dishes, she watched the people coming in to fill her tables. Carlo Mastrobuoni was eating alone, the mayor was with his mother today, and Augusto and his friend Francesco Rossi had taken their usual spot in the far corner. The place was completely full when the American and his mother arrived. They stalled in the doorway, faces falling as they realised every chair was taken.

With a hand in the air, Assunta attracted their attention. 'One moment,' she called, making her way out from the kitchen to the table in the far corner.

Her father was deep in conversation, a wine glass in one hand. Assunta picked up the carafe and put it in his other.

'You want me to leave? But I only just sat down,' Augusto complained.

'I need the space. Go next door instead, I will bring your food.'

Augusto knew better than to refuse, but still grumbled as

he rose from the chair and shuffled away, Francesco behind him.

With grateful thanks, the mother and son came and took their places and Assunta brought them a fresh bread basket and a full carafe of wine.

'I am Caterina Campanella,' the woman told her, removing her jacket and pulling the silk scarf from her neck. 'This is my boy Tony. We hoped that perhaps you might have time to talk today, that we could share some memories?'

Assunta nodded. 'Later, yes? First I bring you some food.'

'Talk is best on a full stomach, that is what your mother used to say,' said the woman, draping the jacket and scarf carefully over the back of her chair.

That stopped Assunta in her tracks. 'I thought it was my grandmother that you knew?'

'I knew her yes, but it was your mother Martina who was my good friend.'

'Mamma?' Assunta was surprised. Her recollections were of a mother who worked long hours and was exhausted by them; there had never been time for friends.

'Martina and I were close,' the woman said, and Assunta noticed how she spoke Italian slowly as though having to fetch back the words from someplace she had left them long ago.

Returning to the kitchen, Assunta tried to work, but her mind was hardly on what she was doing. Instead she searched back through the years for memories that might make sense of what this woman had said. She had known her mother as a woman who moved through life like a light breeze while her grandmother had been the hurricane. It was difficult even to recall her features now, except as drawn and pale. Was it possible she had been close to this stranger?

Distracted by her thoughts, Assunta barely noticed how Sarah-Jane had slotted in and taken over, portioning food onto plates and delivering them to the tables. She kept an eye on the Americans as they ate their food. Both had appetites, tackling two courses, emptying the bread basket and draining the carafe of wine. Once they had finished, she went to clear their empty plates.

'That was wonderful, every mouthful, thank you,' Caterina said to her.

'I am glad you ate well.'

'And your daughter is such a good worker – you are lucky.'

'My daughter?' Realising she must mean Sarah-Jane, Assunta added. 'That is not my daughter. I have no children.'

Caterina's gaze dropped to the fingers of Assunta's left hand and she stared for a moment. 'You aren't wearing a wedding ring – did you never marry?'

When Assunta shook her head, she frowned. 'Then you are completely alone now, with Martina and your grandmother gone?'

'I have my father still.'

The frown deepened. 'Your father, you know him?'

'Yes, you met him,' Assunta reminded her. 'The man you were talking to in the bar the other day, Augusto.'

'That man, no, he is not your father,' Caterina said firmly.

'Of course he is.' The old woman's mind must be failing, so Assunta was gentle. 'Augusto, you don't remember him? You must have known each other if you were Martina's friend.'

'Perhaps I did know him a little, but he is not your father, that is impossible.' She sounded certain.

'Mom, you may be remembering things wrong,' her son cautioned. 'It is all such a long time ago and you do get confused.'

'There are some things you never forget,' insisted Caterina.

Assunta was disappointed. She had hoped for some keepsake of a memory, a moment in Giuseppina's life, a different impression of her; instead there was only this nonsense.

'Who is my father if it is not Augusto?' she demanded, less kindly now.

'Your mother never told you?'

'Told me what?'

Caterina's face clouded and, reaching for her jacket and scarf, she rose from the chair. 'This is not my story ... I shouldn't ... I can't.'

'Mom? Where are you going?' asked her son.

Pushing her arms into the jacket's sleeves, clutching the scarf to her chest, she turned on him. 'It was a mistake coming here, I told you so. The past is best left undisturbed, isn't that what I said?'

'Mom, wait, we haven't paid the bill yet,' her son reminded her, as she fumbled for her stick and made to go.

'I shouldn't have said anything.' She was speaking to him, but the words seemed meant for Assunta. 'Forgive me. I am sorry, very sorry.'

'My mother is not herself.' He apologised, pulling out some cash and dropping it on the table. 'I'm sorry too.'

Wordlessly, Assunta watched them leave. Once they had disappeared she took a breath and began stacking their dirty plates, her hands falling into the habit of work while her mind was still distracted.

'What was that all about?' asked Carlo Mastrobuoni who, sitting alone at the nearest table, was positioned to hear every word.

Assunta tapped her head. 'Crazy, I suppose,' she said.

'I think so,' he agreed. 'Poor old thing.'

'Do you remember her at all, this woman, from the old days?'

Carlo thought for a moment then gave a half-shake of his head. 'I don't think so, but I never paid much attention to adults back then. They always had a task that needed doing or some rule I wasn't meant to break. Usually I avoided them.'

For Assunta the opposite was true. As a girl she had preferred the company of her elders, but if Caterina Campanella was ever among them, she hadn't noticed.

'Will you say something to Augusto, mention what she told you?' Carlo wondered.

'No, it is not worth bothering him,' Assunta said dismissively and went back to work. She needed to finish the lunch service, clear up and make the necessary preparations for dinner. There was no space for worrying about the muddled words of an elderly person, someone who might have been important to her family once, but probably wasn't.

Even so she was glad to have Sarah-Jane there to help. Assunta felt the way she often did at the beginning of a migraine – as if there was a blank spot in her vision where she ought to have been able to see something.

Sarah-Jane

I don't know how Assunta would have managed if I hadn't been there. There were whole stretches of the afternoon when she seemed off her game, quieter than usual and gruff when she did speak; I put it down to the aftermath of her migraine. Still, it wasn't a problem pitching in to help; there was nowhere else I needed to be, and I enjoyed working.

Later we took some lunch over to Renzo in the bar, where she lit a cigarette and cradled a glass of black herbal liqueur, seeming intent on smoking and drinking in silence. Her father, more eager for company, beckoned me over to his table. Augusto turned out to be a talker and full of stories about Montenello, the lively place it had once been, and the efforts to make it that way again.

If you believed everything he said then the one-euro house scheme had been entirely his idea and he had handpicked the very first buyers. It appeared that he knew everyone in town, had been best man at Edward's wedding and was godfather to the mayor's daughter. As he held forth, Francesco nodded along in agreement.

'You are staying in Montenello for the summer,' Augusto said, and it was more a statement than a question.

'Only until my car is fixed.'

'But you are working in the *trattoria*. We saw you there at lunchtime, and two days ago, assisting in the kitchen, waitressing too. Didn't we, Francesco?'

His friend nodded, saying nothing.

'I am very happy that Assunta has found some help at last. You can cook, yes?'

'Well yes, but—'

'That is what she needs. It is too much to keep running the place alone. I tell her this, but she is stubborn and won't listen.'

I tried to put him straight, but apparently Augusto wasn't interested in hearing me.

'Of course, it is good timing because,' he dropped his voice, 'I have some confidential information. The mayor is about to announce the release of several more of the one-euro houses. This will be the last of it, I think, the end of the scheme. You should put in an application.'

'But I don't—'

'There is one particular house, very nice, perfect for you. I can't make any promises but I do have some influence.'

'I don't need a house though. As soon as my car is ready, I'm leaving.'

'What about your job at the *trattoria*?' His eyebrows soared in surprise.

'Well, like I said—'

Again Augusto interrupted. 'Think about it,' he urged. 'If you need my help, I am here. This is a very good house. It will need some work but all of them are very rundown; that is why the *commune* is giving them away. You will take a look.'

'Maybe I will,' I said, although I didn't have the slightest intention of doing so.

Augusto smiled at me. 'Of course, of course.'

When we returned to the kitchen, Assunta continued to seem unfocused. She had a dinner menu planned and the ingredients ready, nevertheless she was happy for me to take over, nodding in approval as I kneaded the dough for pasta and not saying a word as I stewed the hearts of artichokes with smoky pancetta and sweet broad beans. Mostly I prefer cooking alone. I like having a kitchen to myself, and working through each task calmly, at my own pace. Cooking for me is almost meditative; it's why I never could be a chef in a big restaurant – all those people, all the stress and noise. But here, with Assunta a quiet presence, it wasn't too difficult to get into my zone. I cooked and it made me feel good.

People came and ate, but it was hot in the dining room, even with the door and windows wide open, so no one lingered at their table for very long. A few of the less elderly ones hung about outside afterwards, chatting and trying to cool down. As the sky darkened, the fairy lights in the branches of the trees brightened the piazza and it made for a pretty picture. Assunta stood, staring through the window, as if she had never noticed it before.

'Are you OK?' I asked. 'Is your head still hurting?'

'My head?' She seemed half dazed.

'If you want to go home then I can finish up here,' I offered.

'You can?'

'It's no problem. I'm pretty sure I know where everything belongs. Should I lock the door when I leave or just pull it closed?'

'Pull it closed,' Assunta said, reaching into the front pocket of her apron and taking out the well-thumbed booklet she used to note down what every customer owed. 'You will need this,' she said. 'Tomorrow I am closed and the next day too. But come on Monday, I will pay you.'

'There's no need,' I told her. 'You helped me when my car broke down, remember? I'm returning the favour.'

'You work, you get paid,' she insisted, peeling off her sauce-spattered apron and putting it in a basket with a jumble of others to be washed.

After she had gone, I fed the last few customers then cleaned every plate and glass and returned them to the proper place. Baxter and I feasted on leftovers, a little of the rabbit from lunchtime, with some of the artichoke dish that I had thrown together for dinner. Tearing a page from Assunta's notebook, I started jotting with her stumpy pencil, notes as reminders: the food had been good and I didn't want to lose it.

By the time I closed the door behind me, I had that sense of well-being that cooking almost always provides; it had felt good to be useful.

The streets were silent as I walked back. There were a few lights glowing behind the drawn curtains here and there, but most places were already in darkness. I wondered what Riccardo was up to. Surely, he was too young to have embraced the slow pace and early nights, but it seemed the only way to live here.

My little house was stuffy from having been closed up all day, so I opened the windows wide, trusting Baxter to wake me in the unlikely event someone tried to climb in through one. Curling up in bed, I let sleep find me.

In the morning, opening my eyes to sunshine and blue skies, it took me a moment to remember what day it was. Saturday and Assunta's trattoria would be closed, so no one was expecting me. I got out of bed to make coffee then called my mum on FaceTime, thinking we could have a long chat. She was wearing her yoga clothes, sitting out on the terrace beside the potted hydrangeas, and the early morning sun was still low.

'Darling, are you OK?' She squinted at the screen. 'Where are my glasses, what did I do with them, hold on a moment ...'

'I'm fine, it's a lovely day here.'

'You saw the news?' Her voice held a note of anxiety.

'I've only just woken up so I haven't seen anything yet – do I need to?' Propping up the phone against a jug of flowers on the dining table, I went to grab my laptop.

'OK, I'm online. What am I looking for?'

'Tom,' she said quietly.

For a second my fingers stilled on the keyboard, then I typed in his name and saw the news was everywhere. Made With Love had gone under, the restaurant had closed its doors, the magazine had folded and Tom was bankrupt. It seemed that he owed creditors a substantial sum although every news website I looked at said something different. A brief official statement told me it was all in the hands of the liquidators.

'Shit,' I breathed. 'This is awful.'

'Some people might say that it's karma,' said Mum. Seeing my expression, she added. 'He hurt my daughter; you can't expect me to feel sorry for him.'

'All those people though, the ones who worked there.' I thought of his assistant Jo; the fresh-faced new HR manager; and Dominique the bossy executive chef – actually it was quite hard to feel sorry for any of them.

'I wonder what happened, he seemed so successful,' said my mother.

'He had a backer, that's how he was funding the expansion.' I didn't know the whole story; Tom only gave me bits and pieces. 'It was a complicated set-up, I think.'

'Obviously it's all collapsed around him.'

'Shit,' I repeated.

'I hope you're not tempted to make contact,' said my mother.

'Shouldn't I send a message at least?'

'No,' she said firmly.

'Made With Love was everything to him,' I argued.

'Maybe if he'd cared about something other than himself then he wouldn't be in this mess,' she said. Her phone was on the floor now and she was in a down dog pose, with her glasses off, and her long plait of fair hair hanging over one shoulder. 'You don't need to be supportive, he doesn't deserve it.'

'Yes, but what if he suspected this was going to happen

when he made me redundant?' It seemed possible that Tom had seen the collapse coming and wanted to make sure I got a decent payout, that it had been his – admittedly clumsy – way of looking after me.

Mum moved up smoothly into a tree pose, and now mostly what I could see of her were legs and a foot. 'I doubt it,' she said crisply.

'I would have stayed and supported him; surely he knew that.'

'I'm glad you didn't,' she said, wobbling a little, then regaining her balance. 'It's better that you're in Italy, living your own life, than back here involved in the mess he's made of his.'

We talked for a while longer, until Mum needed to lie down for Savasana. Leaving her to relax on her yoga mat, I trawled back through the news websites, re-reading everything I could find about Made With Love. It was mostly the same information but with a gallery of different pictures – Tom cradling a freshly baked loaf of sourdough, Tom drizzling melted white chocolate sauce over a tray of lemon lava cakes, Tom forking up spaghetti. *CELEBRITY CHEF GOES BUST*, screamed the headlines, *MADE WITH LOVE ON THE ROCKS*.

I had put so much of myself into that business and it was hard to believe it was suddenly gone, disappeared into nothing. Sitting there with my laptop on my knee, I thought about the early stages, late nights spent together dreaming up plans over wine or coffee, and the fun we had together; how much we laughed.

The ideas may have been mine but Tom was always the one with the drive to make them happen. To me he had seemed unstoppable, a force of nature, and I wondered how he was coping now with such a huge and very public failure.

Whatever my mother said, it was impossible not to feel sorry for him. Besides, Tom had made sure I would be OK financially and distanced me from this whole disaster. I had to be grateful for that.

My phone was in my hand, and I was trying to decide whether to send a message, when I was interrupted by the sound of someone knocking. Baxter raced to the door with a series of excited barks and I followed behind, intent on getting rid of whoever it was as quickly as possible.

'Not again,' said Edward, taking in my appearance as I opened the door. 'You can't sit around in your pyjamas all morning; we're going for brunch.'

'Sorry but this isn't really a good time,' I told him, standing in the jasmine-scented doorway, bees humming in the flowers above my head.

'It's the perfect time,' he argued. 'There are no weddings happening.'

'On a Saturday?'

'The couple cancelled,' he said. 'Unexpectedly.'

'Why?'

'I don't know for sure, but I can imagine.'

'Heartbreak,' I guessed, and he nodded.

There was a lot of it about, apparently. I knew Tom would be with Jo right now, sitting at the pine table in his light-filled kitchen, holding their baby. I could picture them clearly, almost as if I was standing in the street looking through the window, their arms round each other and heads together, newspapers scattered over the table, the remains of breakfast and empty coffee cups. I imagined Jo saying all the things I would have liked to say: He could rebuild, this wasn't the end, she was there to help. Tom had chosen her, not me and I still wasn't sure what she had given him that I couldn't. Leaning against the doorframe, staring out at Edward, I felt it again, almost as keenly as ever. Heartbreak.

'Not that I don't love the pyjamas but even here we tend to make more effort.' Edward clapped his hands to hurry me up. 'Come on, get dressed, brunch at the hotel is on me.'

'You're really kind.'

'Yes I am, and I'm also ravenous, so get moving.'

'OK, give me ten minutes,' I agreed.

The hotel restaurant was quiet, only a few other tables were occupied, and by people who looked to be tourists. Still, there was a generous buffet laid out with fresh fruit, buttery pastries, a tart of tomato and soft goat's cheese, breads flecked with caramelised onions and rosemary, dense home-made fig preserve and creamy buffalo yoghurt.

'We're famous for our weekend brunches; at least we'd like to be,' Edward said to me.

After the morning's news I wasn't hungry, but filled my plate anyway, and once I started nibbling on a corner of the tart, my appetite began to rally.

'This is good,' I said, loading brioche with a dollop of fig preserve. 'Very good.'

'We've got a great chef here, a local guy.'

'That's what I heard; I think Riccardo told me.'

'Ah, your hot mechanic? My car is with him too at the moment. It's in for a service.'

That worried me. How many cars could Riccardo work on at once? Mine was unlikely to be a priority when he had local customers who could offer him repeat business.

'I saw your Saab actually. It doesn't look like you'll be going anywhere in it for a while,' continued Edward, far too cheerfully. 'It doesn't even have four wheels at the moment.'

'Don't say that,' I groaned.

'Let me know when you've got an idea of how much longer you might need the house. It shouldn't be a problem, but it would be good to get the booking sorted.'

'I'd better talk to Riccardo again, see what he says.'

'Aren't you meant to be having lunch with him?'

'Yes, but I think I'm going to cancel.'

'He'll be disappointed,' Edward warned me. 'He mentioned

it to me this morning when I dropped off the car, said he's booked a table in the olive grove. It will be gorgeous.'

'I don't need the complication.'

'It's lunch,' he pointed out, 'how complicated can it be?'

Edward gave me that look again, the searching one that seemed to sum me up, see beyond my appearance (same shorts as yesterday and a silky orange top Mum had brought back from India) to some deeper, more significant place.

'I'm listening,' he said.

'To what?'

'Your story; whatever happened that made you think it was a good idea to climb into a highly unreliable vehicle and drive across Europe, whatever makes you sit around in pyjamas half the morning and refuse to go out on lunch dates.' Edward smiled sympathetically. 'I told you all my problems after all.'

With close friends it was always too difficult; there was so much story and I wasn't sure where to begin. Several didn't know about Tom and me at all, and none really understood how I felt about him. They would be hurt that I had never confided properly, then they might demand every detail or overwhelm me with unwanted advice, and definitely they would be keen on sitting around drinking too much wine, endlessly agreeing that 'all men are bastards'. With Edward, whom I barely knew, honesty seemed less fraught. Sitting there at a table dotted with plates of fruit and sweet pastries, as a waiter brought us icy glasses of pomegranate juice, I opened up.

'Tom Whiffen dumped me personally as well as professionally.' I stared at my glass rather than into his face as I said it. 'That's what happened.'

'Ouch, that must have hurt.'

'I was crazy about him,' I admitted. 'And I must have misread the signals because I assumed he felt the same way. It was my mistake.'

'I doubt it,' said Edward. 'I think you'd have to be pretty stupid to misread those sorts of signals, and you don't strike me as stupid.'

'Inexperienced then,' I countered. 'Tom's the only man I've ever been that involved with.'

Edward sighed. 'No one explains the rules, do they? No one tells you how it works. They should teach it at school, it would be more useful than algebra.'

'Once I might have been keen to sign up for that class, but not anymore.' I looked up from the glass of juice that was still warming in my hand. 'Who says you need to be one half of a couple anyway?'

'It can be wonderful, the very best thing,' he told me. 'I miss Gino. I hate us being apart like this. We're better when we're together.'

'And I miss Tom,' I admitted. 'But if I can't have him then I don't want anyone.'

After eating we took a long walk through the town, crossing the causeway and following a rough path in a stretch of woodland, until we reached a lookout point where we stood and stared back at the town. Viewed from here it seemed as if the houses were clinging to the mountain like barnacles to a rock. It looked like an unfriendly place of closed doors and dark windows.

'Dramatic, isn't it,' said Edward.

We paused for a while, catching our breath, and I told Edward about my stint at the *trattoria* and how I had helped Assunta when she seemed a little off-colour.

'Now her father seems to be under the impression that I'm permanently on the staff,' I said ruefully.

Edward laughed. 'Be careful, if Augusto decides on something then it tends to happen.'

'He seems very eccentric.'

'You might think so, but actually he is one of the sanest people I know.'

On the walk back, Baxter was panting in the heat, so we slowed our pace to a stroll to suit him, and he responded by dawdling even more, stopping for a thorough sniff of every bush.

'Is he OK?' Edward wondered.

'Just lazy; Baxter has never been a fan of super-long walks. He'd prefer to be stretched out in the shade somewhere.'

We crossed back over the causeway, pausing to look down into the ravine at the thread of a river twisting through it. Then we followed the winding road around the mountain that took us past Riccardo's workshop as Edward thought his car might be ready and I wanted to set eyes on my Saab and see how hopeless things looked.

We found Riccardo sitting in the sun, taking a break. Baxter perked up at the sight of him, wagging his tail so hard that his whiskers quivered, and Riccardo ruffled the wiry hair on his head before getting up to greet us. Shaking Edward by the hand, he told him that his car should be running smoothly now.

'What about mine?' I asked.

'Yours is a work in progress,' he admitted. 'But I hear there may not be such urgency now? You have taken a job with Assunta at the *trattoria*?'

'Did Augusto tell you that?' I asked, exasperated.

'He told my father who mentioned it to me – this is how it tends to work around here.'

'Well, it's not true,' I was quick to point out. 'I was only helping out because Assunta had a migraine. Augusto got it wrong.'

'Wishful thinking, maybe,' said Riccardo. 'She used to have somebody to help. There have been waitresses and kitchen hands, but no one for a while.'

Edward nodded in an understanding way. 'It can be a

nightmare finding good staff who want to turn up every day and work hard. I can see why it might seem easier to manage by herself.'

The doors to the workshop were open, and I took a few steps closer so I could peer inside. Edward's car was parked there, modern and gleaming, next to my dusty-looking Saab with its open bonnet. Sure enough, I noticed it was up on blocks now, as two of the wheels were off. Edward was right; I wasn't going to be driving it any time soon.

His gaze followed mine. 'Like I said, the house is available if you need to take it for longer.'

I turned to Riccardo. 'How much longer do you think? A few more days? Another week?'

He gave an expressive shrug. 'Maybe ... to be on the safe side.'

If I had been Baxter I might have put my tail between my legs, possibly even whined. I envied my dog never having to pretend.

'A week then?' I said, trying not to sound as exasperated as I felt.

Again Riccardo shrugged. 'I have tracked down most of the parts and believe they are on their way.'

'What happened to the wheels?'

'Those tyres didn't have much life left in them and you have a long drive ahead so I thought we should replace them. You want to be safe,' pointed out Riccardo.

'Yes, I do,' I agreed with a sigh.

Both Baxter and I were flagging now, so Edward offered us a ride the rest of the way in his car. Opening the passenger door to climb inside, I turned to Riccardo. 'Oh yes, about tomorrow.'

'Our lunch in the olive grove.' He smiled and his turquoise eyes gazed into mine. 'We will come to pick you up at midday.'

'The thing is ...' I began and then faltered because Riccardo was still smiling, and it occurred to me that lunch with him in an olive grove actually wouldn't be so awful.

'We are looking forward to it,' Riccardo added.

This time I picked up on what he had said. 'We?'

'Papa and I,' he explained. 'I asked him as you suggested, and he has surprised me by saying yes. I hope that is OK.'

'Yes, of course,' I said brightly. 'Your father is coming, perfect. I'll see you both tomorrow then.'

'*Ci vediamo*,' Riccardo said.

Driving away, Edward gave me a sideways glance, his lips twitching.

'That didn't quite go according to plan,' I admitted.

'No,' he agreed.

'It's only lunch though, right?'

'Exactly.' He sounded amused. 'Lunch with the family.'

The rest of the afternoon was spent composing messages to Tom then deleting them again. Some were long and still didn't manage to say what I wanted. The short ones were too casual. It was tricky even settling on the best way of making contact – text, email, a WhatsApp message. There were too many choices and none of them seemed right.

By early evening, I was rereading what had to be my final attempt. This version was at least free of clichés. I hadn't told Tom that my thoughts were with him, or urged him to stay strong, or offered him a virtual hug. I had said only the most important things: that I was sorry to hear about Made With Love. I hoped he was OK.

I came close to sending that one, then hit delete again. Instead, what I sent was an emoji, a single red heart; it was enough, it said everything.

Assunta

Assunta was determined not to dwell on what the American woman had said. It wasn't worth a moment of time. She knew who her father was, there was no doubt about it, and to suggest it was anyone other than Augusto was absurd.

But at the edges of her mind was something half forgotten that she couldn't quite catch hold of. Assunta kept reaching and finding it gone. She tried again and again, but whenever she focused, it shifted. Her mother and Giuseppina ... she pictured them together talking, then noticing her and falling silent. There must have been secrets, truths that they had shielded her from; perhaps she had overheard a few words and not known what to make of them. For the rest of the afternoon and into the evening, she stood in her kitchen, thinking about the two women, until her head began to ache again.

It was Sarah-Jane who had shouldered the hard work, and Assunta was prepared to let her. She needed to be away from the clamour of her customers, to escape the hissing and bubbling of her pans, to sit in silence and be alone.

At home in her armchair, with no sound except the ticking clock, her mind still felt cloudy but she saw where she should be looking. Augusto was a way into this mystery. She remembered him from her childhood, always handsome and often smiling. He had liked to give her treats, sugary things her mother thought she shouldn't be eating. He would take her and Renzo for walks and show them things, stitching together tales that involved whatever they happened to come across.

As a child, she accepted the way her life was as normal. Only looking back later on did she see the things that weren't. Other children had fathers who lived with them, who were there when they went to bed at night and when they woke up, but Augusto's house was in another part of town and she rarely saw him in the company of her mother. He wasn't married to her or to Renzo's mother, or in fact to any woman. He was a man that people gossiped about in corners.

Later on she understood that, while many people might have disapproved, few could dislike him for it, because what Augusto lacked in morals, he made up for with kindness. And he was a good father, better than a lot of men, never stern or cruel, generous with his time. Assunta felt his love; she knew he loved them all.

If there was any truth in what this American woman had said then even he had been taken away. Assunta was alone in the world, she had no father and no half-brother, no real family left at all. Sitting in her armchair inside her house on a hot summer evening, the thought chilled her.

That night, any sleep she had was snatched between episodes of wakefulness and worry, and in the morning the ghost of a headache still haunted her, but Assunta knew what to do now. Dressing quickly in a nice dress that she always saved for the weekends when it wouldn't be covered by an apron, she slipped out of the house and made her way to the hotel.

Behind the reception desk was a young woman she didn't recognise. At Assunta's request she tapped on a computer then gave a brisk shake of her head. The American visitor Caterina Campanella and her son had checked out half an hour earlier. They hadn't mentioned where they would be going next.

'Do you have any other details for them? A phone number?' Assunta asked, frustrated.

'It is our policy to respect the privacy of our guests.'

'She was a friend of my late mother and I hoped to stay in touch with her but hadn't realised she would be leaving so soon. Is there an email address?'

'No, it is not possible.'

She and the young woman locked eyes. Nobody spoke. Assunta took a fifty-euro banknote from her pocket and put it on the counter. In response the woman glanced at her computer screen then scribbled on a white square of paper that she put down beside it.

'I am sorry I was unable to help you today,' the woman said, reaching for the cash.

'It is OK, I quite understand,' Assunta replied, glancing at the square of paper then putting it in her pocket where the money had been. She would send an email later and hope that Tony Campanella would pass on a message to his mother, tell her that she had said too much and not enough, that Assunta needed an explanation.

From the hotel she walked along a series of lanes twisting steeply down the side of the mountain that led eventually to Augusto's house. It was her habit to drop in on him at some point every weekend. He was at the age when most people struggled to take care of themselves and she liked to cast an eye over the place, be sure it was clean, see there was food in the cupboards, laundry hanging from the washing line, and that the rooms smelled only of the wax he used in what was left of his hair and the cologne he patted on his cheeks after shaving.

This was where Augusto had lived for as long as Assunta could remember, a small house with ivy-covered stone walls. This morning she found its doors and windows open and rock music booming out: the Rolling Stones, one of his favourites. Assunta liked them too, but not at this volume, throbbing from the sleek Bose speakers in his living room. Thankfully most of his neighbours were as old and deaf as he was.

'I was listening to that,' Augusto grumbled, when she turned the music down.

'Yes, but I need to talk to you and I am not going to compete with Mick Jagger.'

'You would lose,' he said matter-of-factly.

'I know it,' she told him.

'You are checking up on me again, aren't you?' Augusto accused her. 'You can't wait for the moment you find a speck of dust or a dirty coffee cup and can use it as an excuse to shut me away in a rest home.'

'No one is putting you in a rest home.'

He still kept a neat and pleasant house, with books and records carefully shelved, cushions on chairs, his latest computer on a desk in the corner, but for years Assunta had been ready to move him into her place as soon as it was necessary.

'What do you need to talk to me about?' he asked. 'Something important, I think, for you to be here at this time.'

At weekends Assunta preferred a slower, lazier start and Augusto knew that about her.

'It is nothing important,' she reassured him. 'I only wanted to ask about those Americans you were talking to in the bar the other day. Her name was Caterina Campanella, do you remember her?'

'I recall talking to her, of course I do. Perhaps you think I have the dementia?'

'No, Papa, I meant do you remember her from back in the old days.'

'Oh.' He thought about it. 'I didn't recognise her face. How am I supposed to? It wouldn't have looked like that all those years ago when she left Montenello.'

'True,' Assunta agreed. 'But did you know her name?'

'Campanella?' He paused in thought again. 'There was a boy in my class called that. Maybe it was her brother ... or a cousin. He was clever, very quiet and serious, I wonder where he ended up.'

So many families had left to search out new lives in places that weren't stalked by poverty, so many people born in these mountains had scattered across the globe, and in the days before computers, when phone calls were expensive and letters slow, they severed their connections, disappeared.

'She said she was a friend of my mother, claimed they were close,' said Assunta, hoping to jog his memory. 'Does that sound likely?'

'Who knows, I suppose she may have been.'

'She said I looked like Giuseppina.'

Augusto stared into her face. 'Perhaps you do, just a little, but only when you smile, which isn't often enough these days. What else did this woman say?'

'Nothing really.'

'Then why are you so interested in her?'

Assunta wondered what would happen if she told him the truth; that she feared he wasn't really her father. Would he be hurt? Unsurprised? Would he confirm or deny it? She wasn't ready to find out.

'I miss them still,' she said quietly, 'my mother and Giuseppina. I suppose she reminded me of that.'

Augusto patted her cheek. The skin of his hand felt papery and his touch was light. 'Of course you miss them, you always will.'

He made a pot of coffee and talked about the old days, reminding her of little things. The way her mother had braided her hair with ribbons on a Sunday. The time Giuseppina took her to the beach and she brought him back treasures, pebbles and sea glass, which he still kept in a box somewhere. The *festa* when there was music in the piazza and stalls selling fresh coconut and sweet *torrone*, even a cavalcade of horses. Assunta had heard those stories many times, but still liked to listen.

As she was leaving, the music started up again – Fleetwood Mac now and as loud as before. Her father would sit there all day if he could, nodding along to it. No wonder the old man was deaf, thought Assunta.

She took the longer route home, through the part of town that hadn't been touched yet, near the tower at its top. Eventually more of the houses she was passing would be refurbished. Someone would smash out their walls, re-tile the floors and fit new kitchens. Progress happened, change was inevitable, but Assunta felt at home with the way things were right now.

She hadn't been up to the top of the tower in years. When she was younger, it was where everyone liked to meet, away from the eyes of their parents, to smoke a cigarette or snatch a kiss. Assunta wasn't a part of the gang who acted like they owned it back then, there was too much to be done at home helping her family, but once in a while she would sneak away to hang out with them.

She pushed at the door, finding it open, like it always had been. Taking the stairs she was careful, touching the wall in the places where the handrail had gone, in case she missed a step in the dim light. Once out on the ramparts, she blinked at the brightness of the sky.

'Assunta?' said a man's voice and she turned to see a familiar face.

'Carlo Mastrobuoni, why are you here?' She squinted at him. 'Are you drinking beer?'

'Do you want one?' He took a can from a cooler bag.

'Why not,' she agreed, and Carlo flipped open the tab and passed it to her.

She took a sip and lowered herself carefully onto the ground beside him. 'Did you set a fire?' she asked, noticing a scorched patch of stone.

'Not me,' he said. 'There must be kids who come here still, and think they are rebels like we used to.'

Carlo had been a regular – him and Maria. It was where

they had done much of their courting, and Assunta pictured them sitting arm in arm in this same spot. It was such a long time ago and so much had happened since, but she supposed that was why he had come now, to feel closer to the memory.

Pulling out her cigarettes, she offered him the packet. 'One won't kill you,' she said encouragingly.

'I am drinking at lunchtime, so I may as well smoke.'

'Still a rebel then,' she said, lighting his cigarette then her own.

They sat together and smoked. Assunta thought he might mention the conversation he had overheard the day before between her and the American woman, but if he was curious, Carlo showed no sign of it.

'This view hasn't changed,' he said, staring out over the low parapet. 'Only we are different.'

'I feel the same,' admitted Assunta. 'Often I glance in the mirror and I am surprised by who I see. It is not how I imagine myself. I don't look like me.'

'Yes, you do,' he said, 'especially in that dress. Didn't you used to wear one in the same shade?'

Assunta's dress was a deep pinky purple. It had cost too much but when she saw it hanging in the window of the shop on a rare visit to Borgo del Colle, she had to buy it as this was Giuseppina's favourite colour.

'My grandmother had a dress that was similar, she used to let me borrow it.'

'She loved bright colours,' Carlo remembered.

'Always,' she said fondly.

The beer was sour and foamy, and Assunta look a long sip. 'This is ... different,' she said, 'being up here again after all these years.'

Carlo smiled. 'I know, it is different for me too. Usually I don't come here and drink alone.'

'Why now?' Assunta asked.

'It is my son's fault. He keeps saying that I am too set in

my ways, and perhaps he is right,' argued Carlo. 'Maybe I have become boring.'

Assunta shrugged. She knew that could be said about her too. She had never been very concerned.

'Riccardo is wrong in one way though,' said Carlo. 'I am prepared to change.'

'And that is why you are up here?'

'I haven't come in years.' He looked down at the empty can of beer in his hand then squeezed a dent in it. 'I don't drink much either these days, certainly not at lunchtime. But I am trying to do different things.'

'You had breakfast at the bar the other morning,' Assunta remembered.

'And today I am reliving my youth.'

Assunta was intrigued. 'What is planned for tomorrow?'

'Tomorrow, instead of cooking chicken at home, I am going out for lunch. My son is taking me to Donna Carmela's restaurant in the olive grove. He insists that I come.'

'Very nice.' Assunta didn't have much time for Donna Carmela, who had taken to making regular appearances in Montenello since her son became the mayor. She found her a showy sort of woman.

'My son has booked a table. He is bringing the English girl, the one whose car he is fixing.'

'Sarah-Jane?'

'That is right,' said Carlo.

'Just the three of you?' asked Assunta.

'The food is good, I hear.'

'I have never eaten there.' It wasn't a place where you dined alone and there had never been anyone to go with. 'They say it isn't bad.'

'Why not join us?' Carlo suggested.

Assunta's first instinct was to refuse. 'No, no ...'

'I would like you to come.'

'Perhaps your son won't be able to change the booking.'

'Three or four people, what difference does it make?'

Sometimes Assunta cooked a Sunday lunch for Augusto and Renzo, but often she ate alone. She never went out.

'It would be a nice thing to do ... different,' Carlo added.

'I suppose it would,' she said uncertainly, as she had been caught unawares by the invitation and wasn't sure what to think of it.

Assunta finished her beer and smoked one more cigarette. As she and Carlo climbed down the tower's winding staircase, he steadied her over a section of the stonework that was cracked and uneven, and they walked together towards the piazza.

'It is kind of Riccardo to ask the girl for lunch,' she remarked.

'Yes, it must be lonely for her with no friends or family here,' he agreed.

Looking at his face in profile, at the strong features that were only beginning to soften with age, Assunta knew that Carlo too was lonely. Unlike her, he wasn't used to a solitary life. He would see the spaces that his wife used to occupy – her side of the bed, the chair she always took at the dining table, even the passenger seat in his car – and be faced with what he had lost over and over each day. It was his loneliness that had brought his son back from Napoli to live at home again. Probably it was why Riccardo was insisting that his father join him for a long lunch he was having with a pretty young girl. He mustn't want to leave him behind on a Sunday.

'She is adventurous, this young woman, to take such a long trip by herself,' Carlo observed. 'She came all the way from England and plans to travel to Sicily before she turns for home. I have never driven so far.'

They were in the piazza now, nearing the bar. Renzo didn't work on Saturdays but still he never went far. Assunta could see him, sitting at one of the tables with a group of other men, noticeably younger than them although his hair was thinning.

Carlo followed her gaze, looking at the old men with their drooping shoulders, curving spines and shiny scalps, the same group that was always sitting there if the sun was shining. He frowned.

'Have we had our lives, Assunta?'

'I don't know ... maybe,' she replied.

Sarah-Jane

Normally I'm a ready-in-a-flash type of person. I don't wear much make-up; my hair looks fine piled up on my head and my clothes are a flung-together mix of vintage and chain-store. But that morning everything seemed to be slowing me down. Partly it was because I still wasn't entirely sure about going out for a long lunch with Riccardo and his father (what would we talk about, might it get awkward?). Also I hadn't done any laundry in ages so a thorough check was required before I decided my yellow sundress could stand another outing. The real brake though was that every few minutes I had to glance at my phone to see if Tom had replied.

I had sent him a single heart; surely there was an emoji he could use to let me know he had received it – folded hands to say thank you, a sad face, even a butterfly. But when my phone did ping, it was my mother to say her usual good morning and Riccardo to let me know he was moments away.

Hearing his knock on the door, Baxter raced up, tail wagging. I shoved a couple of sparkly clips in my hair, dabbed on some tinted lip balm and put a few essentials in my bag – sun lotion, keys, credit card – then followed. My phone stayed in my hand; if Tom contacted me then I didn't want to miss it.

'*Buongiorno*.' Riccardo smiled as I opened the door to him. 'You are ready to go?'

'I think so,' I said, noticing that his skin was smoothed of stubble, his hair freshly trimmed and there wasn't a speck of oil on his hands. Also he smelled fantastic.

'Papa plans to meet us there,' he told me.

'He is driving down separately?'

'Yes, because he is bringing a guest, Assunta. I hadn't realised she and Papa were such good friends,' Riccardo said, as we walked towards his truck with Baxter trotting ahead of us. 'Apparently he thinks she is having a difficult time and needs cheering up.'

That was fine, the more the merrier as far as I was concerned.

'Papa doesn't drive his old Fiat very far these days,' Riccardo added, sounding concerned. 'I have told him to take it slowly.'

We climbed into his truck and he negotiated the steep, narrow streets with his usual confidence. As we were crossing the causeway, my gaze flicked down to my phone again, but still nothing from Tom.

'They must have known each other all their lives,' said Riccardo into the silence.

'I'm sorry?' I had forgotten what we had been talking about.

'My father and Assunta, they were in the same class at school so would have been friends even back then.'

We drove a ribbon of road through densely forested hills. Gradually the landscape changed, with the mountains becoming steeper and scrubbier, until we began winding down towards a valley filled with olive groves. As we sped along, Riccardo started talking about his mother again, how she was strong in her mind but very often her body let her down. It seemed that she had been sick on and off throughout his whole childhood.

'My father was dedicated; they were together all the time. He looked after us all when she couldn't. Towards the end he did everything.'

Both of us had lost a parent, but my dad had been young and strong, never a sick day as far as I could remember, and his death came as a complete shock. I wasn't sure whose situation was sadder or more terrible.

'While I was living in Napoli, I would imagine she was still here,' said Riccardo in a quieter voice. 'I tried to think of her in the kitchen cooking, or resting in bed with one of the magazines she loved to read and a jug of fresh lemonade that Papa had brought her. I had those pictures in my mind all the time. But now ...'

'I know,' I said, because even though I was a child when my father's helicopter dropped out of the sky, I still understood how a loss like that never left you alone and how much you wanted to escape it.

'It has been hard for Papa,' said Riccardo. 'I don't think he will ever get over losing her. They should have had many more years and grown old together. Instead he is on his own now.'

He told me about his ongoing attempts to encourage his father to move on with his life, find new interests, or at least break out from his routine.

'I don't think he can ever change much though, not really. He is a man of habit. But Papa has agreed that trying something new every now and then might not be such a bad idea. The other morning he ate breakfast in the bar instead of at home. This for him was huge.'

'Perhaps he needs some suggestions. My mother explored a few different things after she lost my dad. She did a homeopathy course and took up yoga.'

'Papa doing yoga – that I would like to see.' He grinned at the idea.

We were travelling more slowly now along dusty lanes that criss-crossed red-earthed land dotted with ancient olive trees and *trullo* houses with conical roofs. Riccardo wasn't using his GPS; he said it was worse than useless in this tangle of back roads, so instead we followed the rustic wooden signs hammered onto fences and power poles at regular intervals – 'Ristorante di Donna Carmela', they read.

We pulled through a narrow gateway and parked near a whitewashed farmhouse with an old stone barn that was vibrant with the bougainvillea climbing its walls. There was a garden planted with prickly pears and all around us were olive groves stretching to the horizon.

'We are here,' said Riccardo, checking to see if his father's Fiat was among the other cars parked on the gravel drive-way. 'I don't think Papa has arrived yet.'

The restaurant occupied the barn and rambled well beyond it into the gardens, with tables spaced out beneath the trees and shaded by striped shade cloths. Already it was busy but this place had been designed with privacy in mind and, once Riccardo and I were seated, it almost felt like we were alone.

Riccardo glanced at his watch and I took the opportunity for one more look at the blank screen of my phone then put it away in my bag so it wouldn't keep distracting me. Baxter lay beside it, secured to the leg of my chair with a leash, in case he took it into his head to go wandering.

A woman came with our menus. She was tiny, with grey-ing hair that curled to her waist, olive skin and gold hoops in her ears.

'Welcome, I am Donna Carmela,' she announced. 'There are four of you for lunch, yes?'

'The others will arrive any moment,' said Riccardo. 'I hope so anyway.'

'Would you like a drink while you wait?' she asked.

'Prosecco?' I suggested.

Donna Carmela nodded and went to fetch the drinks but returned with a chilled sparkling rosé for me instead. 'This is a local wine, better than the Prosecco,' she assured me.

As I sipped and conceded that it was delicious, she started to collect up our menus, declaring that we would have a far better lunch if we allowed her to be in charge of feeding us.

'I am good at knowing what people want,' she promised.

I might have preferred to hold onto my menu and have some say in what I ate, but I wasn't going to make a fuss because as a rule I don't in restaurants. Besides, Riccardo seemed happy enough with the idea.

Donna Carmela strode away purposefully and when she returned a few minutes later, it was with Carlo and Assunta at her heels. This was the first time I had seen Assunta away from the *trattoria* and, instead of her apron and plain work clothes, she was wearing a bright teal dress covered in a print of roses. She looked a little flushed and much prettier.

'I am hungry,' she announced, joining us at the table. 'What is good today?'

'Can I suggest the red shrimps to begin with,' said Donna Carmela.

'How are they cooked?' Assunta wanted to know.

'They are baked in a sea salt crust. I also think you need to have the swordfish carpaccio.'

'It is marinated in lemon and chilli?'

'Yes, and also a little garlic and parsley.'

Assunta ran through the dishes, asking Donna Carmela questions about each one. Had she bought in or made the orecchiette that was served with a scattering of pistachios and a light lemony sauce, exactly which vegetables had she put in the caponata, could the gratin mussels be served with a little diced tomato in the dressing? Only once she had sighted the prawns (prior to their encounter with the salt crust to be sure they were entirely fresh), was Assunta prepared to order.

There was more discussion, the back and forth of it moving so fast I lost its thread. Watching the two women duelling over the menu, Riccardo caught my eye and gave a resigned shrug as if to say, this was bound to happen, there is nothing to be done, and I smiled back at him.

Finished at last, Assunta sat back in her chair, satisfied.

'Everyone says your food is very good,' she said graciously.

'I look forward to your opinion,' Donna Carmela replied, before disappearing to summon our antipasto course.

While we were waiting for the food to come, all our talk centred on Montenello and the mayor's plans to release a final cache of one-euro houses. I was sure Augusto had said that this was confidential information, but it appeared that everyone already knew. Some locals didn't want more foreigners buying up the houses; they thought the town's young people should be encouraged to come home, like Riccardo had.

'The mayor should give you priority,' Carlo argued.

'I haven't even said that I am applying yet,' pointed out Riccardo.

'You would be crazy not to,' his father declared.

'But they are no better than ruins, these places, the mayor saved the worst till last,' Riccardo argued.

'They are not so bad,' insisted Carlo. 'I had a good look around that part of town yesterday.'

'It will be expensive, even if I do a lot of the work myself. I don't have the money.'

'I can help you,' his father told him. 'This is an opportunity and there won't be another like it.'

They might have continued bickering except a small flock of waitresses descended on us at that point and started crowding plates onto our table, surely more than we had ordered. Glancing at Assunta's narrowed eyes, I suspected that Donna Carmela had struck back by sending out extra little tastes of things she thought we needed to try.

'Eat and be sure to tell me what you think,' she said with a generous smile, passing by the table.

For a moment I only wanted to look at the glossy red prawns dusted with salt crystals, the translucent slivers of white fish dotted with herbs and chilli, and the caciocavallo cheese deep-fried in breadcrumbs and doused in a garlicky white wine sauce. Then I realised that everyone was waiting for me to pick up my fork, so I began.

It was all good, very good, and Assunta obviously thought so too as I saw her nodding in approval.

'It is such a long time since I have eaten food that I haven't made myself,' she said thoughtfully. 'I had forgotten.'

'Forgotten what?' I wondered.

'How flavours can surprise you.'

'Do you never go to restaurants?' Much as I love to cook myself, part of the joy of eating is discovering new tastes and textures in other people's food.

'Never,' admitted Assunta.

Carlo was loyal. 'Why would she, when she makes the very best herself?'

'What about the hotel in Montenello – you haven't been there?'

Assunta shook her head.

'Neither have I,' admitted Carlo.

'Why don't we go then?' I suggested. 'We could have dinner one evening next week.'

Assunta wasn't enthusiastic. Even on days when her *trattoria* was open only for lunch, she was too tired for anything but a quiet night. Carlo felt the same; his custom was a light meal and an early bedtime if he had to be up early for work the next day.

'We could try the weekend, if it is not booked out for weddings,' said Riccardo.

'I will have left by then,' I reminded him. 'My car will be fixed, won't it?'

'Maybe, maybe not,' he said, shrugging. 'I have no control over how long it takes for the parts to arrive.'

'Is there no one you could call to hurry things up?' I asked.

'I can try but you must understand we are in Italy.' Riccardo held up his hands, palms open, in a gesture of defeat.

'Some things can't be hurried,' agreed Carlo.

'They take the time they take,' contributed Assunta.

I was exasperated and rested my fork on my plate, not hungry for any more of the fried cheese or raw fish. That twitchy feeling of wanting to check my phone had been coming and going the whole time we were eating, but up till then I had managed to resist it. Now I felt my handbag vibrating against my ankle. It might have been my mother calling, or any of my friends, but I had the strongest sense that it wasn't. This was Tom at last ready to talk. I was so sure that my heart started hammering.

'Are you OK?' asked Riccardo, staring at my face.

Making an excuse that I needed the bathroom, I grabbed my bag, which had stopped vibrating by now. The circuitous pathways between the trees had seemed adorable when we arrived, but now, hurrying for privacy, they were only inconvenient. I found the bathrooms on the far side of the barn and, shutting myself in a cubicle, pulled out my phone. The number wasn't one I recognised and whoever it was hadn't left a message. Staring at my screen, I willed them to call back. Around me I heard toilets flushing and the murmur of a conversation out beside the washbasins.

I took my time in the cubicle but couldn't lurk in there forever. Convinced it had been Tom, instead of heading back to the table, I walked out into the car park and tried the number. It rang for a while then a recorded voice informed me that the person I was calling wasn't available right now.

'Damn,' I muttered.

Wandering back through the trees, their branches waving as the afternoon grew breezier, Tom's face was in my mind. All I wanted was to talk, tell him everything was going to be OK, that a man with his talents wouldn't be kept down for long. No, actually all I wanted was to hear his voice.

At our table, I found Riccardo alone.

'Where are the others?' I asked.

'They are taking a walk between courses, for their digestion. My father believes it is unhealthy to be still for too
long.'

'He may have a point.'

Sitting down, I put my phone on the table, then picked it
up again and stared at the blank screen. It might ring again
and it might be Tom. Did I want to talk to him for the first
time in so long, right there, with Riccardo beside me? It
would be impossible to say any of the things I needed to
say. At best we would have a terse and awkward exchange.
So my phone went back into my bag, which I placed on the
ground before I could change my mind.

Stroking Baxter, patting his hairy little head, I steadied
myself. Still I kept my right foot pressed against the bag in
case it started vibrating again.

Riccardo poured me a glass of wine; he was drinking very
little himself as he had to drive home.

'My father and those one-euro houses,' he said despair-
ingly. 'He is obsessed.'

'Perhaps he's right though; it may be a good idea to apply
since you're planning on staying in Montenello.'

'They are at the very top of the town, right by the tower,
have you been there?'

I nodded. 'Yes, the views are amazing.'

'I came home to be with Papa, he needs me. How can we
spend enough time together if I am always up there rebuilding a ruin?'

'He may enjoy helping to renovate it with you.'

'It would be hard and dirty work; I can't ask that of him.'

'He's right that it's an opportunity. If you didn't want to
live in the house once it was finished then you could rent it
out; maybe the guys at the hotel will want it for their guests.
Those views.'

'Why don't you apply then?' asked Riccardo.

'I'm leaving soon.'

'You are making friends here, you have a job with Assunta now, why not stay in this part of Italy, instead of travelling from place to place all the time?'

'I don't actually have a job, you know,' I reminded him.

'Maybe not officially, not yet, but Assunta would take you on, she needs the help. And you like Montenello, don't you?'

'I'm getting to like it, definitely.'

'From here you could explore so much of the south and always have a home to come back to instead of being among strangers.'

I considered the idea. It might be possible to stay on in the jasmine-covered house if Edward could arrange a longer-term rental. If I did, I would get to know other local people and feel more a part of the place. It wasn't a terrible plan.

'I still want to see Sicily,' I reminded Riccardo.

'Sicily isn't going anywhere,' he promised. 'And you have plenty of time, don't you?'

Just then the handbag, still resting against my right foot, started to vibrate again. I froze, barely noticing that Riccardo was still speaking, hardly even catching a breath, until it stopped. This time I couldn't go rushing off to the bathroom; I would have to wait. Still my fingertips itched to reach down and grab it so I could see if it was the same number. My hands clenched into fists to prevent me.

When I felt it vibrate once more with a message, I had to know whether it was Tom and what he was saying.

'Sorry,' I told Riccardo. 'I think a friend is trying to get hold of me. I just need to check.'

Glancing at the screen I found a text, sent from the same number.

Sarah-Jane, are you there? Just wanted to tell you, I messed up.

It was definitely from Tom. For a moment I stared at the screen, trying to decide what to do, then quickly typed a reply.

Can't talk right now. Call you later? Read about Made With Love. I'm so sorry.

Once it had been sent, I held onto my phone, and asked Riccardo a question about the one-euro houses, so he would talk and I wouldn't have to. It was several minutes before I felt the phone vibrate with the reply I was waiting for.

That's not what I meant, Tom had written. *I meant you Sarah-Jane, I messed up with you.*

I clutched my phone more tightly; I couldn't wait to speak to him.

Assunta

Assunta was pleased to be wearing flat-soled sandals. Walking with Carlo between the rows of olive trees, higher heels would have sunk into the soft red earth, and might have rubbed and blistered.

Not that Assunta had lots of shoes. Mostly she wore sturdy slip-resistant footwear to see her through the hours on her feet at work on floors that grew slick when food was spilt. Hidden away in the corner of a cupboard were a couple of smarter pairs, dusted off if she needed to go somewhere else, shoes she had owned for years that could still pass for new because she hardly ever wore them.

After the unexpected invitation, she had pulled them out – her flat-soled sandals and a pair of heels she must have bought for some wedding or party. Not especially elegant heels, not pointy-toed or strappy, but smarter than anything else she owned. Which pair should she choose for lunch with Carlo?

As a rule, men didn't invite her out, even men who were old friends, so it felt like an occasion, one she should make some effort for. Deciding on a dress hadn't been difficult. Her favourite was the deep pinky purple, but she had sat down while wearing it on the dirty ground at the top of the tower and now it needed a careful hand wash. That only left a floral frock she had bought for Augusto's eightieth birthday celebration. Whether to match it with the sensible flat shoes or the dressier ones, she was uncertain.

Assunta tried each pair on her feet, thinking about Carlo sitting up on the tower drinking beer, alone with his memories. It had been a surprise to find him there. And now another surprise: she was going to spend a Sunday with him, drive to Donna Carmela's restaurant in his old Fiat, enjoy lunch then drive home again. Higher heels or flat-soled sandals – which was appropriate? She thought about it, off and on, all evening long.

She had made the right choice, Assunta decided, strolling among the trees with their twisted boughs and silver-backed leaves, with Carlo who seemed in no hurry to return to their table. He was talking about his son, worrying the way parents seemed to, and confiding his worries in her.

'We all have to make our own mistakes, I know that, but it is hard to watch when it is someone you love,' he was saying.

'What mistakes is Riccardo making?' Assunta wondered.

'For a start he should have stayed in Napoli where he had more of a future.'

'He seems happy to be home.'

'In that case he should apply for one of the houses. A single euro, that is all it will cost.'

'And a pledge to renovate it within the next three years,' Assunta reminded him.

They were walking alongside a wall made of loose boulders. In the spring there would be wildflowers growing from its cracks, but now in the heat of summer there were only dry stalks and withered leaves.

'My son needs his own place,' Carlo told her. 'It is hard for him living at home, and every day being reminded that his mother is gone.'

'Hard for you too,' said Assunta.

'I was with Maria as she got sicker, there for all the treatments and the appointments with doctors when we learned they hadn't worked. I knew she was dying, I saw it before my eyes every day. But Riccardo was in Napoli for all those years.'

'I remember,' murmured Assunta.

'He would come home and be shocked to see how sick his mamma was, and then he was shocked to lose her. I feel for him, I worry. If he had one of those houses to renovate, a project like that, it would be good for his mind and his future.'

'You work at the Town Hall – can't you use your influence?'

'I will try, but first Riccardo has to put in his application.'

They were too far away now to hear the music playing, the clinking of crockery or the murmur of conversation. The air smelled of warmed earth and was filled with the sound of cicadas singing.

'Would you be lonely if he moved out?' Assunta wondered.

Carlo turned to her. 'My son needs to have his own life.'

Together they retraced their steps, the restaurant seeming further in the distance than Assunta remembered having come.

'Have you digested?' she asked Carlo. 'Are you ready for the next course?'

'Digested, yes.' He patted his still-taut stomach. 'Also we have given those two young ones some time together.'

'Riccardo likes her,' agreed Assunta.

'Is she a good person?' Carlo asked. 'Does she like him too?'

Assunta thought about it. 'I don't know her well enough to say.'

'But she works for you?'

'No, no.' Assunta shook her head. 'Although if she wanted to …'

Taking their seats back at the table, everything looked the same but Assunta sensed a shift in atmosphere. The change was in Sarah-Jane. She seemed preoccupied, her phone in one hand, and she kept glancing at the screen. She was subdued but also brighter-eyed. And when the second course arrived, she fed scraps to her little dog beneath the table, not eating much herself. As for Riccardo, Assunta couldn't miss how he kept glancing at the girl, his expression serious, as if he had noticed the shift himself and didn't know what to make of it.

Their lunch felt as if it might be drifting to an end but there was still food to taste. Pasta with salted ricotta and a resinous hint of rosemary. Cuttlefish stuffed with breadcrumbs, capers and anchovies. Chicken braised with porcini mushrooms. And then Donna Carmela came fluttering around them again, ushering in even more they hadn't ordered. A little something she was testing for the menu and would be grateful for Assunta's opinion on: fresh produce from the garden she thought they would enjoy.

'Very impressive,' said Assunta, because the food was good and it would have been churlish to find fault with it.

'I have eaten in your *trattoria* many times,' Donna Carmela replied. 'I am happy at last you have come to eat in mine.'

'I should have come before,' conceded Assunta.

They ate as the heat built and the afternoon wore on. Carlo drank strong black coffee because he didn't want to be sleepy driving home on such a full stomach. He was a good driver and Assunta felt safe with him even if his Fiat was ancient. Cramped in it together, with the windows down because there wasn't any air-conditioning, and the radio tuned to a station playing the music of their youth, she had felt almost carefree.

'I will make sure you don't fall asleep on the way back,' she promised.

Donna Carmela wasn't finished with them yet. Her final touch was small silk bags filled with sugared almonds, *bonbonnière* that she presented to them as they were leaving.

'A little sweetness to remember us by,' she said, pressing a bag into Assunta's hand. 'I hope we will see you again before too long.'

She had presence, Assunta had to admit it. A small woman, and easily in her fifties, Donna Carmela drew the eye and held it. She was focused on charming Carlo now, talking to him about the Town Hall where he worked with her son, and Assunta saw him smiling as he accepted the *bonbonnière* from her.

'Certainly we will be back soon,' he was agreeing.

They found the little Fiat as hot as an oven and had to open up its doors and wait a while before they could get inside, waving at Riccardo roaring away in his big, air-conditioned truck, Sarah-Jane at his side.

'We'll catch you up,' Carlo called, and Assunta laughed as she climbed inside.

As Carlo pulled out through the narrow gate and onto the dirt road, dust flew into the open windows, but it was too hot to close them. Assunta fanned herself with her hands and he was apologetic.

'Maybe my son is right, it is time for a new car, especially if I am going to be driving further from home.'

'Do you think you might?'

'Why not?' Carlo glanced at her, then back at the road. 'I could go to the coast, swim in the sea, eat a pizza on the beach … it is not too far.'

'Not far at all,' said Assunta, who hadn't been to a beach in years.

'I enjoyed our lunch,' said Carlo. 'It was good to go somewhere new, try food that was different.'

'Yes,' she agreed.

'Though I prefer your cooking,' he told her, eyes still on the road ahead. 'That is the sort of food I want to eat every day.'

He turned on the radio and Assunta recognised the song playing as a Spanish one that had been popular almost thirty years before. '*Vamos a la playa,*' two male voices sang over and over to the point of monotony, and Carlo joined in, surprisingly tunefully.

'*Vamos a la playa*,' he said, as it finished. 'Let's go to the beach.'

Sarah-Jane

I held onto my phone because it was the closest thing to holding Tom. All the way through the rest of that lunch, in Riccardo's truck driving back to Montenello, and as I thanked him and he promised to let me know about my Saab, the phone stayed in my hand. Saying goodbye out on the street seemed to take forever and require a lot of polite chatter (for some reason Riccardo seemed particularly keen on keeping me talking). The moment I got away and was safely inside, with the front door closed, I rang Tom's number, willing him to answer.

'Sarah-Jane?' Hearing that familiar deep and steady voice speaking my name had been worth waiting for.

'Tom,' I replied.

'Where are you? What are you doing?'

I told him about Montenello, describing my jasmine-covered house, how peaceful it was high up on a mountain, how remote it felt.

'What about you?' I asked. 'I saw all those articles about Made With Love ...'

Tom sighed. He said it had been really tough, that he tried to keep the business afloat, cut costs, looked at ways that at least a part of it could be saved, but in the end he had to accept the only option was to let it all go. He sounded entirely unlike the Tom I knew, beaten and down.

'So what will you do?' I wanted to know.

'I'm not finished yet,' he promised, his voice taking on a more bullish tone I recognised. 'I can't tell you much yet, everything is confidential. And right now I need to keep my head down. The tabloids won't leave me alone; that's why I had to change my number. I can't go anywhere without the paparazzi tailing me.'

'What a nightmare,' I said sympathetically, because I knew how much he hated having his privacy invaded.

'Yeah, it's been intense.' His voice softened. 'But losing the business wasn't the worst of it, Sarah-Jane. Shit, I've been such an idiot. The way I handled things with you. That's what's killing me.'

There was a static-filled silence. Clutching my phone tighter, I forced out the question. 'What happened?'

'How do I explain ... where do I start?'

'At the beginning,' I told him.

I sat in the window-seat looking out over the valley as Tom filled in the gaps, telling me everything I hadn't understood about why my life had changed. How following a few glasses of after-work wine, he had given into the temptation of a one-night-stand with Jo. Regretted it straight afterwards but then learned she was pregnant and decided he was going to stand by her – it was the right thing to do. And then both of them realising what a mistake it had been because they didn't fit as a couple and having a baby boy together only made that more obvious.

'I'll always be a part of Charlie's life, of course; it's a beautiful thing to be a father,' said Tom, 'but Jo decided she wanted to move back in with her parents and I wasn't going to stand in her way.'

'So you're not together now?' I asked, wanting to be completely clear.

'We split up not long after Charlie's birth. He's gorgeous – I'll send you a photo. I've got about a million on my phone already.'

'I'd like that,' I said, wondering if the child looked like Tom.

'And you'll meet him – at least I hope so.'

That was when Tom said he loved me. He said it more than once. The phone pressed hard against my ear, I listened to him saying all the things I had wanted to hear. That we belonged together, that he didn't know if I could ever forgive him but he hoped so, because he needed me in his life.

'I've made some huge mistakes,' he said, 'but they've helped me realise what's important ... and who matters.'

'You hurt me,' I managed.

'I know ... I'm sorry. But I only wanted good things for you, Sarah-Jane. With the way everything was going, I was convinced you'd be better off without me. And you're OK now, aren't you?'

'Yes.' I needed to believe Tom had only ever had my best interests at heart all along. 'I'm fine.'

'Will you give me another chance? Can you trust me again?'

'I don't know,' I admitted.

'But you love me?'

'Yes,' I breathed.

'And you've missed me? Because God I've missed you.'

This time I only managed to breathe.

'I wish I was there with you in Italy. I want to put my arms around you Sarah-Jane, touch you, every bit of you.'

I felt a heat rising inside me.

'I'd like to show you how much I love you.' His voice deepened.

'Tom.'

'Do you want that?'

'Yes.'

I wanted to be with him but didn't know how to make it happen. My car wasn't going to be ready for days and it would take more time to drive home. If Baxter and I flew, he would have to travel in the cargo hold and I hated that idea. But there was no one here to leave him with. When I said all that to Tom, he told me London was a terrible idea anyway, there was too much attention on him, too much stress, and no way would he want me exposed.

'I can't have you affected by all this bad publicity.'

'Could you come to Montenello then?' I wondered. 'It's really quiet here, nothing happens, and we'd have total privacy.'

'Would you like me to come?'

I didn't want to pressure him, not if he had business negotiations happening. And there was his little boy to think of now. 'Yes of course but …'

'If I could get away, Sarah-Jane, it would save my sanity right now.' He said it longingly. 'A bolthole is what I need.'

'This would be perfect then. Could you come, might you manage it?' I hardly dared believe it was possible.

'I can't promise anything at this point, but I'll try,' Tom said. 'I want us to be together.'

'Me too.'

'I wasn't sure if you'd even want to hear from me after everything that happened.' His voice dropped again.

'Can we forget all that? Start again together?' There was nothing I wanted more.

'I love you, Sarah-Jane,' Tom said again, and it sounded as wonderful as it had the first time. 'That's the most valuable thing I've learnt from all of this. It's the only thing that's important.'

After I put down the phone, I started tidying the house, folding clothes and washing dirty coffee cups, as if Tom was going to arrive any minute. Baxter followed me from room to room, seemingly perturbed at the onslaught of activity. Once the place was entirely in order, I didn't know what to do, but I felt too restless to settle. What I needed was fresh air and open spaces so, picking up the leash, I whistled Baxter, and we went out for a walk together.

Half the townsfolk seemed to have had the same idea.

Dressed more smartly than usual, they were strolling along the streets and milling about the piazza. As people passed, some gave me a brief glance, others offered a polite *buonasera*. None had the slightest idea that I was a person whose world had just quaked and shifted. I could hardly believe it myself.

I wanted to tell someone but not my mother because I sensed she wouldn't be entirely pleased to hear it. All I really needed was to say the words out loud to another person. Tom and I were together again. He loved me.

Crossing the piazza, scuffing through drifts of confetti, which hadn't been cleaned up – evidently the street sweeper didn't do Sundays – I walked towards the hotel. I didn't expect Edward to be at work but he was there, behind the reception desk, wearing a smart suit and a pressed shirt, greeting me with a smile.

'Sarah-Jane, how was lunch at the olive grove?'

'Oh yes ... fine.' I had almost forgotten eating; it seemed a lifetime ago.

'Everything went well?'

I stared at him vaguely.

'The food?' he prompted. 'The company?'

'All great.'

'So is there something I can help you with this evening?'

'No, not really.' I leaned forward against the reception desk. 'Actually yes, the house I'm staying in, how much longer is it available for?'

'Definitely another week, but might you want it for longer?'

I nodded.

'Then I'll have to check. It belongs to the mayor's wife and occasionally she likes to keep it free for family.'

'If you could let me know.'

'I was under the impression you were keen to leave?' said Edward. 'Has there been a change of plan?'

'Yes, there has.'

He raised his eyebrows enquiringly. 'Lunch with the mechanic went *that* well? Or the car really is a hopeless case?'

'No, this has nothing to do with any of that.' I smiled and then couldn't stop smiling.

'Are you going to tell me or make me guess?' asked Edward.

I placed my hands over my heart. 'Remember how it was broken, smashed to smithereens?'

He nodded. 'Of course.'

'Now it's mending ... because Tom says he wants to be with me, it's all fixed, we're getting together again.' The words sounded as sweet as I had known they would.

'Tom Whiffen? Didn't I read somewhere that his business had gone under?'

'There have been some difficulties.' It jarred to be reminded of the bad news. 'He's coming over to have some time out and reboot.'

Edward's eyes held mine, but he didn't say anything.

'I'll introduce you. Maybe there's a chance of some sort of collaboration in the future once he's up and running again.'

'That would be cool,' Edward said lightly. 'When does he arrive?'

'I'm not sure yet, we'll have a better idea in the next day or so.'

'In the meantime, I'll check on the house,' he promised.

'Hopefully it'll be available. It's perfect for us.'

'Us' and 'we'; it was so good to say those words, to feel like one half of a whole, when the other half was Tom. The happiness was exhilarating, and I imagined being here with him, having brunch upstairs in the restaurant and a glass of Prosecco in the hotel bar, spending lazy days together with nowhere we needed to be and nothing that had to be done.

Walking home through the narrow streets, I imagined us having lunch together at the *trattoria*, watching the sunset from the top of the tower, taking a trip to the olive grove restaurant because he would love it there, and going to the coast, maybe even continuing the rest of my trip together. Deep in daydreaming, I almost lost track of Baxter, who rather than trotting ahead, had fallen behind to sniff lamp posts. I whistled then called him, but he only looked up, cocking his head and went back to sniffing. Mildly irritated, I walked back and snapped the leash on him.

Tom and I were OK again. He loved me. Those two things ran through my mind as I strolled back to the house, as I sat beneath the jasmine with a glass of wine, ate slices of ripe melon and paper-thin slices of prosciutto for dinner, and as I curled up in bed hoping my dreams would be of him.

It wasn't until the next morning that I called my mother. She was in the middle of making coffee, grinding the beans, steaming the milk, her morning ritual, and I pictured her with the phone tucked beneath her chin, pottering around the kitchen in yoga pants and an old T-shirt, the one with the words 'Just Dream It' printed on the front.

'Good morning darling, how was your lunch yesterday?' she asked over the sound of the coffee machine whirring.

'Yes, fine, lovely.'

'Is it hot there? It's quite chilly in London today. I almost put the heater on when I got up. I'm glad you're enjoying a decent summer because I think ours may not be happening—'

'Mum,' I interrupted. 'I've got some news.'

'The car is fixed at last?' she guessed.

'Much better than that. I heard from Tom, he called me.'

The coffee machine noise stopped. I couldn't even hear crockery clinking. 'OK ... and what did he say?'

'He loves me.'

All that my mother said was, 'Oh, Sarah-Jane,' and there was so much doubt and worry in those few words.

'Be pleased for me,' I begged her. 'Because I'm happy.'

'I know, but are you sure?'

'Yes, absolutely.'

'It seemed like you were getting over him and I couldn't bear to see you hurt like that again.'

'It's different now – everything has changed.'

Then I made coffee too, piling the grounds into the Moka and putting it on the stove as I relived Tom's conversation (most of it anyway), my phone tucked under my ear like hers must have been.

'He made a mistake,' I said. 'He asked me to forgive him.'

'There's a child now though, isn't there?' Mum pointed out.

'A little boy, Charlie. I'll get to know him, you will too, he'll be a part of our lives.' That was one of the things I had thought about when I was too stirred up to sleep properly. I was going to be a stepmum. I loved Tom and now I could love his son too.

'Take things a little slowly,' my mother cautioned. 'Let them unfold.'

'I'm going to,' I promised. 'Tom's coming here and we're planning on having time together, just the two of us, and getting back on track.'

'What about his business? Shouldn't he be trying to get that back on track?' she wondered.

'He's handling it,' I said, wishing she didn't have to keep looking for problems. 'It's not going to stop him coming though.'

'Good ... that's good news,' she said, and although it sounded forced, at least she was trying to be positive.

'It's the best news ever,' I told her.

We kept talking as we made coffee and drank it together. Mum didn't seem to want to hang up but there were messages pinging through to me, hopefully from Tom, so once the coffee was finished, I ended our call.

He had sent me a picture of Charlie, a downy head nestled in the crook of his bare arms. Jo must have taken the shot, and I felt a twinge of sadness at what they had shared, moments like this one, with a newborn they had made together. Then I reminded myself of the story behind the picture; things can't have been happy, they hadn't fitted together and it was over now.

I sent Tom a shot of my view, then went outside and took a photograph of the jasmine-covered doorway and sent that too. A message came back straight away.

Looking at flights right now. Think I can get there tomorrow.

No way had I expected him so soon. Holding my phone, staring at the screen, I felt slightly panicked, although it wasn't as if there were any special preparations to make. The house couldn't have been tidier. I didn't need to get my hair done or have a pedicure or buy a new outfit. Tom had seen me so many times flushed from the heat of the kitchen, hair frizzing, not a lick of make-up and my Made With Love apron spattered with flour and oil. I didn't need to pretend for him, to put on a shiny coating; he knew who I was deep down, he loved the real me. The only issue with him arriving the next day was going to be waiting that long.

My phone pinged again.

Can't wait to see you. Then he sent a lot of emojis: hearts, kissing lips and single red roses.

Tom and I were back together again. Still holding onto my phone, I skipped right round the room, circling Baxter, who sat in the middle, blinking and watching.

Assunta

There was a girl in a white dress standing beside the fountain. This bride was bare shouldered in the heat but before long the days would cool and they would come wearing fur shrugs and sequinned wraps, until winter bit hard, when they would disappear altogether until spring and the piazza would be cleaned of confetti and dusted only with snow.

She was a good sign, this high-summer bride, she showed that the town was booming and its future hopeful. Still Assunta loved the quiet, cold days, when Montenello belonged to its own people. The winds that swept the piazza didn't worry her, the hard rains or overcast skies. In her small *trattoria* she provided warming food and her customers braved the weather to come and eat it.

It was humid days like these that were hardest on her, when Assunta cooked to the sound of whirring fans and faced a constant battle to keep the place free of flies. This morning she had half expected Sarah-Jane to appear and take over some of the work without being asked, but the hours flew by without her.

Assunta cooked pasta with sardines, fennel and pine nuts, a dish that made her think of her mother who had always been hungry for it. She would sit at the corner table, the one Augusto preferred these days, finish a bowl and ask for more. Assunta tried to remember if she had ever seen her parents eating a meal together. Surely they must have, although her mind found no clear images. As far as she knew, Augusto only started coming to eat here once the others had gone. He was her father, keeping an eye on her. Now it was her turn to watch over him.

Today he shuffled in with Francesco, a little later than usual, full of some story about one of his suppliers trying to sell him spoiled peaches. Assunta had heard this same tale before. Her father and this man had been feuding for years and it had become a game between them. This time Augusto had won and the peaches had been returned. He was running late but he came triumphant.

She left him to enjoy his food. Later in the bar she would get him talking about the old days, slip in a few more questions about the past. Assunta wanted to believe that Augusto was her father and Renzo her half-brother, but she had been thinking about how little she looked like them. She was broad when they were narrow, her skin was a darker olive and her face had grown plumper as she got older while theirs had winnowed down to cheekbones and hollows. No one could miss those differences. And every time she remembered what the American woman had said, it felt as if her brain was sparking at something it couldn't quite catch at, something small and important.

By the time her customers had lingered over a last glass of wine, and the latecomers had been served and the kitchen cleared, Assunta was longing to take the weight off her feet. Outside was not much cooler than the kitchen had been. She sat with Augusto at a table he had pulled beneath the dappled shade of a tree, while Francesco dozed in a chair beside them and Renzo brought out a lemon granita without her needing to ask. Even holding the icy drink was refreshing.

Augusto still seemed overexcited, although it wasn't the feud that was energising him now, but the news heard from a very good source that this was to be the day the mayor announced his final-ever release of one-euro houses.

'You must let your friend know urgently,' he said.

'You mean Carlo?' she asked.

'No, it was Carlo who told me.' Augusto was impatient. 'I am talking about the English girl, the one who is working with you.'

'Sarah-Jane? Is she interested in buying a house here?' Assunta was surprised.

'Of course, of course, and she must get in quick, apply as soon as it is announced, then I can use my influence.'

Her father and the mayor were very good friends so it wasn't unlikely that he still had some sway at the Town Hall, although it was years since he had worked there.

'If Sarah-Jane comes by, I will let her know.'

'There is no time to waste. You should go and find her right now,' Augusto insisted.

'Right now I am resting.'

'Rest later.'

'Papa, stop,' Assunta complained. 'You are driving me crazy.'

'This is an opportunity,' he said stubbornly. 'She mustn't miss out.'

'I will go and find her once I have had a chance to catch my breath,' promised Assunta.

'She is in that house belonging to the mayor's wife, the one with the jasmine.'

'I know it.'

'I could come with you,' Augusto offered. 'It is almost on the way to my place.'

'Not really, but come if you want.'

Maybe walking with him, side by side, she would find the right questions, because here and now, Assunta wasn't even sure how to begin. Are you my father? If not, then who was? Careless words could hurt him, and it was the last thing she wanted.

'I think Carlo was hoping his son would apply for one of those houses,' she said, instead. 'But he seems reluctant to apply.'

Augusto shrugged. 'Parents want what is best for their children … but the children don't always see it. That is a worry.'

'I wasn't so bad, was I? You didn't have to worry about me.'

'Of course, of course, I still worry,' Augusto told her. 'For you and Renzo.'

'What about?'

'Many things.'

'Name one.' Assunta couldn't think of a single reason for him to be concerned about either of them.

Augusto let out a heavy sigh. 'Ouf.'

'Papa? One thing that worries you, about me or about Renzo?'

'It is the same thing,' he admitted. 'What will happen to you once I am gone. You will be alone.'

'We have each other,' she pointed out.

'Yes, and I am glad you are close, but I wanted more for you.'

Assunta spooned some of the bittersweet shaved ice into her mouth and held it there until it melted. She looked at Augusto, his face bristly with the hairs he had missed that morning when he was shaving. His shirt was worn out, but he refused to throw it away and buy another, so she would have to take this one home and turn the collar for him.

'You hoped we would marry,' she said. 'I never realised that.'

'Not necessarily marry, but have someone to love and take care of you. A man or a woman, I wouldn't mind.'

'A woman? I am not gay, Papa.'

'Not you,' Augusto said and looked towards Renzo standing, with an empty tray in his hand, exchanging a few words with the mayor and Edward, who were meeting over coffee.

'What are you trying to tell me, Papa?'

'I thought when they came it would make it easier for him,' said Augusto.

'When who came?' It wasn't like her father to talk in riddles, and Assunta was exasperated.

'Edward and Gino, men who are like him, I hoped it might help.'

'You think that Renzo is gay?' This was a bombshell; she couldn't believe it.

'Of course, of course, what did you think?'

Assunta realised her mouth was hanging open. Surely it couldn't be true. Renzo was her half-brother and all her life he had been her best friend; if he were gay she would know it.

'Did he tell you this?' she demanded.

'He didn't need to, I have always known, ever since he was a boy.'

'How have you known?'

'He is my son,' Augusto said simply.

Renzo was gathering empty coffee cups, wiping down the table, saying goodbye to the mayor and Edward who were packing up their phones and laptops, ready to head back to work.

'There was never anyone else like him here,' Augusto said. 'How hard must that have been?'

'Are you sure about this?' Assunta was still stunned.

'Yes.'

Assunta watched her brother as he shook the mayor's hand and exchanged a quick embrace with Edward, carefully holding the tray to one side so the cups wouldn't be jolted. Everything about him was familiar. The way he moved, quietly and carefully, doing everything with the least fuss possible. His smile hadn't changed since he was a boy. The plainness of the clothes he wore, in muted blacks and greys, almost fading into the background if he were still and silent.

'He has always been on his own,' observed Assunta. 'There has never been anyone in his life.'

She had assumed that Renzo was content to be his own

man, working long hours, living simply in his neat rooms above the bar. She saw him almost every day; he never seemed unhappy.

'I worry it is too difficult for him, too late. But it is not too late yet for you, *cara*,' said Augusto.

'For what?' Again he seemed to be talking in riddles.

'For you to find someone to take care of you after I have gone.'

Assunta stared at him. Maybe the old man's mind was fading far faster than she realised.

'Papa, I can take care of myself.'

'I know,' he said, and his face was dappled with shade but she could still see his expression was sad.

Renzo had disappeared into the bar. Most of the tables had been pulled outside, so it was quiet in there. Assunta looked at her father, and at Francesco still dozing beside him.

'We need coffee,' she decided, standing.

'You won't say anything?'

She shook her head. 'No.'

'Maybe even Renzo doesn't know. Believe me, this is possible. I learned it on the internet.'

'You have been doing research?'

'There is a lot of information now; it is very good.'

'You wanted to help him?'

'Of course, of course.'

Augusto always wanted to help. Even if it meant interfering in things that were none of his business, he could never resist. At times Assunta found that frustrating but she loved him for it too.

'Coffee,' she repeated, and left her father there listening to Francesco snoring.

She took her empty granita glass inside and set it on the counter. Renzo glanced in her direction then moved behind his big old-fashioned espresso machine.

'I can bring them out,' he told her.

'One for Francesco too; if he is going to drive that truck home then he needs to wake up.'

Renzo smiled. 'One day that will be me, an old man snoozing under the trees.'

'I will be snoozing next to you.'

'I expect so.'

She watched as he made up the tray. A bowl of sugar, a few *biscotti* from the jar he kept behind the counter, water glasses and a jug, paper serviettes.

'You have heard that today there will be the announcement?' Renzo asked as he worked.

'The one-euro houses, it is all Papa has been talking about.' Assunta took one of the hard-baked *biscotti* and snapped it in two with strong fingers. 'Do you think your friend Edward will want to buy another for his hotel?'

'Not this time.'

'And what about the other Australian, his husband, when is he coming back?'

Renzo shrugged. 'Who knows?'

The old machine roared as the coffee was made. It was so loud you couldn't hold a conversation if you were standing right beside it and Assunta often worried that it would deafen Renzo in the end.

'I will take them,' she said, when he had finished putting the full cups on the tray.

'Let me,' he replied.

She followed Renzo out of the bar and over to the table. Her father might be right about him or he might be wrong; either way it didn't matter, she decided, as she sat down next to her father and his sleeping friend.

'Papa,' she said, seeing Augusto's eyes were closing drowsily now too.

He startled awake. 'Of course, of course ... Francesco old man, you can't snore all day.'

'We will drink our coffee then go and talk to Sarah-Jane, tell her about the houses in case it is true that she is interested in buying one,' Assunta said.

'Of course it is true, of course.'

'You are coming with me?'

Augusto thought about that. 'Did you say that Carlo is worried about his son? Then perhaps I should go to see Riccardo instead, have a word.'

'Papa ...' she sighed.

'I have always got on well with the boy. He likes me.'

'Yes, but—'

'There are only four houses, Assunta. They need to apply. Then I can use my influence.'

'OK, Papa, OK,' she said, knowing from experience there was no point trying to argue.

'You should never miss a good opportunity,' he told her.

As Assunta walked towards the house where Sarah-Jane was staying, she tried to make sense of it all. She wondered if it was possible for so much of what you knew about your own life to be wrong. The man who might not be her father, the half-brother who might not share any of her blood at all, and now this, something she had never considered before. Renzo was gay.

The little dog began barking when she knocked on the door and by the time Sarah-Jane arrived to open it she could hear him jumping up, his claws scrabbling at the wood.

'Oh, hi.' Sarah-Jane seemed surprised to see her. She was holding her phone and tapped out a few words on it with her thumb before looking up again. 'Would you like to come in?'

'Thank you, but I only came to let you know they are releasing the one-euro houses today. My father seems convinced you want to buy one and plans to help by using his influence.'

'That's very kind but I'm not interested in any houses. I've no idea what gave him that idea.'

'I am not sure what is going on in his head either,' Assunta said.

Sarah-Jane's eyes were pulled back to the phone. She stared at the screen, frowning.

'I am disturbing you,' said Assunta.

'No, sorry, you're not at all. There's a good friend coming to stay and we're working out how he's going to get here. I'm just waiting for his message.'

'No problem, I have things to do also.'

'I can't wait to bring my friend to your *trattoria*. He's a chef too.'

Assunta gave a shrug. She wasn't curious about who this good friend was or what their relationship might be. The intricacies of Sarah-Jane's life held no interest at all. All she wanted was the familiarity of home. Her own life was complex enough. It was becoming too much, more than she knew how to deal with.

'There will always be a table for you,' she said politely, turning to go.

Sarah-Jane

Tom was coming. All morning we had been making plans. He was going to fly to Bari then hire a car – nothing too large, I warned him, because the roads were impossibly narrow. If everything ran to schedule he would be with me tomorrow evening, before dinner time. After that we might not want to go anywhere for a while. I needed to fill the fridge so we could feast when we were hungry, buy cheeses and prosciutto, fresh bread and good wine. But for now I was too distracted by the back and forth of messages to manage anything practical. Even Baxter had missed out on his walk.

'In a while,' I told him, as he paced around, wagging his tail hopefully.

Tom was coming and I tried to imagine what he would think of this little house, wondering whether I ought to try for someplace more glamorous, maybe splash out on a few nights at Edward's palazzo, because I wanted everything to be perfect. Then I remembered that drawing attention to ourselves was the opposite of what Tom wanted. He was coming to escape the glare, to have a quiet life, a simple one. High-ceilinged rooms with marbled floors and frescoed walls weren't necessary. This little house would do fine.

The heat seemed to build all through that afternoon. I opened up the doors and windows so any hint of a breeze would flow through and switched on the ceiling fan. Baxter gave up nagging for a walk and lay on the tiles, panting in his sleep. Instead of going shopping, or mopping floors or changing bed sheets, I hung onto my phone, sending messages to Tom, waiting for his replies.

I can't wait to see you
I always wanted us to be in Italy together
The flights are booked
The car is sorted
I've started packing
I'll bring champagne
I'll see you soon
I love you

All the hurt that he had caused, the days of me being too depressed to get out of bed, the times my mother had to plead with me to eat, the pain of it wasn't forgotten exactly but this was salve to the scars and every time Tom said he loved me, they faded a little more.

I love you too

I must have fallen asleep because I woke to the sound of footsteps echoing down the hallway, a familiar voice calling my name and the soft thumping of Baxter's tail against the tiled floor he was still stretched out on.

'Sarah-Jane, you are home?'

'Riccardo.'

He was standing in the doorway wearing his overalls rolled down to the waist and a vest in a shade of blue that very nearly matched his eyes. His skin was lightly tanned and his hands and forearms darkly etched with oil stains.

'I am sorry,' he apologised, 'the door was open, I didn't realise you were resting.'

'That's OK, I just dozed off.' The sun had shifted and, glancing at my phone, I saw that half an hour had passed and I had missed a message from Tom, a couple of heart emojis, a cocktail glass and a sunset.

'Augusto sent me,' explained Riccardo. 'He said you wanted to see them.'

'See what?' I asked, confused.

'The one-euro houses.' Riccardo held up a set of keys. 'He insisted on giving me these.'

Baxter's ears were twitching at the sound of his voice. Smiling down at him, Riccardo crouched to give his head a scratch, and the dog's tail thumped against the floor again appreciatively.

'Once that old man gets an idea in his head there is no point trying to argue.'

'But I'm not interested in buying a house,' I told him.

'No, still I thought you might be curious to take a look.' He clinked the keys in his hand. 'These will get us into the two that Augusto says have the most potential.'

What I wanted was to stay with my phone, coming up with arrangements of emojis to send back to Tom. But the pair of them were gazing at me so hopefully, Baxter who needed a walk and Riccardo who was looking for company.

'I may end up owning one of these houses whether I want to or not,' he said, ruefully. 'My father seems determined and now Augusto too.'

'I guess we'd better go and check them out then.' Getting up from the couch, I stretched and yawned. 'Just give me a minute.'

Giving my appearance a tidy-up, finding my bag, grabbing the dog's leash, moving through air thickened by humidity, took me several minutes. By the time I was ready, Riccardo was sitting on the chair in the entranceway, Baxter on his knee.

'He seems to like you,' I observed.

'We like each other,' said Riccardo.

The three of us walked together up the steep, quiet streets towards the landmark of the tower. It must have always been a poorer part of town as there were no houses here to match Edward's palazzo, and some of the places we passed, barred and boarded up, looked like nothing more than hovels.

'Lots of these houses are empty,' I said. 'Why only sell four of them, why not get rid of them all?'

'According to my father it is a difficult process. They have to trace the original owners and give them an opportunity to pay any taxes they owe. Some families think they may want to return one day and aren't prepared to give up their property.'

'But if they're neglected like this they won't be habitable anyway,' I pointed out.

'Exactly, but these people have dreams, I suppose. They don't want to let go of the idea of coming home.'

I tried to imagine walking away from a place, not knowing if you would return but always being aware it was there, the life you used to have, waiting in case you decided you wanted it again. And in the meantime walls would crumble, ivy spread ever upwards and smother them, weeds sprout from cracks in the stone and grow from broken gutters, and eventually your house would look like the building Riccardo and I had paused in front of.

'This does not seem to have much potential,' he said dryly.

'Are you sure it's the right one?'

He negotiated the broken steps up to a wooden door slumping from its hinges, and began trying keys in the rusted lock. To my surprise one of them fitted and turned, and with a strong shoulder Riccardo pushed the door open. There was a lot of creaking and we both peered into the dim, dusty hallway.

'Shall we?' asked Riccardo.

'After you,' I replied.

There was still plenty of life in this house. Spiders had woven a whole metropolis of webs, legions of flies had died on the floors, and mice had scurried over them leaving hard pellets of droppings. It was noisy too. Every floorboard we stepped on complained with a creak and the shutters sighed when they were forced open.

'It's awful,' I said, once the place was light enough for us to see properly.

'Terrible,' Riccardo agreed.

The rooms were so small they felt oppressive, ceilings sagged, walls bowed, the air was stale and damp; no wonder whoever had abandoned this place didn't want it back.

'I would pay money not to own it,' I told Riccardo.

Only Baxter seemed delighted, trotting from room to room, his nose to the ground and ears pricked.

'He is rat hunting,' Riccardo observed.

'Ugh, let's get out. Will we even bother going to see the other place?'

'I have promised to make a full report to Augusto.' Riccardo began taking photos with his phone: the bathroom with its cracked porcelain and rusted taps, what was left of the kitchen, a couple of the poky living area.

I waited outside for him to finish, shaking off the gloom of the place, breathing the fresh air, with Baxter clipped onto his leash so he couldn't slip back inside.

'The next place is at the top, right beside the tower,' said Riccardo, as he emerged and pulled the door shut behind him.

'I'll come for the walk, but I might not go inside with you,' I told him. 'There's something so depressing about a house that no one wants.'

'Yes,' he agreed, 'and all I can see is the work that needs to be done – that is depressing too.'

From the outside, the second house looked much the same. A garden was growing from its walls and gutters, its stonework was scarred, its door and shutters rotting. I let Riccardo go inside alone, and after a few moments he came back out again.

'I think you should come and see this – maybe it is not so bad.'

It must have been the view that made him think that, west-facing with the whole sweep of the valley and mountains in the distance. There was a terrace looking out over it, and while the tiles that covered it were faded and cracked, and the whole structure looked unsafe, I could imagine sitting there with a glass in my hand, watching the sunset. The rooms weren't quite so cramped, the ceilings seemed slightly higher, and even though cobwebs hung from its beams and I was stepping on more dead flies, this felt like a place where people had been happy once and might be again in the future.

'What do you think?' asked Riccardo.

'It isn't so bad,' I agreed.

'The terrace will need to be rebuilt and the inside completely gutted. But Augusto is right, this one has potential.'

'Maybe it's worth putting in an application.'

Riccardo pushed his hands into the deep pockets of his overalls, shrugged his shoulders and sighed. 'Even if it has potential, do I want to own it?'

'Most likely you don't have a chance. Surely there will be hundreds of applications?'

'When the one-euro scheme first started, there were thousands. But times have changed and now they don't get many at all.'

'And Augusto will use his influence,' I remembered.

Riccardo smiled. 'I am sure he will. Also I am a citizen of Montenello so perhaps they will give me priority. If I want this place then I think it may be mine.'

I tugged Baxter away from some mouse droppings that he was trying to eat, and walked through the rooms again. There was nothing in them to be salvaged, but I could imagine it cleaned and rebuilt, walls painted white, floors re-tiled, red geraniums in the window boxes, jasmine climbing over the terrace.

'This could be very like the place I'm staying in,' I told Riccardo. 'Really charming.'

'With some work,' he agreed.

'Yes, with a lot of work, but you could transform it.'

Riccardo scuffed his feet through a drift of dead flies. 'Could you imagine living here?'

'I can't imagine living in Montenello, but if I did then this house would suit me. Not too big but not too small either, and that view.' I looked out across the terrace. 'I'd live in a place with a view like that.'

We stayed for long enough to discover that the plaster on the walls crumbled beneath our fingers when we touched it, that the door to the terrace was jammed and rats had nested in a cupboard in the master bedroom.

'I wonder what happened to the people who owned it,' I said, as Riccardo took more photographs.

'They left for a better life – hopefully they found it.'

The sun was sinking, the light was pink and gold, the sky lilac-stained, and we stood for a moment watching, neither of us speaking.

'We should go before it gets dark,' said Riccardo.

'Yes,' I agreed, although it was a shame to miss a moment of this sunset.

'Perhaps once I am certain the terrace is safe enough, we will come back and share a bottle of Prosecco out there to celebrate.'

I turned to him. 'You are going to buy it then?'

The light had changed his face. His skin glowed gold like the sky and his turquoise eyes sparkled.

'Yes, I am going to spend one euro,' he confirmed.

I found myself hoping that some day in the future I might come back here again, to see what he had done and made of it all. It seemed like this house had plenty of potential.

'I'll celebrate with you,' I promised.

Assunta

It took Assunta a while to compose an email to the Americans. She wrote it out by hand over and over. Words had never been her strength and she struggled for the right ones. What she needed was more information, anything Caterina Campanella could tell her about her mother, or who her father had been, any snippet at all. But how to ask in a way that was firm yet polite, that made it clear there was a responsibility to share whatever she knew, so that Caterina would understand she really didn't have a choice.

After several attempts, Assunta decided the final draft she had written would have to be good enough. She couldn't come up with anything better. But then she had a dilemma because her phone was a basic one and she didn't own a computer. On the rare occasions she might need to send an email or look up something on the internet, she went to Augusto's house and he helped her use his computer. That wouldn't do this time, neither could she ask Renzo. Staring at the sheets of paper covered in her spidery handwriting, Assunta tried to think what to do.

There was only one other person who knew what the American woman had said that day because he had been sitting at the table right next to her and overheard every word – Carlo. Since he worked at the Town Hall, Assunta assumed he would own some sort of computer, or at least his was the kind of modern phone that emails could be sent from. Hadn't he once told her to ask if she ever needed his help?

In the evenings, once she was home, Assunta preferred

to settle, and it was rare for her to go out again. But now she took off the comfortable clothes she wore to relax in, put on her bright floral dress and ran a brush over her wiry salt-and-pepper hair.

If you knew the shortcuts, Carlo's house wasn't too far from hers and Assunta was on his doorstep in no time. He looked surprised to find her there but was more than willing to help when she said what she needed.

'Come in, come in,' he invited her.

'Are you sure it is not too much trouble?' asked Assunta, hesitating on the doorstep.

'I was watching something dull on television and am grateful for the interruption,' he promised.

She heard the show blaring down the narrow hallway. Assunta had never been inside this house before. It was a small place to have raised three children in and the most spacious room must have been the kitchen that he showed her into, with a long dining table at the centre and a television on the wall at one end. This would have been where the family spent most of the time, where his wife Maria had cooked, and his son and daughters had eaten meals and done their homework. The smell of whatever Carlo had made for his dinner still hung in the air and a single soup bowl and spoon sat in the sink, waiting to be washed. Everything else was tidy.

While Assunta waited for him to fetch his laptop, she browsed the framed photographs arranged on the sideboard. There were lots of Maria, wedding portraits and shots with the children, pictures of her as a much younger girl, usually with Carlo and smiling.

'Here we are,' he said, returning with the laptop. 'I will set you up here on the table. You have eaten yes? Would you like a *digestivo*? And maybe something sweet, a few *biscotti*?'

'Thank you, thank you,' said Assunta, who wasn't used to other people going to so much trouble for her.

'You need some help getting started?' he wondered. 'It

may be different from the computers you have used before. Would you like me to open up a new email for you?'

'Please,' she said, pulling out the sheet of paper she had folded into her jacket pocket and setting it down beside the laptop. 'This is what I want to say.'

'You would like me to check it?'

Assunta nodded. 'Please.'

Carlo found his reading glasses and took a seat beside her, then read through the letter, carefully.

'What do you think?' she asked when he had finished.

'You have made some good points here and what you are asking is fair. This woman has left you with questions about your family and it is wrong to leave you wondering. There is no reason to, as far as I can tell. Your mother is gone now and nothing can hurt her.'

'My father might still be alive, whoever he is.'

'Perhaps this woman is completely wrong though, and your father is Augusto.'

'I hope so,' said Assunta. 'But she has put the doubt in my mind now and I can't seem to be rid of it.'

'In that case you should send this email. It is worth a try.'

Assunta typed it out slowly with two fingers, then read it back over, correcting the mistakes she had made and asked Carlo to press send before she could change her mind.

'I will keep an eye out for a reply and let you know as soon as it comes,' he told her.

'I hope this isn't an inconvenience.'

'Not at all, Assunta, you must never hesitate to ask for my help.'

This was something people often said, but Assunta sensed that Carlo really meant it. 'Thank you.'

'I don't drink in the evenings, not usually,' he said. 'But do you think a glass of wine would be a good idea? Out on the terrace since it is such a hot evening. We could watch the sunset.'

'A glass of wine would be a very good idea,' she agreed.

His terrace was set into the mountain and to reach it they negotiated a steep flight of steps. Carlo lit citronella candles to keep the mosquitoes at bay and opened a bottle of white wine that tasted of honey and herbs.

'You have a good view,' Assunta observed.

'I spend too much time inside watching television and not enough out here enjoying it. I think when Maria was sick we got out of the habit of coming down.'

'She was sick a long time.'

'Years and years.'

Carlo's wife had wanted to keep coming to the *trattoria* even when she needed a wheelchair and barely looked at the food, never mind tasted it. When a week or two had passed without seeing them on the usual days, Assunta had known the end must be near. Then the funeral notices had been pasted on the wall beside the Town Hall and Assunta had dressed in black and gone to the church to pay her respects but hadn't followed the procession of family and close friends to the mausoleum. Not long afterwards Carlo had started coming to the *trattoria* again, on the usual days but now on his own, and Assunta always made sure to stop and exchange a few words with him because she knew how lonely he must be.

'I will make the effort to come down more often,' Carlo decided. 'I used to grow tomatoes and herbs here. My son is right, it is time to start living again.'

'Where is Riccardo?' wondered Assunta, realising he should have been home from work by now.

'He texted to say that Augusto had given him keys to the one-euro houses.'

'He has gone to see them?'

'Apparently your father insisted.'

Assunta smiled. 'I can imagine.'

The sun was growing fiery in the sky, splashing it with

shades of pink and lilac. Carlo poured out a little more wine from the bottle and they clinked glasses.

'Hopefully Riccardo is looking at one of those houses right now and deciding to buy it,' said Carlo.

'I think my father will insist that he does.' The wine was relaxing Assunta, blurring the hard edges of her day.

'Then I will be grateful to Augusto. My son needs to think of his future now … and so do I.'

Assunta turned to look at him. The sky was reflecting pinks and gold, lighting up his face and for a moment he looked as much the boy she remembered as the man he had become. Without thinking, she reached out the hand not holding a wine glass, touching his arm, resting it there for a moment or two.

'Thank you for your help this evening,' she told him. 'You must tell me if ever there is anything I can do to help you.'

Sarah-Jane

Waking up on the morning of Tom's arrival felt like being a child at Christmas who had to wait to unwrap all the best presents. He wasn't expected until later that afternoon and I was desperate to see him. I planned for us to sit out beneath the jasmine, drinking Prosecco and talking, calmly and honestly, about everything that had happened and how we felt about it. With the air between us clear, we could start thinking about rearranging our lives so we could be together.

My morning routine now was to make a coffee then call my mother while I drank it, sitting outside and making the most of the coolest part of the day. Today we tried to stay away from discussing Tom too much. I knew exactly what she thought and Mum was aware I didn't want to hear it. Instead I told her about my visit to the one-euro houses.

'And you're not even slightly tempted?' she asked. 'Not dreaming about it at all?'

'Hell no, it would be a complete nightmare. Imagine dealing with tradespeople here and not speaking their language properly.'

'Other English people must have done it,' she pointed out. 'You could ask for their advice.'

'Have you rented out my flat to someone else, is that why you're saying that?' I teased.

'Of course not, Sarah-Jane.' Her voice sounded serious. 'That flat is always yours; the whole house will be some day. But wouldn't it be nice to have a foothold in Italy since you're a little bit Italian. It would mean something.'

'This isn't where Dad's family came from though,' I reminded her.

'You might never find that town. But you have found Montenello.'

It was true that I was starting to settle into the slower pace of life, and I did like this little house and being peaceful. But what I planned was to share it all with Tom for a while, before heading off together on our next adventure.

'I'm not staying,' I told my mum. 'Not for much longer. I'm going places.'

It was what I wanted, I was sure of it, even so I would be sorry to leave Montenello. If my car had to break down somewhere, then I was glad it had happened here. Unexpectedly this had turned out to be one of the best parts of my trip so far.

The day was a busy one. I stopped at the bar for another coffee, this time with Edward, who seemed downcast because his husband Gino was showing no sign of coming back from Sydney. I spent longer than intended chatting with him and afterwards it was a rush to buy everything I needed – wine, cheeses, prosciutto, a tray of syrupy rum-soaked cakes from the *pasticceria*, a loaf of fresh crusty bread – before the shops closed. On the way home I stopped to say a quick *buongiorno* to Assunta.

'My friend Tom is arriving later today.' I was bubbling with excitement and wanted to tell everyone.

She stared at me blankly. 'What about your other friend? Where is he?'

'I'm sorry?'

'The little dog, Baxter, he isn't with you today?'

I looked down at my feet, then behind me, then out into the piazza. Baxter was always around somewhere, now suddenly he wasn't. Rushing out of the *trattoria*, I called his name, looking from left to right, expecting to see him sniffing at a tree or skulking round a table outside the bar hoping to be offered treats.

'Baxter!' I called. 'Baxter!'

There was no sign of him. His leash was lying useless somewhere in my basket because I had got used to not bothering to clip it on his collar, trusting him to stay at my heels.

'Perhaps he saw a cat and chased it,' I said to Assunta, who was standing in the doorway, her eyes searching the piazza with mine.

'He won't have gone far,' she reassured me. 'Papa will help you find him.'

Augusto's truck had rolled into the piazza earlier than usual. He was standing beside it chatting to the mayor. Assunta beckoned him over but he held up a hand and shook his head at her.

'*Papa, vieni qua subito*,' she called crossly. 'We need your help.'

This time he came, although with some complaining. 'You interrupted an important discussion. I was using my influence, making sure the house is Riccardo's if he wants it, which of course he will.'

'Never mind that now,' said Assunta. 'The little dog has disappeared. We don't know where he has got to.'

'Baxter? He is missing? How long?' Augusto sounded alarmed.

'I'm not sure when I lost him,' I admitted, trying not to panic too much, because Baxter had never been one of those dogs that goes wandering and was usually too lazy to want to walk far. 'He was definitely with me when I bought the wine, but after that I don't remember seeing him.'

I was still looking around, expecting to spot him at any moment but also starting to have upsetting thoughts. People kidnapped dogs, didn't they? Or Baxter might have been hit by a car. I should have kept him on the leash. I should have been more careful.

'I will help you,' said Augusto. 'Don't worry, we will find him.'

It was much the same scenario as the day the Saab broke down, with Augusto recruiting the old men sitting outside the bar to help, and calling on those loitering in the piazza. This time I was more grateful. He stayed at my side as we searched, and his thin voice joined mine calling, 'Baxter, Baxter.'

At the hotel Edward confirmed that Baxter had definitely been with me at the bar but he hadn't seen him since then. Next Augusto and I walked all the way down to Riccardo's workshop; however, the doors were closed and there was no sign of him.

'Baxter, Baxter,' I called more loudly, really worrying now.

'Where else could he be?' Augusto wondered.

'We went to see the one-euro houses yesterday. Perhaps he's gone back up there.'

'Ah yes, you went with Riccardo.' The news seemed to please Augusto. 'Let us go and take a look then.'

We walked all the way to the tower, winding through the offshoots of streets on the way, and then back down to the piazza. Assunta glanced at us through the window of her *trattoria,* and Augusto gave a quick shake of his head.

'Perhaps I should go home,' I suggested. 'He might have turned up there.'

'Good idea,' agreed Augusto tiredly.

Collecting the basket of groceries I had left with Assunta, I hurried to the house, hoping to see Baxter on the doorstep, sleeping in the shade. But no little dog was there.

Slumping onto a chair I put my head in my hands and let the tears come. Crying didn't help but there was nothing else to do.

When my phone rang, I almost didn't pick up but then saw it was Riccardo.

'I don't know what to do ... I've lost Baxter,' I told him.

'Yes, that is why I am calling, I have a stowaway,' he told me.

'He's with you?' The relief was a rush.

'He must have jumped into the car earlier when it was parked in the piazza. I had left the doors open to keep it cool and he curled up on the back seat without me noticing.'

'Is he OK?'

'He is looking very pleased with himself.'

'Oh thank God, I was so worried.' I felt almost dizzy with relief.

'Don't worry, he is fine.'

'Where are you?'

'I am heading to a few places. I have to replace a battery in a car, then I need to go to pick up some parts and finally collect a car from Borgo del Colle and tow it to my workshop. So it is going to be some time before I can bring him back to you.'

'I'm sorry you've been put to so much trouble. I can't believe he's been this naughty.'

'Perhaps he wanted an adventure.'

'You'll be careful?' I was thinking about all the things that might go wrong. 'Don't leave him in the car in the hot sun, don't let him wander off.'

'No problem,' he promised. 'I have a piece of cord I can use as a leash and will remember to give him water. Baxter is safe with me. Today he gets to experience being a mechanic's dog.'

'Thank you so much, Riccardo.'

'I will enjoy his company.'

After the call ended, I was quite shaky. I wouldn't feel entirely happy until Baxter was back here with me. Realising I needed to tell Augusto the news so he could stop looking, I put away my shopping quickly, and headed back to the *trattoria* which was busy now with people eating the grilled swordfish coated with crushed sweet dried peppers that Assunta was serving for lunch.

'Baxter's with Riccardo,' I told her. 'He's fine.'

'OK, I will text Papa.' Assunta took her weird little mobile phone out of her pocket. 'Sit down, I will bring you something to eat.'

'Thanks but I—'

'Some food, a little time to rest,' she insisted. 'Sit at Papa's table. He and Francesco won't mind.'

Showing up ten minutes later, both Augusto and his friend were amused to hear of Baxter's escapade. They seemed to think it was a sign the dog had spirit and Augusto didn't mind that he had walked halfway across town looking for him. If anything he was energised and as we ate, regaled me with the town's latest news.

'Soon the mayor will make an announcement.' He dropped his voice, looking about for those who might be trying to eavesdrop. 'The *festa* will return. This is what I am hearing.'

I listened to him talk about how gloomy and empty the place had been before the one-euro scheme had saved it. Only elderly people had been left and each year more of them died.

'Now we have many young people – diversity.' He said the word as if he was particularly pleased with it. 'It is very good I think and now we are holding a *festa* to celebrate.'

How Augusto managed to talk so much and still finish a meal, I have no idea, but his pasta bowl was empty and Assunta was bringing his second course of swordfish and still he was telling me about the people who had bought the houses, how they had come from all over the world, although some had paid their one-euro and not renovated as promised so the places had been confiscated again.

'These are the final houses to be sold, there will be no more,' he reminded me.

'I know, but I still don't want one,' I told him.

'Of course you do, of course.'

After lunch I stayed in the bar rather than returning to

an empty house. Renzo brought me a granita, shaved ice flavoured with bitter orange, and I sat with the regular group of old men, listening to them chat, tuning in and out of the conversation, not really understanding much except that Augusto seemed to be the leader, and when he talked, the others paid attention.

My phone was on silent but held in my hand so I could feel the vibration of any messages coming through, hoping for one from Tom. When it came it was disappointing.

Plane was delayed and now I'm in an endless queue for my rental car. What a nightmare.

Five minutes later he sent a string of angry-faced emojis, and ten minutes on there was another message.

Queue not moving. Some sort of fight going on at the desk. I may be here my whole life.

Poor Tom, there was no hurrying people here and it was pointless getting frustrated, but he didn't know that yet. In his old life everything was arranged for him whenever he travelled, priority check-in and boarding, then a driver waiting at the other end holding up a sign with his name on it. He wasn't used to any of this inconvenience.

My phone buzzed again but this time the message came from Riccardo. He had sent a shot of Baxter sitting in the driver's seat, peering through the steering wheel, panting in the heat. Next there was a message:

I think he would like a gelato.

No!

Just a small one?

Absolutely not!

A while later another photo came. This was a selfie, a massive *gelato* in the foreground, and behind it Riccardo and Baxter's faces side by side. Laughing, I showed it to Augusto, who smiled.

'He is having nice day out with Riccardo, your little dog.'

'Apparently.'

After that there were more messages from Tom. The queue had moved slightly. The airport was unbearably hot. There was a family behind him and their baby was screaming. He seemed to feel the need to tell me about every last irritant and I had to keep coming up with sympathetic responses. Then there was nothing for quite a long stretch and I hoped that he was getting served at last.

When Assunta appeared, I joined her on the stools up at the bar for a coffee and *digestivo*. As I finished my drinks, another message came through.

Success! Not the car I booked but it will have to do. See you soon.

My stomach fluttered with excitement. It wouldn't be too much longer. Soon we would be together, his arms around me, my face against his, breathing the familiar scent of his skin, hearing his deep voice say my name.

'My friend has arrived in Italy,' I told Assunta. 'He is on his way.'

She nodded. 'Very good.'

'I'll bring him for lunch to your *trattoria* tomorrow.'

'Tomorrow I make the spaghetti with sardines,' she told me.

'He will love it.'

I was impatient to set eyes on him, but at the same time hoped he wouldn't rush and drive too fast on the twisty roads. Walking back to my house I tried to remember what sort of driver Tom was and wasn't sure if I knew. Most of our time had been spent in my flat, steering clear of paparazzi and fans demanding selfies with him. I don't think we'd even been in a taxi together. A lot about our relationship hadn't been normal but now hopefully we would get the chance to make up for it.

There were no more messages from anyone and I tried to keep myself busy, but there was really nothing to do. Take a cheese from the fridge to bring it to room temperature, polish two champagne flutes and set them on the counter, change into my yellow sundress and free my hair from its top-knot because Tom liked me to wear it down over my shoulders.

I had sent him a photograph of the house so he would recognise it and had left the front door open so he didn't need to knock.

'Sarah-Jane?' It was his familiar voice at last.

'Tom, hi Tom.' I was nervous suddenly.

'Oh there you are.' He sounded relieved. 'Thank God for that.'

Tom was standing in the doorway, a set of matching luggage out on the street behind him, his shirt crumpled, and his face reddened from the heat.

'The GPS sent me on some sort of crazy tour,' he complained. 'You said the streets were narrow but bloody hell. Then I couldn't park anywhere near here so I've had to drag my bags for miles. Is it always this hot?'

'Tom,' I said, because I couldn't quite believe he was here. 'Tom, it's so good to see you.'

'Sarah-Jane.' Smiling, he held his arms wide and I rushed towards them. He held me back for a moment, looking me up and down, taking in every inch of me.

'You beautiful, beautiful girl,' he said and then he pulled me close, his face touching mine, his cheeks bristling my skin.

The smell of jasmine was heavy in the air and it mingled with the muskiness of his warm skin. I touched him, breathed him and closed my eyes as we kissed. The taste of him was exactly as I remembered.

I hadn't intended for it to happen so fast. The plan was that we would sit down and talk before we did anything else. But Tom's hands were sliding beneath my sundress and when I tried to speak, he silenced me.

'Shhh, not now, let's go to bed.'

'OK then,' I agreed because he was already leading me down the hallway.

Everything was familiar, the weight of him on top of me, the feel of his hands, the width of his hips between my legs, even the way he groaned my name just a little sooner than I wanted, as the pleasure flashed across his face.

'Sarah-Jane, I've missed you so much,' he said, leaning against me, his heart thudding into my chest.

'I've missed you too,' I told him.

Afterwards, Tom opened the bottle of Prosecco I had chilling in the fridge, and we had a glass together in bed.

'I suppose we'd better get dressed,' I said reluctantly.

'Let's relax for a while,' Tom replied. 'It's been a long day for me.'

'I'd like to but Riccardo will be here at any minute.'

'Who's Riccardo?'

'He's a friend. Long story, but he's got Baxter.'

'Baxter?' Tom's brow furrowed. 'You mean your dog? He's here in Italy with you?'

'Yes, we've been travelling together.'

'Seriously?' He sounded astonished.

'Well I couldn't leave him in London.'

'You could have,' argued Tom. 'There are boarding kennels, isn't that what they're for?'

'I didn't want to come without him.' I was slipping back into my sundress and tying up my hair.

Tom started trying to get dressed too, looking round for his suitcases and realising they were still outside, muttering 'Damn' beneath his breath. He didn't want to put his dirty, sweaty clothes back on so I went and fetched the bags for him, managing to lug them up the steps. He had brought a lot of stuff and as he opened them up in my little bedroom, pulling out clothes and toiletries, hanging up his jackets and piling his books on the bedside table, it started to feel like our place rather than only mine.

'Why is your dog with this guy anyway?' he asked, semi-distracted by the unpacking process.

'I think Baxter must have jumped into his truck earlier when Riccardo was parked in the piazza.'

'But why would he do that?' Tom wanted to know.

'Riccardo's a mechanic, he's fixing my old Saab, and we've spent a bit of time together. Baxter seems to really like him for some reason.'

Tom looked at me, with a raise of his eyebrows and a tilt of his head. I knew exactly what he was thinking.

'Nothing like that,' I promised. 'We're just friends and he's been nice to me.'

Tom shrugged, pulled on a grey T-shirt and some black skate shorts, and poured us more Prosecco.

'What is there to eat?' he asked.

So many days and nights that Tom and I had spent together started with that question. I loved to feed him and always kept special things in my fridge and pantry so I could create a small feast at a moment's notice. Jars of marinated white anchovies to serve on crostini with a slick of roasted red pepper puree. Marinated mushrooms to sprinkle with pine nuts and drizzle with a herby olive oil. Soft goat's cheese with truffled honeycomb and figs. And Tom's favourite, my homemade tigelle, the small soft-crusted flatbreads filled with cured meats and cheeses then toasted. He was careful about what he ate, there was never too much and it all had to be very good.

'I've got a fantastic cheese,' I told him, 'a sharp, savoury pecorino. There's some salami spiced with *peperoncino*. Green olives, really plump, delicious ones, smoked trout and good bread. I was going to do an antipasto platter and a tomato salad, keep things really simple.'

'That sounds perfect,' Tom told me.

I was in the kitchen, chopping juicy ripe tomatoes, when I heard a knock on the door. Tom was frowning over his laptop checking emails so I wiped clean my hands and went to open it.

Baxter shot in, tail wagging, thrilled to see me, dancing round my legs, and I smiled at Riccardo, who was looking down in amusement.

'Thanks so much for looking after him,' I said.

'He has been in the car all day and had no exercise,' said Riccardo. 'But if you like we could take him for a walk now.'

'Sorry I can't, I have a friend here,' I began.

Suddenly Tom was beside me. He moved into the doorway angling his body in front of mine, shook Riccardo's hand, called him 'mate' and said he was pleased to meet him. Tom can charm anyone; he has an easy way and that gift of being comfortable in any situation. Riccardo, though, didn't seem entirely charmed.

'You are in Italy for a holiday?' he asked.

'Yeah not sure for how long, just chilling out with Sarah-Jane.' Tom smiled at me.

'You are staying here?' There was a slight furrow of a frown between those turquoise eyes.

'That's right,' Tom confirmed. 'Anyway, great to meet you. We'll see you around, I expect.'

'OK, *ci vediamo*.' Riccardo bent and patted Baxter, who wasn't dancing anymore but sitting, quietly and solemnly, at our feet. 'And see you soon, *mio amico*.'

I wanted to ask about the one-euro house, whether he had put in an application, how long it was likely to be before he heard if it had been successful. But Tom was tugging Baxter by the collar, pulling him inside, saying *ciao* and shutting the door on Riccardo.

While he returned to his emails, I finished making our quick and simple meal, Baxter skulking around the kitchen with me. Assuming he was hungry after his joyriding adventure, I poured some biscuits into his bowl but he only sniffed them and walked away.

'Shall we eat outside?' I asked Tom. 'I have a little nook set up under the jasmine.'

'Sure,' he said, putting the laptop to one side, standing and stretching, moving behind me and running his fingers down my spine, leaning closer, hot breath on my neck, kisses on my bare shoulder. 'Whatever you want is fine by me.'

It was a degree or two cooler outside. I had put out a stool to serve as a table and Tom and I sat on either side of it, grazing on antipasti and sipping chilled Prosecco. Every now and then one of my neighbours went by, smiled and nodded in our direction, or called out 'buonasera'. I recognised most of them by now: the couple that were always arm-in-arm, the elderly man who walked with a stick, the various women with their shopping trolleys.

Pulling Baxter up onto my knee, I offered him a slice of the pecorino and was relieved when he took it from my fingers.

'It was so awful when I thought I'd lost him,' I told Tom, who was staring in my direction.

'Yeah I bet,' he said, reaching over and giving the hairs beneath Baxter's chin a playful tug. 'I still can't believe you brought him with you though.'

'He's been great right up until today. I don't know what got into him.' I gave my dog's hot, hairy little body a fierce hug. 'I ran all over town looking for him.'

'Don't do that again, buddy.' Tom warned him. 'We have better things to do than worry about you – we've got a lot of lost time to make up for.'

I smiled at him. 'I'm so glad you're here.'

'Me too, this place is great.'

'It's not too small for you?' I knew his house in Hampstead was practically a mansion.

'Small is good,' he told me. 'It means we'll be close to each other all the time.'

'Tom,' I said, lifting Baxter from my knee and setting him on the floor, where he stayed beneath my chair, looking sulky. 'I think we ought to have a proper talk about what happened.'

He put his hand on my leg where the dog had recently been. 'We do need to talk but not about the past. I'm all about moving on now, I'm only interested in the future, and that's what I want us to talk about. I've got plans, really big plans. Do you want to hear them?'

'Yes, of course.'

Tom took my hand, pulled it to his lips and kissed my wrist. 'I'm rebuilding Made With Love, it'll be better than ever, and you're going to be part of it. And not behind-the-scenes anymore, Sarah-Jane, I want everyone to know how talented you are. You and me together – we'll be the faces of Made With Love.'

His eyes were shining and his voice brimmed with excitement. I could never resist Tom, but when he was like this, full of ideas and passionate about them, he seemed especially powerful.

'I'll do anything I can to help,' I told him. 'But I'd rather stay behind the scenes. You're the star.'

'Not anymore. I'm going to make a star out of you.'

'Really, I'm happier not to be in the spotlight,' I insisted. 'It's not my thing. I wouldn't be good at it.'

'I have this vision, Sarah-Jane. I'm going to make it happen and it will be amazing.' Tom sounded so certain. 'You'll be good, I know you will.'

That was when I had my first flicker of doubt, just a sensation really, that what Tom wanted might not be the best thing for me. I damped it down, not wanting to spoil the moment by thinking that way. But I didn't want to be a celebrity, it was my idea of hell being the centre of attention, and I was surprised that he didn't get that.

'Actually you'll be incredible.' Tom beamed at me. 'And when you hear exactly what I've got planned, you're going to love it.'

Assunta

Assunta didn't like emails. She trusted that a letter would be returned when it didn't reach the person it was intended for, that a fax machine would report if it had failed to transmit. With emails, you sent them and might never know if they had been read or just disappeared into the ether. And so she half expected a silence from the Americans. Perhaps they didn't check their messages regularly, or hers was hidden in a junk folder, or had become lost somehow on its way to them. Assunta had sent it and that was the important thing; she could do no more, except hope for a reply.

She needed to know the truth about who her father was. Thinking about it so much was draining her energy. At home that evening she was too exhausted to cook a meal and had no appetite anyway. Instead she sat in her chair, feet up on a stool, head resting against a cushion, and spent the last of her energy thinking some more.

Assunta groaned on hearing the knock at her door but eased herself out of the chair and answered it anyway, to find Carlo on her doorstep. Outside the light was fading and his face was in shadow so only as he stepped forward, holding a sheaf of papers in his hand, did she realise he was smiling.

'I have a reply for you,' he told her, 'from the person you emailed.'

'Come in, come in,' she said, stepping aside.

'You don't want to read it in private?' he checked.

To be alone with whatever this message said was the last thing Assunta wanted. Taking the papers from his hand, she repeated. 'Come in, please.'

Carlo had printed off a copy of the email and two versions of the black-and-white photograph attached to it, in small and larger sizes. The quality was poor but Assunta recognised the two women standing with their heads close and their arms around each other – her mother and the American woman, very young versions of them, smiling for whoever had been standing behind the camera.

'I couldn't help looking at the photo,' said Carlo. 'It is your mother, yes? When do you think it was taken?'

'Before I was born maybe? I don't ever remember seeing her smiling like that.'

'So they were friends, that part at least is true, but it doesn't mean the rest is.' Carlo held one of the printouts and looked down at the blurred image. 'This was taken in your *trattoria*?'

'It was.' Assunta had recognised the wall she stared at every day, noting that some of the ceramics still hanging on it were already in place. The photo was all shades of grey but she knew their bright colours.

She looked at the image a little longer, before reading what had been written in the email.

My mother wanted you to have this photograph. It is one of very few she has from those days and she brought it with her to Italy hoping to find her friend, or at least some memories of her. Mom is still very upset about what she told you. It was a mistake, something that slipped out. If there were things your family didn't want you to know, then it is not her place to reveal them. That is what she asked me to say. Mom wanted you to have the photograph though because she believes it is one you will never have seen before. She did say some things about your mother – that she was kind and funny, a good friend, that she always regretted losing touch with her. The rest she hopes you will forget. And she begs you to please forgive her.

Wordlessly Assunta passed the email to Carlo, watching his face as he read it. He looked solemn, his eyes widening.

'I can forgive her, but I can't forget what she said. I have tried but it is impossible,' said Assunta.

'Of course it is,' he agreed.

'What shall I do now?' She needed someone else to have the answer.

Carlo gave her question some thought. Then he crossed the room to her drinks cabinet, found the brandy bottle and poured her a glass, and stared at the photograph again.

'Is there anyone else left from those days who might remember?' he asked.

'Francesco perhaps.' Even as she said it, Assunta knew her father's old friend wouldn't be able to help. He was a man of few words, kind but simple-minded, someone her father had always looked after but was unlikely to confide in.

'You could try asking him, but I think you would be wasting your time,' confirmed Carlo.

'The others are all gone or their minds are fading.' Assunta took a sip of the brandy and it burned her throat pleasantly as she swallowed. She went and poured another glass and passed that one to Carlo.

They sat together, she in her worn old armchair, him in the one beside it that barely anyone used so its fabric was still smooth and the cushions plump.

'Augusto is the only one likely to know the truth,' said Carlo.

'I keep thinking about asking him,' Assunta admitted.

'What is stopping you?'

'I am worried about hurting him. He has been such a good father to me. Why would I want another? It seems ungrateful.'

Carlo sipped his brandy, deep in thought and silence, and the trace of a smile crossed his face.

'What are you thinking?' asked Assunta.

'I am remembering that even as a boy, I knew of your father's reputation. He was a scoundrel, yes? How many women did he make pregnant?'

Assunta shrugged. 'Who knows?'

'It was a scandal. My own parents loved to talk about it. In those days a man was made to marry a woman if she found herself expecting a baby, but Augusto never did marry anyone. How did he get away with it?'

'They all left,' Assunta said. 'Only Renzo's mother and mine stayed. And he looked after them.'

'He is a good man.'

Assunta sighed. 'I know.'

'Don't underestimate him. I understand that you don't wish to cause hurt. But right now you are the one that is hurting, and Augusto wouldn't want that.'

Assunta felt tears pricking at her eyes and brushed them away roughly with the back of her hand. 'You think I should talk to him, ask who my father is?'

Carlo nodded. 'Find a way to do that, yes.'

'But how?' Assunta couldn't imagine the words she would use.

'Be honest – tell him what you heard and how you are feeling. He will understand.'

'Maybe.' Assunta wasn't convinced.

'He can tell that you are unhappy right now,' Carlo told her.

'How do you know that?'

'Because I can tell too.'

This time there were too many tears for Assunta to dry with a sweep of her hand. Carlo passed her his handkerchief, pressed into a neat square and faintly scented with the lemony cologne he used, and gratefully she pressed it to her face.

'I am sorry,' she said. 'I don't know what is wrong with me.'

'There is no need to apologise.'

'It feels like I knew exactly who I was, and now I am not sure anymore.'

'You are the best cook in Montenello, the kindest woman I know, my childhood friend, Renzo's half-sister, Augusto's daughter. You haven't changed and neither has any of that.'

'Thank you.' She looked down at the handkerchief. It was fine linen embroidered with his initials in one corner. Maria must have done that; she had used blue thread and the stitches were neat. Now Carlo laundered and ironed it just as carefully as his late wife always had. 'Thank you but I shouldn't be bothering you with any of this.'

'I am glad you have,' he told her. 'I hope you will not hesitate to bother me again.'

Assunta passed back the handkerchief and Carlo folded it into his pocket.

'Tomorrow I will talk to Papa and maybe solve this mystery,' she decided.

'You must be prepared though,' he cautioned. 'If your mother and Giuseppina lied to you then there must be a reason. You may not like what you hear.'

'I want to know the truth, whatever it is.'

He finished his brandy then let himself out, closing the front door softly behind him, leaving Assunta in her quiet living room, listening to the clock ticking and staring at the grainy photograph in her hand. Her mother looked happy. She was the prettier of the two, with curly hair and her brows heavily pencilled, a film star look that Assunta thought she must have copied from one of the magazines she loved to read. She had been a woman with dreams, a person with secrets, and this American stranger had known her better than her own daughter did.

Assunta felt heavy and tired. She had no energy for any of

the things she normally did before going to sleep. She didn't drink a cup of camomile tea, listen to the radio or read a few pages of a book. It was a relief to be in her bed, with her head on the pillow and the faded old quilt pulled high over her shoulders.

She placed the photograph on the nightstand beside her, although Assunta didn't need to look at it as the image was seared on her brain already, the two women, arm in arm and smiling. Tomorrow she would show it to Augusto. As a child she had loved his stories; this time she would ask to hear the one he had never told her.

Sarah-Jane

I woke up and felt for Tom beside me, but the bed was empty. Then I smelled coffee and heard him moving round in the kitchen. Lying in bed a few minutes longer, I enjoyed the feeling of knowing he was there, sharing my little house. I could still hardly believe it.

When I got up, he was on the sofa, his laptop on his knee and his phone beside him.

'Is the Wi-Fi always this slow?' he complained.

'Yeah, it's not the greatest,' I said apologetically, although to me it seemed pretty good for a place in the middle of nowhere.

Baxter had slept the night on his own bed in the living room for a change. He gave me a woeful glance as I walked past but, when he heard me pouring biscuits into his bowl, trotted over and started eating, which was a relief because I had been worried he seemed off colour after his adventures the day before.

'That dog whiffs a bit,' Tom told me, eyes still on his computer screen.

I liked Baxter's smell, it was familiar and comforting, but I conceded that it might have got a bit stronger in the summer heat.

'I'll give him a bath later,' I said, opening the windows to let in some fresh air, 'although poor boy, he'll hate it.'

Focused on what he was reading, Tom didn't reply. The coffee pot was empty so I got on with making more and turned on the oven to warm the pastries I had bought the day before.

'Only fruit for me,' said Tom, still frowning at his screen.

Leaving him to his work, I had my breakfast out on the front step, sitting in the morning sunshine, with Baxter curled up beside me.

'Sorry,' Tom called through the open doorway. 'Just a couple more emails.'

I could hear him tapping on his keyboard, muttering, then tapping some more. Waiting for him to finish, I thought about the conversation we'd had the night before. Tom's new vision for Made With Love, a back-to-basics approach. No more flashy restaurants and French chefs. Instead, Tom wanted us to move somewhere rural, ideally not far from the coast, where we would have a vegetable garden, teach kids how to grow food and cook it, produce a book of family-friendly recipes based on the meals we had grown up on, dishes that would nourish as well as please; essential, simple, honest. Tom outlined his plans and I listened. Everything he said seemed to make sense. This was a time for families to be together, cook together, eat together; that was what made people happy.

'We can give them the skills, show them the way,' Tom enthused. 'It's a chance to do things like I always wanted to. It had got too big, all I did was manage staff and sit in meetings. Why did I ever think that was a good idea?'

I worried about the practicalities, how Tom was going to repay all those debts, how we were to fund this new rural coastal lifestyle. Sitting in the morning sunshine, listening to him send emails, I had to trust he had a plan. There were financial backers and business advisers; he was busy communicating with them now and they would figure it out. As for pushing me in front of the cameras, Tom would see it wasn't my talent that people were interested in, and that he was the starry one with all the glamour and magnetism.

As I was daydreaming out on the front step, I heard the sound of running water and realised Tom must have stopped work and was taking a shower. I thought about him naked and wet in the steamy bathroom and went inside to join him. As I pushed open the door he had his back to me, and his face upturned to the jets of water. For a moment I watched through the glass wall of the shower. Tom worked out at the gym and surfed in Cornwall whenever he could, so his body was strongly muscled. His torso seemed to have thickened a little and he had gained a few kilos, but it suited him.

Turning to see me watching, he grinned. 'Are you going to come in?'

'I'm tempted. Have you finished working?'

'I'm all yours for the rest of the day,' he promised.

This time we took things more slowly, soaping each other, pressing our mouths to each other's skin. When the hot water started to cool, we abandoned the shower and stood in front of the bathroom mirror and as the steam faded our bodies were revealed, bit by bit, until there we were, Tom and I.

'We look good together,' he said, smiling at our reflection.

Afterwards we lay in bed, listening to the morning sounds of Montenello through the open windows, people calling to each other, a piano playing, church bells, birdsong – neither of us in any hurry to move.

'It's another beautiful day out there,' I remarked lazily. 'Probably we should get up and enjoy it at some point.'

'What have you got planned?' asked Tom.

'There's not a huge amount to do here,' I admitted. 'But we could go for a walk and I'll show you the town and then I thought we'd eat lunch at a little *trattoria* in the piazza. It's my regular spot.'

'Whatever suits you, I'm happy.'

I was happy too. Breaking up with him had been terrible but perhaps the time apart had been good for us because we had realised how important we were to each other.

I pulled on my frayed denim shorts and a floaty smock top I had taken from my mother's wardrobe, a vintage piece from the 1970s, brightly embroidered with flowers.

'Very boho,' Tom said, glancing at me. 'We're going to have to go shopping.'

'What do you mean?' I thought I looked fine. The top was one of my favourites.

'My vision is for you in lots of natural fabrics, in whites, creams, oatmeal, clean and fresh. That will be your new look.'

'Not really clothes to cook in though,' I pointed out.

'It's about image, everything is these days, and those shades will play well on Instagram.'

'I'm not really sure oatmeal suits me,' I said. 'It makes my skin look sallow. My colours are brighter.'

'You'll look great; you might just need to fake tan every so often in winter, keep up a radiant glow. But right now you're glowing naturally.' He tangled his fingers in my hair and bruised my lips with a fierce kiss. 'You're beautiful, Sarah-Jane. I don't think I've ever told you that enough.'

Tom made me feel beautiful. As we walked through the streets of Montenello, arm in arm, with Baxter trotting beside me safely clipped to his leash, it felt like every dream I'd ever had come true. We walked up to the tower and I showed him the view, and then we circled back down to the piazza because both of us were hungry.

'It's a very simple little *trattoria*,' I warned him. 'No frills and no choice in what you get to eat, no menu at all.'

In his old life Tom had dined at all the big-name restaurants – Noma, Atelier Crenn, The French Laundry, El Bulli before it closed. His choices had been dictated almost entirely by Michelin stars. But this new version of Tom might be more open to cheap and cheerful. Ducking through the doorway of Assunta's *trattoria* he declared it charming. He liked the bright ceramics on the walls, thought the baskets of coarse bread on each table were a nice touch and he enjoyed the first dish of spaghetti with sardines, although to me it didn't taste quite as good as it had the first time I ate it.

Assunta was wearing a distracted, half-dazed look as she moved about her kitchen and ferried plates of food, and I wondered if she was coming down with another of her migraines.

'Are you OK?' I asked, when she brought over the second course of slow-cooked mutton in a garlicky sauce with broad beans.

She nodded and shrugged, but said nothing.

'This is my friend Tom, he's staying with me for a while, visiting from London.'

'Very nice,' she said gruffly.

'I've been telling him how great your food is,' I said.

'Thank you,' she replied. 'Enjoy.'

Again the lamb was fine, but not so deeply savoury and silky-sauced that I wanted to hold every forkful in my mouth for a few seconds longer to make the most of the flavours. It was as if some small but vital ingredient had been missed, and I couldn't pinpoint what.

'It's usually better than this,' I told Tom, disappointed because I wanted him to be wowed by the little *trattoria*. 'Honestly I've eaten some of the very best Italian food I've had in my life here.'

He took another bite of the softly shredding lamb. 'It's fine, honest food, there's nothing wrong with it. Probably we could use a few of her recipes, they might be useful. Where else have you been eating?'

I told him about brunch at the hotel and lunch in the olive grove and Tom pulled out his phone and started to google. 'The olive place looks interesting,' he agreed. 'I'll add it to my wishlist.'

Then he read out that list to me: a Michelin-starred cave restaurant in Matera, an award-winning place in Lecce, a palazzo hotel established by Francis Ford Coppola. 'I did some research before I came,' Tom explained. 'Made a few reservations.'

'Oh OK,' I said, surprised.

'These rustic places are great. The one in the olive grove sounds exactly right for us. I'll email now and see if I can get a table on one of our free days. We're pretty booked up.'

'We are?'

Tom glanced down at Baxter, who was sitting quietly at my feet, hoping for treats but undemanding. 'Yeah and you'll have to leave him at home. I can't imagine any of the good places are going to welcome dogs.'

'Lecce is a really long drive,' I pointed out. 'I can't leave him locked indoors on his own all day. And it'll be too hot for him to stay in the car.'

'Can't that guy look after him? The one who had him yesterday?'

'Riccardo?' I said, dubiously because it seemed too big a favour to ask. 'I suppose he might not mind once or twice.'

'Great.' Tom was upbeat. 'We're booked into Vitantonio Lombardo tomorrow for lunch. That's the one in Matera. It's a tasting menu and then we'll want time to look around the town so you'd better see if your friend is available.'

I glanced at my little dog. He seemed to know that we were talking about him and cast a woeful look back at me.

'Baxter will be able to come with us sometimes though,' I said hopefully. 'At the hotel and the olive grove they were fine with him.'

'I don't know if we'll be eating at the hotel. There might only be time for a drink there.'

'How busy is our schedule?' I wondered.

Tom took me through it when we were sitting outside the bar, finishing off our lunch with a pomegranate granita and a glass of darkly herbal *digestivo*. There were plans for almost every day for the next fortnight. Some of the restaurants had been booked up when Tom contacted them but he sweet-talked even those who had never heard of him into finding us a table.

'That means you're staying for at least a couple of weeks then?' I realised. We had never talked about the end of Tom's visit; I was too excited about it beginning.

'That's right, and then I've booked us on the same flight from Bari to London.'

'Really? You've booked a flight for me too?' I asked, with a small but unmissable flare of frustration. 'I haven't finished my trip yet. The plan is to drive around Sicily then back up north. There's a hill town in Abruzzo I want to visit and I'd like to spend time in Venice.'

'I know, I'm sorry.' Tom reached his hand to mine and his fingers stroked my palm. 'I need you, Sarah-Jane. We'll come back to Italy, I promise, once everything is back on track.'

'But my car is here,' I pointed out. 'And what about Baxter?'

'The best thing would be to get that guy who is fixing the car to sell it for you once he's finished,' suggested Tom. 'And you can fly the dog home surely.'

This wasn't how I had imagined my adventure ending. I tried to explain this to Tom, but he didn't want to know. He needed me, he couldn't do this without my help, it was the two of us now, or nothing at all. That is what he kept saying, leaning across the table, clasping my hand tightly, staring into my face.

'I want us to be together, Sarah-Jane. I know it's selfish but I can't wait while you explore the rest of Italy without me. I need you right now. We're launching a new business, remember.'

'I thought there would be more time to think about it, to be sure it's what I want,' I told him.

'There'll be time, of course there will.' Smiling, Tom released my hand. 'Let's go back to the house now. I want us to spend the rest of the afternoon in bed together.'

I definitely wanted that. The afternoon, the days, the years ahead, I wanted them with him. But at the same time, I felt pushed off-course and disoriented. Perhaps all I needed was time to reset myself, but for now my head was spinning.

'Hang on,' Tom said, as we were getting up to leave. 'You should take some shots of me here. Use my phone, the camera is better.'

He thought that a pomegranate granita would look perfect in the picture because the colour was pretty, so we had to wait for a fresh one. Then we repositioned the table, so the shade wouldn't dapple his face, and angled a chair for the light to be exactly right. Tom and I had worked on a lot of photo shoots and we knew what we were doing.

He was an expert when it came to posing as well, leaning forward and tilting his head so any fold of chin wouldn't be obvious, smiling in a way that lit his face but didn't overly crinkle his eyes, holding his arms away from his body with muscles slightly tensed.

'You look great,' I told him. 'Now pretend to eat a spoonful of the granita. Lovely.'

He did it in slow motion, pausing for me to take shot after shot with his new iPhone. The message flashed up as I was doing it, only one line and from Jo. I couldn't help reading it.

Babe please call me really need to talk ♥

Hurriedly I passed back the phone, pretending I hadn't seen what was on it. Tom gave the screen a quick glance before pushing it into the pocket of his chinos. Neither of us mentioned the message.

Why did Jo need to talk? What was his relationship with her now? How had they negotiated a break-up when they shared a baby? I had so many questions but didn't ask any of them. Instead I walked with him, arm in arm, back to my little house, Baxter trotting behind us.

There were bound to be complications, I reassured myself. But we would sort them all out. The important thing was that we did it together. I tried to push aside the doubts, but they were there still, taking up space in my head, and I couldn't get rid of them.

Assunta

Impatience had never been among Assunta's flaws but today all she wanted was for her customers to eat and leave. There was a conversation she needed to have and no one was going to keep her waiting any longer than necessary. If the mayor thought he would enjoy one of his leisurely meetings over lunch, Assunta put him straight by clattering pans and crockery, so he was forced to shout his conversation. If Maddalena Marino was waiting for the tables to empty so she could raid the baskets for bread, Assunta hurried her along by wrapping a leftover loaf.

'For you to take home,' she said gruffly.

'How kind,' replied Maddalena, who lived in one of the finest houses in town where the mattress was probably stuffed with all the money she hated to spend. Assunta didn't care. She only wanted her gone, and for the others who were left to quickly follow.

Augusto had eaten his lunch and was sitting outside at a table Renzo had placed in the shade of a large plane tree. She kept an eye on him through her kitchen window. It looked as if he and Francesco were dozing.

The last pair of customers drained their wine glasses, settled their bill and gathered their belongings. Assunta stood and watched them go. Then she left everything behind: empty water glasses and bread baskets on tables, a saucepan soaking in soapy water in the sink, carafes that hadn't been polished and put away. Ignoring it all, she pulled the door of her *trattoria* closed and made straight for the two old men still dozing in the shadows.

'Papa,' she said softly, taking a seat beside him.

Augusto blinked, his eyes focused on her and he sighed. 'I am resting,' he told her. 'It is good for my digestion.'

'I know that, but there is something I have to talk to you about.'

'Of course, of course.' Augusto yawned then took a sip of water. 'I am awake now, what is it?'

Assunta took the photograph from her apron pocket. It was the larger of the two prints that Carlo had made for her, and she set it on the table between them.

Her father patted his pockets then located his reading glasses on top of his head. He peered at the shot for a moment and nodded. 'Your mother I recognise, and the other woman … maybe she is familiar, I am not sure.'

'Caterina Campanella.' Assunta told him. 'She is the American woman you were talking to in the bar the other day.'

'Is that so?' He looked more closely. 'Ah yes … poor lady, how the years have changed her.'

'This photograph proves that what she said is true – she and Mamma were good friends.'

'It seems so,' Augusto agreed.

'There is another thing that she told me.' Assunta felt her heart hammering; she had come this far, she had to keep going. 'This time it was about you.'

'Can't people stop gossiping about me now I am such an old man,' he grumbled. 'I haven't done anything interesting for years.'

Assunta took another breath. The last thing she wanted was to hurt him but there seemed no other way to reach the truth. And the truth was what she needed now.

'I suppose it is yet another story about what a rascal I was back in the old days. I am sure I will have heard it before.'

'Not that,' Assunta told him.

'Then what? It is not like you to hold back from speaking your mind. Can it be so terrible?'

'Caterina Campanella says you are not my father.' Now the words were out and she felt shaken to have said them.

Augusto stared into her face, and for a long time he said nothing.

'Papa, please. Is it true?'

'I have always felt like your father,' he said finally.

'But you are not?'

Reluctantly, Augusto shook his head. And sitting there in the piazza, surrounded by her customers, people she had known her whole life, Assunta had to hold her breath to stop the tears falling.

'Who then?' she asked, once she could manage to speak.

'I don't know.'

'You must.'

'I wouldn't lie to you, Assunta.'

'You have been lying to me my whole life,' she pointed out.

'That was different; I didn't tell you the whole truth.'

'I want it now,' she said. 'The entire story.'

Augusto reached for a paper serviette and dabbed his forehead with it, then took another shallow sip of water, coughing as he swallowed.

'It is not much of a story. Your mother was pregnant, and everyone assumed I must be the father because ... you know ...'

'Because you were the obvious person to blame?'

Assunta had never asked her father about his reputation. It was an unspoken thing between them. She didn't want to know how many women there had been, what was true and what only rumour. And while there were several more half-siblings out there in the world, Renzo remained the only one she was ever close to.

'It had been your fault all the other times?'

'Of course.' Augusto nodded resignedly. 'And your mother never denied it so neither did I.'

'But why?' This was the part of the story that made no sense to Assunta.

'I liked her, we were friends, and if she was keeping a secret then I was happy to help.'

'You never talked to her about it, not even once?'

'Not really.' Augusto stared up towards the leafy canopy, his papery-skinned face lit by the shafts of light that penetrated it. 'She thanked me before she died, said it made her feel better knowing I would be here to keep an eye on you, but by then you were my daughter, I thought of you that way, I had forgotten anything different.'

'Why though?'

'Because I care about you, that is why.'

Assunta's sadness was edged by anger. The truth was meant to be a clear and obvious thing, not a story that told her almost nothing at all.

'I care about you too,' she said, her voice almost breaking on the words. 'Of course I do. But even so, I want to know who my real father was.'

'That man, he never bothered with you, so why would you bother with him?' asked Augusto.

'I need the truth. Who am I, if I don't know who he is?'

'Sometimes there are things we never know.'

'That is not how it should be,' insisted Assunta.

'And what are we to do about it?'

'Papa ...' she began.

'You still call me that?'

'Of course.'

'This stranger.' Augusto jabbed at the image of Caterina Campanella. 'She should have stayed quiet. What business did she have telling you something that your mother preferred you not to know?'

'Why though, why did Mamma keep it a secret?' That was what Assunta most needed to understand.

'It was her choice, that is all I can tell you.'

'Was there anyone in her life back then, any man at all?'

Augusto shook his head. 'As far as I can recall she didn't have a *fidanzato*, she wasn't courting, and her days were spent cleaning other people's houses. She worked at the hotel too for a while in those early years.'

'I am not sure if I ever knew that.' Assunta cast her mind back and found only blanks in her memory. 'The hotel – what did she do there?'

'She was a chambermaid but she left that job after she became pregnant with you and never went back to it.'

Assunta wished she could travel through time and find out what had really happened; watch it like a movie, her family's untold story.

'So my mother had a secret and you helped her keep it. You never asked questions,' she said.

Augusto nodded.

'And you never told anyone else that I am not your daughter.' She looked towards Francesco, still snoring in his chair beside them.

'You are my daughter, *cara*. Of course you are, of course.'

Assunta stared at the face of a man she had loved all her life. There was one truth she already knew. Without him and Renzo, she would be left with no one at all.

Sarah-Jane

The long, lazy afternoon that Tom and I spent in bed together should have been perfect, except I couldn't relax. That short and mystifying message from Jo was playing on my mind and I kept wondering about it.

Babe please call me really need to talk ♥

There was every reason for them to be in touch, they had a child together, but why the heart emoji? And Tom hadn't called her, he seemed to have ignored the message altogether; I didn't know why. Was he avoiding Jo? Did he not want me to overhear whatever they talked about? Were there things he was still hiding from me? The questions kept coming. As much as I wanted to trust Tom, I wasn't sure if I ever would again, at least not completely, and the thought made me anxious and sad because I really wanted to trust him.

That evening we walked back up to the tower, with a bottle of Prosecco, to watch the sunset. Afterwards I cooked a simple pasta dish, with ripe tomatoes, white anchovies and crushed dried red peppers. We ate outside beneath the jasmine, with candles flickering on the steps around us, and the music of crickets chirping. And then we went back to bed together. It should have been perfect, except it wasn't.

The next morning I couldn't decide what to wear for our lunch in the Michelin-starred restaurant. My favourite yellow sundress seemed too casual, my gypsy skirt and ruched tops too boho, the floaty Indian tunic and the frock made from recycled sari fabric quirky rather than chic. Perhaps Tom was right and I would need to go shopping if I was going to fit into this new life he was planning for us.

I chose a leaf-patterned wrap dress in bright shades of orange and pink, pairing it with sneakers in case we did a lot of walking. Tom didn't say anything, so I assumed he didn't hate it too much.

'Are we going to drop off Baxter on the way?' I asked.

Thankfully, Riccardo had been happy to look after the dog, saying he would be at the workshop all morning and we could bring him any time. Although I was sure he would take good care of Baxter, I still felt bad about having to ask him.

'That stinky little thing is not going in my rental car,' Tom told me.

'It's only a short drive,' I argued.

'I signed an agreement: no pets. I thought you were going to bath him?'

Baxter really didn't smell that bad and I was getting a bit sick of Tom being so mean about him. Mind you the dislike seemed mutual. I had noticed the dog tended to shrink away if Tom approached and left the room whenever he came into it.

'Fine, I'll walk over to Riccardo's place then,' I said, not wanting an argument.

'Better get moving.' Tom was busy checking emails. 'I'll be finished with this soon, and ready to go.'

I wondered if, with me out of the house, he was going to take the chance to phone Jo. They shared a child so there was every reason for them to talk, but still. She had called him 'babe'. And she had used a heart emoji.

I didn't hurry, as instructed, not exactly, because I was starting to get a bit tired of Tom telling me what to do. Instead, I stopped at the bar for a quick coffee and found Assunta there, having breakfast with Carlo, so deep in conversation she only nodded a greeting.

I drank my coffee and as I was heading out, bumped into Edward.

'No weddings today?' I asked.

'Just a small one, an evening reception in the palazzo, so I'm seizing the chance for half an hour away from the hotel,' he said tiredly. 'Do you have time for another coffee?'

'Sorry, not really, my friend Tom is here.'

'Ah yes, the celebrity chef. And how is that going?' asked Edward.

'Fine,' I told him. 'I haven't forgotten I promised to introduce you. I'll bring him to the hotel for a drink soon.'

'Come for dinner, or at least lunch,' he urged.

'We'll try,' I said doubtfully. 'We're going to Matera today, to Vitantonio Lombardo.'

'Very fancy.'

'I'm dropping Baxter off with Riccardo. He's looking after him for the day.'

'He takes care of your dog, fixes your car, is there nothing the man can't do?' said Edward.

'Actually, there's no sign of the car being fixed,' I said worriedly, because if Tom continued being so fussy about the rental, then I would need my Saab. 'But Riccardo's being really sweet with Baxter.'

'He's a great guy,' said Edward.

'He is,' I agreed. 'And Baxter seems to love him.'

As I was heading away, Edward reminded me to be sure to let him know when Tom and I would be in for dinner. 'We'll come up with something special for your celebrity chef.'

'Will do,' I agreed, doubtful I could convince Tom it was worth making some time for him.

Walking down the hill, I passed several people I recognised. The English woman with the expensive handbag said a cheery 'good morning', the street sweeper a gruff '*buongiorno*', an elderly woman exchanged a smile with me and a young woman with a toddler stopped to pat Baxter.

Pop music was playing on the radio at Riccardo's workshop, the usual engine parts littered the ground, and he was underneath a car, lying on one of those stretchers on rollers, with only his lower body and legs sticking out. My Saab was still parked there, and I was thrilled to see it had all its wheels attached now. One rear door was open, and the windows were down.

'Good morning,' I called out over the music.

As Riccardo rolled himself out from under the car, Baxter strained at the leash to reach him.

'He is fine, let him go,' said Riccardo.

'I'm worried he might run away or try to follow me.'

'It is OK – I have a plan.'

Riccardo had made up a bed for him on the back seat of the Saab, with a couple of tartan wool rugs and a cushion. Baxter hopped in and settled down immediately.

'He will feel at home in there,' Riccardo told me. 'I can take him for a walk later and we will have lunch together. Not a Michelin-starred lunch, but still something good.'

'Thank you so much for this.'

'No problem,' Riccardo promised. 'Working here all day on my own can get lonely. It is good to have a friend.'

'I'll text and let you know what time Tom and I will be back.'

'You will want to take a look at Matera. See the *Sassi*, the cave dwellings.'

'Yes,' I agreed, although there hadn't been the chance to do any reading about the place, so I wasn't sure what he was talking about.

Time was ticking by and Tom was waiting for me. We had a day of eating and sightseeing ahead and a journey to get there. But I was reluctant to say goodbye to Riccardo and leave my dog curled up on his own in my Saab, probably imagining that I was about to get in with him and drive somewhere.

'If Baxter is still with me later this afternoon, he will be paying a visit to the Town Hall, to the mayor's office, in fact,' Riccardo announced.

'He will?' Then I realised what he had meant. 'Oh, you are applying for the house?'

'I did that already,' Riccardo told me. 'Today I will pay my one euro and sign the documents, and then the place is my problem.'

'You got it, that's great.'

'Papa is pleased, certainly. I will go with him to take another look and if the terrace seems secure then you must come and have a glass of Prosecco out there one evening to toast its future. Bring your friend too, of course.'

'We'd love to,' I said, fearing that yet another outing wouldn't fit in with Tom's schedule. 'And I'm really pleased for you. It's good news.'

'I hope so.'

Leaning into my Saab, I gave Baxter a last pat and said goodbye. Leaving without him was unsettling. I was so used to his leash in my hand and the quiet jangle of his collar at my heels.

I arrived back at the house to find Tom impatient to get away. The place was a mess, his clothes strewn around the bedroom, dirty dishes in the sink, little piles of things everywhere, coins, keys, phone and laptop chargers. I was itching to tidy it all up but there was no time. He was ready to whisk me out to the car, which was parked a couple of streets away.

'I've packed everything we need into the boot, and you're all I've been waiting for,' he said, a note of complaint in his voice. 'What took so long?'

He seemed broodily silent as he drove down through the narrow streets and over the causeway. But before long his mood was upbeat again, and he started chatting away, reciting things he had learned about Matera and its history, how people had lived in the caves for 9000 years and were still living there in poverty in the 1950s.

'The place has been reborn, transformed,' he explained.

'It's an example of what can be created when you have the vision and the drive. I've been wanting to see it for ages.'

'Montenello has been reborn too,' I told him, as the car wound through forested roads. 'It was in decline, turning into a ghost town and it's been saved by the scheme to sell off the houses.'

'But Matera is on a much more impressive scale,' he responded. 'The place is a tourist mecca now. It's what success looks like.'

Tom told me more about it as he drove. His memory for facts and figures was amazing. I listened and looked out of the window, so I got the first glimpses of our destination.

From a distance this town wasn't unlike Montenello. It gave the same impression of being hewn from the volcanic rock that it rose out of. There was that familiar pattern of layered terracotta roofs and church spires piercing the sky, that sense of a landscape ancient and unchanging.

'Do we have time for a walk around before lunch?' I wondered. 'What time is the table booked for?'

'Actually we have a meeting set up. Sorry, it's just a coffee,' Tom said lightly. 'There might be the possibility of a collaboration with this guy so I didn't want to miss out on the chance to catch up with him.'

Business meetings over coffee are frustrating. There is so much time wasted talking about everything except what you're there to discuss. This is Tom's super-power, of course. Being charming, putting people at ease, and guiding the conversation patiently to whatever end he has in sight. I had sat through plenty of those meetings with him, but never one in a bar on the edge of a southern Italian town that I was desperate to explore.

Tom's contact was a chef or hotelier, possibly both, I couldn't be certain. He introduced himself as Silvestre Brichese and he seemed to know everything and everyone. Older than Tom, but not by much, he had a raffish air, in his tailored linen jacket, mirrored Prada sunglasses and two thick gold chains round his neck. He spoke in fast, accented English, directly to Tom as though I was only present as a decorative element. Tuning in and out of their conversation, I watched groups of tourists drifting past towards the labyrinth of cave dwellings, and longed to follow them.

Tom was talking about money now, so this was some deal he was thrashing out, not a collaboration at all, but an investment. I listened to him drop dizzyingly high figures and watched the other man nod as if they were reasonable. Then I looked up at a church silhouetted against the bright sky, swifts swirling around its tower. And down at the gorge beneath us pockmarked with abandoned caves and scored by walking tracks. The morning was almost over.

'We have a lunch booking,' Tom said regretfully. 'At Vitantonio Lombardo, so I don't want to keep them waiting.'

'Let's talk about this later over a drink,' suggested Silvestre. 'You are here for just one night, yes?'

Tom flicked me a quick glance. 'That's right.'

Silvestre took the sunglasses from the top of his head, and covered his eyes. 'OK, I will come to your hotel for a spritz this evening then.'

We all stood, and Silvestre shook Tom's hand then kissed me on both cheeks, before strolling away. I waited until he was out of earshot before turning to Tom.

'Our hotel?' I asked him. 'What's he talking about?'

'It was meant to be a surprise,' he said. 'I've booked us into this fabulous place, a cave hotel, super-deluxe. Don't worry, there's a bag in the car with a change of clothes and our toiletries. I've thought of everything, I promise.'

'But you didn't think about Baxter,' I pointed out. 'What's going to happen to him?'

'That dog, he's constantly an issue.' Tom sounded irritated now. 'I don't even know why you brought him with you. What were you thinking?'

221

'He isn't an issue,' I said defensively. 'I love having Baxter with me.'

'Everything we want to do, he's the reason we can't,' argued Tom. 'You should fly him home, get your mum to look after him.'

'No!' I felt a jolt of pure fury and it took me by surprise. 'I'm not sending Baxter away. And I don't want to stay here overnight either.'

'Please, Sarah-Jane.' Tom's tone was wheedling now. 'This guy Silvestre, he's got a lot of money and he needs a place to put it.'

'What is he, some sort of gangster?'

'Well, I wouldn't call him that exactly,' Tom said uncomfortably.

'What sort of people are you getting involved with?' I was frustrated enough to have raised my voice and Tom put a finger over my lips to hush me.

'People who can help us achieve our goals, Sarah-Jane.'

'They're your goals, not mine.'

'We're doing this together, remember, we're a team, you and me.'

'If that's the case then you need to tell me exactly what's going on.'

'What I need is for you to trust me.' Tom rested a hand on my arm. 'But let's not argue and spoil things. We're going to have a beautiful lunch and a really special night. Your friend will take care of the dog, it won't be a problem, I'm sure.'

I resented having been manoeuvred into this. I was angry and upset. But short of wresting the car keys off him, I didn't know what to do. I was stuck in Matera, whether I liked it or not.

'I thought you loved surprises,' he said, trying to coax me into a better mood. 'That's why I planned all this for you. Get hold of your friend, make sure everything is OK with the dog, and then we can relax and enjoy ourselves.'

'Fine,' I said, a bit tersely. 'But if he isn't willing to keep Baxter overnight then we'll have to go home.'

'He will be,' promised Tom.

Reluctantly I tried Riccardo's number. When he didn't answer I left a quick message, asking him to call as soon as he had a chance. Then I followed Tom to a restaurant, a narrow room with only a few tables, spot-lit and covered in crisp white linen and I did my best to have a good time.

We were seated side by side beneath the limestone arches and Tom ordered a bottle of Bollinger and the twelve-course tasting menu. Over the next two hours we ate pizza blackened with charcoal, placed on a truffle sauce swirled with ricotta. A pasta dish topped with shrimp, layered with colour and rich with foie gras and brandy. Pork cheek simmered in the same herbaceous *digestivo* that Renzo served in his bar. Salted cod and sweetbreads, more truffle, lamb. Some dishes were only a bite, a single explosion of perfect flavour, arranged on a round of tree trunk or a piece of tufa rock, intricate and artful.

We ate in silence, Tom and I, which wasn't so unusual with a meal like this, which demanded concentration, except I wasn't focused on it because my head was halfway to Montenello.

I was worried that Carlo might not be keen on letting Baxter stay overnight in his house. If so, then Riccardo might be prepared to sleep at my place, but we had left it in such a mess, and besides it seemed too much to ask. I checked my phone once or twice between courses but there hadn't been any calls. Most likely the radio was playing so loudly in his workshop that Riccardo hadn't heard his phone ringing.

When the final dessert course arrived, in the form of lips we were supposed to kiss up from the plate, I wasn't as amused by it as I might have been.

'Sensational,' said Tom, as the head chef emerged from

his kitchen to wish us farewell. 'World class, one hundred per cent.'

A bear of a man, he hugged us both and we managed a conversation, in my half-broken Italian and his sparse English, about the way he had taken the traditions of Basilicata's food, and remade them as his own.

'I wonder what Assunta would make of it,' I said to Tom afterwards. 'I'd love to bring her here.'

'The woman in your little *trattoria*?' He dismissed her with a shrug.

'So many of the flavours he used have their roots in the food she cooks,' I pointed out.

'You're not comparing the two of them though, surely?'

'They're linked, they're part of the same story.' I was surprised he couldn't see it. 'Their food has the same history and ingredients.'

'He's an artist and she's just a cook.'

'Isn't that what Made With Love is all about now?' I pointed out. 'Simple, heartwarming cooking, nothing flashy?'

'Everyday food for ordinary people,' agreed Tom. 'Yes, that's the brand, but it's not how we have to eat ourselves.'

His words didn't surprise me. I had always been aware of the gap between the way the public saw Tom and the person he really was. But now it seemed much less like smart marketing and far more like deceit. And that was unsettling – yet another reason not to trust Tom as much as he wanted me to.

Our hotel was a short walk up a steep slope. We were to sleep in a candlelit cave, furnished sparsely with antiques. Tom had taken the most expensive suite, of course, and it had creamy pocked stone walls arching into a high roof and a worn, smooth sloping floor. The bags Tom packed for us had been brought in and left on a luggage rack and set on a low bureau was a large vase of white flowers that he told me he had arranged to have sent.

'How much is all this costing?' I wondered.

Tom shrugged off the question. 'Don't worry about money; very soon it isn't going to be a problem.'

'Because of that guy Silvestre?'

'I have a consortium of investors. Hopefully he will be one of them.'

Although the cave was fairly large, it had hardly any natural light which made it feel like a tighter space, and as he lay back on the white linen-covered bed and started talking about new TV shows and Netflix deals and going international, Tom seemed to fill it with his personality. I felt a little trapped. For the very first time I didn't really want to be near him, and it was the strangest feeling, like the magic was wearing off.

When my phone rang and I saw it was Riccardo, it gave me an excuse to get away. I went outside to answer it and sat on a bench overlooking the cave-studded hills beyond the gorge.

'Baxter is fine,' Riccardo told me. 'Were you worrying about him? Is that why you called?'

'No actually, I've got a bit of a problem,' I admitted.

When I explained the situation, he sounded unfazed. To sleep in a cave hotel would be an experience. Baxter could stay on overnight with him, there was no problem at all.

'Will your father be OK with that? Do you think you should check with him?'

'I am sure he won't mind. And anyway, who knows what time he will be home. Papa has gone to the beach for the day, together with Assunta.'

'Really?' When I had spotted them in the bar that morning they both looked ready for work, Carlo in his suit, Assunta in her apron. 'Is that something they do very often?'

'Never before.' Riccardo sounded slightly bewildered. 'In Papa's message to me he said it was hot, and they wanted to swim in the sea. They are driving there in his Fiat. I hope it is up to the trip. That car is old and usually he doesn't go so far in it.'

'I hear the mechanic who looks after it is the very best.'

'This is true. And that mechanic has some good news for you. Your Saab is ready – I finished it this morning and it is running beautifully.'

'Oh, great.' I had been so impatient for the car to be road-worthy again and now I wasn't as pleased as expected.

'I am sorry it has taken so long,' said Riccardo. 'Will you continue with your journey, see the rest of Italy?'

'Maybe,' I said. 'If I can.'

'Don't worry about the bill being very expensive. I will charge you, how you say, the friend's rates.'

'You don't have to do that.' I was sure it must be a struggle for him building a new business.

'But you are a friend,' he said.

After we ended the call, I stayed sitting on the bench and thought about Montenello. I was still an outsider there, but I had been tugged into the life of the town, caught up in its story. I wanted to know what Riccardo was going to do with the house he had bought. Would Edward's husband come back and help him keep the hotel running? I wondered what dishes Assunta would serve in her *trattoria* when the days grew wintry and cold, and how the town looked when it was dusted in snow, and I didn't want to miss the *festa*.

Tom's voice broke into my thoughts. The door of our cave room was open and he was leaning out of it, bare-chested, calling my name.

'Sarah-Jane, Sarah-Jane ...'

Reluctantly I let him pull me from my thoughts.

'Are you going to come back inside and spend the rest of the afternoon in bed with me?' He was wearing that famously boyish smile, his skin was lightly tanned, his hair silvering against it.

I glanced away from him, towards the view of this town with its houses and churches burrowing into the rock, and its labyrinth of back streets waiting to be explored. I was sick of Tom assuming I would go along with whatever he wanted.

'No, I don't think so. I want to see a bit of Matera; in case I never get to come back here.'

'Really?' The smile slipped from his face.

'Why don't you come too?' I said, just in case he might want to do something for me.

'I need a rest,' he replied. 'Just don't get lost, OK – drinks with Silvestre at six.'

Getting lost seemed such a good idea. I didn't have the slightest desire to see creepy Silvestre again, no matter how much money he was worth. And I needed a break from Tom because it was starting to feel like I couldn't breathe properly when he was around. Leaving the hotel, I turned off my phone and walked where my feet took me. Up steep stepped streets and through narrow passageways, to a church that rose from a rock, and higher still, along a stone-flagged path perched above the ravine, until I couldn't go any further. Then I circled back through another warren of tight streets and squat houses, and it felt like parts of Montenello, only more ancient. As I began to tire, I chanced on a wider piazza and stopped for a drink, sitting outside a café. I loved this place. I liked watching people drifting past, tourists with nylon backpacks, narrow-hipped Italian boys in tight white jeans, a glamorous *nonna* with long silvery hair and Prada sunglasses. I loved Italy; I wasn't ready to leave yet.

I stayed at the café until the light faded, nibbling on the snacks they brought out, ordering another drink and watching people as they came and went. Mostly I passed the time thinking about Tom; the man he really was, not the one I wanted him to be. Had he always been so controlling? So selfish? Was he ever really listening? I knew he was a man who loved success but now I found myself wondering if it was all that mattered. He seemed to want it so much he was prepared to accept cash from some dodgy guy. What other lengths would he go to? How many lies would he tell?

Those weren't happy thoughts. They made me feel truly lost. Finally, I decided not to be lost any longer and followed my feet back to the hotel. It was late by the time I found it. Tom must have given up on me and gone somewhere for dinner because to my relief he and Silvestre weren't among the few people still drinking in the candlelit courtyard and our room was empty. I took a bath to wash off the dust of the day and lay there still deep in thought while the water was cooling. Tom kept saying he needed me, and it was the one thing I suspected was true. I wasn't quite so certain that I needed him anymore. All those weeks travelling solo through Italy, I'd been fine, hadn't I? Even when things went wrong, I coped. Besides I had given my heart to Tom once and he hadn't looked after it. Was I really going to let him have it again?

Climbing from the bath and turning my phone back on, I ignored the missed calls and messages from him and speed-dialled my mother.

'Sarah-Jane?' She answered straight away. 'Is everything all right?'

'Not really,' I admitted. 'I'm worried I might have made a big mistake.'

'We all make mistakes,' my mother said. 'How are you going to fix it?'

Assunta

On days when she made pasta by hand, Assunta started work early. She never resented the time it took to knead the dough and form it into thick ribbons or curls of *cavatelli*. This morning she had arrived at her *trattoria* before dawn, after a long and sleepless night, and made the pasta because she couldn't think of anything else to do. When it was finished, Assunta left it spread out on trays to dry and went next door for her coffee.

She was still thinking about her mother. All night long she had struggled to gather the memories, but so many of them were small and unimportant. Her mamma soaking tired, swollen feet in a bowl of warm water and vinegar that Giuseppina had brought her, complaining about the mess the wealthy people made in the homes they expected her to clean, letting Assunta massage rich cream into her chafed hands, closing her eyes and sighing. There were the cigarettes she rolled each evening with a machine she kept up on a high shelf because one of her chief pleasures was to smoke whenever she had a spare moment. There was the house where Assunta still lived, always clean and tidy, because her mother never allowed dust to settle on shelves or gather in corners. She had seemed a simple person, honest and open, not like a woman with a secret.

With the pasta made, Assunta needed coffee. Next door in the bar she found Renzo talking to Carlo, who was sitting up at the counter, drinking a *caffe con latte* and eating a pastry.

'This is becoming a new habit, eating your breakfast here,' she said to him.

'It is a good way to start the day,' Carlo replied.

Assunta settled onto the stool beside him, helped herself to a sugar-dusted pastry from the piled-high platter, wrapping one end with a paper serviette and biting into the other.

'What does the day hold for you?' she asked Carlo, once she had swallowed a buttery mouthful.

'More meetings,' he said, casting his eyes to the ceiling, 'endless meetings but never any decisions. I am a part of the committee that is organising the *festa*. It is a disaster.'

'What is going wrong?'

'Half of them have impressive ideas, the other half have reasons that are impossible. And so we argue day after day.'

'It does sound like a disaster,' agreed Assunta.

'Just the thought of spending more time trapped in a room with those people.' Carlo shuddered. 'I would rather be almost anywhere else.'

Renzo had made Assunta's coffee, two shots of espresso with a jug of steamed milk so she could pour the amount she preferred. He put it down on the counter in front of her, and she took a sip.

'Even the date is in question,' said Carlo. 'The *festa* of San Bernadino always used to happen in late August but we will not be prepared to celebrate our patron saint by then. Even if there is only a procession with his statue, some music in the piazza and a few stalls selling food, we can't be ready at least until September. And people want more than that. Much more.'

'What sorts of things are they suggesting?' asked Assunta.

'Fireworks, a cavalcade of horses, a carnival, street illuminations.' Carlo counted the ideas off on his fingers. 'The problem is that no one wants to organise any of these things.'

'Do you think it will happen, this *festa*?'

'The mayor says it will, so it must. And he has decreed that it will be an annual event so whatever happens, we must do it all again next year and the year after.' Carlo sighed tiredly. 'Perhaps it is time for me to retire, make way for a younger person.'

'You need a holiday that is all, a break from it all,' said Assunta, sipping the last of the coffee.

Renzo cleared away her empty cup, and replaced it with another, this time a strong espresso that she stirred a spoon of sugar through.

'Even one day off would be nice,' agreed Carlo.

'What about today then?' suggested Assunta, as the caffeine buzzed through her pleasantly. 'What if you didn't go to work and instead went home, changed out of your suit and did something nicer?'

'It is an interesting idea, but what would I do?' Carlo wondered.

'Didn't you want to go to the beach?'

'Yes, but not by myself.'

Assunta thought about the trays of freshly made pasta laid out next door. None of it would spoil, only dry a little more, and she could still cook it tomorrow.

'It will be hot again today,' remarked Renzo, who was wiping surfaces and clattering coffee cups but, as Assunta knew, always half listening. 'And I hear the air conditioning in the Town Hall isn't working properly. Is this true?'

'It is true, by mid-afternoon it will be unbearable,' said Carlo.

Her *trattoria* had no air-conditioning, only whirring fans to move the warm air through the dining room. Assunta thought about golden sands, a light breeze, and the chill of waves lapping her legs as she waded into the Ionian Sea. How long was it since she had done that?

'I will come with you,' she told Carlo. 'To the beach.'

'Now?' he checked. 'Today?'

'If you can get away from work, take a sick day, make some excuse.'

Carlo frowned. 'I have never done anything like that before.'

Renzo was putting some *panini* into a brown paper bag. He added two serviettes, twisted the ends, and gave it to Carlo, who looked at him questioningly.

'A picnic for the beach,' Renzo explained. 'Cheese and prosciutto. They can argue about the *festa* without you for a day. Nothing much will change.'

'You are right.' Carlo stared at the bag in his hands, glanced at Assunta then back at Renzo. 'Maybe you have a couple of cold beers too? I will put them in my chiller bag when I pick up the car.'

'If we are going to the beach then I need to get my swimming costume.' Assunta wasn't sure where it was or even if it still fitted her. 'And I have some ripe peaches that Papa gave me, they need to be eaten.'

'I will come by and pick you up,' Carlo told her.

'You should go now then,' said Renzo. 'Before it gets any later.'

Assunta found herself smiling as she hurried home. This wasn't like her at all, and she felt pleasantly bold. Searching out a few essentials – a towel, her wide-brimmed hat, sunglasses, the one-piece bathing suit she found at the very bottom of a drawer, a loose kaftan-style garment to drape over it – she was ready in no time and waiting impatiently when Carlo's little Fiat pulled up outside.

He chuckled as she climbed into the car. 'Look at us, at our age, running away from work, stealing the day for ourselves like teenagers.'

'Misbehaving,' said Assunta, fastening the seat belt. 'I hope we don't get into trouble.'

'I told them I had a cold coming on.' Carlo still sounded amused. 'I even made my voice sound croaky.'

'My customers will think I have another migraine.'

'Your brother is right, they can manage without us, just for one day, that is all.'

They drove to a beach backed by dunes, where the sand was almost white and the sea clear and shallow. Carlo paid for sunbeds beneath a brightly coloured parasol at the very edge of the water. Assunta went to get changed then lay in the shade, shrouded in her kaftan, while he stretched in the sunshine, rubbing cream into his bare chest and long, lean legs.

She felt shy suddenly, as if they were strangers, and wished she had thought to bring a book or magazine. What would they do for this whole day together, what would they talk about?

'I can't believe we are here,' said Carlo, gazing out at the wide blue band of sea and sky. 'I hope this beach is OK for you? I looked it up on the internet and it seemed the best one that wasn't too far to drive.'

'You have never been here before?'

He shook his head. 'Maria didn't like beaches. She preferred hotels with swimming pools.'

'She didn't like beaches?' repeated Assunta, finding it difficult to believe.

'Sand sticking to her, the saltiness of the water, the walk from the car carrying all our things, she didn't enjoy any of that.'

'I love it,' said Assunta, filling her lungs with the fresh, clean air. 'Thank you for bringing me.'

'Shall we swim then?' he suggested.

Self-consciously she stripped off her kaftan and together they ran barefoot over the hot sand and rushed at the waves, Carlo diving under and resurfacing, water streaming from his body, Assunta floating on her back.

He was a much stronger swimmer than her, and struck out further and deeper. Assunta watched the sun glinting from his arms as he powered on. Then he turned and swam back, and they trod water together. All this beauty was here every day, she realised, looking back at the beach. Waves lapped at the shoreline, silvery fish skittered through the shallows, spiky tufts of Marram grass waved from the dunes. It was like this while she was busy working or worrying. It would be like this again tomorrow and the next day, all blues and pale gold, beautiful.

'I needed this day away,' said Carlo, when they were back on the beach, letting the sun warm their skin dry.

'So did I,' said Assunta.

They spent the day there, picnicking on what they had brought, then ordering more drinks from the bar, plunging into the sea when they were hot, dozing away a good part of the afternoon, talking about everything and nothing.

'We should do this again before summer is over,' said Carlo, as they took their final dip in the sea and watched the sun sinking into it.

'I would like that.'

They were standing with their feet on the sandy seabed, letting the water buffet them. A stronger wave caught Assunta by surprise. She was pushed forward and under, then teetered sideways into Carlo who caught her. They both laughed and Assunta pushed her wet hair off her face and blinked the water from her eyes. Carlo was still smiling. He turned to her and very softly, very gently, their lips touched. Assunta wasn't sure which of them had moved towards the other, but it was Carlo who apologised.

'Don't be sorry,' she told him.

'Really? Are you sure?'

Assunta nodded.

He smiled again. 'Look at us, at our age, behaving like teenagers.'

Sarah-Jane

Everyone makes mistakes, that was what my mother told me, but she never had, not when it came to love anyway. Mum married a man who adored her and when he was snatched away, she didn't try to find a replacement because they were meant to be together; I felt that as much as she did, and there was nobody out there to match him. Once I had hoped Tom could be that for me, dreamed he was anyway. And it wasn't easy coming to terms with how wrong I had been.

Sitting in the dark, on the bench outside my cave room, the phone heating against my ear, we had a long chat, Mum and I.

'I think he's using me,' I told her. 'Maybe he always was.'

'Yes,' she said, carefully. 'I know.'

'Why did I let him?' It seemed ridiculous to be so naive.

'You thought he was the person you were looking for. Plenty of others seem to have been charmed by him too, if that's any consolation.'

'I thought he was perfect, wonderful, amazing – but it's only ever been about him and the business, right from the start hasn't it? How can it have taken me so long to work that out?'

'Don't be so hard on yourself. You're hardly the first woman to fall for the wrong guy.'

'He keeps saying he loves me. He says it all the time.'

'They're easy words to use and he knows how much you want to hear them.'

'Not if it's a lie I don't.' My voice almost broke on the words. 'Do you think he was always lying?'

I still half-hoped Mum was going to reassure me, say Tom's feelings must have been genuine at least for a while, make me feel a little better, but she was much too honest for that.

'Oh, Sarah-Jane, I'm so sorry.' She sounded very sad.

'He thinks I'm coming back with him to rebuild Made With Love.'

'I very much hope you're not.' Now she was indignant.

'What am I going to do though? What will I say?' I could imagine how Tom would take the news that I didn't want to be a part of his grand vision.

'Forget about Tom for a minute and tell me what you want. Would you like to come home, for instance?'

'No, I'd far rather stay here in Italy a while longer. There's no hurry for me to come back is there?'

'Say that then,' Mum advised 'Tell him you're in no rush to leave so he'll have to find someone else to do all the hard work for him. Doesn't that about sum things up?'

'He'll be furious.' The thought made me sad because for so long I had wanted to matter to Tom, really matter, not just for my cooking skills.

'It's that girl who had his child I feel sorry for,' said my mother.

'Jo?'

'She's stuck with him, one way or another, whereas you can break free. I'd never tell you how to live your life, Sarah-Jane, but I have to say I'm relieved.'

'You never liked him.'

'It's been quite an effort trying to hide it,' my mother admitted.

'I wish you'd said something.'

'You needed to find this out for yourself.'

My mother was right; I had believed in Tom so much that nothing anyone said would have changed it. Now it was like a mist had cleared, and I could see him clearly, all the things I hadn't noticed. And I didn't believe anymore.

'Baxter can't stand him,' I told my mum. 'It's taken me a while to realise that too.'

I was in bed when Tom got back to the room. He smelled of whisky and wine, and I lay very still, hoping he would think I was asleep. I felt the spring of the mattress as his weight rolled onto it then listened as his breathing slowed and changed into a snore. He must have drunk a lot with Silvestre and I was glad not to have been with them.

Tom slept better than I did. There was too much going on in my head for proper rest and in the end I gave up trying and went to sit outside on the bench, staring up at the stars. I was beginning to feel better about the future now because I knew where I wanted to be, and that had to be a start.

Somewhere in this long boot-shaped country were people whose blood I shared, if only a few drops. Perhaps I would never meet them, or even find out which town my father's family came from, but there was a place in Italy where I was beginning to feel at home and find a few friends, a little town on top of a mountain.

I was still sitting outside when the staff arrived to prepare the breakfast. Seeing me there, one of the kitchen hands brought me a cup of coffee and a warm bread roll spread with creamy butter and sweet-sour cherry jam.

When Tom woke, I needed to talk with him. I needed to say that I wasn't going to buy a new wardrobe of taupe-coloured clothes, or move to rural England and fake a perfect life, to make it absolutely clear that Made With Love wasn't going to be made with any more of my love. Through the open door I could hear him snoring, the sound of it echoing from the cave's high ceiling and rough walls. Not wanting to wait a moment longer to set things straight, I went inside and called his name.

Tom struggled to rise into consciousness, rolling away and pulling the sheet over his head, demanding coffee in a croaky hungover voice. I fetched a cup from the breakfast room and when I returned he was still in bed, propped up on pillows.

'What happened to you last night?' he asked testily.

'I got a bit lost and you'd left by the time I made it back.'

'That was dumb.'

'Not really, I didn't want to come out with you and Silvestre anyway.'

'I told you he's important for the business,' Tom said impatiently. 'But I closed the deal anyway, so it turns out I didn't need you.'

'That's good,' I said, taking a breath and steeling myself. 'It's really good that you don't need me. Because I'm staying in Italy.'

He stared at me disbelievingly. 'What do you mean you're staying here? What about everything we've talked about, our vision?'

'It's your vision, not mine, like I keep saying.'

'I don't understand,' he said. 'You wanted to be part of it. You were excited.'

'No I wasn't. I've been trying to tell you that. It's not what I want at all.'

'Sarah-Jane, what's wrong with you? This is such an opportunity.' He was still tangled in the rumpled bed sheets. 'You're making a huge mistake.'

'I don't think so.'

'But we're perfect together, you and I.' Shrugging off the sheets and climbing from the bed, Tom reached for me. 'We're going to have the kind of life other people dream of.'

'No,' I said, stepping away, not feeling anything much except how strange it was to feel nothing.

'I've been working hard, making these plans for both of us, you can't let me down now.' Tom's voice was starting to fray.

'I had other plans and you just expected me to drop them,' I pointed out.

'No, what I expected was some support,' he said bitterly. 'It was me who gave you a start when no one else was interested, remember. You were a nobody and I made you.'

'I've never minded being a nobody,' I told him. 'It's fine by me.'

Tom shook his head as if what he was hearing made no sense. 'Look at what I've done for you so far. Now I'm prepared to do even more – but you're turning me down? Seriously?'

'Yes.'

'You'll regret this, you know that don't you?' His eyes were cold and his face flinty. 'This is a stupid move, throwing everything away. I didn't think you were stupid, Sarah-Jane, but apparently you are.'

Saying nothing, I stared at him.

'Stupid and a bit boring, if I'm honest. That's why you need me. I make you more interesting.'

'At least I know what you really think.' I was reeling at his words, hurting now. 'If I'm that boring, you'll be glad to be rid of me.'

'No.' His voice changed; now he was contrite. 'God, I'm sorry, you know I don't mean it.'

'It sounded very like you did.'

Tom moved towards me again, resting his hand on my arm, then frowned as I shook it free. 'It's just that I'm struggling with this OK? I thought I could count on you. And I'm a bit gutted … devastated actually. You're everything to me, Sarah-Jane.'

He gave me a look, pleading and rueful, a heart-softening look that might have worked on me once, but not anymore, not now his dazzle had gone. All that was left was a man who I didn't trust very much.

'What can I say to make you change your mind?' he asked.

'Nothing, nothing at all.'

'I can't bear to lose you. I love you. How much do I need to tell you that before you believe me?'

This time I did let him pull me into a hug, but I was the first to break away.

'Please,' he said, his voice low and sad.

'No,' I told him, surprised at my own strength.

'This is it then?' he asked, still sounding like he didn't quite believe it. 'I'll beg if that's what you want?'

'No.'

'Money then? A share of the business?'

'None of that.'

'Are you completely sure?'

I looked at him, handsome despite the hangover, at the crinkles round his green eyes and the shadow of designer stubble on his skin, at the face I wasn't going to be able to avoid because it would still be in magazines and newspapers, on TV and all over social media.

'I'm sure,' I said.

The drive back to Montenello was mostly made against a soundtrack of Tom's music played slightly too loud: Dire Straits and Coldplay, quite a lot of Snow Patrol. None of it music I liked but I didn't ask him to turn it down because at least it filled the silence.

'I'll pack up my stuff and go then, shall I?' asked Tom frostily as we were crossing the causeway into Montenello.

'OK then,' I said, and his expression was pained.

'If I'm lucky, I'll get on a flight tomorrow. I guess I have to find a hotel in Bari tonight though,' he said.

I nodded my agreement.

'I certainly won't miss this town,' he told me, turning onto a steep, narrow street. 'It's nothing special, is it?'

I remembered how I had thought the same thing that first

day when I arrived and walked around, before I got to know the place properly.

'Just another mountain town,' finished Tom. 'A bit of a shithole really.'

'I like it,' I told him. 'I'm thinking of staying a bit longer.'

'Good luck to you then, you'll need it.'

While Tom packed noisily, I sat outside listening to the sound of cupboard doors slamming and his footsteps echoing through the rooms as he gathered up bits and pieces he had dropped around the place.

'That's me then,' he said, dragging his bags out of the house and down the steps, leaving them on the street in a small pile, where they had been when he arrived.

'Take care of yourself,' I told him. 'I hope everything goes really well with the business.'

'It will,' he promised. 'Dedication and drive – that's what it takes to succeed, and I've got that, Sarah-Jane.'

'You do,' I conceded.

There was an awkward moment when I think he was trying to decide whether to hug me again.

'Bye then,' I said. 'Drive carefully.'

'Yeah, see you around.'

Tom picked up his things, slung the strap of his computer bag over his shoulder, and wheeling a suitcase behind him, walked away without turning back. I watched him go, listening to the rumble of wheels over cobbles. The house was mine again and it was such a relief – like I had been holding onto a deep breath and could finally let it go. And while my heart might have been a little sore, it definitely wasn't broken.

Assunta

Assunta left her hair in stiff salty ringlets and her skin dusted with crystals of white sand. She didn't want to lose the feeling of the beach or forget the brief moment when her and Carlo's lips had touched and any of what came afterwards – holding hands, as they lay side by side on their sunbeds letting the heat dry their skin. Driving back to Montenello with music playing and the windows of the Fiat wound down. Saying goodbye, smiling into each other's faces, knowing something between them had shifted, but saying nothing for now.

Home again, Assunta couldn't settle. Her house felt too still and empty. She didn't want to sit in her favourite chair, or cook an evening meal, or take a shower. Glancing into the bathroom mirror she saw that she had caught the sun and her skin was glowing. Still no one would know from seeing her how changed she felt inside.

Downstairs on her dresser were the photographs she saw every day: Giuseppina and her mother through the decades of their lives. She knew those faces like her own and thought it meant that she knew the people too. Staring at herself in the mirror, Assunta moved a finger to her lips, and tingled at the memory the touch brought. Everyone had secrets.

The house felt too small to contain her so lacing her feet into comfortable shoes, Assunta went out and began walking. She had no destination in mind, only needed to move, to take long strides through the cooling air, become breathless up the hills. She thought of Carlo as she went and wondered if he was alone at home, thinking of her.

If Assunta walked anywhere in the evenings, it was only ever the same route, from her *trattoria* to home. Now as darkness fell, she passed through streets that were less familiar, although she recognised the faces of the people she saw, knowing them for what they preferred to eat, even when she couldn't recall their names. A whole life spent in one town, and Assunta had never felt restless before.

Aside from the piazza, Montenello was poorly lit at night and when she rounded a corner and saw the hotel, chandeliers glowing, fairy lights twinkling, Assunta thought how pretty it was and stopped walking. Upstairs a wedding feast was in progress and she could see white-coated waiters moving through the crowded rooms. There was the sound of music coming through the open windows, of laughter and conversation.

This hotel was where her mother had worked, although in those days it was rundown and neglected, not somewhere people stayed unless they had to. It had long been boarded up before the Australians arrived to change its fortunes. The building was so transformed her mother would barely recognise it; nothing about it was the same. She may have worked in those rooms that were now a part of the restaurant, making beds and mopping floors. Assunta tried to imagine it.

She didn't mean to go inside but the door lay open and the warmth of the light was inviting. Edward was sitting behind the reception desk and he looked up at her tiredly.

'Assunta, is everything OK?' he asked.

'Yes,' Assunta replied. 'No.'

'Yes or no, which is it?'

'Both.'

'It can't be both,' he told her.

'But it is,' she insisted. 'Some things are OK, others are not.'

'Right,' he said. 'Is there something I can help you with then?'

'Maybe ...'

He waited in silence as Assunta tried to decide exactly what it was she wanted. The expression on his face looked like one he might keep for difficult guests, patient and understanding.

'I have found out that my mother worked here a long time ago,' she said at last.

'Right, I didn't know that,' said Edward, 'but then I don't know much about the history of the hotel, only that it can't have been very successful. What did your mother do here?'

'She may have been a chambermaid but I am not sure. Perhaps you have some records?'

'Unlikely,' Edward said. 'We cleaned out boxes of mildewed paper that someone had left behind, burned it all.'

'There is nothing left?' Assunta was disappointed. She had hoped to find something of her mother here.

'Only a few documents that Gino thought were interesting. He had them framed and hung on the wall of the office. Come up and have a look if you like.'

'You are busy,' she said awkwardly.

'Always,' Edward agreed.

He took her upstairs, away from the rooms filled with wedding guests and along a narrow corridor past several closed doors.

'Here we are,' he said, unlocking the furthest and showing her into a small space with not much in it apart from a wooden filing cabinet, some shelving and a spindly-legged desk. Hanging on the wall were the framed documents he had referred to. A yellowing laundry docket, a breakfast menu, a crinkled black and white postcard showing the hotel as it had once been. Each item was in a wooden frame and mounted on stiff white card.

The final frame held a handwritten list of seven names. Assunta found her mother's third from the bottom – Martina

Marotta. 'This is her,' she told Edward, pointing it out. 'I think it is a staff list, so she must have worked here.'

A couple of the other surnames belonged to families who still lived in Montenello, but the others weren't familiar. She supposed that one of them might have been her father.

'I'm sorry there isn't anything more,' said Edward. 'Gino doesn't like clutter.'

'My mother was here, at least I know that.'

'Are you looking for anything in particular?' he asked.

'Not really,' she said, because the truth was too complicated.

Edward removed the frame from the wall, passing it to her. 'You should take this. It means more to you than us.'

'Are you sure you don't mind? There is an empty space on the wall now.'

'That might bother Gino, but he's not here, and it doesn't bother me.'

Assunta followed him back down to the reception area, holding the frame carefully, wondering about the names on it and if there was anyone left who might remember these people. She was about to leave when Edward stopped her.

'Would you like a drink?' he asked. 'I'm about to have one.'

'Why not?' she agreed, because there was no reason not to.

The bar area was empty. Edward showed her to a seat beside the window and went to mix the Negroni she asked for. In a square glass with a coil of orange peel and a large ball of ice, the ruby red drink looked stylish.

'*Saluti*,' she said, raising her glass.

'Cheers then,' he replied.

'You work long hours,' she observed.

'So do you.'

'I am thinking of changing that,' she admitted. 'I want time for other things.'

'Will you close your *trattoria*?' he asked. 'Open it on fewer days?'

'I haven't decided yet.'

'I envy your freedom. Me and Gino have so much debt we'll be working until our last breath.'

'How is he, your husband?' It had been a while since Assunta had seen them together. 'Is he coming home soon?'

'I wish I knew,' said Edward wryly.

Their wedding hadn't been so long ago. They had flown back to Australia for it, and held a second celebration here in Montenello. Assunta hadn't been a guest at their party, but her father and Renzo were there, and she watched the newlyweds pose for photographs beside the fountain, both in pastel-coloured suits – one pale turquoise, the other blush pink – looking very handsome.

'Gino keeps finding reasons he needs to stay longer in Sydney,' Edward told her.

'Australia is very far away.' Assunta couldn't imagine travelling such a distance, never mind flitting back and forth.

'About as far as it's possible to get,' Edward agreed. 'We talk on Zoom all the time but it almost makes things worse, seeing someone and not being able to touch them.'

'You have been together for many years?'

'Since we were kids. We've never been apart for this long before.'

How other people lived was their business and Assunta made a point of never prying. But she was curious about these two men who loved each other. For once she wanted to know more.

'Here in Montenello we never had a gay couple before you came,' she told him. 'At least not as far as I know.'

'Yeah,' Edward nodded. 'That was something Gino worried about. He thought it might be an issue. It was your father who put our minds at rest.'

'You are friends with Papa?'

Edward smiled. 'I love Augusto, he is priceless.'

'And my brother Renzo too.'

'He's a great guy.'

'Can I ask a question?' Assunta hesitated. 'It is in confidence.'

'Sure.'

'Do you think Renzo is like you?'

'Like me? You mean gay?' Edward sounded surprised.

'Yes …' Seeing him frown, Assunta tailed off uncertainly. 'I am sorry, maybe I shouldn't have asked you this.'

'No, that's OK. I'm just not sure why you expect me to know.'

'You are his friend, I thought he may have talked to you.'

'He's a very private man, your brother, isn't he,' observed Edward. 'He doesn't give much away.'

Assunta nodded. 'Even to me and I am his sister.'

'You're worried about him though?'

'I worry that he is alone, that is all.'

'If it's any comfort, I don't think I've ever met a man who seemed more content than Renzo. He spends all day surrounded by his friends. He never looks stressed or worried. He knows who he is and where he belongs.'

'I would like my brother to have what you have, you and Gino.'

'That's not working out so well for us right now though, is it?' Edward sounded as bittersweet as the cocktail he was drinking.

'I wish Renzo could find a companion.'

'You live alone though, don't you? You're happy?'

In Assunta's mind was an image of her pulling up outside her house in Carlo's little Fiat and staying there, engine running, not wanting the day to be over. They had made plans for more time together, another trip to the beach perhaps, a lunch, breakfast. The last thing Carlo had said was that he would see her very soon.

'I am happy,' she confirmed.

Sarah-Jane

I walked over confetti as I went to fetch Baxter, scuffing it aside with my shoes without a second thought. Other people had been busy knotting their lives together while I was feeling pleased to have mine to myself. The white paper petals fluttered away from me in the breeze.

My Saab was ready. It was parked in Riccardo's workshop next to the car he was working on, with the top down and my dog sitting on the back seat. His tail wagged as I walked in and he twitched his eyebrows at me.

'Baxter is ready for you to drive him away,' said Riccardo, turning down the volume on the radio that was blaring.

The keys were in the ignition. Opening the driver's door, I eased inside and put one hand on the steering wheel then started the engine with the other. It rumbled to life and I listened to it for a few moments, pressing my foot on the accelerator. It certainly sounded like it was ready to take me up hills again, along winding coast roads and stretches of *autostrada*. But I didn't entirely trust that car anymore; it was just something else I had fallen in love with that ended up letting me down.

Riccardo was leaning into the open window, listening to the engine's roar, his tanned forearms resting on the rim of the door.

'You are going to take a drive now? Test it out?' he asked.

'I suppose so,' I said.

'Where is your friend, will he go with you?' He glanced at the doorway as if Tom might be skulking out there ready to appear.

'My friend has gone,' I told him, switching off the ignition.

'Ah,' he replied. 'A pity.'

'It turns out he wasn't such a good friend,' I admitted.

'In that case, not a pity at all.'

Perhaps it was the memory of all those engine parts littered over the workshop floor, or Baxter's anxious bushy-browed gaze from the passenger seat beside me, or something about the look in Riccardo's eyes as they met mine. But I found myself asking, 'I don't suppose you would come for a test drive with me? Is that part of the service?'

He grinned. 'Why not?'

'How long do you have?'

'As long as you like.'

I strapped Baxter into his safety harness while Riccardo cleaned the oil from his hands with a squirt of gel then jumped in beside me. Then I edged out of the garage carefully and turned down the hill. I wanted to avoid the centre of town for now, so I drove towards the causeway. The forested roads beyond it were wider, but the traffic moved fast and, gritting my teeth a bit, I sped up to match it.

After a few kilometres my grip on the worn leather steering wheel lightened and I lost some of the stiffness from my shoulders. I remembered how good driving could feel with the roof down and the wind in my hair, and nothing but sky above my head.

'This car is fun,' said Riccardo.

'You see now why I bought it?'

He nodded. 'It suits you.'

We turned before reaching Borgo del Colle and drove back towards home. Maybe because I knew my way around now, even the tightest streets seemed a little more navigable and before long we had reached the piazza.

'Shall we stop, have a coffee?' asked Riccardo.

'This is where I broke down,' I reminded him.

'It won't happen this time, I promise.'

Assunta emerged from the *trattoria* and stood in the doorway, watching me park. A man walked past and patted the bonnet, saying something affably in Italian. From a table outside the bar, Augusto and his friend smiled in our direction.

'It is running well now? No need to push it anywhere today?' called Augusto.

'I hope not,' I said, releasing Baxter from his harness and climbing out of the car.

They made space for us at the table, fetching more chairs, and Renzo brought a bowl of water for Baxter, a lemon granita for me and a strong black coffee for Riccardo. Assunta came to join us, Carlo walked over from the Town Hall, and Edward stopped for a brief chat. Everyone wanted to know where I was going to drive my Saab to next.

'Why not stay here a little while longer,' Edward suggested. 'Use Montenello as a base and take some day trips.'

Immediately Augusto started listing places within easy reach. He borrowed Assunta's stubby pencil and jotted on a paper serviette. Restaurants, beaches, historic towns, impressive cave systems, everyone added something.

Sitting outside the bar, the afternoon drifted effortlessly into evening. Renzo brought more drinks, an Aperol spritz for me, a beer for Riccardo, and a bittersweet liqueur for Assunta, who lit a cigarette then let it smoulder away untouched in the ashtray.

Her *trattoria* was closed but everyone was hungry so she decided to cook a little pasta she had left over, with a simple tomato sauce, maybe a salad. I went to help her prepare it, lining a plate with thin slices of fennel, blood orange and crisp red onion. Then we carried the food next door, Renzo bringing us a bottle of red wine and we had a sort of impromptu dinner party out on the pavement. As the sky darkened, fairy lights glittered in the trees and the fountain was illuminated.

To finish there was another round of liqueurs. Renzo joined us because the bar was empty and we kept talking and drinking until it grew later than we realised. When Augusto started to look tired, Assunta decided to take him home, so Riccardo helped me clear the table and together we washed up plates and pans, drying everything and putting it all back where it belonged.

Not wanting to risk driving home after I had drunk so much, I left the car where it was and Riccardo walked with Baxter and me through the dark, deserted streets. We said goodnight on my doorstep.

'That was really lovely but I'm sorry for distracting you from work,' I told him.

'No problem, the work will still be there tomorrow.'

'I'll see you soon then.' Although it struck me that I wouldn't need to, not now my Saab was fixed.

It was time to go inside but instead I stood there, listening to the night-time chirping of crickets, feeling the whisper of a breeze ruffling my hair, reflecting on what a good time we'd had together. I didn't need a mechanic anymore and I was going to miss him.

Baxter scratched at the paintwork of the front door, asking to be let in.

'He thinks it's time for bed,' I told Riccardo.

'It is getting late and he is probably right. Goodnight, Sarah-Jane, sleep well, and yes, see you soon.'

Riccardo turned away, heading back the way we had come and standing in the doorway, I watched him taking long strides through the scarce pools of light cast by a few streetlights.

Inside the house, I could sense the musky smell of Tom's fragrance still lingering so I opened up the windows to let it drift out and disappear. Only when all I could breathe was fresh air did the place feel mine again. Making myself a cup of tea, I pulled out my map of Italy and set it on the table. It was inked with my route, where I had already been and the places I planned to go. My finger traced a line south through Calabria and into Sicily. There was nothing to stop me going now. But there was nothing to stop me staying either.

Assunta

Assunta shook the last cigarette from the packet and frowned. Why had she even started smoking? It was so long ago she could barely remember. Perhaps only because her mother smoked and she wanted to be like her. Renzo gave her an ashtray, still she stared at the cigarette without lighting it.

'Are you opening the *trattoria* today?' he wondered.

'Probably,' she replied.

When the butcher's truck pulled up outside, Assunta didn't bother to move. The door of her *trattoria* wasn't locked so the boy could carry the shoulders of lamb inside without her help. She planned to roast the meat in the oven on a bed of crisp potatoes and a mix of fresh and dried tomatoes, scattered with breadcrumbs, crushed garlic, chopped rosemary and grated lemon zest. *Lamb alla Lucana*; she could make it today or tomorrow, it didn't really matter.

'And what about the *festa*? Will you be serving the food there?' Renzo wondered.

'Carlo has asked me the same thing.' The plan was for trestle tables in the piazza and for people to sit down and enjoy a feast that everyone assumed she would take care of cooking. Assunta still hadn't decided, one way or another.

'It will be a lot of work,' she observed.

'You would need some help,' agreed Renzo, busy wiping up spilled sugar from the counter.

'True,' said Assunta, who didn't want to think about it.

'Perhaps the English girl, she can cook, yes?'

'But she will leave Montenello before it is time for the *festa*.'

'Not if she has a reason to stay.'

Through the window Assunta could see Sarah-Jane's car parked where she must have left it the evening before, after the meal they had eaten together. The salad the girl had made, with fennel, orange and red onion, had mustard whisked in with the dressing and flaked almonds scattered on top, which had never been Assunta's way. She might try it next time though. It hadn't been too bad.

Renzo cleared away the clean ashtray and her unsmoked cigarette, replacing them with a glass of iced water.

'There is a list,' she told him.

'What list?' Renzo paused in his work for once. 'What are you talking about?'

'A list of people who used to work in the hotel; my mother's name is on it.'

'And why is it important, this list?'

'It is the only clue I have.'

She started to explain, but Renzo already knew the details: that Augusto wasn't the man who had made her mother pregnant, that she needed to find out who was.

'Papa told me,' he admitted. 'But he didn't mention a list.'

'It is next door.'

'Show me then.'

Assunta went to fetch it, and then watched her brother's face as he studied the names. His expression gave nothing away.

'Guido Raggi and Fabbio Galeazzi,' he repeated aloud. 'You think one of these men might be your real father?'

'Perhaps.'

'What does Augusto say?'

Assunta hadn't wanted to risk seeing any more hurt on the old man's face and knowing she was the cause.

'I haven't asked him.'

There was also Carlo, who might help by typing the names into his computer or looking at records in the Town Hall.

That morning she had eaten breakfast with him and drunk two cups of coffee. Things were changing between them and who knew what those changes would bring. For now they were being careful with each other. So Assunta hadn't asked him either.

'Leave it with me then,' said Renzo.

'What will you do?' she asked.

'I don't know,' he admitted. 'I must think about it.'

He took the list upstairs to the apartment he had lived in for as long as Assunta could remember. It was rare for her to follow him up there. He had only a few rooms, sparsely furnished, where he slept each night and occasionally cooked a meal. Renzo's true home was this bar, filled with the people who came day after day, and he knew the details of their lives as well as how they took their coffee. Who was hiding troubles, who was making plans, who was celebrating, who was worrying; he heard most of it and guessed the rest. If anyone could learn more about the names on that list, it was Renzo.

Sitting at the bar, staring through the window, Assunta saw a little dog trotting across the piazza, and watched for the English girl following behind. There she was, in a bright smock top and frayed denim shorts, walking with a swing in her stride, whistling at Baxter and heading towards her car. The smell of coffee must have drawn her towards the bar instead, and she smiled as she saw Assunta.

'Good morning,' she said cheerfully.

Wordlessly Renzo slipped behind his Gaggia, grinding beans and heating milk, while Sarah-Jane helped herself to a pastry from the piled plate on the counter, wrapping it in a paper serviette, sugar dusting her face as she bit into it.

'Where will you drive to in your car today?' asked Assunta.

'I'm not sure I'll drive anywhere. It's nice just to be here.'

There was no sign of the friend she had been so pleased to have visit her. Renzo thought he must have left town and, if that was so, it didn't seem to have made her unhappy. She was smiling now as she accepted her *cappucino*, taking a sip and giving a soft sigh of appreciation. Sitting up at the bar, with her tanned legs crossed and her glossy dark hair spilling over her shoulders, she looked like she belonged.

'I need to get hold of Edward.' Sarah-Jane glanced at her phone. 'I'm not sure how much longer I can have the house for.'

'There will be other houses,' said Assunta.

'I know, but I like that one.'

'So you are planning to stay for a while?'

'Possibly.' She frowned at her phone. 'I sent Edward a message earlier but haven't heard back yet.'

'He is busy, so many weddings this summer,' Assunta murmured. 'And without his husband here.'

'That's what I was thinking,' said Sarah-Jane. 'I wondered if he might need some extra help, even for a short while?'

'Maybe,' said Assunta.

'I could work in the kitchen or the bar, do some waitressing, admin, anything really,' said Sarah-Jane. 'The trouble is my Italian might not be good enough.'

Assunta said nothing and Renzo fixed her with a look that she tried to avoid by staring into her empty coffee cup until he moved it away, off the counter, and spoke up himself.

'My sister needs help,' he told Sarah-Jane.

'You do? In the *trattoria*?' The girl turned to her, sounding hopeful.

Assunta wanted more than help. She needed someone who could be trusted to take her place when her head hurt or her spirits were low, at times when the knives felt heavy in her hands and the heat of the gas jets made her kitchen stifling, and on days like this one when her body knew what she had to do, but her mind couldn't meet the thought of it.

'If you work, I will pay you,' Assunta said brusquely.

'When would you need me to start?'

'Today ... now.'

'So I have a job?' She looked bewildered and sounded uncertain.

'If you want one.'

'Oh, yes please.' A smile lit Sarah-Jane's face. Jumping down from the stool, she hesitated for a moment, then threw her arms round Assunta. 'It would be fantastic to work with you, thank you. I'd love it.'

Assunta wasn't accustomed to being hugged by other women. She stiffened a little and patted her shoulder. 'It will be hard work.'

'Yes,' agreed Sarah-Jane.

'I must be able to rely on you.'

'Yes, yes.'

'On days when I can't be there, I may ask you to take over.'

'That would be fine, but I'd need some recipes. I can't cook exactly like you do.'

'Then do it your way.'

'Really?'

'Why not? Today though we will do it the way I always have. Lamb alla Lucana ... come and I will show you.'

The work was never effortless, but with two of them it was easier. Sarah-Jane peeled and chopped the potatoes, while Assunta seared the lamb shoulders. Together they laid the lamb, tomatoes, herbs and lemon on the bed of potatoes. As the meat sizzled in the oven, Assunta stepped back and let Sarah-Jane take her place, watching as the first course was prepared, a simple soup of wilted greens, dense chicken broth, salty pancetta and lots of olive oil.

'More,' advised Assunta, as she drizzled oil into the pan too sparingly. 'Always a little more than you imagine you need.'

The meal was ready and, when her customers crowded in, Assunta had enough time to move from table to table.

She greeted Donna Carmela, who was lunching with her son, the mayor, and had brought in a bottle of Prosecco so was probably celebrating something. She chatted with lonely Maddalena Marino and supplied her with extra serviettes so she could wrap her bread and take it home. She exchanged a few words with Carlo while he waited for Riccardo to join him. There was even time to sit down with Augusto for a while, to perch beside him and Francesco on a bench seat, and taste a little of the soup that Sarah-Jane brought for her to try.

'She is working for me now,' Assunta explained to her father.

'Of course,' he replied.

'She will be remaining here for a while.'

Augusto nodded, then frowned. 'The one-euro houses, unfortunately the decisions have been made, it is too late for her to apply.'

'She likes the house she is staying in.'

'Then she must buy that one,' he said, as though the matter was settled.

At best Assunta hoped to keep the girl through to autumn if the weather stayed warm. Surely when the sky turned stony grey and misted Montenello in cloud, when the icy rains came and the windows of the *trattoria* steamed with condensation, she would choose to leave the place behind, and Assunta would be alone again.

She planned to make the most of the time between then and now.

Sarah-Jane

There are some places where you feel at home and for me Assunta's *trattoria* was like that. I was comfortable with her worn-handled knives and scorched metal trays, knew where to find each thing, how to move around the small space. That lunchtime I could sense her watching me, but there was no interference as I pulled the meat from the oven and served up portions on her mismatched crockery: golden potatoes and tender lamb, sweetly roasted onion and tomato, a crunch of scattered breadcrumbs, a hint of nutty pecorino cheese. She must have been starting to trust me.

The dining room was full of people. Some greeted me by name, although I wasn't sure what many of them were called, not yet anyway. Cooking here day after day, I would get to know them surely. In such a small place, it would be almost impossible not to.

Baxter had been dozing on the floor in a shady spot. Now he moved, and sat beside Riccardo, panting hopefully, in case there were titbits.

'Don't feed him,' I warned, as I took over plates loaded with *Lamb alla Lucana*.

'Never,' promised Riccardo, and I could tell from his smile that he would slip the dog a few treats.

Back in the kitchen, piling more plates with food, I couldn't quite believe the turn my day had taken. That morning I had set out hoping to find some sort of work, and now here I was wearing an apron and my face flushed from the heat of cooking. I had a job.

There was still the matter of where I was going to live

to worry about. Really I wanted to stay on in my jasmine-covered house if it was at all possible. With lunch over, instead of drifting next door to the bar with the others, I whistled Baxter to my side and walked down to the hotel. For once there was no wedding being celebrated and no sign of Edward either. The woman working behind the reception desk offered her help, but it seemed better to talk to him, so I decided to try the palazzo.

Baxter tugging on the leash, I walked down winding streets and narrow passageways and before long we were standing in front of the graceful old mansion with its golden walls and shuttered windows.

It took a while for Edward to respond to my ringing on his doorbell. I was about to give up and head away when the solid wooden door creaked open. The face that looked into mine was tired. His eyes were shadowed and the lines that scored his forehead seemed to have deepened.

'Sarah-Jane?'

'Sorry to disturb you, is this a bad time?'

'No, it's fine, come in.' He opened the door wider. 'I was about to make some coffee.'

Inside everything was perfect. Surfaces gleamed, cushions were plumped and vases filled with fresh flowers. I could imagine what it must take to keep a house this size so rigorously organised, even with a fleet of cleaners, and thought it wasn't too surprising if Edward seemed exhausted.

He showed me through to a large reception room with frescoed walls and then disappeared to get the coffee, returning with it arranged on a silver tray, with a plate of roughly shaped little biscuits shiny with white sugar fondant.

'I hear your friend skipped town,' he remarked conversationally, setting it down.

'Really?' It was disconcerting to think that people were talking about me.

'It might have been Renzo who mentioned it. Nothing much happens around here without him noticing.'

'Well, it's true. Tom has gone.'

'So how is the heartbreak now?' Edward asked sympathetically.

'I'm OK … it was me who ended things this time.'

'That's good then, it's progress, yes?' he said, pouring out two tiny cups of espresso, with the distracted air of a man who had too much going on in his own life to care very deeply about mine. 'I take it you're leaving now too. You want to check out?'

'Actually no, the plan is to stay for a while.'

The frosted biscuits were brittle and laced with aniseed. Nibbling on one, trying not to get crumbs everywhere, I told him about my new job and how I was hoping to keep the house longer term. As he listened, Edward's face clouded.

'Bad timing, I'm afraid. The mayor and his wife have decided to sell.'

'When did that happen?' My simple, jasmine-scented house was a part of what I loved about Montenello and I was flooded with disappointment.

'It's been in the works for a short while,' he said. 'They're cashing up so they can buy this place from me and Gino.'

'The palazzo – you're selling?' I was taken aback. 'But I thought this was your dream.'

'Yeah, it was.' Edward looked round the grand room with its crystal chandelier and plastered walls painted with Cupids. 'I love this house, but still I'm breaking up with it.'

Edward confided then, about the size of the debt crushing him and Gino, how they had borrowed all that money feeling bullish when business was going well, never fearing there might be a downturn.

'Even with the hotel busy again, we can't make up the lost ground. Gino knew it, that's why he went to Sydney where he can earn good money making furniture, more than we'll ever make here.'

'So you're leaving? Going home?'

'Actually no, the plan is to stay.'

A little of his weariness seemed to lift as he told me that, with the palazzo sold and their debt scaled down, Gino could afford to come back. There were a couple of rooms in the hotel for them to live in for now and, although it would be cramped, noisy at times, and not ideal, at least they would be together.

'I had it all wrong,' explained Edward. 'I assumed he was over there because he didn't want to be with me. You'd think after all this time we would know each other better.'

Fresh from getting everything wrong myself, I could see how these two men might have misunderstood each other. How Gino had assumed he was responsible for sorting the financial mess they were in, how Edward had felt rejected.

'Anyway it's all fine now,' said Edward. 'We had a big talk, sorted out a few things, and agreed to sell this place, it's the solution to everything.'

'And the mayor is going to buy it.'

'It was agreed with Salvio and his wife Elise this morning – great for me, but not so much for you, sorry. We'll find you something else though, I promise.'

'Couldn't I stay on until they're ready to put the house on the market?'

'I can ask.'

'It may take a while to sell,' I said hopefully.

'Possibly, but I wouldn't bank on that. It's fully renovated, after all.'

Absent-mindedly I bit into another biscuit, imagining what I might do to improve my little house if I owned it. Gauzier curtains over the windows so the view was never blocked completely, a wicker chair outside by the front door, maybe a fancier kitchen. It wouldn't take much for it to be perfect.

'What will you do with all your stuff?' I asked Edward, thinking how much furniture and art there was in just one room of this mansion.

'Some of it Salvio and his family will keep because it was designed for this house, a few special things will go into storage, the rest we'll sell. I've been making lists.'

'They must be long lists, you've got a lot of stuff.' I couldn't help thinking life might be nicer without so many objects that needed dusting.

'Too much,' Edward agreed.

'If I can help at all ...'

'That's an offer you might live to regret.'

'I'm good at organising things and packing,' I told him. 'I write a neat label.'

'I'll bear that in mind.'

I was aware that despite my best efforts, I was surrounded by a small hailstorm of biscuit crumbs. When Edward was busy pouring more coffee, I scuffed them with my foot in the hope he wouldn't notice what a mess I had made.

'Don't worry about it,' he said.

'Oh no, sorry.' I was mortified.

'Seriously, there have been hen parties in this room. People have trashed it.'

'But it's so pristine.'

'That's Gino, he trained me. I'm naturally untidy but he got me young and made a few improvements.'

'How do you think it'll be, living at the hotel together after being here?'

'We'll cope,' he said. 'We have to. It's only a house and I'd much rather lose it than lose him.'

I looked around the airy room and all his beautiful things, and was happy for Edward having someone in his life who was more important than any of it.

'You on the other hand do need a house,' he said.

'I do, I really do,' I agreed.

'So what exactly are you looking for?'

I was pretty clear about it. A nice place to live in for a while as I worked with Assunta, and learned to cook the way she did, not following rules and recipes, but using all my senses. I wanted a place that was fairly compact, light and bright, with good views and a spare bedroom so people could come and stay. It would be nice to have an outdoor space to grow a few pots of herbs, but not a huge garden to care for.

'To be within walking distance of the piazza, ideally somewhere furnished, and nothing too pricey.'

'Like the house you're in then,' said Edward.

'Exactly like that,' I agreed.

'Why not buy it?'

'I'm staying a few more months, not forever,' I pointed out.

'All I'm saying is, if you like it that much ...'

I had never envied Edward his palazzo, as impressive as it was. I was happy in a smaller space with only the essentials. And I did love my simple house. Saying goodbye to him and starting on the walk home, it struck me that owning it wasn't beyond the bounds of possibility. I still had savings and my mum would help; we could rent out my flat if we needed to, so there were ways to make it happen.

Instead of the shortcut, I took a longer route home, passing through the piazza, thinking I might stop in at the bar if anybody was around. It was that stage of the afternoon where many people were at home for a siesta but I noticed the English woman, the one with the stylishly cropped hair and fancy handbag. She was sitting alone, bent over a large sketchbook, and as we passed by, Baxter stopped and obstinately refused to walk on.

'Hello, you're very cute,' she said, stretching down to pat him. 'What breed are you?'

'He's a Border Terrier,' I told her.

'He's got such an expressive face. Do you have a moment?

'I'd love to make a quick sketch of him.'

'Sure,' I said.

'I'm an illustrator,' she explained, giving me a quick glimpse of the elaborate drawings covering the page. 'I'm working on some ideas for a children's picture book. And I love the way your dog looks, sort of rascally, like he'd enjoy an adventure.'

'He definitely would,' I agreed.

'I'm Mimi, by the way.' Turning to a fresh page, her pencil began flying.

'Sarah-Jane.'

'You're working next door at the *trattoria*,' she remarked, glancing at Baxter, then back at the sketchbook. 'That will be nice for Assunta.'

'And you live here, don't you?' I asked.

Baxter was sitting down, head tilted and ears pricked, almost as if he knew his likeness was being taken.

'I bought one of the original one-euro houses and renovated it,' Mimi told me as she continued sketching. 'Come and visit some time, if you want. I love showing it off.'

'That would be great.'

'To begin with there was a small group of us, just me, Edward and Gino, and Elise who bought the little place I believe you're renting. She's married to the mayor now,' Mimi explained helpfully.

'Yes, but they're selling that house I've been staying in,' I told her. 'Buying Edward's palazzo.'

'Really? You're up with play,' said Mimi, sounding impressed. 'When did this happen?'

'I think it was all signed today, meaning I'm homeless, unfortunately.'

'You could buy it, Elise's house I mean. It's very sweet.'

'I've been flirting with the idea.'

'Ah yes, that's how it starts,' she warned. 'With the flirting.'

Her drawing of Baxter captured him exactly, with his otter-shaped head, bushy beard and quizzical eyebrows. I liked it so much that she tore it from the notebook for me to keep. Renzo brought out coffee and I sat down to enjoy it, while Mimi continued sketching and chatting.

'It took me a while to come round to the idea of buying my place,' she admitted. 'It seemed such a risk, a crazy thing to do, and I suppose it was. But now I sit in the sunshine beside my swimming pool and my life in London seems ages ago.'

'You've got a pool.' I was envious.

'I've got pretty much everything I always wanted. I do miss my sons, but they're grown up with their own lives, and they visit, especially over summer.'

'Do you get back much? To London?'

'Not as often as I'd imagined I would. This feels more like home now.'

'I only ended up here because it's where my car broke down,' I said, looking at the Saab still parked very near to where it had happened.

'That must have been fate at work,' said Mimi, finishing her sketch then showing me another version of Baxter rendered in lines and shading.

We swapped phone numbers, and she urged me to pop in for a swim while the weather was still warm. As I left she was sketching again, absorbed in her work, as the afternoon sun slanted in, lighting her face.

I left my Saab where it was because there seemed no hurry to move it now, and wandered back to the house that could be my home, if I wanted. There were reasons not to buy it, sensible ones, but it wasn't too hard to discount them. I could rent out the place when I needed to. I could sell if I changed my mind. Rounding the corner and seeing it, just a squat stone building with jasmine hanging low over its doorway, not flashy or even very special, and certainly no space for a swimming pool, it seemed to be what I wanted.

As soon as I stepped through the front door, I called my mother. She was at home in her kitchen, concocting something to give her friends for dinner. She sounded excited and started running through the menu: a rice salad with a pesto she had made from nasturtium leaves foraged from the park, a nut roast that was looking a bit crumbly. And then she paused. 'Sorry darling, did you call for any particular reason?'

'Yes,' I told her. 'I think perhaps I did. What would you say if I told you I'm thinking of buying a house here?'

Assunta

The exhaustion was like nothing Assunta had known before, a deep-down bone weariness that slowed her steps as she walked home. Sitting heavily in her armchair and closing her eyes, she wondered if this was a migraine coming on or a sign of something more serious. There was no reason to be so tired; Sarah-Jane had done most of the work that day and would be there to help again tomorrow. But perhaps lightening the load had made it more obvious how much she had been carrying. As Assunta eased out of her shoes and put her feet up on the coffee table, all she knew for sure was that she didn't want to move.

She must have slept for a while because drifting back to consciousness, she noticed the sun had shifted and the light was softening. Assunta yawned and considered getting up. She did feel slightly better, the nap had been what was required, but she was glad there was no need to open the *trattoria* this evening.

The knock she heard at her door wasn't welcome, but Montenello was a place where you tended to open your door to neighbours so, spurred by habit, Assunta got to her feet and went to see who needed her.

Carlo was on her doorstep. She felt a girlish lurch of pleasure at the sight of him then steadied herself.

'I am disturbing you?' he asked.

'No, no,' said Assunta, ushering him in. 'I was sitting here doing nothing at all.'

'That sounds nice,' he said wistfully. 'I have been working

on plans for the *festa* all day; I could happily sit and do nothing for a while.'

'Then sit,' Assunta urged, nodding towards her armchair.

Carlo stayed standing, looking at her, as if he wanted something and didn't know how to say it.

'You have come to talk to me about the *festa*,' she guessed. 'I still haven't decided whether I will cook. Even with the English girl to help, it would be a lot of work.'

'That doesn't matter now. It is not why I came,' Carlo told her.

'Why then?' she asked a little gruffly.

'I wanted to see you, Assunta. Is that OK?'

The uncertainty in his tone surprised her. 'Yes, of course.'

'I was walking home then found myself coming here instead.'

Assunta stared into his face. She wasn't tired any longer. Her heart was beating faster, her nerves were singing and there was a feeling like electricity coursing through her.

'I like it when we are together,' Carlo said.

'I like it too.'

Afterwards, Assunta couldn't remember how their bodies had come together but the kiss felt natural, like something meant to happen. As the day dwindled to dusk, they didn't move from where they stood. Finally Assunta rested her head against his chest and he held on to her tightly.

'This is why I came,' he said, a smile in his voice.

'Better than talking about the *festa*?' she asked.

'Better than doing nothing at all?'

'Much better.'

Assunta moved from his arms and opened a bottle of wine, a good red that she had been saving. She couldn't imagine a better time than this to enjoy it. They went outside to her garden, Carlo put a rug on the ground and she brought food for them to eat if they grew hungry. Salty *taralli* biscuits, sharp caciocavallo cheese, salami spiced with wild fennel, all set out on a low table. They ate sparingly and sipped the wine, and as stars lit the sky, they lay on the rug together in a circle of citronella candles to keep the insects at bay.

'Imagine if people could see us now,' said Assunta. 'How they would talk.'

'Let them,' said Carlo, rolling to face her and resting a hand on her hip. 'We can do whatever we want and anything is possible.'

'Is it?' To Assunta this moment felt unreal.

'I think so. But we can take things slowly, if that is what you would prefer.'

'What do you prefer?' she asked, putting her hand over his, pressing it more firmly against her.

'I don't want us to be slow,' he said huskily.

'Me neither,' Assunta admitted. 'There seems no reason for it.'

She might have felt awkward, but the wine helped and so did the darkness, and soon Carlo made it easy for her to forget to be self-conscious. It was a hot night but even if her neighbours heard their cries through open windows, her garden walls were high and there was a leafy tree to shield them. Afterwards Assunta lay in the crook of Carlo's arm, until they had caught their breath and then both of them started laughing. The more they laughed, the funnier it seemed, and they held onto each other, rocked by the joy if it.

'I meant what I said,' Carlo told her, brushing the tears from her eyes and then his own. 'Anything is possible, we can have a new life together, go anywhere.'

Assunta had never wanted to travel far; she didn't even own a passport and those cities she had visited seemed a confusion of noise and traffic.

'Where would we go?' she wondered.

'What have you dreamed of?'

'This,' said Assunta, simply.

Carlo cupped her cheek in his hand. 'Me too,' he told her.

They lay there until the candles burned down and the mosquitoes nipped their ankles, driving them inside to Assunta's bed for a few more hours together. At dawn, Carlo slipped out from beneath the sheets and began to dress.

'I have to go home,' he said. 'I can't arrive at work in the same clothes I wore yesterday.'

Assunta watched him putting on his trousers and buttoning the shirt he picked up from the floor.

'I will see you for breakfast in the bar though? The usual time?' he asked.

She nodded. '*Va bene.*'

'And tonight, and tomorrow, and every day after?' he said, his voice soft.

'Yes,' agreed Assunta, and her eyelids closed, and she felt his lips on hers as he kissed her goodbye.

Afterwards she lay in bed a while longer and pressing her face into his pillow, breathed in the spiced scent of him. Assunta ought to have been tired because she had barely slept. But for once she felt as though she had the energy for anything life asked of her. She had never known a feeling quite like it.

Sarah-Jane

I learned to make the short, wide ribbons of pasta they called *lagane* served with crushed, dried Senise peppers, bread-crumbs and lots of grassy-green olive oil. Assunta showed me how to prepare baked pasta with calamari and almonds, the way her grandmother always had. Each mealtime, there was something new to know, a secret to improving a sauce, a flavour used in a way I had never considered. And perhaps because she had a helper at last, someone to rely on, Assunta seemed to change day by day; she smiled more, hummed a song as she worked, and when we went next door to the bar, she didn't doze in her chair, but joined the conversation.

'The *festa*,' she said, one afternoon as we sat and drank a coffee with Augusto and his friend Francesco. 'It will be so much work, such a commitment, I cannot decide if it is possible.'

She had already told me about the proposal for her to cook the feast that was planned, and I knew she was reluctant.

'Edward might be interested in the hotel doing the cater-ing,' I suggested. 'Or there is the mayor's mother, Donna Carmela – perhaps she would be willing to take on the job.'

It was Francesco who replied and, because he rarely said anything, we all stopped to listen.

'*Stranieri*.' He made a tutting noise. 'No.'

'Donna Carmela isn't foreign,' Assunta told him. 'She comes from Puglia, she was born there.'

The old man pinched his fingers and thumb together, shaking his hand at her dismissively.

'Well, it is true.' She brushed off his gesture with a shrug.

'This is the first *festa* in Montenello for more than twenty years,' Augusto pointed out. 'My old friend is right – we should not ask outsiders to cook for us.'

'So what do you want me to do?' asked Assunta, sounding exasperated.

'Little paper cones filled with fried seafood; squid and prawns; octopus tentacles,' said Augusto promptly. 'Crisp strips of zucchini, maybe a few arancini.'

'*Una pasta*,' put in Francesco.

'A baked pasta ... cannelloni?'

'No, no.'

'The one with the sauce of walnuts and anchovies then,' said Augusto.

'Anything else?' asked Assunta tartly.

'Porchetta or lamb, whichever you think best.'

'And how am I supposed to prepare enough of this for the whole town?' Assunta demanded.

Everyone turned and stared in my direction.

'I'm not leaving before the *festa*,' I promised. 'I can help you, definitely.'

What I didn't mention was that, with my mum's help, I had made an offer on my little house. It was considerably more than one euro and we weren't sure it would be enough, but while we waited to find out, I wasn't going anywhere.

'I really want to see the procession and the firework display,' I told them. 'But otherwise I'm happy to be helping in the kitchen.'

'And I will be there to help you too, *cara*,' Augusto promised her.

'Wonderful, all my problems are solved,' Assunta said dryly.

I was almost certain she wouldn't be able to resist feeding the whole town. Assunta was never going to stand by and watch the hotel's chef do the work or allow Donna Carmela to take over.

273

'There will be plenty more people willing to help,' I told Assunta.

'Such as?' she wondered.

'We could ask Riccardo,' I suggested, because I couldn't think of anyone else I knew well enough to volunteer and surely he would be willing to dice vegetables, stir sauces and take dishes to the trestle tables they were going to lay out end to end in the piazza.

All the details of the *festa* were supposed to be a secret but inevitably they had leaked out. There was to be a concert in the piazza, with bands playing local music. In the Town Hall they were lining the walls of the reception rooms with a photographic exhibition about Montenello's history. The big event was a procession with a statue of the town's patron saint carried through the streets, and a special Mass. And after the feast on the final night, fireworks were to be set off at midnight.

The whole town was buzzing, people were swapping nuggets of information everywhere I went, especially the elderly ones, because they had memories of the festivals held here in the past, and no one ever imagined another one would happen.

'If the mayor comes and asks me himself then we will do it,' decided Assunta. 'This is his *festa*, he is getting all the glory so he can make some of the effort.'

'If I tell Salvio, he will come,' promised Augusto.

'And I will make a baked pasta, not the one with the sauce of anchovies and walnuts,' she added stubbornly.

'Of course, of course,' agreed her father.

I had stopped keeping notes for every dish that Assunta showed me how to cook, because I never referred to them. I learned by watching and doing, and then trusted myself to balance flavours and bring ingredients together without a set of instructions.

When I wasn't working, I liked being home, just me and Baxter, enjoying the peace of my house and the view from its windows, making the most of it all. I tended to fritter away time on social media, seeing what my friends were up to, or checking the *Daily Post* website for news. And that was what I was doing when the headline grabbed my attention: *CELEB CHEF'S AMAZING NEW LIFE – TOM WHIFFEN IS BACK.*

I tried not to click but couldn't help myself and there it was, the plan Tom had come up with for him and me. The rural retreat, the organic vegetable gardens, the cook school, the restaurant championing local produce, the scheme to foster talented young chefs. As far as I could tell, he didn't have a location yet, but Tom had a talent for making things sound good, and this sounded amazing.

In the photograph he was with Jo and holding his baby. Both of them wore beaming smiles so I assumed that must mean they were back together, or had never broken up properly in the first place – not that it mattered much now, either way. 'I'm doing this for my family,' he told the reporter. 'This is a fresh start and we couldn't be happier than we are working together towards a better future.'

I stopped reading, closed my laptop, and tried to decide how I felt. It would have been fair to hate Tom, but I didn't, not completely. There was only a sense of relief that it wasn't me in the photo beside him. I didn't envy Jo and if the *Daily Post* was going to keep writing about them then I would have to switch to a different news website, because from now on I didn't want to know what they were up to.

If anything I felt lighter after reading that article, freer too. I patted Baxter as I went to put the kettle on for a celebratory cup of tea. I was pretty sure he wasn't missing Tom much either.

The next day the mayor came and formally requested Assunta's services for the *festa* and after that everything went crazy. She was transformed from a woman who seemed to take each day as it came to a demon planner. Soon there were lots of lists pinned up in the kitchen, ingredients and costings, a day-by-day countdown of the necessary preparations, lists of people who we were going to ask to help and exactly what they would do.

'You will speak to Riccardo, yes?' Assunta reminded me.

It had been a few days since he had been in for lunch and I missed seeing his face. Assuming he was busy fixing cars in his workshop, I wandered that way after we had finished work. But the doors of his garage were closed and the scrawled note stuck up on them only said the word '*Chiuso*'.

'Closed,' I said to Baxter. 'I wonder why.'

The dog twitched his eyebrows at me, then whimpered and scratched at the door.

'He's not here, but maybe you're right, we should walk back to his father's place and see if he's there.'

There was a hint of autumnal coolness in the air and Baxter trotted beside me as we headed back up the sloping street. When I got no response to my knock on Riccardo's door, I tried his phone but he didn't answer. So Baxter and I kept walking further into the labyrinth of narrow lanes and steep stone steps towards the house Riccardo had bought for one euro.

As we drew closer, I heard the scream of an electric drill and the sound of hammering. The front door lay open and there was that metallic dusty smell peculiar to building sites as I stepped through into the hallway.

'Hello?' I called.

It was clear he had been busy. An archway had been knocked out from the wall that divided the living and dining areas, and carefully I edged past the rubble.

'Hello? Riccardo?' I cried, more loudly.

The power tool stopped screaming and I heard his voice calling back to me. 'Who is there?'

He was working out on the terrace, wearing a mask and goggles, stripped down to his singlet, dusty and sweaty.

'Sarah-Jane.' He sounded pleased to see me. 'Be careful there.'

'Sorry to disturb you,' I apologised. 'Assunta sent me over to see if we could count on your help for the *festa* but it seems like you're busy.'

He looked around as though taking in the scene for the first time – the piles of timber, the rubble of old stones, a lot of dirt and a litter of tools. 'It is a bit of a mess,' he agreed. 'But things aren't as bad as they look. I can help you.'

'You're sure? She has you down for kitchen prep and wait staff.'

'I won't argue with Assunta,' he said with a smile.

Riccardo talked me through what he was doing with his house. He planned to open things up so it flowed out to the terrace, put in a new kitchen and an en-suite with a clawfoot bath, to expose the stone walls in the living room and re-tile the floors.

'You're brave,' I told him. 'I'd never tackle anything this big.'

'Brave or crazy, I am not sure, but I hope it will be worth it in the end. I don't have any particular deadline; I will work on the place whenever I find time and Papa will help out sometimes on weekends.'

'You'll get there,' I told him. 'And it's going to be beautiful.'

'Right now I am focusing on making the terrace safe because on Saturday I would like to have a celebration, just some drinks for a few friends. I hope you will come.'

'Saturday? Do you think you'll be ready for a party by then?' It seemed unlikely.

'Not a party, only a glass or two of Prosecco to toast the

future, so don't dress up,' he warned. 'Wear something you are happy to get a little dusty. And bring Baxter, obviously.'

I almost told him about my offer to buy the jasmine cottage. But I wanted to wait until I knew for sure that it was mine and, as everyone kept telling me, in southern Italy these things could take time.

'By the way is there something wrong with your car?' Riccardo asked, as he ushered me back through the debris to the front door. 'Only I see you have left it in the piazza.'

My Saab had been abandoned in the same spot for well over a week now. I kept thinking I should move it but there didn't seem much point. The *trattoria* supplied me with the food I needed, coffee was drunk at the bar, and the butcher's boy gave me offcuts for Baxter. It was easier to walk everywhere than deal with narrow streets and a lack of parking space.

'No, it's fine, I just haven't been anywhere,' I told Riccardo.

'An old car like that, it is better to take it for a run from time to time.'

'Do you think so? OK, I'll go for a drive.'

'Are you busy this evening? We could head into Borgo del Colle and eat a pizza,' he suggested. 'It would give you a reason to drive it.'

'That would be great,' I agreed, because who doesn't love pizza?

'*Va bene*, let's make it a little later though, as I have to finish here. See you in the piazza at eight?'

'See you then,' I agreed.

I heard the whine of the drill starting up as I walked away down the hill, tugging along Baxter who didn't seem to want to leave. I was looking forward to it already, the drive to Borgo del Colle with the roof down, a wood-fired pizza in some little local place, a glass of Aglianico wine. And I was looking forward to being with Riccardo as well, to hanging out with him; I couldn't think of any other way I'd rather spend the evening. The realisation was unexpected. It took me by surprise.

Assunta

Assunta's days began with Carlo's kiss as he left her bed. A little later they would meet for coffee and brioche in the bar, and hold the secret of that kiss between them. In a town where people knew everything about her, Assunta liked that nobody knew this one thing. Her brother Renzo might have guessed it. He had given them a long, steady look that morning, his eyebrows arched, but Assunta had only smiled and he hadn't said a thing.

'I want everyone to know about us. I will shout it from the rooftops,' Carlo kept insisting.

Assunta dreaded other people getting hold of this and making what was beautiful seem ugly. She preferred not to be talked about in corners of the piazza.

'Exactly which rooftop do you think you are going to climb, old friend?' she asked him.

'I can get up to the top of the tower and shout from there,' he pointed out.

'OK, but not yet.'

It was two years since Maria had passed, although she had been caught up in the long, slow, messy business of her dying for a long time before that. Aside from the town's gossips, there were her children to consider, Riccardo and the two girls. For now, Assunta thought it better to have her life with Carlo when other people weren't looking.

'You are a widower and it is too soon,' she reminded him.

'People will notice before long. We will give ourselves away,' he had warned.

But Assunta knew it was possible to have secrets, even

here in this small town. Her mother had managed it, after all.

She and Carlo took every opportunity to see each other, if only for a look or smile exchanged across the crowded dining room of her *trattoria*. The nights were for them alone, and Assunta could hardly wait for darkness to fall and the sound of the key she had given him being turned in her front door. If she was already in bed, he would climb in beside her. Other times she was waiting on the other side of the door, ready for his kisses.

In the morning, over coffee and pastries, both of them remembered but tried not to let it show in their faces. They sat at the counter, a respectable distance apart, and talked with Renzo about other things.

Preparing for the *festa* was the concern of the moment, for everyone in town but especially Assunta. She had never cooked on such a scale before and kept making lists as if they were the answer, but in truth she was worried. The food was the most important part of this celebration; good or bad, it would be what everyone remembered.

'You should come over and see the photographic exhibition we are installing in the Town Hall,' Carlo said as they finished their breakfast. 'Most of it is up now.'

'I don't have time.' Assunta needed to talk to the butcher about the meat he would supply. Porchetta or lamb, she still hadn't decided.

From his place behind the bar, Renzo spoke up. 'I would like to take a look.'

'Sure, come over any time,' Carlo told him. 'It will be interesting to know if there are faces you recognise.'

With a nod, Renzo moved away to serve another customer. Carlo and Assunta held each other's gaze for a few moments more and then he picked up his jacket.

'I must get to work.'

'Will I see you at lunchtime?'

Carlo shook his head. 'There is a meeting and they are bringing in food from the hotel, so I won't be able to get away.'

'Later then,' she said softly.

'Later,' he agreed.

Assunta remained at the bar after he had gone, thinking how much there was to do before she saw him again. Only a stretch of piazza separated her from Carlo's office in the Town Hall but they might have been miles apart and the days were long. Later they would make up for it though. Gazing out of the window towards the grand old building, flags fluttering in the warm breeze, Assunta held on to that thought.

Soon she saw Sarah-Jane crossing the piazza, wearing her bright yellow sundress, dark hair caught up in a top-knot. She was on time, as always, and heading towards the bar for her coffee before they started work.

'*Buongiorno*,' she called coming in, the dog at her heels.

Glancing towards her, Renzo began to froth the milk for a *caffe con latte*, and Sarah-Jane took the stool that Carlo had just vacated.

'Good news,' she announced. 'I have a helper lined up for the *festa*. Riccardo is happy to do whatever we ask of him. So with the staff from the hotel, that's plenty of people, isn't it?'

'I hope so,' agreed Assunta, wishing she could shift the feeling that whatever she cooked for this *festa* might not be good enough.

'Porchetta or lamb?' Sarah-Jane was asking. 'Riccardo reckons lamb, slow-cooked, with a sauce of anchovies. And what about hiring a wood-fired oven, and doing the vegetables on it as well as lots of little flatbreads? Shall I look into it?'

'Why not,' said Assunta, because the plans were getting bigger and bolder whether she liked it or not, and besides, it was a good idea.

'We ate pizza last night at a place in Borgo del Colle,' Sarah-Jane continued. 'There's something about scorched bread isn't there, all smoky and hot, a bit oily. It'll be great with the lamb and the vegetables. Riccardo thought so too.'

'You ate a pizza with Riccardo?'

'My car needed a run, so it seemed like a good idea.'

'Ah yes, and it was good, this pizza?'

'It was fine.'

'He is a great guy,' ventured Assunta.

Sarah-Jane drank an inch of her milky coffee then covered the cup with a lid she had fashioned from a serviette, and took it next door to sip on as she began the preparations for lunch. Assunta couldn't understand this habit of carrying a drink from place to place, even when there was time to sit down and finish it. But the girl did the same thing every morning.

She was a good worker and too talented to be slicing onions in a small *trattoria* that didn't even have a name. Assunta knew she would want more from life than this. She was here only for a while, recovering from whatever disappointment she had suffered, then she would be on her way.

They cooked together without needing to speak much. Today they made a first course of pasta stuffed with ricotta and summer herbs from her own garden, and a second dish of salt cod baked in tomatoes and onions, as outside the sun brightened the morning and the piazza filled with people.

'Today's bride is older,' Sarah-Jane remarked, as she laid out baskets of bread on the tables.

Assunta looked up, and saw the bride was about her age.

'She looks happy,' said Sarah-Jane.

Lit by sunlight, the bride in her long cream jacket and matching high-necked dress tossed her bouquet high into the air. There was the sound of squealing as several women scrambled to catch it and a cheer as the winner held the flowers aloft.

'Have you ever caught a bouquet?' asked Sarah-Jane, still watching.

Assunta shrugged and shook her head.

'Me neither.'

Assunta had no need for white roses or a cream satin dress. She didn't want people gathered round and a photographer capturing the moment so she could keep it in a frame for ever. Those things didn't matter now.

Looking up at the blank windows of the Town Hall, she knew exactly which one Carlo would be sitting behind. She thought perhaps she had always known.

Sarah-Jane

The thing I like most about parties is getting the invitation. When the evening arrives, more often than not I find myself in the mood to stay home. My mum always encouraged me out. She would help me choose a dress to wear and insist I was going to have a great time, then pretty much push me through the front door. At most parties I ended up busying myself heating sausage rolls to pass round on platters or slathering French bread with garlic butter. The kitchen was the one place where I knew exactly who to be and how I was meant to behave.

'But you'll have a great time,' Mum said, predictably enough, when she heard that I wasn't sure about going to Riccardo's party.

'It's only drinks and the house is pretty much a building site,' I said dismissively.

'Even so, you don't know who you'll meet there.'

'I won't know any of his friends,' I pointed out. 'And you remember what it's like when you're the one throwing the party – Riccardo will be too busy to have time to talk to me.'

'You need to make an effort to mix with people,' my mother insisted.

'I mix with lots of people, at the *trattoria* and in the bar.'

'You're too old to be shy, Sarah-Jane,' she continued, ignoring me.

'I'm not shy, I'm a sociable loner.'

'Put on something nice and go, just for one drink, OK?'

Mum made me FaceTime with her through my wardrobe

and she picked out a cornflower blue ruffle dress that I thought was too much.

'Wear it with your Converse and a denim jacket,' she advised.

'Maybe,' I said.

'And brush your hair, darling,' she urged, before we ended the call.

I left my hair the way it was, caught up in a cloud on top of my head, with messy tendrils hanging down. But I put on the dress, like Mum told me, and emptied most of the contents of my fridge onto a platter that I put on the passenger seat of my car, thinking I might as well drive up to Riccardo's house as I was only staying for one drink, after all.

Day was turning to dusk by the time I arrived and the whole place was lit with fairy lights. Holding the platter defensively in front of me, with Baxter at my heels, I made my way inside. Riccardo had done an impressive job of tidying up. All the rubble had been swept away, there were more fairy lights and lanterns strung up, and a crowd of people was spilling out onto the terrace. I heard Italian pop music playing loudly and in one corner of the room saw Augusto, hovering over two turntables and a stack of records.

'Are you the DJ for the evening?' I had to shout to be heard.

'Of course, of course,' he replied happily. 'You have a request? I have Bee Gees, Elton John, Talking Heads; tell me what you like and I will play it.'

Looking round the room, there were more faces that I recognised. Carlo was out on the terrace with Assunta, and I saw Edward talking to Renzo.

And then there was Riccardo. He had his back to me and was wearing dark jeans and a fitted black shirt with the sleeves rolled up. The woman he was chatting to looked over in my direction and he turned, smiling as he saw me.

'Sarah-Jane, I thought you weren't coming.' He came to

take the platter from me, setting it on a small trestle table. 'You didn't have to bring food, but thanks – this looks great.'

There was no kitchen here for me to hide in, it had been demolished, and the hum of conversation around me was all in Italian. One drink, like I had promised Mum, and after that I would be leaving.

'Come and meet some people.' Taking my arm, Riccardo led me out onto the terrace. 'And you need a cocktail.'

Someone put a margarita in my hand, the Italian version with a sweet kick of amaretto. Riccardo introduced me to a girl he knew from school, and a guy he had grown up with, and we said hello to his new friend from the bar in Borgo del Colle and a couple of other guys. I gulped my drink and when it was topped up again from the cocktail shaker, didn't say no.

'Have you met the mayor, Salvio, and his wife, Elise yet?' Riccardo asked. 'No? But she is English too.'

The mayor was often to be seen out and about, having lunch at the *trattoria* or holding meetings in the bar. Now he was with a heavily pregnant woman who I also recognised because she tended to be on the fringes of the bridal parties while they were being photographed in the piazza.

'Elise is the wedding planner, right?' I asked.

'Yes, she is great, you will like her.'

They were a perfect-looking pair, him dark and her very fair, and both quite gorgeous, one of those couples that seem better lit than other people. There was a cluster of friends around them, and I might have held back, but Riccardo tugged me forward and made the introductions.

'Sarah-Jane is staying in your house,' he explained to the mayor's wife. 'She has found herself spending the summer there.'

'Oh, you're the one.' Elise seemed more interested, suddenly. 'And you want to buy it, you've made an offer?'

'You have?' Riccardo turned to me, in surprise.

'I really love it,' I told them. 'It's special.'

'Isn't it,' Elise said warmly. 'I'd rather not sell, but Salvio wants a proper mayor's residence, and our family is growing so we could do with more space.'

'You are trying to buy the house?' Riccardo said to me, sounding a bit bewildered.

'I'd like to have a place here,' I explained. 'But my offer hasn't been accepted yet.'

Elise was quick to apologise. 'We're supposed to be waiting to see if we get a better deal, but really what are the chances?'

'Have there been any other offers at all?' I wondered.

'So far, yours is the only proposal of purchase we've had,' she admitted. 'Can I ask if you're planning to use it as a holiday rental or do you actually want to live there?'

'The idea is to live in it, at least for now.'

Riccardo was staring at me. 'You are planning to stay here? In Montenello?'

'Well, I do seem to have a job ...'

'And friends?' wondered Elise. 'Or do you have family here?'

'My dad's family were Italian, way back, generations ago,' I explained. 'I always imagined finding the town they came from and somehow feeling at home there.'

'This is the town?' guessed Elise.

'No, I'm pretty sure it isn't. But I do feel at home; I'm starting to anyway.'

Riccardo turned to Elise. 'You should sell Sarah-Jane your house,' he urged. 'It is perfect for her.'

'I'll see what I can do to speed things up,' Elise promised.

'You're definitely staying?' Riccardo double-checked with me.

'I want to,' I confirmed.

'That is great news.' He turned to Elise again, grinning at her, his turquoise eyes sparkling. 'It is fantastic, isn't it?'

'I guess it is,' she replied, sounding amused for some reason.

'We need more drinks; we are celebrating,' declared Riccardo, heading off in search of the cocktail shaker, leaving me standing beside Elise who watched him go, smiled fondly, then said, 'He's such a great guy, isn't he.'

'So everyone keeps telling me.'

'As long as you know.' Elise leaned into her good-looking husband, who wound an arm round her waist and rested it on her baby bump. 'It would be a real shame not to notice.'

That was one party I did enjoy and it wasn't only the tequila, although I'm pretty sure that helped. Augusto cranked up the music and everyone started dancing, even Assunta with Carlo, doing some sort of old-style jive. There was pizza delivered from the hotel, a long metal tray of it, layered with torn basil and melted mozzarella. We drank some more, then Riccardo and I started dancing and, as the crowd began to thin, we were still there, taking over the terrace, dancing together until we were breathless.

When everyone else had left, Riccardo rifled through his vinyl collection to put on something more soulful. He filled our glasses with sparkling water and fetched the last of the pizza, and we sat out on the terrace feeding bits of it to Baxter.

'It's late, I should go,' I told him, although I didn't really want to.

'But this is the best part of the evening, when everyone has had a good time and we can just relax. Stay a little longer.'

We talked for a while about the people I had met and he shared snippets of local knowledge. The mayor's wife was having twins. All the one-euro houses had sold. Riccardo's business was picking up.

'And I thought Montenello was a place where nothing ever happens.'

'I haven't mentioned the most interesting news yet,' he told me, hesitating for a moment before adding. 'It is about my father. I believe he is having a secret love affair.'

'Really?' I was surprised and intrigued. 'What makes you think that?'

'He has been leaving at night and coming home when it is nearly morning – he thinks I don't hear him, but the stairs creak and the doors are too heavy to close quietly.'

'He hasn't said anything?'

'Not yet, but I keep waiting.' Riccardo lifted Baxter onto his knee. 'Perhaps he likes to have a secret.'

'It's far more likely that he's worried you'll be upset, because of your mother,' I pointed out.

Riccardo stroked Baxter's head absent-mindedly. 'If you had asked me a year ago what I thought about my father being with another woman, I might have been a little upset. But now, if it is the right person, then I wouldn't be unhappy.'

'Do you have any idea who she is, this woman?'

'Only a suspicion,' he told me, 'I think it may be Assunta. Did you see the pair of them tonight doing that old-style dancing?'

At first it seemed unlikely, but then I considered how the two of them were often together. Carlo ate lunch at the *trattoria* almost every day. In the mornings it wasn't unusual to come across them having breakfast at the bar. This evening they had mostly danced with each other. And it started to seem like a possibility.

'Assunta,' I repeated, finding the idea really quite romantic. 'If that's the case then she knows how to keep things to herself. Will you say anything?'

'I am not sure how to.' Riccardo ruffled Baxter's ears then set him down on the ground again.

'I wouldn't be either. I don't know what I'd do if I found out my mum was seeing someone,' I admitted.

'She never has?'

I shook my head. 'My father was the love of her life. There was never anyone for her but him.'

Riccardo looked troubled. 'He has been gone a long time, your papa?'

'Yes, but Mum's happy on her own, she doesn't need a man, doesn't want one.' Saying it, I realised that I hadn't ever asked her; it wasn't a subject we talked about.

Busy pouring more water into our glasses, Riccardo said nothing.

'She still loves my father,' I told him.

He nodded in apparent agreement.

'We're close,' I added, in case he wasn't completely convinced. 'We tell each other everything.'

'She is your mother, you know her best,' he said carefully. 'But there is more than one person for all of us, Sarah-Jane.'

'If you want it, then yes I suppose there is,' I replied.

He was looking at me with a serious expression and I had the distinct sense we weren't talking about my mother anymore.

'I am happy that you are staying in Montenello,' he said, very softly.

'I might not get the house,' I reminded him.

'You will get it. I have a good feeling. I hope you do, anyway.'

I had drunk too much tequila to drive home and so left the car outside Riccardo's place and he walked with Baxter and me through the quiet streets. The town looked beautiful this evening. There was a full moon making the light silvery and the stone of the old buildings gleamed.

We were still a way from home when Baxter started falling behind, walking slower and slower, until I was half dragging him along with the leash.

'Is he OK?' Riccardo sounded concerned.

'Just lazy, I think. He gets like this sometimes when he thinks we've done enough walking.'

'He seems tired,' decided Riccardo. 'I think it is best if I carry him.'

Reaching down, he scooped Baxter up into his arms. The dog gave a happy sigh and, as we walked on side by side, rested his head on one of Riccardo's shoulders.

'I hope he's not smelly,' I worried.

Riccardo sniffed his fur, shrugged and kept walking with the dog in his arms all the way to my jasmine-covered doorway. The white blossoms had dropped in the dry heat of summer but with any luck I would still be here next spring, when flowers scented the air again.

'Goodnight then,' I said, reaching for Baxter who seemed to have fallen asleep.

There was a moment while Riccardo was passing him over, when our bodies met, and my skin tingled where we touched, arms, hands, shoulder, a series of tiny static shocks that took me by surprise and left me shivery. If he hadn't been holding onto Baxter so firmly, I might have dropped him.

'You will call tomorrow? Let me know how he is?' Riccardo asked, once the dog was safely in my grasp.

'OK,' I said, my heart thudding.

It was late and I had drunk all those cocktails; that was the only explanation. Even so, putting Baxter on my bed and climbing in beside him, it stayed in my mind, that strange fizzy feeling, I kept getting little flashes of it, as I lay there not quite falling asleep, trying to remember if I had ever felt anything like it before and deciding, just as I was drifting off, that no, I definitely hadn't.

Assunta

Assunta felt as though her life had been unmoored. They were still there, all the familiar landmarks, but she was seeing them from a different place. Day after day she walked to the piazza, sat in the bar, worked in the *trattoria*, just as she had year after year. Nothing seemed quite the same.

'You have given up smoking,' Renzo observed, removing her unused ashtray from the counter of the bar.

'It was a bad habit. I think I only began because Mamma always smoked and I was trying to be more like her.'

'You didn't look alike,' observed Renzo.

'I wished I did, but no.'

'I think you look like your father.'

'You know something?' She had given him the framed staff list from the hotel and since then Renzo had said nothing about it.

'I may have found a clue.'

'Where? Show me.'

'You will have to wait until the Town Hall opens. It is in the exhibition they are putting up.'

'A photograph?'

Renzo nodded.

'We will go as soon as they open, then.'

Carlo had already left for work, but he had taken the back entrance, the one all the staff used, and the Town Hall's heavy wooden doors wouldn't be unlocked for another hour. The time passed slowly for Assunta, impatient to see the photograph, to find whatever Renzo had noticed. At work, starting the preparations for lunch, she kept hoping it would tell her something.

The moment she saw her brother hovering in the doorway, she removed her apron and flung it towards the hook on the wall. 'I am going out for a while,' she told Sarah-Jane. 'You will be OK?'

'Sure.' The girl sounded surprised, and Assunta sensed her eyes following them as they walked across the piazza together.

The exhibition was in the entrance foyer. Several stands had been set up to display photographs and there were other items too: a blue flag showing the coat of arms of Basilicata, with its distinctive blue waves; a memorial of the earthquake that had damaged much of the region; some fragments of ancient pottery.

Renzo led her to one of the stands and in the centre there it was, a black-and-white photograph of all the staff, standing outside the hotel, among them her mother, smiling.

'She looks so young and pretty,' said Assunta, gazing at it. 'Like she has no troubles at all.'

'No troubles, but perhaps a secret, even then,' said Renzo, and he lifted a finger to point at the man beside her. He was heavy-set, with a broad nose and a square jaw, features that Assunta shared.

'There is a resemblance,' she conceded, finding more similarities as she spoke, the shape of his eyes, the fullness of his cheeks, even his hairline. 'He looks like me.'

'You look like him,' Renzo agreed.

There were five people in the photograph, two women and three men. Each was spaced apart quite evenly, except her mother and this stranger who were close, hip-to-hip, almost touching, their hands held behind them.

'Who is he?' she wondered. 'Have you managed to find out anything?'

'What I know is that he managed the hotel. But he went away years ago.'

Assunta stared at the man whose features she shared. 'Where did he go?'

'To London, with his wife and children.'

'He was married?'

'Yes.'

'You think my mother loved him, had an affair, and then when she fell pregnant—'

'He didn't stand by her,' finished Renzo, softly. 'Instead Augusto did.'

'How do you know so much? Are there records?'

'I recognised his name. Fabbio Galeazzi, he was my mother's cousin.'

'You remember him?'

'Not very well, he must have left town when I was small. But I looked in Mamma's old album and found some photographs of him there.'

'He is still alive?'

'I am not sure and can't ask Mamma.' Renzo's mother was in a care home in Borgo del Colle, and she remembered nothing of the life she'd had, didn't even recognise her son. 'I suppose Augusto might be able to tell us. They must have known each other.'

'Could I see the other photographs, the ones in your mother's album?'

'Yes, I will get them for you.'

Assunta wanted to examine this face from other angles and in different lights, to be sure the resemblance was as strong as it seemed. Staring at the stranger now, it felt quite possible – this was the man whose blood she shared.

'If Fabbio Galeazzi is my father and he was related to your mother, that means we share blood, you and I,' she said, turning to Renzo. 'We are still family.'

'Of course,' he said, matter-of-factly. 'We have always been family.'

*

As they left the Town Hall, a wedding party was gathering on the steps. An older woman fussing with her hat, a little boy uncomfortable in his suit, girls in pretty dresses holding posies. The mayor's wife was there too; so pregnant the seams of her maternity dress were beginning to stretch. She was calming a groom, nervously waiting for his bride.

Had her mother hoped for this? Had she believed herself caught in a love story? Whatever promises were made, whatever dreams she might have had, a man had let her down. She was always a sweet-sour woman, *agrodolce*, and now Assunta understood how disappointment must have settled on her, when life hadn't turned out how she expected.

'The photo album is with my mother,' Renzo said as they parted. 'I will close the bar later and go to visit her.'

'I can look after the place for you,' Assunta reminded him, 'now that I have a helper.'

'And you will talk to Augusto?'

'Maybe.'

'You could write to that American woman again,' her brother suggested. 'Tell her what we have learned, see if she confirms it.'

'Maybe,' Assunta repeated.

'I won't forget to fetch the album for you,' he promised.

Through the open doorway of the *trattoria* there came the reassuring waft of food being cooked, onions sizzling in oil, pumpkin roasting sweetly. Sarah-Jane smiled more broadly than usual as she came in.

'Something has happened?' Assunta guessed.

'Yes, I've got good news,' she replied. 'My offer on the house has been accepted.'

'So you are staying? And you will continue to work here?'

'If you want me to – the news wouldn't be so good if you didn't.'

'This job is yours as long as you want it.'

Already they cooked so well together that the kitchen felt

as peaceful as when Assunta had managed alone. This morning, though, the girl's news had made her talkative, and she was listing all the things she needed to do: register her residency at the Town Hall, talk to the notary about proceeding with the contract, deal with the tax office.

'It sounds complicated,' said Assunta, relieved that all her places in the world had been decided for her.

'It will be worth it,' Sarah-Jane replied, then began speaking of what she planned to do: install a smarter kitchen, put fresh paint on the walls, buy outdoor furniture.

Assunta looked round at her *trattoria* and tried to see it through her younger eyes. Did the walls seem shabby and in need of painting, were the plates that hung on them old-fashioned and the tablecloths too bright?

'Perhaps it is time to make some improvements here,' she said.

'Don't do anything.' Sarah-Jane sounded horrified. 'It's perfect as it is.'

'Augusto thinks we should have music.'

'No, definitely not.'

'I like it this way too,' Assunta agreed. 'But you must tell me if you think it is necessary to change something. Things can't always stay the same.'

Among the people who drifted in for lunch that afternoon were Carlo and Riccardo. They came in almost every day now, and were in the habit of taking a table near the window. Seeing them together, it struck Assunta that the son was the image of his father. There was hardly any of Maria in him. He reminded her so much of Carlo at that age.

Carlo had been the only boy she ever noticed. All those years she had watched him with Maria, as each of their children was born and grew, as they got old together; all those years and she had kept how she felt sealed up inside her. He belonged to another woman; he was happy with her.

Now Maria was gone, although at times Assunta still expected to see her, coming into the *trattoria* a step ahead of her husband, her face hollowed by illness, skin yellowing, wearing the bright scarf that hid what had happened to her hair. For so many years his wife had fought to stay at Carlo's side. Had she accepted that some day he would find a future without her? Had she wanted him to be happy again with another woman? Assunta would never know for sure, but she didn't think so. It was what worried her when she woke in the night and lay listening to Carlo breathing beside her. It unsettled her in the quiet and empty moments.

Trying to bury that feeling now, she carried over a basket of bread and a carafe of wine.

'Today we have a pasta with pumpkin and pancetta,' she told them.

'My favourite,' said Carlo.

'Mine too,' agreed Riccardo.

It was possible to take after one parent and not look like the other; Assunta had the proof of that before her eyes right now. And soon she would have more photographs to show that she took after a stranger, a man with a solid body, full cheeks and muddy brown hair, a man who had belonged to someone else and broken her mother's heart. The sadness that swept over Assunta was unexpected. She was rocked by it as she turned to fetch the bowls of pasta and it still weighed heavily on her as she watched father and son eating, an empty chair beside them where Maria might have been.

Sarah-Jane

I kept thinking about Riccardo. Even while I was trying to focus on more sensible things like the house purchase and all the formalities that needed to be completed, he occupied my mind. His smile and the way it made the turquoise of his eyes sparkle. There was something so solid about him; he could fix things (although admittedly not very fast), he was reassuringly practical, a man who got his hands dirty. Most of all I thought about that sensation when our bodies connected, the tequila-fuelled surge I still couldn't make sense of. Had Riccardo felt it too?

Seeing him the next day in the trattoria, everything seemed as usual. Riccardo was with his father, I was cooking pasta, and as we exchanged a few words about Baxter (who thankfully was his normal perky self again), that moment on my doorstep might have been imagined, except I knew it was real, I had felt it.

Now a morning later, sitting up in bed drinking coffee, I was still thinking about him, idly, pleasantly, knowing I should get up and ready for work, but not in any real hurry, just sitting there happy.

When my phone started ringing, I saw it was my mum so reached for it and answered, saying '*Buongiorno*' in what I thought was a convincing Italian accent.

'Are you looking at the *Daily Post*?' she asked straight away.

'No, I've stopped reading that,' I told her. 'I don't want to know another thing about Tom.'

'Oh, I think you'll want to see this.'

'Is it about him?'

'Yes, and I shouldn't gloat but …'

She made me stay on the line while I grabbed my laptop and found the news report among the column of 'Don't Miss' celebrity items.

MADE WITH LOVE CHEAT BETRAYED ME: THE TRUTH ABOUT CELEB CHEF TOM WHIFFEN, said the headline and clicking, I found a photo of Jo looking pale with shadowed eyes, alongside another more glamorous shot of her, with Tom, in happier times.

'Have you found it, are you reading?' demanded my mum.

'Yes, give me a minute.'

The interview was a furious tell-all. Jo revealed that Tom had been cheating on her with other women for the entirety of their four years together, and that every time she found out he would beg for forgiveness, but enough was enough, she couldn't take it anymore.

'Four years,' I said to Mum. 'That means he was already with her when we got together.'

'I know. Keep reading.'

She said Tom was vain, that his charm masked a man who only cared about himself, and she felt stupid for not realising it sooner. She called him a terrible father who never kept his promises and seemed to treat his son like an accessory. And then in the final paragraph she mentioned me.

'Tom doesn't even come up with his own recipes. His world-famous carrot cake and his perfect chicken soup were all the work of his assistant Sarah-Jane Santi. Tom's not an especially good cook actually. Everything he made for me was really tasteless.'

I couldn't help laughing at that, and heard my mother on the other end of the line laughing with me.

'Not an especially good cook,' I said. 'Poor Tom.'

'Don't give me "poor Tom", he deserves every word of it,' responded my mother.

'I wonder what he did to make her so angry that she went to a newspaper.'

'Whatever it was, I'm glad he's out of your life.'

'Me too.'

'You'll meet somebody lovely now, I know you will, now you're free of him,' she added encouragingly.

'I don't need anyone,' I told her reflexively.

'No, but you might want someone.'

'You never wanted anybody else after Dad died though, did you?'

There was a brief silence then the sound of her voice again, softer now, 'It's not quite the same, is it?'

Baxter clambered up onto my lap, nosing the laptop aside, settling in, and I hugged him to me. 'Isn't it?'

'I was sad for a long time,' she pointed out. 'And then I had you to think about. I don't know if you remember, Sarah-Jane, but you made it very clear that you liked it being just the two of us.'

'So, it was me that held you back?' The thought was troubling.

'I wasn't unhappy to be held back.'

'What if you'd met someone lovely?'

'There has been no one lovely. And Sarah-Jane, I'm fine, not at all lonely, entirely content with the way things are.'

'So am I.'

'But you're young.'

'You're not old. And Dad's been gone a long time.' I echoed the words Riccardo had said a couple of nights earlier. He wasn't entirely wrong.

Mum gave a sigh. 'Sometimes it seems ages ago, sometimes not long at all, and besides, I have my life arranged the way I like it.'

'If that changes, I'd hate for me to be what holds you

back.' As much as I disliked the idea of her with any other man, that much was true.

'I'll bear it in mind,' she promised. 'But Sarah-Jane? Please don't let what happened with Tom be the thing that holds you back, because I'd hate that. You're in Italy now, making a fresh start, and not all men are like him.'

'I hope not,' I said.

'I know it,' Mum replied. 'And I also know you deserve someone lovely – everyone does.'

At the *trattoria* the next day, Riccardo's father came in alone. I watched for any signs that he and Assunta were more than usually friendly, catching them smiling across the room at each other, but not sure if I was reading too much into it.

'Carlo seems lovely,' I remarked later, after the last customer had disappeared and Assunta and I were busy cleaning up.

'Yes,' she agreed.

'You danced together a lot at the party the other night,' I continued, pulling clean plates from the dishwasher.

'Yes,' she repeated, stacking them away on the shelves.

Even by Assunta's standards, this was cagey. If something was going on, she wasn't about to admit it. But I found myself hoping there was, because just like Mum had said, everyone deserves someone lovely.

Carlo came in alone for lunch the next day, and the day after. I didn't see anything of Riccardo, although I looked for him every time I walked across the piazza or went into the bar, and kept expecting him to be among the customers arriving in the *trattoria*. There was no reason to message him or call into his workshop, no need to see him at all, except that I wanted to.

My car was still parked beside his house, where I had left it on the night of his party. If I walked up there to get it, there was a chance I might find him. But what if it was awkward?

What if that strange fizzy sensation hadn't meant much? What if it had been all me, and he hadn't noticed anything?

In the end I actually did need the car (to drive to Borgo del Colle and pick up paint charts). Walking up Montenello's steep streets on the way to collect it, I told myself that Riccardo might not even be there. Then nearing the house, Baxter started trotting ahead, tail wagging and I saw that his truck was parked outside, with several long planks of wood on the back. There he was, struggling to carry one inside.

He was wearing denim shorts and an old T-shirt dusted in wood shavings, his tanned skin lightly sheened with sweat, and he looked hot and frustrated.

'Do you need some help?' I called.

'Sarah-Jane.' Balancing the plank against the door frame, Riccardo pulled up his T-shirt, wiping the moisture from his face, exposing the long line of his belly. 'I have a problem, the angle of the hallway – it may not even be possible to get them inside.'

'What if I hold the back end and you take the front?'

'OK, let's give it a try.'

As he hefted the plank up onto his shoulder, I moved beside him and took some of its weight. Riccardo was right, the hallway was awkward, and the plank required a lot of shuffling back and forth, and tilting at exactly the right angle, but working together we managed the first one, and after that each one was easier.

'Thanks for the help,' said Riccardo, when we finished. 'I couldn't have done it without you.'

'I'm not much use at renovating but I'm happy to lend a hand with the painting when you're ready,' I offered.

'That is not going to happen for some time,' Riccardo said, looking round at the shell of a room. 'As you can see.'

'I'll still be around. I'm not going anywhere.' We were standing on either side of the large stack of wood, both of us dusty and hot, staring into each other's faces.

'I thought once that old Saab was fixed, you would get into it and drive away for ever,' Riccardo said.

'That was the plan.'

'If I could have worked on that car even more slowly, then I would have.' Riccardo pushed his hands through his hair and gave me a bashful smile. 'To be completely honest, I may have taken a little longer than I needed to.'

'All those times I came to visit and found pieces of my engine all over the ground ...?'

'I didn't want to put them back,' he admitted.

'You didn't?' I was stunned.

'I was in no hurry to finish. I wanted to keep you here.'

'So you could have fixed my Saab quicker?'

'Of course, much quicker ... but aren't you glad I didn't?'

The kiss was inevitable. I leaned across and touched my lips to his, and as I did, my nerve endings sparked and my heart beat faster in response. Gasping, I pulled away and he looked back at me, eyes widening, turquoise bright.

'Sarah-Jane?' Reaching across the stack of wood, Riccardo took me into his arms, lifting me high and swinging me over. As our bodies came together, he touched my face, and my hands slipped under his T-shirt.

'Yes,' I said in a whisper.

He was hard and muscled, and his mouth was on mine. 'Yes,' I repeated, as he was stripping off my clothes, and pulling free of his own. 'Yes,' as he was lifting me against the rough stone wall, parting my legs, and pushing hard inside me. 'Yes, yes, yes.' It was hot and messy, it was fast then slower then fast again; it felt like I had been half asleep before and he was waking me up. It felt amazing.

By the time Riccardo let my legs drop to the floor both of us were breathless. I looked around the bare room, its floor carpeted in sawdust, its walls bowed and window panes cracked, almost dazed to find myself there. And then I looked into his eyes again.

'Yes,' I told him.

'What do you mean, yes?' He gave me an uncertain half-smile.

'Yes, I'm glad you didn't fix that car any faster. Very glad.'

Afterwards we went back down the hill to my place. This time I didn't stand on my doorstep watching as Riccardo walked away. Instead we went inside and took a shower together, soaping each other clean of sweat and dust, kissing as the hot water streamed over us. Then he towelled me dry, patting the moisture from every part of me, his lips touching me in places the towel had reached, making them wet again. And greedy for more, our bodies shuddered against each other.

Assunta

People needed to eat, they came, and she cooked for them – it was the certainty Assunta clung to, and at the end of each night, the thought in her head that most comforted her. In many other ways, she wasn't the person she used to be. Assunta was changing, just like the town she lived in. She had never imagined that would happen.

As promised, Renzo had brought her the album of his mother's photographs, a worn leather volume with thin sheets of translucent paper separating each page. There were only three pictures of the man they believed to be her father: one at a wedding wearing a suit, another beside the fountain in the piazza and the last with a young woman who wasn't her mother. Assunta saw herself in this man's face whenever she looked at it. At first she couldn't stop looking. She considered trying to peel the pictures from the pages they were stuck to or holding onto the album because surely Renzo's mother wouldn't notice it was missing. But then Carlo took some photographs of them using his phone, and then Assunta found she could zoom in and look even more closely at the features that resembled hers, so the album was returned.

While Assunta may have changed, the rest of life went on almost as usual. In Montenello, the *festa* was all anyone seemed interested in and all they cared to talk about. Parties, noise and crowds of people had never appealed, and she might have let it happen around her, but her family insisted on being a part of things. Renzo particularly wanted to follow the procession on the evening the celebrations began, as the statue of San Bernadino was carried from one church to another, taking the longest route possible, winding through the town with everyone following. Most of the events they would be too busy to enjoy but this procession had its roots in tradition and he couldn't bear to miss it.

The hope was for fine weather but a cool night with a threat of rain was what arrived. Despite this, most of the town turned out, including Augusto, who walked between her and Renzo, as they took turns to hold his arm.

'What a wonderful day, what an occasion,' he kept repeating to one, then the other.

The statue was heavy and the men carrying it needed to keep resting, which offered them time to rest too. As her father caught his breath, Assunta scanned the crowd. There was Edward with his husband Gino, finally returned from his travels. There was the mayor and his family, Donna Carmela too. There was Carlo and Riccardo, with Sarah-Jane and her dog on a leash. There were the people who ate in her *trattoria* and faces she remembered from school, and their children and grandchildren.

'What an occasion, what a day, I never thought to see this again,' said Augusto, as with a loud cry the statue was lifted again.

'Do you want to keep going the whole way, Papa?' asked Assunta.

'Of course,' he replied. 'If I miss it this time, who knows if I will be here for the next?'

She and Renzo exchanged a glance over his head. The old man was stubborn and neither wanted to be the one to argue. Determinedly, Augusto kept going all the way to the church and stayed for the candlelit Mass, singing in his quavery voice while Assunta fretted that the walk home would be too much for him.

Leaving the church, she was relieved to find an old Fiat car waiting outside, its engine running, and Carlo at the wheel.

'Do you need a ride, signore?' he called to Augusto through an open window.

The old man tried to object as they encouraged him inside, but sinking into the passenger seat, he closed his eyes with a thank you.

'There is the carnival tomorrow, music in the piazza,' Assunta reminded him. 'More to enjoy.'

'Of course, of course,' he muttered, as Carlo leaned across to wind up the window, exchanging a quick smile with Assunta.

They watched as the car drove away, then she and Renzo began walking, and Assunta slipped an arm through his, drawing heat from his nearness, as the breeze started to chill them. Behind them knots of people were loosening and drifting apart, calling 'buonanotte'.

'You haven't said anything to Papa about this man we believe is your father,' observed Renzo.

'There is no point – it doesn't change anything.'

'What if Fabbio Galeazzi is still alive?'

'Then either I would have too much to say to him or nothing at all.'

'So you will leave this thing now?'

'I will leave it,' Assunta said. 'I know where I come from and that has to be enough.'

Very gently Renzo squeezed her arm to his side. 'You know where you belong, and that is more important.'

Heads down as the breeze stiffened, they quickened their pace. Rain began to fall, fat droplets spattering from the sky. Assunta heard voices calling her brother's name and a flurry of footsteps racing up behind them, then two large umbrellas arched over their heads.

'You two are going to get soaked,' said Edward, moving alongside her.

'The hotel's not far, come with us for a nightcap,' suggested Gino, closing in on Renzo's side.

Even without the cocktail, something with brandy, ginger and spice, Assunta would have been sleepy. Resting on a banquette in the hotel bar, it was a struggle to keep her eyes open. She heard only snatches of the conversation, not enough to make any sense of it, but it was good being there with them, warm and dry, her brother and his friends.

Assunta left when the rain stopped, walked the short distance home and found Carlo in her bed, already deep in sleep. He muttered as she rolled against him, and without waking properly, rested an arm across her belly.

This was their world, this queen-sized bed in a room that had been hers since childhood, in the house her family had left her. Assunta kept worrying that the neighbours might see Carlo leaving early one morning, but so far no one had said a word. She was a private person, and now almost superstitiously so, because it seemed the more discreet they were, the better.

Carlo stirred, breathing her name, tightening his arms around her.

'Thank you for driving Papa home,' she murmured back at him.

'He had a good time tonight, he was fine,' said Carlo. 'Tired though.'

'So am I,' she sighed.

'Too tired?' he wondered.

She rolled to face him, rubbing her cheek against his. 'Not too tired.'

For as long as possible, she thought they would go on leading this life together without attracting attention, quietly behind closed doors, not disturbing anyone.

People needed to eat and assumed that Assunta was there to feed them. They saw the same woman they had always seen, diligent, a little dull, unremarkable. Few would believe, that like her mother, she had a secret. Assunta relied on that; she worked hard and stayed quiet. And with the *festa* in full swing all anyone would care about was feasting and parades, music and dancing. Assunta was safe in her secret, at least for now.

Over the next seven days, there was barely time for anything but work. The piazza was filled with people and they crowded into the bar and *trattoria*, strangers as well as those she knew, attracted by the music and costumed children, by a carousel that was illuminated at night-time and stalls selling *torrone*, shaved coconut and bags of honeyed nuts.

Assunta couldn't have managed alone, but together she and Sarah-Jane got through the days and evenings. They cleaned plates and scrubbed pans; cooked and carried food to tables out in the piazza; cleaned more plates; cooked and carried more food.

Very late in the evenings, when finally they got to eat, sitting in the half-lit *trattoria* with dishes of leftovers on the table, and outside the music still softly playing, Carlo and his son would come and join them, Renzo might wander over with his friends, Augusto might be there dozing in a corner, everyone tired but happy to be together. Often they finished the night singing.

Somehow Sarah-Jane always ended up beside Riccardo. Everybody noticed this but no one bothered to mention it. Neither did they say anything when the little dog jumped up on Riccardo's knee. Or comment as he put an arm around Sarah-Jane's shoulder. They were young and free; there was nothing to stop them.

'It has taken him long enough,' Carlo complained, but only in Assunta's hearing. 'I thought it would never happen. And now they can't keep their hands off each other.'

'They are happy together,' said Assunta.

'And we are happy too,' Carlo reminded her. 'I want everyone to know it.'

'Not yet,' she said, when what she meant was not ever.

The ghost of his wife Maria was always there. She had

walked through this piazza and sat at a table in her *trattoria*. She had drunk coffee in the bar and queued for fruit and vegetables beside Augusto's truck, bought pastries at the *pasticceria*, and rested on the benches beneath the trees. At least she had never visited Assunta's home. With its doors closed and curtains drawn, she felt they were free there.

The feast for the final night had been planned very carefully. Lamb was to be spit-roasted outside beside the wood-fire where they would be baking bread all day. There were to be stalls, manned by staff from the hotel, frying seafood and vegetables to serve in paper cones. And the ovens of the *trattoria* would be filled with trays of pasta. Assunta occupied her mind with this, worrying over every detail, even when she and Carlo were alone together.

'We will need to be quick because people won't want to sit there and wait for too long,' she told him. 'There is enough pasta to feed an army but I am concerned we may run out of the lamb. And the plates Sarah-Jane has insisted we use, they are made from potato starch not plastic – will they be strong enough?'

'My love, we have been worrying about this *festa* for months,' Carlo said patiently. 'It is happening now, it is a success and everyone is happy. Your feast will make them happy too. Stop worrying.'

Assunta couldn't explain that the feast was the easiest thing for her to worry about. That it filled her mind and stopped other things crowding in. She couldn't mention Maria, couldn't even say her name, fearing that if she did, it would ruin everything. Carlo still carried her photo in his wallet, like people expected him to.

As discreet as they were, some day it would have to end, this thing between them. She was sure of that. Because they weren't young like Sarah-Jane and Riccardo, they had the past to consider. So, for now and as long as she could, Assunta would hold tight to their secret.

'Biodegradable,' she said to Carlo. 'All the tableware, cutlery too, Sarah-Jane insisted.'

'It is important nowadays, people expect it,' he told her.

Assunta shrugged. 'If that is what they expect, then we must give it to them.'

The feast was on the final night of the *festa* and Assunta had wondered if there might be some who were tired of partying by then, if the older ones would have retreated to their beds and worn earplugs to shut out the noise. But apparently no one in town was alone and at home. When she had a chance to glance up from her work, Assunta thought she had never seen the piazza so busy. The fountain was masked by people and there was a queue for the carousel, people were sharing food from paper cones and drinking a terrible cocktail made with red wine, limoncello and sweet vermouth that Augusto kept bringing over glasses of.

Even with the extra help, with Riccardo and Carlo waiting on the tables, with Sarah-Jane in the kitchen, with Edward and Gino next door helping Renzo, even so it was too busy. Tomorrow the trestle tables would be packed away and the carousel dismantled and the music would stop. No one wanted to miss out on a moment of the enjoyment before then.

'We must finish serving food well before midnight,' Carlo reminded her. 'Everyone wants to see the fireworks. If people haven't eaten by then, they have left it too late.'

'There will still be lots to do though,' Assunta fretted. 'Tidying, cleaning.'

'Tomorrow, it can all wait till tomorrow, and there will be other people to help us,' he reassured her.

When Carlo announced that it was time to stop cooking and serving, Assunta was reluctant. He was insistent, removing a tray of pasta from her hands and setting it on the stovetop, untying the strings of her apron and hanging it on the hook. 'You have done enough, more than enough. It has been a triumph. Now we are going and we need to hurry.'

'We can watch the fireworks from here, through the window,' she pointed out. 'There is no need to hurry anywhere.'

'Yes, but I have somewhere better in mind.'

Carlo took her by the hand, even though there were people all around who might notice. 'Quickly Assunta, this way.'

Soon they had escaped the lights of the piazza and were rushing through the maze of empty streets, Carlo pulling her forward, so fast she was breathless.

'Where are we going? Why the rush?' she wanted to know, as they were almost running up the steep, half-dark streets.

'Be careful, don't trip,' Carlo told her. 'Keep going.'

He took her all the way to the tower, using the light of his phone to guide them up the steps and at the top they stood panting, looking down at the town, the piazza a burst of light below them.

Carlo moved forward towards the parapet. He glanced at his phone, waited a few moments, then cupping his hands around his mouth, he let loose a loud shout.

'My name is Carlo Mastrobuoni and I want everyone to know: I love Assunta!'

There was the echo of his voice and then a silence, while Carlo waited, poised on the parapet, expectant. Still nothing.

'No,' he said. 'No ... where are they?'

Assunta understood and began laughing. 'You timed that for the fireworks.'

'And they are late. I don't believe this. I had it planned exactly for a few seconds before midnight, and then there were meant to be skyrockets and the whole sky exploding with light. But nothing.'

The sky was dark and empty; there was only starlight and silence, even the music in the piazza seemed to have stopped.

'Do you think anyone heard you?' wondered Assunta.

'Maybe not, but I am going to keep shouting.'

'No,' she told him. 'What will people think?'

'What does that matter?'

'You are a widower.'

'I know that,' Carlo said patiently.

'People expect …'

'I don't care what they expect; I can't be ashamed of being happy with you. Are you ashamed of loving me?'

'No,' she admitted.

'Well then.'

'I love you, yes, but I am not going to shout it at the top of my voice like a crazy person.'

'Fine, leave that to me.' Carlo turned, cupping his hands around his mouth again, and calling even more loudly: 'I love Assunta!'

There was another moment of silence, and then from the piazza below they heard the crowd chanting, calling for the fireworks, impatient now.

'I ought to have known it, of course they would be late,' said Carlo. 'It was inevitable.'

At last there was the sound of cheering, followed by several fiery tails of light shooting upwards, and the bangs as they exploded, showering the sky with purple and gold.

Assunta moved closer, leaned into him, took his hand and said in a normal voice, not shouting like an idiot. 'I love Carlo Mastrobuoni. I want everyone to know it.'

Sparks fell from the sky, glittering around them.

Sarah-Jane

The fireworks might have been late but they were worth the wait. Riccardo and I stood in the doorway of the *trattoria*, our faces tilted to the sky as it filled with colour and light. Although the piazza was more crowded than I had ever seen it, everyone fell silent and the whole show might have been for us, to mark our new beginning.

If I hadn't bought an unreliable car, if I hadn't lost my job, if I hadn't fallen for the wrong man, then I might never have met the man who felt like the right one. It seemed worth sending rockets high into the sky for that.

This *festa* had been such hard work. Every night I had fallen into bed exhausted, my hair and hands still smelling of whatever we had cooked, not sure if I could do it all again the next day, or even if I wanted to. But Riccardo was always there and he knew how to make me feel better. Somehow we got through it.

Standing with him, watching the last bright ball of colour burn out against the dark sky, I was almost glad it was over. Tomorrow street-sweepers would come and clear away all the streamers and empty firework shells. The sound stage would be dismantled, the equipment removed, things in Montenello would go back to normal.

'Please don't tell me we have to clear this up tonight.' Riccardo was looking at the chaos behind us, piles of blackened oven trays, smeared dishes and dirty plates. 'Surely Assunta doesn't expect that?'

'Where is she anyway?' I looked out into the piazza, but

there was no sign of her and Carlo among the groups of people saying goodnight and heading home.

'They left before the fireworks – I saw them go,' Riccardo said.

'They missed it all?'

'Maybe,' he shrugged. 'I don't think they will be back again this evening anyway.'

'Should we make a start?' I suggested unenthusiastically, surveying the mess.

'I don't think so. It has been a long night, a long week and anyway ...' Riccardo smiled at me. 'I have a better idea.'

'I'm sure you do,' I said, smiling back, because so far, in the moments we had managed to find for ourselves, every time seemed better than the last and, while surely that couldn't go on, we deserved a chance to find out.

I turned out the lights and closed the door, saying goodnight to Renzo who was about to take his father home. There was a food truck still serving fried doughnuts, and the air smelled of gunpowder and burned sugar. Rivers of people were flowing into the streets leading out of the piazza, with everyone heading home. There was no way to hurry, we could only follow at the same pace and listen to the sounds of chatter and laughter, at friends calling one to the other, even someone singing an old Italian love song.

We were halfway home when we spotted them, walking hand in hand in the opposite direction, Assunta and Carlo. They paused when they saw us, and we kept walking towards them, until the four of us met in the circle of light from a street lamp.

'Well,' said Riccardo, 'what happened to you?'

'We went up to the tower, for the view, and also ...' Carlo looked sideways at Assunta, then down towards his hand, clasping hers.

'The fireworks started late,' remarked Riccardo. 'Wasn't the plan for them to begin exactly on the stroke of midnight?'

Carlo gave a resigned shrug. 'I know, but what can you do?'

'There is always next year,' said Riccardo.

'Next year, yes,' agreed his father. 'There will be another *festa* surely, and more fireworks.'

'Perhaps then we will come up the tower with you and the four of us can watch together? If the view is so much better?' said Riccardo.

Carlo nodded. 'Yes, I would like that.'

We stood there, a small island in the eddy of people, and then Riccardo grinned at his father.

'Well,' he said.

'Well,' Carlo repeated, smiling back.

'*Buonanotte*, have a good night, Papa.'

'Yes, and you ... both of you.'

We moved on then; us going with the crowd and Carlo and Assunta still against it, calling out, 'Goodnight, *ci vediamo*, see you in the morning.'

'They seem happy,' I said.

'I think so.'

Reaching my house, I unlocked the door and went to go inside but Riccardo stopped me.

'It's late,' I said. 'Aren't you coming in?'

'But this is the best part of the evening,' he said. 'When everyone else is gone, and it is just you and me.'

'Shall I get some wine and a rug then, bring them outside and we'll have a last glass?'

'I'll fetch it,' he told me.

We sat together swathed in the woollen rug, drinking red wine, talking a little and kissing a lot, until needing more than kisses, we threw off the rug and abandoned the half-drunk bottle out on the doorstep. Then we went inside, the three of us, me and my dog Baxter, and Riccardo, my someone lovely.

Acknowledgements

Dear Reader,

This isn't the novel I intended to write. My original plan involved setting a book in Siena, a town I haven't visited for many decades, and I planned to spend time there soaking up the atmosphere. It was early 2020 and ... well, I think we all know how that turned out!

Instead, whilst in lockdown, I started on a different sort of novel, one that took me to the south of Italy, to revisit favourite places and old friends, at least in my imagination. I wanted to write a happy book that readers could escape into, and I wasn't going to have any hint of a pandemic in it.

Of course, now I've finished I realise how much this novel has been flavoured by what was going on around me. It is a story about loneliness, about the importance of connecting with friends and family and how, when surrounded by people you love, it is possible to be content leading a relatively small and simple life.

I want to thank everyone who has helped me to keep working at a time when my thoughts were often scattered. In particular my friend Mandana Ruane who, a few years ago, actually did drive around Italy with her Border Terrier Jezebel, and who inspired Sarah-Jane's journey. And thanks to all the fellow writers, friends and colleagues who have been such a supportive community and especially my husband Carne Bidwill, who mixes an excellent Negroni.

Also thanks as always to the teams at Orion, Hachette Aotearoa NZ and Hachette Australia and to my agent

Caroline Sheldon. I'm not sure how you all kept on doing what you do.

By the time you hold this book in your hands who knows where we'll be at. Maybe we'll be hugging each other, travelling again and doing all the normal things, although as I write this, that day still feels a long way off.

In the meantime this story is for you, with love. I hope it's taken you to Italy.

Credits

Nicky Pellegrino and Orion Fiction would like to thank everyone at Orion who worked on the publication of *To Italy, With Love* in the UK.

Editorial
Charlotte Mursell
Sanah Ahmed

Copy editor
Clare Wallis

Proofreader
Laetitia Grant

Contracts
Anne Goddard

Design
Joanna Ridley
Nick May

Editorial Management
Charlie Panayiotou
Jane Hughes
Alice Davis

Finance
Jasdip Nandra
Afeera Ahmed
Elizabeth Beaumont
Sue Baker

Audio
Paul Stark
Jake Alderson

Production
Ruth Sharvell

Marketing
Yadira Da Trindade

Publicity
Brittany Sankey

Operations
Jo Jacobs
Sharon Willis
Lisa Pryde

Rights
Susan Howe
Krystyna Kujawinska
Jessica Purdue
Louise Henderson

Esther Waters
Victoria Laws
Rachael Hum
Ellie Kyrke-Smith
Frances Doyle
Georgina Cutler

Sales
Jen Wilson

If you loved *To Italy, With Love*, don't miss
Nicky Pellegrino's next gorgeous novel . . .

P.S. Come to Italy

Available to pre-order now!

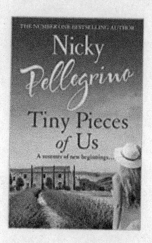

My heart is less than 1% of my body, it weighs hardly anything; it is only a tiny piece of me, yet it is the part everyone finds most interesting.

Vivi Palmer knows what it's like to live life carefully. Born with a heart defect, she was given a second chance after a transplant, but has never quite dared to make the most of it. Until she comes face-to-face with her donor's mother, Grace, who wants something in return for Vivi's second-hand heart: help to find all the other people who have tiny pieces of her son.

Reluctantly drawn into Grace's mission, Vivi's journalist training takes over as one by one she tracks down a small group of strangers. As their lives intertwine Vivi finds herself with a new kind of family, and by finding out more about all the pieces that make up the many parts of her, Vivi might just discover a whole new world waiting for her . . .

Join Vivi as she discovers second chances at life are anything but easy . . .

*For sale: historic building in the picturesque town of Montenello,
southern Italy. Asking price: 1 Euro*

Cloudless skies, sun-soaked countryside, delicious food . . . In the
drowsy heat of an Italian summer, four strangers arrive in a beautiful
town nestled in the mountains of Basilicata, dreaming of a new
adventure. An innovative scheme by the town's Mayor has given them
the chance to buy a crumbling historic building for a single Euro – on the
condition that they renovate their home within three years, and help to
bring new life to the close-knit local community.

Elise is desperate to get on the property ladder. Edward wants to
escape a life he feels suffocated by. Mimi is determined to start afresh
after her divorce. And there's one new arrival whose true motives are yet
to be revealed . . .

For each of them, Montenello offers a different promise of happiness.
But can they turn their dream of Italy into reality?

The best adventures are waiting for you to follow your heart . . .

Kat is an adventurer, a food writer who travels the world visiting far-flung places and eating unusual things. Now she is about to embark on her biggest adventure yet – a relationship.

She has fallen in love with an Italian man and is moving to live with him in Venice where she will help him run his small guesthouse, Hotel Gondola. Kat has lined up a book deal and will write about the first year of her new adventure, the food she eats, the recipes she collects, the people she meets, the man she doesn't really know all that well but is going to make a life with.

But as Kat ought to know by now, the thing about adventures is that they never go exactly the way you expect them to . . .

Can you change your life by swapping your home?

'It was a curious sort of feeling, being so cherished by a stranger . . .'

Imagine swapping your house for a stay in an Italian villa . . . and falling
in love with the owner's life.

After Stella's boss dies suddenly, she's left with nothing to do apart from
clear the studio. It seems as though the life she wanted has vanished.
She is lost - until one day she finds a house swap website and sees a
beautiful old villa in a southern Italian village. Could she really exchange
her poky London flat for that?

But what was just intended as a break becomes much more, as Stella
finds herself trying on a stranger's life.

Can Stella overcome her grief and find her way into a new future?